THE LION'S DEN

THE LION'S DEN

KATHERINE ST. JOHN

HEADLINE

Published by arrangement with Grand Central Publishing,
a division of Hachette Book Group

First published in Great Britain in 2020
by HEADLINE PUBLISHING GROUP

1

Cataloguing in Publication Data is available from the British Library

ISBN 978 1 4722 7641 4

Offset in 11/16 pt Bembo Std by Jouve (UK), Milton Keynes

Printed and bound in Great Britain by Clays Ltd, Elcograf S.p.A.

Headline's policy is to use papers that are natural, renewable and recyclable
products and made from wood grown in well-managed forests and other
controlled sources. The logging and manufacturing processes are expected
to conform to the environmental regulations of the country of origin.

HEADLINE PUBLISHING GROUP
An Hachette UK Company
Carmelite House
50 Victoria Embankment
London EC4Y 0DZ

www.headline.co.uk
www.hachette.co.uk

For my girls

The only known predators of lions are humans.

Day 1

I've always thought myself immune to the dizzying effects of fabulous wealth, but the sight of sleek jets lined up on the tarmac ignites an unexpected giddiness in me. How liberating to be able to move about the world so easily, without the inconveniences of mass transportation. No lines at the ticketing counter, no taking off shoes and disassembling carry-on bags, no body scans, no cramped leg space or short connections, no luggage belts or lost bags.

Yeah, I could get used to that. Summer certainly has.

I'm reminded of when I was first introduced to caviar at a swanky dinner party many years ago. My date was a pretentious bore, but I'll never forget his voice in my ear as I stared with wonder (and perhaps a shade of apprehension) into the little glass bowl of tiny black eggs carefully balanced on a bed of ice before me.

"It's easy not to crave caviar if you haven't tasted it," he said.

He went on to warn me as I put the opalescent spoon to my lips that once sampled, the delicate taste is not so easily forgotten. He was right. I could see how if the opportunity arose to make it a regular part of my diet, I might come to require it. I suppose the trappings of wealth that seem indulgent at first soon become necessities.

But I'm only a guest in this world, and I figure a week is not enough to develop a dependency on grandeur, so: I will not be turning down any caviar.

Nor will I be turning down any bread, cheese, butter, chocolate, or gelato. Or, for that matter, any of the other delicious foods I've been denying myself for an entire month. I've kicked and punched and crunched and starved myself into the best shape of my life in anticipation of a full week in a bikini, and I am ready to indulge.

I rip my eyes away from the spectacle on the runway to rummage through my bag one last time. Passport, check. Wallet, check. Phone, check. Watch. Shit.

"What is it?" my sister asks as I dump the contents of my purse into my lap.

"My watch," I moan. "I swear I had it this morning, and now I can't find it."

"Do you really need a watch on a yacht trip to the Riviera?"

"Just help me find it," I beg.

She tucks a wisp of blond hair behind her ear and paws through the junk in the center console. Lauren is the spitting image of our mother, petite and blond, while I'm our father, lanky and brunette. And yet our faces are similar enough that she could always get away with using my ID in the four years before she turned twenty-one. Not that she needed it—my little sis spent even more time in the college library than I did. All that studying paid off, because she's starting law school in the fall, and I couldn't be prouder.

Finally, I unzip the side pocket of the little round crossbody Gucci insignia bag Summer gifted me and wrap my hand around the watch, right where it should be. "Oh." I breathe a sigh of relief. "Got it."

Lauren studies me. "You're kinda wired this morning. You have too much coffee?"

I fasten the watch on my wrist. "I guess I'm just a little nervous about this trip," I confess. "I'm not totally sure why I'm still invited. I've hardly seen Summer recently."

"But you guys have been BFFs forever," she says, surprised. "Didn't she just give you that ridiculously expensive bag a few weeks ago?"

I nod, fingering the red-and-green stripe down the middle. It's the most expensive bag I've ever owned, and despite myself, I love it.

"What happened?" she asks.

"I don't know."

But I do.

I unload my roller suitcase from the trunk of my beat-up Prius and give Lauren a hug through the open window. "Thanks for letting me borrow your car," she says with a smile. "Have fun. And please don't come back with a boyfriend twice your age."

"Haha," I return. "I'm not Summer."

She gives me a wry smile. "I've never understood what you see in her. But the most exotic place a friend has ever taken me is Lake Michigan, so I guess you win."

"Okay, now get out of here before anybody sees me with this beater." I slap the roof of the car for emphasis. "Ow!" I jerk my hand away from the blazing-hot metal.

"Keep me posted!" She blows me a kiss.

"Give Grannie my love!" I shout after her.

As she drives away, I feel a twinge of regret I won't be road-tripping with her to see Grannie perform the title role in *Mame* for the community theater at her new retirement condo in Lake Havasu. I blame Grannie for passing on to me the acting bug and always relish an opportunity to see her in her element. But as sad as I am to miss her in the part she was born to play, sometimes life demands that you sacrifice senior dramatics for a week on a yacht in the Mediterranean.

I roll my bag past the rows of expensive cars baking in the summer sun to the two-story stucco building that serves as the waiting room for the small private airport and ring the buzzer. The woman on the other end politely informs me that the crew for my plane has not yet arrived and the passenger list has not yet been published, so she can't yet let me in. "I'm sorry," she says. "New security measures. Check back shortly."

Fantastic. I'm three minutes early and clearly the first to arrive, already sweating in the impractical vintage sundress I was so excited to find at a garage sale in Beverly Hills last week. The fabric is too thick for this weather, the bodice too tight. I wish I'd worn something loose and cotton, but I was doing my best approximation of stylish on a shoestring budget, so here we are. At least I have the purse.

Desperate for shade, I haul my suitcase over to the curb and stand in the strip of shadow cast by a lone palm tree, watching the activity on the airfield through the chain-link fence. Shimmering waves of heat rise from the tarmac, distorting the horizon. Past the line of jets, a yellow twin-engine Cessna takes off. Helicopters come and go from a couple of helipads in the distance.

Out on the runway, I count twelve men in suits descending the steps of one of the jets, holding their jackets closed against the wind, and watch an NBA player I recognize but can't name board another with what must be his wife, three kids, two people who look to be assistants, and four big dogs.

I wonder if that woman is happy. She surely must be *comfortable*. Certainly more comfortable than I am, melting here in my stupid dress. Money has never been a part of the dating equation for me, but suddenly I have to wonder: What if I'm wrong? What if love *doesn't* conquer all and money *can* in fact solve all your problems? Summer's clearly placed all her chips on that bet.

My not-so-illustrious acting career has been studded with bit parts and waitressing jobs that have sometimes put me in the path of hunky celebrities, and on occasion I've been the recipient of their passing attention. But I've never followed through, always horrified by the thought of becoming a witless flavor-of-the-week dangling from the arm of some star until he dumps me for the next famous model. I can almost hear Summer's voice whispering in my ear, suggesting that this sentiment is only my lack of confidence hampering my Hollywood ending.

I laugh out loud, realizing I must look like a madwoman if anyone's watching. Surely the heat is going to my head. Or maybe it's the jets. I'm not Summer. I would never go as far as she has in the pursuit of gold.

Before I can totally lose my mind, a silver BMW SUV pulls into the spot beside me and a voice chirps, "Hey, lady, what are you doing out here?"

I wave and drag my suitcase over to the car as Wendy emerges from the driver's side, glancing at her dainty gold watch. "Lemme guess, Summer's late."

"We're the first ones here," I confirm. "And they wouldn't let me in yet."

"No wonder you're melting," she says as we air-kiss.

Wendy's black with Disney princess dark eyes complemented by perfectly arched brows and a flawless complexion. Always stylish, today her petite frame is draped in the quintessential flying-on-a-private-jet-to-the-South-of-France outfit: freshly pressed white linen pants paired with tan wedges and a billowy golden top, her signature long wavy raven extensions covered by a floppy white sun hat.

My uncomfortable vintage dress suddenly just feels old. I am never as aware of my appearance as when I'm around Wendy and Summer. It's not their fault; they're just effortlessly chic. If I am ever chic, there is definitely full effort involved. My brain simply doesn't work that way. I see a dress and think it's an outfit. They put together a whole *look*.

Wendy's roommate, Claire, gets out of the passenger side and joins us at the back of the car, where we repeat the air-kiss ritual. I notice she's cut her usually long dark hair into a flattering lob, accented with beachy waves and caramel highlights that bring out her blue eyes. "Love your hair," I say.

"Thanks!" Her dimples twinkle as she smiles. "Have I not seen you since I cut it?"

"Not since Wendy's birthday dinner back in June, I think."

"Claire's never around since she started dating Mr. Major League," Wendy teases.

"My boyfriend's in Chicago, so I'm there a lot now," Claire explains. "He's a baseball player."

"That's great," I enthuse.

Claire's an incredibly sweet elementary school teacher originally from Miami who's soft-spoken when she speaks, which isn't much, and... well, I'm not sure what else, to be honest. We've known each other probably four years, and I'm ashamed to admit I don't think we've had a meaningful conversation in that entire time—probably because she's always overshadowed by Wendy, who is hands-down the most outgoing, energetic, popular person I've ever met. When we first became friends at UCLA, Wendy was president of her sorority as well as head of the Greek Society, somehow balancing maintenance of a 4.0 GPA with planning fundraisers and beautification projects for the school grounds. These days she's an event coordinator turned publicist, and knows—I'm not kidding—everyone in Los Angeles. Well, everyone from a certain social set, anyway. The social set that would go to fancy events and need publicity. But trust me, that's a *lot* of people. Like a politician, she has that gift of making you feel like she actually cares when she's talking to you. Which makes sense, because her father's a state senator in Ohio.

I asked her about her overwhelming charm once, thinking it was just a natural part of *being Wendy*, but it turns out it's a technique. She told me it was all about light touch and eye contact. She tried to show me how to do it, but I just came off as creepy. You'd think that because I'm an actress, manipulation would come easily to me, but I've always just tried to be a decent human—and foolishly expected everyone else to as well. Unrealistic, I know. I'm working on it.

"I had dinner at Cove last night and stopped by the bar after, but I didn't see you," Wendy says.

"I took the night off so I could pack," I fib. A casting director I've auditioned for numerous times yet never quite booked through was having a party there, and I didn't want her to see me bartending. But Wendy got me the job (for which I am grateful), so I can't tell her that. It's not that I'm embarrassed to be a bartender per se. It's just that after a year of being able to pay all my bills acting, I feel... Okay, maybe I'm a little embarrassed that things haven't turned out quite the way I imagined. I've hit a slump, as it were. A speed bump. That's all it's going to be, because things are going to be different when I get back from this trip, I swear it.

Wendy opens her liftgate, revealing a completely stuffed trunk. "Overpack much?" I tease.

"The big one's for clothes, the medium for shoes and bags, and the small for hair products," Wendy says, indicating a matching set of maroon luggage. "You know me and my weave."

"I was gonna say, it's looking especially gorgeous today," I laugh.

She gently sweeps her hair over one shoulder with a smile. "Thanks, it's fresh for the trip."

"I swear I had a regular-size bag until Wendy got involved," Claire says as the three of us lift her gargantuan suitcase onto the pavement.

"Sounds familiar." I give her a meaningful smile.

A chauffeured black Suburban rolls up as we're unloading Wendy's trio of bags, and Summer's mom, Rhonda, her sister, Brittani, and another girl I don't recognize spill out, juggling coffee cups, cell phones, hats, and purses.

Here we go.

"Had to stop at the outlet stores on our way into town," Rhonda announces with a flourish. As if to punctuate her declaration, a shopping bag tumbles out of the car before the driver can catch it, spilling three boxes of shoes onto the pavement. "Wouldn't wanna be underdressed in the *South of France*!"

Brittani gives her mom a high five, and they make spirit fingers like cheerleaders.

Besides a few extra pounds and some unfortunate cosmetic tweaks that have left her looking persistently surprised and curiously puffy, Rhonda hasn't changed much in the ten years since I last saw her: blond-streaked hair piled on top of her head, makeup just a little too done, leopard-print top stretched taut across her ample chest.

I haven't laid eyes on Brittani in as long, either, and I'm immediately surprised that despite their different fathers she's grown up to look exactly like her sister—leggy, blond, and beautiful, with enviable cheekbones and a perfect bow of a mouth. Only, where Summer is always dressed as though she's just come from brunch on the Upper East Side, Brittani looks like she's headed to spring break in Cancun. She's wearing a tight pink T-shirt with WHAT HAPPENS IN VEGAS . . . spelled out in rhinestones over cutoff jean shorts, and her hair is brassy from peroxide. Which is to say she's clearly inherited her mother's sense of style.

"Girls' trip!" Brittani whoops as she gallops over.

I flash a bright smile. "Brittani! Rhonda! So good to see you guys!"

"Listen to you! 'You guys'! You can say 'y'all' with us. We all know you're from the South!" Brittani exclaims, putting on a Southern drawl. She hip-checks me, sending me stumbling into a Porsche.

I regain my balance, managing a good-natured, "Wow, you look great. I think you were twelve the last time I saw you."

"Well, I'm twenty-two now! Whooooo!" Spirit fingers again. "Are you still trying to be an actress?"

I smother my irritation. Brittani can't possibly mean to be as condescending as she sounds, can she? "I'm still acting, yeah," I say, forcing a smile.

"What have you been in?" she asks.

A logical question, which shouldn't bother me nearly as much as it does. There's no good way to answer, and though I know intellectually that I'm still building my career, it only ever makes me feel like a failure. None of the movies I've done are big enough that she would have heard of them, and the parts on television are small enough she wouldn't remember me. So instead I say the one thing that I'm actually proudest of, which will be the least interesting to her and hopefully shut her up. "I'm nominated for a Webby Award for a web series I did," I say. "It's called *Junk*, and it's about—"

Aaand I was right. She doesn't even let me finish before beckoning to her friend. "Come meet Summer's sidekick!"

A week on a boat with Brittani. Didn't fully consider that when I accepted this invitation.

Her friend has long dark hair streaked with purple and is dressed more like she's going to Ozzfest than the Riviera. A black jean mini-skirt rides low on her hips, held in place by a heavy studded belt that matches her black-and-silver spiked platform heels, and her limbs are laced with ink. She's not wearing a bra under her slinky black tank top, but she doesn't need anything to hold her sizable boobs in place. They're high profile.

As she saunters over, I can see she's quite beautiful, with smooth, tan skin and delicate features, and there's something exotic and rebellious about her. But most remarkable are her startling violet contacts.

Strange. I knew Summer was allowing Brittani to bring a friend "to keep her occupied," but I'm more than a little surprised *this* is the friend she sanctioned. Summer's always been image-conscious, and has become rigorously so as John's girlfriend, meticulously cultivating a facade of sophistication to conceal her less-than-cultured upbringing. Wendy and I fit into her aesthetic, sufficiently attractive and socially graceful enough to make her look good, but not quite so beautiful or accomplished as to be rivals.

I can understand inviting Claire, who she hardly knows—Claire's agreeable and well mannered, pretty in a nonthreatening way, a safe solution for filling six slots on a boat when you only have two friends. Brittani and Rhonda are family, of course, who'd have given Summer all kinds of hell if they weren't invited (and Summer's already disclosed to me her plans to adjust their wardrobe once we're on the boat). But this girl...It's not just that her style clashes with Summer's; the bigger offense is that she's undeniably, unforgivably sexy.

I extend my hand to her with a smile. "I'm Belle."

Her many bracelets jangle as she awkwardly shakes my hand. "Amythest."

"Like the stone?" Wendy pipes up.

"But spelled different," she clarifies.

I can't help but wonder which came first, the name or the purple contacts.

Rhonda stretches the neck of her leopard print and blows down her shirt. "Hot out here."

I give her a moist hug. "I know; it's terrible. This is Wendy, and Claire."

"Oh, Wendy, I've heard so much about you!" Rhonda says.

Wendy adjusts the brim of her big white hat, laughing. "All good, I hope!"

"Summer won't shut up about you. It's so great to finally meet you." Rhonda turns her attention to Claire. "Tell me your name again," she says, throwing an arm around Claire's shoulders.

Claire begins to speak, but Rhonda cuts her off. "No wait, I know it! It's Abby!" Claire shakes her head, embarrassed. "Amy! Ashley! Amber!"

"Claire," Claire says quietly.

"I could have sworn it started with an 'A.' And how do you know—"

Wendy takes Rhonda's arm as though they're old friends, effectively rescuing Claire from her focus. "We're all gonna have such a good time!"

We troop through the arctic cool of the tiny terminal, where our passports are checked against the passenger list, then out the double glass doors onto the roasting tarmac. The jet's crew is nice enough to take our bags, but a stout flight attendant in a structured khaki dress who can't be much older than we are politely informs us that it's strict policy not to allow anyone on the plane until Mr. Lyons arrives.

So back we go across the asphalt toward the terminal. But before we can reach the oasis of air-conditioning, she heads us off. "My apologies. Mr. Lyons prefers for guests to be ready to board as soon as he arrives so that we can take off promptly."

"Okay, great. We'll be ready." Rhonda throws a thumbs-up as we continue toward the terminal.

"So much for a girls' trip." Wendy sighs.

I laugh. "He hardly lets her out of his sight. You really think he was going to send her to the Riviera on his jet without coming along?"

The stewardess rushes ahead of us, flustered. "No, no, I'm sorry," she calls, sweat glistening on her brow. "What I mean is that you should stay put. They'll be here any minute."

No one moves. "You mean here in the sun?" Brittani asks, incredulous.

"Yes. It's better that way," the stewardess insists, a hint of desperation in her voice. "Please, come this way. You can stand in the shade over here."

Which is how we wind up sweltering in the shade under the nose of the plane for close to an hour.

By the time the white Bentley arrives, I have to pee something awful and sweat is pooling in the underwire of my bra. Summer emerges from the driver's side looking like she just stepped out of a Bogie and Bacall movie. She's always been my most glamorous friend, but this is a whole new level. She's dressed in a beige wrap dress with big dark glasses, a Chanel scarf covering her tastefully blond hair, and she's positively beaming, completely oblivious that their hour delay has caused us all to wait standing on the tarmac.

Her cool elegance sparks a flame of resentment within me. It's not too late to bail; I could say I don't feel well, probably even get most of my shifts at the bar back. No sane person would accompany her on this trip after what she's done. But no. In spite of everything, I have to be here. I resist the urge to check my watch, douse the plume of sedition, and power up my smile.

Emerging from the passenger side of the Bentley in a bespoke gray suit is her boyfriend, John, not a day over sixty-three to her twenty-six, a wiry slip of a man who may almost reach Summer's height if you factor in the two inches of perfectly coiffed silver hair and the stacked heels on his handmade Italian leather shoes. Summer's not overly tall, but I notice she's in Chanel flats to match her scarf, no longer allowed heels lest she dwarf him.

"Look what John got me for my birthday!" she exclaims, dashing over to us. She pushes back her sunglasses, her eyes like emerald pools sparkling in the sunlight. "Come see! It has my name stitched into the leather!"

Her delight is infectious. We all gather around the exorbitantly expensive vehicle, *ooh*ing and *aah*ing appropriately—it is, after all, something magnificent—as the bags from the trunk are loaded onto the plane.

I give Summer a hug, trying to recapture our old familiarity. "It's gorgeous, and so are you."

"I'm so glad you could come." She squeezes my hand. "Nice sunglasses."

"Thanks!" I finger the large black knockoff frames. "I thought you'd like them. I found—"

"Honey, does this mean I can have the Mercedes?" Rhonda interrupts.

Summer smiles, but her eyes convey a different message. "Mom," she cautions with a little shake of her head.

"I'm joking! Tell my daughter to give her old mom a break," Rhonda appeals to John as Summer looks on, clearly having second thoughts about having invited her mother.

"Rhonda, you're not old." John flashes his Cheshire-cat grin. "And the Mercedes is yours."

Rhonda drops her chin and squints at him over the top of her sunglasses, trying to tell whether he's serious, but he's already turned his attention to the valet, confirming he'd like the car parked in his usual spot.

As the Bentley pulls away, Wendy lays a light hand on John's arm. "You're such a great boyfriend. Thank you so much for this trip. We're really looking forward to it."

I turn up the wattage in my smile. "Yes, thank you."

"Thank you," Claire echoes softly, lowering her eyes.

He nods magnanimously. "My pleasure. Glad to have you girls along."

And with that, he's off toward the plane, precipitating a flurry of activity as the crew prepares to greet him.

The couple of times I've met John he's been pleasant, if deliberately so, with the occasional flashes of brilliant charm common to a man who's gotten as far as he has in life. He and I have only had briefly superficial conversation of the type you'd expect with a billionaire whose age is somewhere between that of your parents and your grandparents—still, I'm never sure that if I dropped dead in the midst of chatting with him and was replaced by another girl of vaguely similar genus, he'd actually notice.

When I was a kid, we had this goldfish with bulging eyes, Eddie.

Periodically, Eddie would die, and my parents would covertly replace him with a new Eddie. This went on for years undetected by my sister or me, until finally one day I happened to be the one that discovered Eddie belly-up in the fish tank, eliciting a confession from my parents (who I now realize were holding back tears of laughter, not grief) that this was in fact Eddie VI.

If Summer's friends are Eddies to John, what does that make Summer? Is she replaceable, too? She admits he's had other mistresses and taken other groups of pretty young things on exorbitant vacations (apparently it's good for business), but seems to genuinely believe he's never felt about any of them the way he feels about her. And she claims to be head-over-heels in love with him. Hasn't been sleeping around on him, either. Not since Eric, at least.

To each her own, I remind myself. It's not like all the guys I've been with were princes, exactly.

Brittani pushes Amythest in front of Summer. "This is Amythest," Brittani says. "She's the best. You're gonna love her."

My brain shorts. In no world would Summer agree to Brittani bringing a friend she's never laid eyes on.

"Hello." Summer's smile doesn't falter as she extends her hand to Amythest, but I can see her taking in the platform stilettos, the violet contacts, the curvy body swathed in black.

Amythest takes Summer's hand with a smile, and for a minute I think she's going to curtsy, before I realize it's just a crack in the asphalt she's having trouble navigating in those heels.

Summer meets Brittani's eye with intent. She's got a great poker face, but I know her well enough to read the distress she's covering. "Can I talk to you for a minute, sis?"

She steers Brittani by her elbow to the foot of the airstair, where John is talking with two men in suits. He takes leave of the men and listens intently with a hand on each of the girls' shoulders as Summer speaks in low tones and the rest of us pretend not to be trying to hear what they're saying, while Amythest fiddles with her bracelets and stares at the pavement. After a minute, Brittani calls Amythest over and introduces her to John. He says something to her that sends her fishing in her bag and beckons to one of the men in suits. Amythest hands the man her passport, and he jogs up the steps to the plane with it in hand while she stands chatting with John, twirling a long strand of purple-streaked hair on her finger.

"Brittani was supposed to bring someone else," Rhonda stage-whispers. "But the girl got sick."

Wendy and I exchange a bemused glance. "Did Summer know there was going to be a switch?" Wendy asks.

Rhonda chuckles, eyeing her younger daughter with admiration. "Sly little bitch didn't ask because she knew Summer'd say no. Didn't tell me, either, until we were picking Amythest up."

"Bold move," I say. Maybe Brittani's smarter than I've given her credit for.

Over by the plane, the man in the suit has a quick conversation with John, who then says something to the three girls, hands Amythest her passport, and trots up the steps.

"I guess she's been approved," Wendy breathes.

"Something tells me that was John's decision, not Summer's," I return.

Summer strides toward us, her expression dark, leaving Brittani and Amythest whispering behind her.

"Everything okay?" Wendy asks as she approaches.

Summer narrows her eyes at her mother. "Why didn't you call me?"

"I didn't know," Rhonda professes. "I can't keep up with her friends, I figured that was the one you okayed."

"No," Summer fumes, sotto voce. "But now John has decided she's fine, so we have to spend the rest of the trip with her. Thanks a lot."

"I'm sorry—" Rhonda reaches out to hug her daughter, but Summer turns and marches toward the jet.

An older stewardess with short gray hair escorts the rest of us to the airstair, where Wendy insists we snap a flurry of pictures before finally boarding. As I step through the door of the plane, my sandal catches on the metal and I trip headlong into John, knocking him into the younger flight attendant, who spills the cup of coffee she was in the process of serving him all over me.

"Shit!" I say. "Shoot. I'm sorry. So sorry."

Well, this is a great way to start off the trip. The stewardess is as mortified as I am. She quickly grabs a napkin and begins dabbing at his suit.

"I'm fine." He brushes her away without a hint of the charm he usually radiates. "Clean her. She's dripping all over the floor."

The stewardess hands me the napkin, which I use to clean my legs and dab my sundress. At least this will provide me with an excuse to change into the more comfortable outfit in my carry-on. I can hear Summer asking John what happened, then apologizing for me.

Wendy grabs my elbow. "You okay?"

I nod, my cheeks on fire as I follow her into the cabin.

The inside of the plane is refined luxury in shades of cream and beige, and refreshingly cool after the sauna we've been baking in for the past hour. Having discovered long ago in the way-back of my mom's station wagon that I get violently ill riding backward, I'm careful to pick one of the forward-facing seats. I slide into the buttery leather captain's chair that would make any first class look like economy and take a swig of cold water from the bottle conveniently placed in the cup holder at my fingertips.

Yeah, I could definitely get used to this.

I've just turned to look for the bathroom when I see the two men in suits that John was talking to outside board the plane, one a large Italian mobster-looking guy in his fifties and the other closer to John's age, bald and rounding at the belly. "Vinny," Wendy whispers, indicating the mobster-looking one, "and the bald one's Bernard."

I'm aware John travels with bodyguards and have met the bald one in passing before, but Vinny is new. "Friends of yours?" I joke.

"They're John's security. I met them at dinner last week."

A dinner I wasn't invited to, clearly. It stings a little—especially since I'm the one who introduced Summer and Wendy—but I'm not surprised, in light of the recent events that have driven a boning knife into our friendship, which neither of us dare speak of.

Vinny and Bernard confer with John, then Bernard holds up his hand for us all to quiet down, which we do. Summer stands at attention next to John, her smile restored; the canary-yellow rock on her finger glitters in the sun that streams through the window, sending flecks of light around the cabin. I don't know anything about carats, but it's gigantic. John clears his throat and curls his lips into a smile. "Thank you ladies for joining us on Summer's birthday trip," he begins. "If you'll all stand up, the crew are going to come through the cabin and show you to your seats."

We all stand obediently as he continues. "Each of you will receive a gift bag with an eye mask, earplugs, and a sleeping pill. Once we take off, the stewardesses will reconfigure the plane for sleep while we have a light dinner. Then Summer and I will sleep in our bed in the back, and the rest of you will sleep in your assigned beds in front."

I think I read a hint of apology in the smile Summer gives us as John takes her hand. They make their way toward the back of the plane while the crew points us toward our seats. Sure enough, I'm assigned one of the two rear-facing seats, next to Amythest, across from Rhonda and Brittani. Why, oh why, did I pack my Dramamine in my suitcase instead of my carry-on?

I quietly get the young stewardess's attention once we have all been seated. "I'm so sorry, but I get sick facing backward. Is there any way I could sit facing forward?"

"I don't have the authority to change your seat," she apologizes, "but I'm sure it would be okay if one of your friends wanted to switch with you."

I look up at Rhonda and Brittani, who chortles, having heard the whole thing. "Sorry, girl, I ain't giving up my seat!"

"I gotta sit next to my baby." Rhonda pats Brittani's hand. "We have so much to talk about."

Should have known better than to ask them. I get up to approach Wendy and Claire, who sit directly behind me, facing forward. "I hate to ask you guys this, but I get supersick facing backward. Could one of you possibly switch with me?"

They look at me with pity for a painfully long moment before Wendy scratches my arm with her French-manicured nails—an incurable habit that I assume evolved from her theory about light touch being ingratiating. "Don't want you retching all over the jet," she teases. "I get a little woozy facing backward, too, but take Claire's seat. Claire, you don't mind, do you?"

Claire shrugs amiably. "Okay."

"You sure?" I ask.

She smiles, gathering her things. "It's not a problem."

"Oh my God, thank you so much. I really appreciate it. And I'm so sorry for making you move. I owe you one."

"I totally understand. Anyway, I'm on a private jet. I really don't care where I sit."

I'm just settling into my seat next to Wendy when the older flight attendant approaches, a look of alarm on her face. "My apologies. I'm going to need you to take your assigned seats for wheels up."

"It's okay," Wendy explains. "Claire switched with her."

The stewardess smiles tightly. "I know. But unfortunately, I'm going to need you to take your assigned seats."

I blink at her. "But the other flight attendant said—"

"Mr. Lyons has requested that everyone take their assigned seats for wheels up." She gestures toward my seat. "Please."

Wow. Okay. I unbuckle my seat belt and collect my things like a toddler punished for throwing her green beans on the floor at a fancy restaurant.

As I move past the stewardess, she mouths, *Sorry.* I can't quite bring myself to smile back.

I sink into my rear-facing seat, again doubting my choice to come on this trip. In a daze, I buckle my seat belt and reach for the airsickness bag tucked into the arm of my chair. At least I'm by a window. Across from me, Rhonda and Brittani are engrossed in a celebrity magazine, tittering over the cellulite of some reality star.

Amythest pats my hand, her violet eyes exuding genuine sympathy. "Sorry," she whispers. "That totally sucks."

"I'm sorry if…" I gesture to the airsickness bag.

"It's okay. I hold Brittani's hair back, like, every Saturday night. And sometimes Fridays, too. And Thursdays. And…Well, you know. I'm pretty much an expert."

As she fiddles with one of her many silver earrings, I notice the script etched into the inside of her forearm. It reads TO THINE OWN SELF BE TRUE.

"Polonius," I smile, recognizing the line. When her eyes flit to mine in confusion, I indicate the tattoo. "From *Hamlet*?"

"Oh, no, that's from a Reba song. 'Fancy'?"

Of course. "Oh yeah. I like that song. Ever been on a private jet before?"

The tiny purple stone in her nostril glints in the sun as she shakes her head.

And with that, the jet is hurtling forward. The ground rushes away faster and faster until we lift into the air. I look out the window, my palms sweating.

The endless grid of Los Angeles lies beneath us in all her glory as we climb into the sky. The dark-blue sea appears to be held back only by the thin line of sand that separates it from the rows upon rows of homes sprawling across the basin and up the sides of green mountains that turn to umber as they rise past the line of irrigation.

"Two kinds of neighborhoods in LA," I say, "the ones with blue pools and the ones with blue tarps."

"I've always wanted a pool," Amythest says. "But I don't know how to swim."

(ten years ago)

Georgia

I lay on a plastic lounge chair in the scorching Georgia sun, staring up at the milky blue sky through scratched sunglasses. The day was still, the rhythmic rise and fall of the cicadas interrupted only periodically by the spray of water from the pool filter as it slapped the concrete, turning the stone darker for just a moment before evaporating.

The oppressive midday heat ensured I had the pool to myself at this hour. If I blocked out the chain-link fence and NEWBURY PARK COMMUNITY POOL sign, I could almost imagine it was my own.

Someday.

Beads of sweat glistened between the round of my breasts in the new string bikini I had to hide from my father. I'd just turned sixteen, and while I'd been a head taller than most of the guys in my class since I was twelve, I was a late developer, so this was the first summer I'd gotten to enjoy having the curves of a woman.

I sat up, took a long swig of my quickly melting blue-raspberry slushie, and contemplated the five feet between my chair and the pool. *Slip on my flip-flops or hazard frying the bottoms of my feet on the blazing stone?* I decided shoes were too much trouble and sprinted the short distance on tiptoe before cannonballing into the pool.

As I dove through shards of light in the aqua blue and flipped upside down for a handstand, I heard a muffled voice calling my name. I surfaced, squinting in the sunlight, to see hot-pink toenails in bedazzled flip-flops.

"You need a pedicure," Summer said.

"I know." I looked down at my fingernails, which still had traces of dirt under them from working with my mom in the garden that morning. "Manicure, too. I was gonna do them last night, but my dad made me play chess with him."

"You guys are such nerds. I love it." Summer perched on a lounge chair and took out a cigarette, frowning across the street at the low line of my house. "Your mom's not there, is she?"

"She's at work."

She lit the cigarette and inhaled. "She's always at work."

"Yeah."

My poor mom had been pulling double nursing shifts at the hospital in an effort to save money. Turned out college was likely gonna cost far more than my parents had thought, and their salaries weren't nearly as great as they'd hoped—just good enough not to qualify for financial aid. But they valued learning, and a higher education free of debt was the one extravagant gift they wanted to give their children, come hell or high water. So while I studied hard in hope of obtaining a scholarship, they worked every available hour to make sure I'd be able to attend the best of the out-of-state universities that boasted the theater programs I was interested in, regardless.

Summer exhaled, and the smoke hung in the air. "God, it's hot out here."

"You should get in. The water's almost cool."

She shook her head. "Just did my hair. Anyway, I gotta go with Rhonda to meet Three for lunch at the club. Wanna come? We could play tennis after."

Rhonda was on her third marriage, to our next-door neighbor, a lawyer I'd heard my dad call an ambulance chaser more than once. Summer never used his real name unless he was in the room.

"Can't. I gotta hang with my sister when she gets home."

Summer flicked her cigarette. "She can just go home with my sister."

"I promised I'd take her to the movies this afternoon."

Our sisters were both eleven, and my mom still made me babysit Lauren, while Rhonda not only let Brittani stay home alone, but also let her watch R-rated movies. My mom, of course, had figured this out and would allow Lauren to go over to Brittani's only if I was there as well. But Summer didn't need to know this.

"Anyway, I was thinking about dyeing my hair pink later," I said.

Summer wrinkled her perfectly upturned nose. "Why?"

"I don't know. I've always wanted pink hair." I pushed out of the water and flopped down on the lounger next to her.

"Nice suit," she said. "God, I wish my boobs were as big as yours. I'm getting new ones as soon as I'm eighteen."

"Well, they're not the same size," I confided. "Righty hasn't quite caught up with lefty."

She stared at my chest. "I can't tell."

"That's because I added padding from of one of my push-up bras." I removed the pad from under my right boob and showed it to her.

Her liquid green eyes crinkled with laughter as she took a long drag of her cigarette, then offered it to me. I didn't smoke, but sometimes I'd have a drag of hers, just for solidarity. "Can't," I said. "Lauren'll rat if she smells it on me."

She shrugged and stubbed it out, then washed away the mark on the pavement with pool water, flicked the butt into the bushes, and covered it up with dirt. "Oh, I almost forgot." She extracted a novel from her purse and set it on the lounge chair. "I finished this last night. It's really good."

"Thanks! That the one about the kids who murder their friend?"

"I don't want to give it away."

Summer was the only girl I knew who was as avid a reader as I was. Most of the girls in our class could barely make it through the assigned reading, but Summer and I could easily rip through a novel in a matter of days if it was a good one.

She gave a little wave as she latched the gate behind her. "See you at class tomorrow. And don't dye your hair pink. Guys hate fashion colors."

★　★　★

The next morning I bounded down the stairs to find my mom sitting at the kitchen island reading the paper in her robe, coffee cup in hand, her wavy blond hair pulled up in a scrunchie. She should've been Summer's mom, not mine. Even at forty-four, sans makeup, she was still what they call a knockout. Of course, I got my dad's genes.

She looked up and smiled. "Morning, honey."

"Morning. I'm late for French. I gotta go."

I noticed her eyes slide to my hastily selected mismatched clothes and unbrushed hair, but she stopped herself from saying anything. "At least grab a banana out of the bowl. I'm late shift tonight so I won't see you, but there are leftovers in the fridge. Kiss?"

She proffered her cheek, and I planted a kiss on it.

Windows down, bumping Snoop Dogg in my mom's old station wagon, I parked near the battered NEWBURY HIGH SCHOOL sign and hurried through the glass doors, down the wide hallway to the one open classroom, marveling at how much quieter the school was during the summer. The new teacher stood with his back to the class, writing French conjugations on the blackboard in front of twenty or so kids.

I slid into the empty desk in front of Summer. "You're blocking my view," she whispered, cutting her eyes toward the front of the class as the teacher turned around. Damn. He looked like a young Johnny Depp, but athletic and without the weird hair and clothes. A ripple of energy passed through the girls around me as he began to speak, welcoming us to class—in French. Well, at least I'd be paying attention this summer.

"Good morning, class. Welcome to French Three, where we will be speaking only in French."

A groan went up from the class.

"I'm Mr. Stokes, and I'll do my best not to make your summer-school experience torture."

When the bell rang an hour later, I gathered up my books, thrilled that our only homework was to watch *Amélie*. "If all our teachers were that hot, it'd be easy to get straight A's," I whispered to Summer.

"As if you don't already," she teased. "Can I get a ride home? It's past noon, so Rhonda's probably drunk."

"Sure."

She threaded her way through the desks to the front of the class, where Mr. Stokes was erasing the blackboard.

"Hey, you look familiar." Summer addressed him easily, as though speaking to someone our age. "Do you play tennis at River Run Country Club?"

He turned, smiled. "Yeah. Can't say I'm much good anymore, though."

"Thought I saw you up there the other day. You didn't look too bad. I'm Summer."

"Summer Sanderson, I remember." He shifted his gaze to me. "And you're—wait, don't tell me—Isabella Carter?"

I smiled. "Isabelle. Nice to meet you. Your class was great."

Your class was great? I was an idiot.

Summer fixed him with those verdant green eyes. "Anymore?"

"What?" he asked.

"You said you weren't good at tennis anymore?" she clarified.

"Oh. I used to play in high school."

"And when was that?" she asked.

"Five, six years ago."

She smiled. "Well, I'll have to challenge you to a game if I run into you at the club, see if you've still got what it takes."

He laughed, but behind his smile I thought I could see him considering the propriety of playing tennis with a leggy blond sixteen-year-old student. Summer gave him a little wave as she sashayed out the door, and I scrambled to catch up.

Once we were safely in the privacy of the station wagon, I burst out laughing.

"What?" Summer asked, feigning innocence.

"You flirted with that teacher like he was our age!"

"Think he liked it?"

"Oh, come on. Of course he did. You should've seen the look on his face as you walked away. Pure gold."

"Turn there." She indicated a strip mall up ahead. "We're getting our nails done. We can't be walking around looking a mess."

The rest of the week flew by in a haze of French conjugations and afternoons by the pool, my dripping manicured fingers riffling the pages of the book Summer loaned me.

On the Friday before the Fourth of July holiday, I joined Summer for a sunset game of tennis at River Run. The afternoon was bone-melting hot and an hour in I'd soaked through my gym shorts and T-shirt, yet somehow Summer still looked fresh in her tennis whites.

I batted the ball over the net. "How are you not soaked?"

"It's this fabric. It dries it out or something." She whacked the ball to the other side of the court, and I didn't quite make it.

"I'm beat," I said, "and I've gotta go over to Grannie's for dinner."

"I got this outfit in the club store," she remarked as we zipped up our rackets. "Just charged it to Three's card."

"That's nice of him."

"Oh, please. He doesn't know. He never so much as checks the balance. It just comes out of his account every month. We could get you an outfit," she suggested.

"No, that's okay."

"Seriously, he'll never know the difference."

"I wouldn't feel right," I demurred.

"Suit yourself." She slung her racket over her shoulder and squinted past me a few courts away. "Is that Ryan?"

"Who's Ryan?" I turned to look. "That looks like Mr. Stokes."

Mr. Stokes and another good-looking guy his age were just breaking for water a few courts away. Summer was already walking in their direction, her tennis racket slung over her shoulder.

I hustled to catch up. "So you're on a first-name basis with our teacher now?"

"Act like you don't see him," she whispered.

As we approached, she turned her head toward me, actively not looking in his direction. I laughed nervously.

"Isabelle, Summer," he called out.

Summer feigned surprise, while I tried unsuccessfully not to act awkward. "Oh, hi!" she exclaimed blithely. "I knew I'd seen you playing here before."

The cute friend extended his hand to me. He had floppy light-brown hair and broad shoulders. "Hi. I'm Tyler."

"Isabelle." He looked me in the eye and smiled as I shook his hand. Was that an interested smile? An electric shock ran through me as I realized he thought we were college girls.

"I'm Summer," Summer said.

"You gals know Ryan from class?" Tyler asked.

"Something like that," Summer eluded. She nodded at the court. "He claims not to be any good. How about you?

"Maybe we should play a round of doubles and you can find out for yourself," Tyler suggested.

"Sounds fun," Summer agreed. "Monday?"

"Around five?" Tyler asked.

"We'll see you then."

Summer gave a little wave as she sauntered away, her skirt flouncing. I followed her up the steps to the clubhouse. "Are you actually going to play with them?" I whispered after the door closed behind us.

"Of course." She shrugged, browsing through the bikinis on the swimsuit rack. "And you are, too."

"He's our teacher. I'm pretty sure we'd get in trouble if the school found out."

"It's just a game of tennis. And they're not that much older than us. Come on." She batted her eyes at me cartoonishly. "Pretty please? Be my partner in crime. It'll be fun."

I couldn't help but laugh. Tyler was cute, and she was right. They were only a couple of years older than us. It could be fun. "I'll think about it," I said.

She grabbed my elbow and nodded toward the cash register, where a curvy blonde was paying for an armful of merchandise with a black Amex. A rock the size of Texas glistened on her ring finger as she put her wallet back in her designer tote, then gathered her shopping bags and breezed out the door, sliding a pair of dark sunglasses over her eyes.

"Haley Youngblood," Summer breathed. "That was the latest Dior bag, and did you see those sunglasses? They're the new Chanel ones with real diamonds on the hinges."

We watched through the window as the girl fired up a white Range Rover with dealer tags.

"Makes sense," I said. "Her dad owns, like, half the city."

"Her husband," Summer corrected me.

"Ew! No! Seriously?"

She nodded. "She's from some Podunk town where he has a farm. Apparently she was his waitress. Lucky bitch."

I pictured her husband's ample frame. "Define lucky."

"She can have whatever she wants whenever she wants it."

"Except love," I said.

She tilted her head, considering. "There's different kinds of love, Belle. And after a while, any dick gets old."

"Literally," I conceded.

The designated Monday rolled around sultry and hot. As Summer and I pulled out of her driveway in her mom's red Mitsubishi, the sun slipped behind dark thunderheads gathering on the horizon. I peered up at the sky, praying for thunder. "We should cancel. It's gonna storm."

"Too late." She turned up the hill that led away from the club.

"Where are you going?"

"Silver Creek."

"Why?" I asked. "I thought we were playing at River Run."

She shrugged. "Ryan changed it. Probably didn't want to be seen with us. They live there, and the courts are pretty nice."

A knot tightened in my stomach. "Oh," I said.

She looked at me, as though reading my thoughts. "I swear I told you when I dropped off the outfit yesterday, and you totally said you were fine with it, or I wouldn't have said yes."

I had no recollection of this, but I'd also been in the middle of a three-page essay in French, so I may not have heard.

"Thank you again." I smoothed my pristine tennis whites. It was the outfit she'd been wearing when we played last week. I wouldn't let her buy me one, so she'd given me hers and bought a new one for herself. The thought that maybe she didn't want to be seen with me in the old one had crossed my mind, but she was my friend, and anyway, my mother taught me you don't look a gift horse in the mouth, so I put it out of my head.

"If you don't wanna do it, I can take you back," she offered. "I don't want you to be uncomfortable."

"No, it's fine." Thunder rumbled overhead. "It'll be fun."

The song on the radio switched to our latest Madonna favorite, and she turned it up. "It's a sign: *You're frozen.*" She sang along, and I joined in, trying to force myself to relax.

The first fat drops of rain were just beginning to fall as we got out of the car at Silver Creek; after dashing the hundred yards from visitor parking to Ryan and Tyler's apartment, we were drenched.

A clap of thunder cracked as Ryan swung open the door. We darted inside, dripping all over the carpet.

"Sorry," I said, shivering in the air-conditioning.

"Tyler, towels!" Ryan shouted over his shoulder.

I wrapped my arms around my chest, acutely aware that my soaked tennis whites were now completely transparent. Summer was unfazed, giving Ryan a kiss on the cheek as though she hung out at her teacher's apartment every day of the week.

Tyler emerged from the back with towels, and I immediately

remembered why I agreed to this. He flashed a lopsided smile and wrapped me up in a big towel, lingering with his arms around me. He smelled of Drakkar Noir. I could feel his muscular chest and strong arms, the scruff on his chin roughing my forehead. None of the guys in my class had strength or stubble like that.

"So I guess we're not playing tennis today," I said stupidly, looking up at him.

"Guess not."

"I ordered pizza," Ryan offered.

"And we have beer and bourbon," Tyler added.

"Perfect," Summer said. "I'm usually more of a Scotch girl, but a shot of bourbon sounds like just the thing to warm me up. Who's with me?"

I, for one, was definitely in need of a drink to loosen up.

"Nice," Tyler said, and we followed him through their sparsely decorated living room to the kitchen. He grabbed a half-empty bottle of bourbon from the top of the refrigerator and poured generous shots into four red Solo cups.

"We don't believe in dishes." He winked. "Bottoms up."

Summer promptly downed her shot, shivering as it slid down her throat. Tyler watched with admiration, Ryan with something bordering on apprehension.

Tyler raised his cup to me, and we threw back our drinks simultaneously. The alcohol hit me like a ball of fire. I'd never actually had bourbon, and in that moment I discovered that I did not like it.

"Yech," I blurted. "Ohmygod." I grabbed Tyler's open beer and gulped, desperately attempting to wash away the taste.

Tyler laughed. "I take it you don't like bourbon?"

"That was the worst thing I've ever tasted!"

"But I bet you're warm now," Summer added.

And she was right. I was. I'd just had what must've been about three ounces of bourbon and half a beer on an empty stomach, and I was feeling much warmer. So warm, in fact, that I noticed I'd dropped my towel on the floor.

"You guys wanna throw your clothes in the dryer?" Ryan asked. "We have sweats you can wear."

"Or, of course, you don't have to put on clothes if you don't want to," Tyler chimed in with an exaggerated wink.

"Sweats sound great." Summer turned to Ryan. "Why don't you show me where they are?"

She followed him to his bedroom, and I heard the click of the door as it shut behind them.

"You want me to get you some dry clothes?" Tyler asked.

It did sound great to be dry, but the outfit I was wearing had a built-in bra, and my push-up pad was wedged under righty. I didn't want to be braless and lopsided in whatever T-shirt he handed me. "No, I'm okay." I picked up my towel and draped it over my shoulders. "This fabric dries fast. I'm almost dry."

"Okay." He cracked open a fresh beer and handed it to me. "We could watch a movie in my room, or..."

I perched on the arm of the brown La-Z-Boy couch. "Isn't the pizza gonna be here soon?"

"Yeah, but whatever."

He swigged his beer; I stared up at the framed Texas flag over the couch. "You from Texas?"

"Yeah."

"Cool." I sipped the beer, trying not to wince. "This is good."

"Yeah, it's cheap, but it's my favorite," he agreed. "And you can drink a lot of it and not get too full, you know."

"Yeah." I nodded, studying my beer. I literally had no idea what else to say to him. What did grown men like to talk about? I didn't know anything about sports, cars, or hunting. The boys I'd dated all knew the same people I did, had the same teachers. But this was a whole different ball game. I looked up to see him gazing at me. I gave him a nervous smile.

"You're really pretty when you smile," he said.

A flush of heat rushed to my head. "Thanks," I mumbled, caught off guard.

He held my gaze, his eyes a soulful muddy brown. My stomach flipped. He reached for my face and pulled me into a kiss, his face rough against my skin as his tongue pried my lips apart, reaching into my mouth with fervor.

The scent of his cologne was thick as he pulled me off the arm of the couch into his lap, his arms encircling me, his hands all over me. I wanted to enjoy it, but he kept thrusting his tongue into my mouth like he was digging for something, and it wasn't as pleasurable as I'd thought it would be. His tongue was big and in there so deep for so long that I had to pull away to breathe, and when I did, he buried his face between my boobs and made an animal-sounding grunt as he pulled my hips forcefully in to his. "Oh God, I just want to eat you." He bit my arm.

He wasn't biting hard, but still it kinda hurt, and I didn't want to be eaten. I wanted to be caressed. But now I wasn't sure I wanted to be caressed by him anymore. Was this how sex was supposed to be? Maybe I was just naive. The farthest I'd gone was dry humping with fumbling high school boys. I'd never been with someone experienced. His tongue again. By this point I was trying hard to like it, but it didn't feel like he was interested in me at all; he just wanted to ravage my body.

He kept his eyes trained on my boobs as he threw me down on the couch, lying on top of me, and I didn't feel what I thought passion should feel like; I just felt squashed and claustrophobic. One hand shot up my top, groping my boob, while the other pawed at my bodysuit.

"Okay." I tried to back away, but there was nowhere to go. I was in the corner of the couch with a two-hundred-pound man on top of me. "Hey."

He was clawing at my hips, trying to get my panties off, but thankfully my tennis outfit was a one-piece, so finally he just gripped the crotch of it and pulled it aside while he pushed his gym shorts down with his other hand.

"Hey," I managed, "wait a minute. Slow down." I was still trying to sound nice, but I was getting a little panicky.

"Oh baby." He held my shoulder down with one hand while gripping his dick with the other. "It's just so hot."

He moved his fleshy torpedo toward my mouth, and I ducked, trying to squirm down through his legs and out from under him, but he was too heavy. "You wanna just fuck, let's just fuck," he groaned, fumbling for my crotch.

I was trapped. I couldn't breathe. I didn't want to fuck him.

"Wait!" I squirmed, trying to push him away. "I don't."

But he didn't hear. "God you're sexy," he grunted, maneuvering his dick between my legs.

"No!" I cried, tears stinging my eyes. "Please." I could feel his dick poking my inner thigh. I mustered all my strength and shoved him as hard as I could. "I'm a virgin! I'm only sixteen, please!"

Immediately he stopped, his dick flopping over the top of his shorts. "What did you just say?"

"I'm sorry," I croaked, my heart in my throat. I rose up on my elbows. "I wasn't trying to have sex. I'm a virgin."

"No, the other thing," he snapped, his eyes dark.

"I'm sixteen," I said quietly.

He scowled. "You said you were eighteen."

"I didn't."

But this only seemed to make him madder.

"Why the hell did you come here?" He grabbed one of the pillows from the couch and whacked it into my chest so hard my head hit the armrest. "What the fuck?"

He stormed into the kitchen, leaving me to quickly scramble to my feet as Summer and Ryan emerged from his room, disheveled, she in nothing but his T-shirt, he in boxer briefs. "What's going on out here?" Ryan demanded.

Tyler stalked out of the kitchen, the bottle of bourbon dangling from his fist. "She's sixteen." He pointed at me. "Did you know that?"

"Calm down," Ryan said.

"Underage!" Tyler pushed Ryan up against the wall, pinning him with his forearm. "What the fuck!"

Summer skirted around them as they yelled expletives at each other and put her arms around me. "Are you okay?" she whispered.

I wiped my wet cheeks with the back of my hand. "I just wanna go home."

"Come with me while I get dressed."

She grabbed my hand and dragged me to Ryan's messy room, where she quickly changed back into her tennis outfit. The guys were in the kitchen talking heatedly when we emerged. We grabbed our purses from the entry table and slipped out the front door without saying goodbye.

Neither of us spoke until we were in the cocoon of the car, safely past the gates of Silver Creek. As we turned onto the road home, Summer asked quietly, "What happened?"

My words tumbled out in a jumbled mess, mixing with tears as I detailed what had happened. "I'm sorry I ruined your night," I finished.

"No! Belle! Are you kidding? That guy's an asshole! I'm just glad he didn't take it further with you."

"Thanks for understanding."

"I'm always there for you," she promised.

"Please don't tell anyone."

"Of course not," she said. Then, "Are you really a virgin?"

"Yeah," I admitted. "I tell you everything. I think I woulda told you if I'd done the deed." She laughed. "Wait, are you?"

She gave me the side-eye. "Not anymore." She grinned.

Thankfully, we didn't have to see Ryan in class the rest of the week because of the July Fourth holiday. Summer tagged along with my family to my uncle's lake house for a few days, ostensibly to get away from Rhonda and Three's constant fighting, but in reality I could tell she was worried about me. I kept turning it over in my mind, wondering if I'd actually led him on.

"It's not your fault," she'd remind me when she caught me chewing my lip with intensity, furrowing my brow. "Guys are just like that." I figured she would know.

When we got back home, a U-Haul was hooked up to the back of Rhonda's red Mitsubishi. Summer sighed when she saw it. "Well, I guess we're moving again. Thanks for letting me know, Rhonda."

We said our tearful goodbyes a few days later, vowing to keep in touch. It was funny—Summer had been in my life less than two years, but I felt like I'd known her so much longer. She swore she'd miss me and made me promise to come visit them in Arizona, both of us knowing it would never happen. At least we'd have Skype and text. As she waved goodbye, I felt like a deflating helium balloon spinning into space.

I returned to French class on Monday to find that Summer wasn't the only one missing. To my relief, Mrs. Price, the regular high school French teacher, was at the blackboard writing conjugations. No one was able to get anything out of her regarding what happened to Mr. Stokes, but she did confirm that he would not be returning.

When I called Summer to tell her, she insisted that there was no way anyone could know what had happened, and maybe she was right. Regardless, I felt lighter than I had in months. That evening I dyed my hair pink.

Day 2

I wake to a hand gently shaking my shoulder, and the voice of the stewardess. "Time to wake up. We're landing in an hour."

The smell of brewing coffee fills the cabin. I struggle to rouse myself, feeling as though I'm surfacing from the depths of the ocean. I extract my arm from the tangled blanket and check my watch. While I managed to make it to the bathroom the three times I threw up, I upchucked the sleeping pill somewhere along the way and counted at least five torturous hours staring at the ceiling while the others slept soundly. So I probably got about three hours of sleep. I should be in rare form today.

I take a deep breath and let it out slowly, making a vow to myself to let go of the whole rear-facing nausea-inducing shit storm that was the oh-so-perfect start to this "dream trip," and spend the next seven days playing my part in Summer's extravaganza.

I push up the sleeping mask to see Amythest's glittery purple toenails three inches from my face. At least they're pedicured. I instinctively pull my knees into my chest, realizing if her toes are on my pillow, mine are probably on hers. She must have the same thought, because she simultaneously jerks her feet away and our knees ram into each other.

"Ow!" We squirm to sit up. Our eyes meet and we laugh. "Sorry," we say at the same time.

"How you feeling?" she asks.

"I think I got three hours. But I'm not nauseous anymore, so that's good."

The cabin is still configured for sleep, with all the seats converted to single beds barely big enough to hold two girls. On the berth behind us, Brittani and Rhonda are still dozing, and across the aisle from us, Wendy and Claire are waking up as well.

Wendy pushes up her sleep mask and stretches, looking refreshed. "Oh my God, I think that was the best sleep I've had in years! How'd you guys sleep?"

"Fine." I force a smile.

"I could sleep another eight hours." Claire yawns, lying back down.

Wendy claps her hands, ever perky, and pulls Claire up. "Oh no you don't!" she chirps. "Private airports in vacation destinations this time of year are a total scene. We've got to freshen up before we land."

As Wendy unwinds her navy silk hair wrap, I notice her makeup is unsmudged, and her face shows no signs of pillow creasing, "But you're already fresh," I grumble. "How is it possible? It's like you're a fucking unicorn."

"It's this pillowcase," she says, removing the satin cover from the pillow and folding it neatly. "Keeps your skin and hair from creasing." She tucks it in her travel bag, hops out of bed, and spritzes her hair with a travel-size bottle of leave-in conditioner.

"I don't know how I live with you." Claire moans, curling up on the bed.

The younger stewardess comes down the aisle with a tray of fresh coffee and sets it on the table near the divider between Summer and John's half of the plane and ours. "If you could all have a seat at the table, we'll prepare the plane for landing."

We make our way over to the table, and I quickly sit down on the forward-facing side, next to Wendy. The stewardess hands us each an immigration form to fill out, and a stapled legal document. I scan the document, emblazoned at the top with LIONSHARE HOLDINGS. It's a nondisclosure agreement.

"What's this?" I ask.

"It's an NDA. Standard procedure. I'll need it returned before deboarding," the stewardess says.

I turn my gaze back to the document, alarm bells ringing in my head.

"Excuse me," Wendy calls to the stewardess, distressed. "It says here no photography. Does that mean we can't take any pictures?"

The stewardess freezes, a deer in headlights. "Um, I don't..."

Vinny steps in. "No photos of John or any of his associates." I look up, surprised. I hadn't seen him, but there he is, hovering behind us. "And anything taken on the boat or the plane will need to be approved by one of us before posting publicly."

We all nod uneasily.

Wendy makes a show of scribbling her name and handing it over, and the rest of the girls follow suit. I'm still less than comfortable signing, but I don't want to rock the boat before the trip's even truly begun, so I do it, providing my parents' address and phone number as my emergency contact.

Wendy eyes me over her compact as she touches up her foundation. "You sure you slept okay? You don't look so good."

"I threw up my sleeping pill," I confess, "so it took me a while to get to sleep."

She hands me her makeup bag. "The little green tube is eye depuffer."

"Thanks." I squeeze a dot of the cream on my finger and gently apply it beneath my eyes.

"You can keep it," she says. "I never use it."

"Must be nice," Summer says.

We look up to see her standing behind us in the open doorway between her section and ours, freshly showered.

"I'll tell you what must be nice," Wendy teases. "A shower."

"You'll have one as soon as we get to the boat." Summer squeezes in next to Wendy and me. "Can you pass me one of those coffees?"

Brittani slides her a coffee and she takes a sip. "Mmmm." She leans in to Wendy and me, speaking under her breath. "I had to have sex with John twice before we could go to sleep. He accidentally took a Viagra instead of his sleeping pill."

"Accidentally?" I chide.

"Seriously," Summer says. "He's blind as a bat without his glasses, and he left them up front."

"Maybe I should slip Wes a Viagra," Wendy comments.

"You guys still aren't having sex?" I ask.

"He's just so stressed over work, he doesn't feel like it. But he bought me these shoes for the trip. Said every girl needs a pair of Louboutin wedges to go to Europe in the summer. How sweet is that?"

She holds up her foot and shows us her tan woven wedges with the telltale red bottom.

"Ooh, I have those in white. And black. I think I have them in navy, too, but I don't have tan. I need to get the tan," Summer gushes.

Her wardrobe sure has evolved since this time last year, when she was borrowing from my limited closet. But then, she's certainly worked for it. I swallow my vitriol. "Good thing we're the same size." I wink.

"Of course, I can't wear them around John," she whispers. "He can't stand it when I'm taller than him." She assesses Wendy. "You're probably fine wearing heels because you're so short, but you shouldn't," she warns, looking at me. "If you didn't bring flats, you can borrow some."

"I have flats. And not wearing heels for a week sounds great."

"Good." Summer pats my knee. Her eyes land on my wrist. "What kind is that?" She indicates my glowing smart watch.

Her appetite for material goods is voracious.

"It's some weird German brand." I finger the gold band. "I just thought it looked cooler than most of the ones out there that I see."

"I like that it's round," she says. "Lemme try it on."

"It's syncing to my body to tell me when I'm gonna get my period and stuff, so I'm not supposed to put it on other people," I demur.

"Weird," she says. "What else does it do?"

"It tracks my sleep. I'm not sure what else. I just got it."

"You've gotta give me the name. I want one."

"It's not quite as nice as yours." I indicate her Rolex. "And that ring is fabulous."

"Thanks." She admires the sparkling yellow stone in the light. "It's a canary diamond. It's worth, like, two million, if you can believe it."

Two million dollars for a ring? Sweet Jesus, I can think of so many better uses for two million dollars than as a finger decoration.

I have exactly $794 in my bank account. Plus eighteen hundred in cash in my freezer, but that's for rent, due the day after we get back. I don't even have a credit card. I just recently paid off the ten thousand in debt I ran up to buy a car and put down a deposit on an apartment, and I don't want to have the temptation of digging that particular hole again.

Wendy gazes at the bauble, transfixed. "It's gorgeous." Her tummy rumbles. "Sorry. I'm starving!"

"Me too," I say.

"Oh, you guys didn't get any Danishes up here?" Summer asks.

"No," Brittani chimes in. "Why? You have some? I'm starving."

"We had a whole basket," Summer says, "but we ate them all. You guys were supposed to have some up here." She flags down the younger flight attendant. "Are there any more Danishes?"

The girl shakes her head. "I'm sorry."

"But wasn't there a basket for up here?" Summer cocks her head.

"There was, but that was the second basket I gave you," she says.

"You ate two baskets? Piggy!" Brittani exclaims.

"There should be more," Summer insists, ignoring Brittani.

The stewardess nods. "Yes, ma'am. Will you be needing anything else?"

"A double latte with coconut milk and agave."

"Wait, you got lattes on here, too?" Brittani asks. "I'll take what she's having."

The gray-haired stewardess approaches, having finished reconfiguring the beds into chairs. "Please return to your seats for landing."

"Just make the one latte, please," Summer instructs with a roll of her eyes. "Brittani can have a sip of mine."

"Thanks, sis." Brittani's tone drips with sarcasm.

"Brittani!" Rhonda chides. "Be grateful to your sister for bringing you here."

"She knows I'm kidding. God!"

Before I can return to my seat, Summer grabs my elbow. "Sit with me." She pats the forward-facing seat next to her at the table.

I slide into the seat beside her and buckle my seat belt, wondering whether I've already gotten myself in trouble. But maybe, I reproach myself, she's just trying to be nice.

Summer watches the flight attendants chatting at the front of the plane. "I got rid of the pretty ones," she whispers.

I never would have noticed if she hadn't said anything, but indeed the stewardesses are plain, made only more so by their dowdy uniforms. But I can understand her reasoning. John did pick her up on a jet.

When I don't answer right away, she continues. "Sorry John can be a little controlling," she confides. "But he's hardly gonna be around. He'll be working most of the time."

"All good."

"It'll be just like old times, only now I have a yacht." She flashes me a grin, and I see a flicker of my old friend, the girl I shared secrets with before the diamonds and the deceit. "Ooh, look." She points out the window, at a strip of road perched atop a mountain overlooking the sea.

"Is that where we're landing?" I ask, alarmed.

She laughs. "Don't worry. We do it all the time."

It's midday when we land at the small private airport on the Ligurian coast. As we step off the plane into the unrelenting Mediterranean sun, we're greeted by a hot breeze and a sweeping view of the sea. I pause to enjoy it, until Brittani bumps into me, also entranced.

"Holy shit!" she exclaims. "It is so fucking pretty here!"

My ears ringing, I bound down the steps to the tarmac, fishing in my canvas carryall for my passport. Summer stops next to me, rummaging in her giant Louis Vuitton.

"I like your bag," I say, hoping to keep up the camaraderie we shared on the plane.

"I got it to match the rest of my luggage, but it's way too big—I can't ever find anything in it. You can have it when we get back."

Once inside the small stone-and-glass building, we hand over our passports to the lone Italian customs agent, who stamps them without ceremony and hands them back to us. Amythest eyes her stamp with admiration.

"First stamp?" I ask.

"First time I've left the States since I came over from the Philippines. When I was six," she admits.

"You were born in the Philippines?" I ask. She nods. "I've never been there, but I hear it's beautiful."

"Ha. Tell that to my mom. She gave up everything to get away from there."

I want to ask her more, but we've joined the others waiting in the airy lobby for the baggage handlers to bring out our bags. Summer is holding court, thumbing through her passport. "Almost full." She displays her stamps. "We've been to so many places, I'm gonna have to get a new one soon."

I point out a Bahamas stamp. "I remember that one," I say with a conspiratorial smile.

"That's from a trip I took with my mom to Atlantis," she says lightly.

I laugh. "No. It's from when I was shooting that movie there and you and Wendy came down to visit." I open my passport to show her my identical stamp, but her voice stops me cold.

"I don't know what you're talking about." Her green eyes lock on mine, making sure I'm aware of the minefield I'm walking across. "I've only ever been to the Bahamas with my mother and with John."

"Right. Got it."

Good thing they don't stamp your passport when you're driving into Mexico, because—

"What are you girls looking at?" John approaches and places his hand on Summer's shoulder.

"Oh, I was just showing them my stamps from all the places we've been," Summer says a hair too quickly.

In a split second I see him recognize that's not the whole truth, consider it, and decide not to engage. "I have a meeting in town." He throws a smile at the rest of us. "Welcome to the Riviera, girls. I'll see you all on the boat later."

Before anyone can respond, he's halfway across the lobby, Vinny trailing after him. The older goon, whose name I can't remember, rounds us up. "Ladies, your passports."

The other girls hand over their passports to him without a second thought, but I hesitate. One of the first rules of international travel is never to part with your passport.

He holds out his hand to me expectantly. "For safekeeping."

"I can just hold on to it," I say, trying to sound casual. "I'm careful."

"It's not a big deal," Summer says. "It's just the way John does things. Believe me, it's easier if we all just go along."

"I'd rather just hold on to it," I repeat, my heart hammering in my chest.

"Belle, please don't be a problem," Summer implores.

I can't think fast enough to come up with an excuse, and clearly they're not going to make an exception for me. But I don't like this one bit. After another few awkward seconds, I reluctantly acquiesce. He slips our passports into his jacket pocket, and we follow him out into the sweltering day, where two black Suburbans wait under the portico, engines running. The goon climbs into the first one. "Summer, Brittani, and Mrs. Brown, you're with me."

"*Mrs. Brown?*" Rhonda balks. "Please. Call me Rhonda."

He nods without cracking a smile. "Okay, Rhonda."

"What about Amythest?" Brittani asks, hip-checking Amythest. "I wanna be with my girrrl."

"Quit your bitching. You're in Italy!" Rhonda says.

"Whoooooo! It-a-ly!" Brittani croons.

I dive into the second Suburban, thankful for a break from that voice.

Wendy, Claire, and Amythest pile in behind me. We all take in the view as we wind down the mountain, past picturesque homes built into the hillside facing the sea. "I can't believe we're finally here," Claire says.

"I can't believe we had to turn over our passports," I grouse.

"Planning on going somewhere without the rest of us?" Wendy teases.

"It's the principle," I say. "Besides, it's weird. I mean, why do they need my passport? Unlike Summer, I don't enjoy being kept on a leash."

Wendy sneaks a glance at the driver. "John does seem pretty controlling," she agrees in a whisper.

"Yeah." Claire matches her whisper. "The NDA was a little weird."

"And the assigned seats on the plane," I add quietly.

"She said he'll be working most of the time, though," Wendy reasons. "I doubt we'll see him that much. And maybe it's superstition or something. A lot of people are weird about flying."

Leave it up to Wendy to be diplomatic.

"How's he so rich?" Amythest asks.

"I don't know exactly," I say. "His company is Lionshare Holdings? He does something with real estate development, I think, moving money around, funding things."

"Sounds shady," Amythest comments.

"I'm sure some of it is," I agree.

"I don't think so," Wendy says. "He just funded the new superhero movie with that superhot Australian guy who just had a baby with the blonde that was in the last installment? It's like number four in the series I think."

"*Midas 4, When the Gold Runs Out*," I recite. I turn to Wendy. "Speaking of movies, don't mention anything about you guys visiting me in the Bahamas. According to Summer, it never happened."

She raises a perfectly arched eyebrow. "Good to know."

"I just wish she'd tell us these things before," I grumble. "How are we supposed to know what not to say?"

"Well, we know John's jealous," Wendy replies. "So probably skip anything that has to do with another guy. And for sure don't mention Eric."

"Who's Eric?" Amythest asks.

"Summer's ex," I say.

"What happened?"

"He died," Wendy says with an air of finality.

"Shit. How?" Amythest presses.

"It's probably better if we don't talk about it." Wendy looks pointedly at me. "Okay?"

"O-kaaaay." Amythest holds up her hands. "Jeez. So what happened in the Bahamas?"

I could bite my tongue, but I'm feeling ornery. "You know Tate James?"

Amythest nods. "I mean, not personally."

Wendy gives me a sharp glance. "Oh, come on," I say, snorting. "I get not talking about Eric, but this is really not that big a deal." I turn my attention to Amythest and Claire, who lean in attentively. "I had a bit part in a movie he was starring in a couple of years ago—"

"Which one?" Amythest interrupts.

"*Black Heart*," I say.

"Who were you?" she asks.

"I played his girlfriend's best friend who gets taken hostage by his nemesis and killed. I had, like, two lines before I got a dagger to the throat."

"That's so cool," she enthuses.

"So what happened with Summer?" Claire asks.

"My scene required rain, and they wanted real rain, God knows why, so I was down there a couple of weeks waiting for it to rain, and Summer and Wendy came down to visit me. Summer ended up hooking up with Tate. Then his wife showed up for a surprise visit, and he kicked Summer to the curb. She was pretty upset."

"Then what happened?" Amythest prods.

"Nothing," Wendy says, fixing me with a glare.

Okay, fine. I won't tell the part about how Summer showed up at his hotel room and confessed everything to his wife while he was on set, triggering that vicious divorce. "See? Not that exciting," I concede lamely. "We had fun before the *merde* hit the fan, though." I turn to Wendy. "Remember that wedding we accidentally crashed?"

Wendy laughs. "And I ended up making out with the best man. Can you believe that was only, like, three years ago?"

"A lot can change in three years," I say.

I lean my head back against the leather seat and gaze out the window as we descend into a little town at the bottom of the hill that seems almost set-designed to be a quaint Italian village by the sea. The street is lined with bakeries and shops that look like they've been there for hundreds of years.

The Suburbans thread their way slowly through cobblestone streets that were not made to accommodate giant American vehicles, coming to a halt in front of a cute little restaurant with red awnings and ample outdoor seating.

"How cute," Claire comments.

Summer, Rhonda, and Brittani emerge from the front Suburban and stroll past the restaurant. "I was hoping we were going to eat," Amythest says longingly as they disappear from view.

The goon opens the door, and the car fills with the smell of spiced roasting meat. "Where's everyone going?" I ask.

"Summer saw a shop she wanted to stop in."

"Can we just pop in that restaurant and grab a bite while she shops?" Wendy asks. "We're all starving."

He shakes his head. "You stick together. Come on."

We pile out of the car, and he herds us up the street and around the corner, into a little boutique where Summer already has an armful of dresses to try on. She holds a peach one up for us to see. "What do you think?"

"That color is beautiful on you," Rhonda raves.

The smell of fresh-baked bread wafts through the store from the bakery next door. I could faint I'm so hungry. I thumb through a rack. Prada. Miu Miu. Versace. The prices are in euros and are nothing I can remotely afford.

"These clothes are gorgeous!" Wendy exclaims.

Claire shows me the price tag on a swimsuit, wide-eyed. Six hundred fifty euros. For a strip of fabric no bigger than my hand. I sit in a chair in the front corner of the store, looking longingly out the window at curvy Italian girls licking gelato from waffle cones.

Upon seeing the armfuls of outfits Summer is taking into the dressing room, the shopgirl pops open a bottle of prosecco and pours us each a glass. The bubbles caress my tongue and the alcohol hits my stomach like a fireball, warming me from the inside out. Without a morsel of food in my belly, soon I'm fuzzy and starting to enjoy myself. The shopgirl keeps the bubbly coming, and before long, we're all merrily sloshed.

When we finally leave the store, Brittani and Rhonda are restyled in the tasteful new dresses Summer bought them and Bernard is overloaded with Summer's giant shopping bags. I'm a little surprised that he's willing to be her cart horse, but I guess he doesn't have much choice. We stumble down the cobblestone street behind him, the impractical four-hundred-euro white silk scarves Summer bought each of us draped around our necks, our laughter echoing down the narrow pathway. The sight of the restaurant where our Suburbans are parked reminds me of how hungry I am, and I immediately feel the downturn of the champagne buzz already beginning to morph into a headache.

Wendy grabs my arm. "Do you smell that? Fresh pizza."

I inhale the scent of baking crust, bubbling tomato sauce, smoked meats. I know I'm supposed to just go with the flow, but my hunger gets the better of me. Weak at the knees, I turn to Summer. "Please can we just stop in and grab a slice of pizza? We're famished."

"Oh! I totally forgot you guys were hungry! Was there not enough fruit and PowerBars in the car?" she asks.

All of us from the second car shake our heads no. "We didn't have anything," I say.

"Oh my gosh, I'm so sorry!" Summer exclaims. "We had them, so I figured you did. We have to get you something to eat."

Bernard looks up from his cell phone and shakes his head. "We go to the boat. John wants you there when he arrives."

Summer sighs and looks at us with genuine pity. "I'm so sorry. You can have whatever you want as soon as we get to the boat," she promises.

We force smiles and nod.

"The tender is down at the water." Bernard points toward the water, a few hundred yards away. "The cars are too big. We'll walk."

We follow Bernard down another picturesque cobblestone street, the reflected light between the buildings turning gold as the sun makes its daily journey toward the sea. The only one of us talking is Brittani, loudly telling Amythest a graphic story about a guy she was having sex with at a fraternity party and managed to throw up on, then passed out naked on his bed, only to wake to two guys standing over her, pouring beer on her. It's nauseating. I want to slap some sense into her, for the sake of womankind. But I know that would be an exercise in futility. I briefly wish my thoughtful, clever little sister were here in her place. Ha! As if Lauren would be caught dead playing the role of eye candy on some billionaire's yacht.

As we near the bottom of the hill, the road empties into a promenade along the sea where lovers stroll hand in hand and children splash in a fountain. The sun is sinking in the sky, taking with it the heat of the day, and a fresh breeze blows off the water, lifting my hair from my shoulders. A row of restaurants overlook the lapping sea, their outdoor tables filled with laughter over afternoon aperitifs. I close my eyes and take a deep breath, feeling the breeze on my skin, inhaling the salt air, and imprint the scene on my mind, for use at a later date when I'm back in my real life.

I open my eyes to see that the others are almost at the bay and run to catch them as they scurry across the wooden planks behind Bernard toward a large white motorized tender. A tall, thin guy about our age dressed in a crisp white uniform with a name tag that reads HUGO hands us into the boat one by one. His shoulder-length curly brown hair is pulled back in a ponytail, his eyes hidden behind aviator sunglasses, but his smile is warm as he warns each of us in heavily accented English, "Careful, slippery," and "Sit in back if you don't want get wet."

I take a seat on the back row next to Summer and turn to appreciate the sight of the town growing smaller as we chug out of the bay. Wendy whips out her phone and begins taking pictures, and all the girls follow suit, snapping a flurry of shots of the town, the sea, and one another. I frame the town with the mountains above and water below, and post it with the tagline "Vacation begins." I briefly worry that I've somehow violated the NDA, but Summer doesn't say anything, so I'm probably okay.

Once we exit the slow zone, Hugo shouts over the rumble of the motor, "Ladies, hold on to your hats," and hits the gas.

Brittani whoops. I do indeed hold on to my hat as the front of the boat lifts up and we skim over the tops of the waves headed out to sea. Summer leans in and shouts in my ear, "I'm sorry about the food. Believe me, there will be plenty the rest of the trip."

"No worries. I'm just glad to be here. I've been needing a vacation. The bar is killing me."

"Don't worry. You won't be there for long. We'll figure something out. You're so talented, and now that John's funding movies, I'm sure we can get you in something soon. I mean, he has the money—he can kinda make them do whatever he wants."

As much as I would love to believe that's true, we both know John would never in a million years stick out his neck for me. "That would be awesome," I say.

Wendy scoots over next to me. "What are you girls talking about?"

"Just plotting Belle's imminent success," Summer says. She grabs our hands and gives them a squeeze. "I'm so glad you guys are here. Now we just need to get you appropriate boyfriends."

I laugh. "I think our ideas of 'appropriate' are a little different."

"Whatever," Summer says. "I'm telling you, you've gotta stop dating these broke artists and meet a real man who can give you what you deserve."

"You date who you meet," I say. "And I meet struggling actors, mostly. Dylan wasn't, though." I study her for a reaction, but she's unreadable.

"You went out with him once," she laughs. "I wouldn't exactly call that dating."

"Because he lives in a different country," I protest. "But we still message each other sometimes."

She raises her brows.

"He's devastated about losing his brother, understandably," I plow on. I can tell I'm getting under her skin now. "His grandmother lives out here apparently, though? He said he might be visiting, so I told him I'd let him know if we were close."

"You probably won't have time to see him this trip," she shrugs, keeping her cards close to her chest. "And anyway, if you guys were really into each other, you would have found a way to see each other again before now."

She's not wrong. "Sorry for bringing it up," I say. I wonder if we both know how far I'm stretching the truth.

"It's okay. Just don't say anything about Eric in front of John." She looks pointedly at both me and Wendy. "You guys know I'm still messed up over what happened, but the last thing I need is everyone talking about it."

"What does John know?" I ask.

"Nothing. And I'd like to keep it that way. Okay?"

Wendy and I nod obediently.

Summer pats my knee, softening her tone. "We'll be having dinner with plenty of John's friends this trip. Maybe you'll meet someone; then you won't have to worry about getting acting parts anymore."

I laugh, a little offended. "I'm not in it for the money." But she could never understand that. "And anyway, I'm good being single right now, just having fun."

"You don't wanna wait too long or it'll be too late," Summer warns. "We're not getting any younger. Once we reach thirty, it's over."

"Oh God, don't remind me!" Wendy wails.

I'm more worried about my career as I move toward my thirties than my marriage prospects—Hollywood isn't exactly known for its supply of amazing roles for women who don't look like teenagers. Nevertheless, I'm interested to hear her reasoning. "Why thirty?"

"Because guys know that girls over thirty want to have babies, like, yesterday."

"God forbid anyone want a family," I say.

"I can't wait to get married," Wendy sighs. "I've had my wedding planned since I was in kindergarten."

"We know," says Summer.

"A vineyard, Vera Wang," I chime in, laughing. "It'll be beautiful."

"Unless his family insists on a church, of course," Wendy adds.

"John has a vineyard," Summer offers. "And a church."

"I think Wes is the One," Wendy says dreamily.

"You've thought that about all of them," Summer ribs.

"Well, of course I did. Or I wouldn't have wasted my time with them."

"Just because a relationship doesn't last forever doesn't mean it wasn't successful," I say.

"Ha! A successful relationship is one that ends in marriage," Wendy declares.

I nudge her playfully with my shoulder. "I'm sorry, what decade are we living in?" I tease. "I'd say a successful relationship is one you learn from, no matter how it ends."

"You're both crazy," Summer says. "It's one you gain from. Duh. *Qui n'avance pas, recule.*"

Well, at least she's honest about her point of view. I don't think that's the intended use of the proverb, but I guess the point of a proverb is that it can apply to many different situations.

"What does that mean?" Wendy asks.

"It literally translates to 'who does not move forward, recedes,'" I say, then smile at Summer. "Somebody remembers her high school French."

"It was rusty, trust me, but we spent some time in Paris in the spring, so I was able to brush up." Summer returns my smile without a hint of acknowledgment of my reference to our shared past.

"I didn't know you guys could speak French," Wendy says, impressed.

"We took it together in high school," I explain. "Though I think we spent more time ogling our teacher than doing conjugations."

Summer laughs.

"Smile." Rhonda points a camera at the three of us. We pose, and she clicks.

The sea is full of yachts. Colossal as cruise ships and streamlined as space-ships, white and black and silver; each is resplendent in her own right. Our tender approaches a sleek white one, large by anyone's standards, but medium in comparison with the others on the horizon. She looks to be about three stories high, sizable enough to have a couple of Jet Skis and tenders docked underneath, not quite big enough for a helipad. THE LION'S DEN is etched in gold block letters across her stern.

"We've ordered a new one with a helipad, but they take forever to build, so we're still in this one," Summer sighs. "So we'll just have to tender everywhere. Sorry."

I stare up at the floating palace. "It'll do." A rush of blood to my head. A week on this thing, huh?

Wendy points to the name and laughs. "Kinda perfect, since you're a Leo and all."

"Oh, you're right. I didn't think about that," Summer muses. "John named it. He kinda has a thing with lions. Because of his last name, I guess."

Two white-uniformed crew members rush over to help secure the tender and assist Hugo in handing us up the ladder onto the lower deck of the boat, where the rest of the crew stands in a semicircle, smiling, their hands clasped behind their backs.

"You have to take your shoes off," Summer instructs as one of the crew comes around with a basket, into which we all deposit our shoes. "Don't worry. We have a pedicurist coming tomorrow morning."

"Good thing," Brittani guffaws. "I think I have something growing under my big toenail."

I cringe.

"Welcome to the *Lion's Den*," Hugo says. "Your home for the week. I introduce to you our French crew."

We all turn to face the orderly line of crew members.

Hugo gestures to a stocky white-bearded man who looks straight out of central casting. "This is Bruno. He is our great captain." Bruno nods at us with just a hint of a smile.

Next to Bruno is a linebacker of a man in his thirties, with a shaved head, his muscles nearly ripping out of his sleeves. "This is Jean; he is first mate. He does all the heavy lifting here, as you can see."

Next to Jean is a good-looking guy of indeterminate race, dark skin and hair, probably around our age. "This is Alexandre; he is second mate."

Wendy elbows me. Alexandre flashes a thousand-watt smile and says, "Dre."

That one I think I'll remember.

Hugo moves on to the next in line, a wiry little guy in his twenties with brown hair and glasses, who looks like he would work at a tech start-up. "Luc is our engineer, anything technology—you can't work the stereo, you drop the iPhone, he can help."

Next to Luc is a well-groomed woman in her late thirties, over-Botoxed, long blond hair in a ponytail, diamond studs in her ears. "This is our chief steward, Julie." Julie gives us a perfunctory smile and nod.

Next to Julie is a slim brunette about our age with sharp features, full lips, and a pixie cut. "This is Emmanuelle. She is our second stew."

Last in line is a petite, dark-skinned girl with freckles, her long black hair in a braid that falls over her shoulder. I'm guessing she's of North African descent, and she can't be more than twenty. "This is Camille; she is our junior stew. And you know I am Hugo. I am the utility man. Anything you need, we make it happen," Hugo says with a little bow.

A man in a white chef's uniform, his salt-and-pepper hair pulled back in a ponytail, appears in the doorway with a silver tray of food in each hand. "Oh," Hugo says, "I cannot forget Jacques, *le meilleur* chef. If you like to take your seat at the table, we have some food for you."

Jacques sets the trays down on a circular table in the shade. "Who is hungry?"

We all slide into the plush white banquettes as Emmanuelle hands out champagne glasses and Julie comes around with a bottle of Dom Pérignon.

"Finally!" Brittani says, reaching over me to snatch a handful of prosciutto and melon.

Silence descends on the table as we fall upon the hors d'oeuvres like a pack of starved dogs. A helicopter buzzes overhead, whipping up the waves as it makes its way to a gargantuan black yacht floating nearby.

"Igor Rajinovsky." Summer waves her fork vaguely in the direction of the yacht. "Russian billionaire. He's a friend of John's. And that one over there"—she points out a white yacht, just as substantial as the black one—"is his wife's."

"Why do they have two?" asks Claire.

"They have an understanding," Summer explains. "On his, he has one floor of Swedish girls, one floor of Thai girls, and one floor of Russian girls. They rotate in and out every week. That's probably a new shipment coming in now."

"Hookers," Brittani clarifies.

"More like a harem," Summer says.

"What's the difference?" Claire whispers in my ear.

"Anyway, their kids are on the wife's boat, so he gets the best of both worlds," Summer continues.

"Who says you can't have your cake and eat it, too," I joke.

"Why don't they just get a divorce?" Claire asks.

"Cheaper to keep her," Summer quips. We all look at her blankly. "When you have as much money as these guys, divorce is so expensive and complicated, sometimes it's just not worth it."

"And she's, like, totally okay with this?" Wendy asks, incredulous.

"It's not exactly her call," Summer says. "And anyway, she gets a three-hundred-foot yacht and the cachet of being his wife, so you can't exactly feel bad for her."

"If my husband gives me a three-hundred-foot yacht, he can cheat on me as much as he wants," Amythest chimes in.

She and Summer clink glasses.

"As long as you get to pick the crew, of course." Wendy cuts her eyes toward Dre, who is doing something with a rope, his sleeves pushed up, muscles glistening in the sun.

"I think somebody has a crush," I chide.

"Me? No. I'm totally in love with my boyfriend!" Wendy demurs, not totally convincingly. "But I do appreciate a nice view."

Summer eyes Dre. "Don't we all."

I stare out over the ocean, my hunger finally satiated, champagne buzz and lack of sleep combining to make me feel slightly removed, like I'm floating.

Which, of course, I am. On a yacht. In the Mediterranean. It's all very surreal, euphoric almost—except for the niggling sensation in the back of my mind like a grain of sand stuck in the gears, reminding me I don't belong here. I shouldn't be here. And yet here I am, thanks to Summer. My old friend. Could I have ever imagined, when I met her at sixteen, all the events that would conspire to land me on this yacht, in this immensely unlikely scenario?

"Belle? Belle." Wendy interrupts my reverie. "Earth to Belle."

They're all standing, trying to move out of the banquette, and I'm blocking the way. "Sorry," I murmur, sliding out of the seat.

We each take a cold bottle of water from a basket offered by Hugo and follow Julie's flaxen ponytail from the outdoor dining area into a large living space with built-in navy-and-white-striped couches that face the sea. "This is the main deck," she says.

She leads us deeper into the boat to a more traditional sitting area. The decor is understated luxury, with muted colors, clean lines, and soft fabrics. "As you see, we have two sitting areas and the main dining room." She leads us into a dining area with a long table and an ornate chandelier hanging over it. I look up at the chandelier and notice a camera in the corner of the room. There's one in every corner of the room, actually. I wonder who's watching them.

"Here to right is the kitchen, where Jacques does the magic," Julie continues. "No need go there. Anything you need is here in the bar and kitchenette." She opens the door to the refrigerator, revealing rows of sparkling and flat water, pressed juices, and wine, as well as fresh-cut strawberries, yogurt, cheese, and other snacks. "You ask and we give anything you require." Julie gestures toward a door down a short hallway past the spiral staircase between the kitchen and kitchenette. "Through this door is Monsieur and Madame Lyons's room."

Apparently the crew has not been informed that the missus is not the wife. Summer gives me a quick wink. "Show it to them," she says.

"Of course." Julie threads her way through the group and opens the door to the master suite.

The king-size bed, with its polished wood headboard and built-in bedside tables, is centered on the back wall, an assortment of pillows displayed atop a woven gold comforter. His-and-hers closets are to the right and left of the bed, window seats centered under the large windows that look out over the sea on either side of the room, a large flat-screen television mounted on the wall across from the bed.

Julie opens a door to the left of the television. "The bathroom."

The entire front wall of the white marble bathroom is glass with a view of the water, a large Jacuzzi tub positioned underneath to take in the vista.

Brittani hops into the Jacuzzi. "Holy shit. I'm so taking a bath in your hot tub!"

On the wall next to the steam shower is a framed picture of Summer. She's lying on her side, naked. Her arm is draped so it just covers her nipples, her top leg positioned to cover her crotch, bedroom eyes directed at the camera. No surprise there. It's the bed she's lying on that draws my attention. The light and focus fall off behind her, leaving the room in soft shadow, but I'd know it anywhere. It's my bed.

I also know who was behind the lens. Which is why I'm surprised to see it displayed here.

I'm careful to hide my reaction, but everyone's focus has shifted to Summer, whose voice takes on a shrill edge behind us. "Julie, where's the comforter set I picked out?" she asks. "This quilt thing looks like it belongs in a Holiday Inn."

"I will find it for you." Julie's smile never wavers. "Always, if there is anything we do to make your stay more comfortable, please to let us know."

We trail behind Julie as she exits the room. She gestures to a closed door just outside the master. "Monsieur Lyons's office. Please do not go there." She heads up the wide spiral staircase in the hallway. "Your rooms are all just down the stairs. We see after the tour."

We follow her into an informal room with comfortable couches and another huge flat-screen TV, as well as a large desk with two sleek computers. "This is the upper deck," she says.

I stare up at the life-size oil painting of John that presides over the room. As I move, his deep-set eyes seem to follow me. It's unnerving.

He does personify power. I'll give him that. And I guess to certain women, money and power are more attractive than a taut jawline and shared cultural references. But John is older than Summer's dad, or Three—or any of her stepdads, for that matter. How do you get around that? I mean, five, ten, fifteen years' difference, no big deal. Even twenty, especially as people get older. But thirty-six years? Maybe it's true love, but let's face it: it's an arrangement you only ever see between very rich men and very beautiful women.

Shut up, Belle. She's clearly made her choice. Everybody has different needs, and God only knows what kind of complexes having Rhonda as a mother and a string of crappy stepdads has given Summer.

Anyway, regardless of our divergent taste in men, my issues with

Summer go way beyond her relationship with John. If only it were that simple.

Julie picks up a remote control and hits a button. Blackout shades silently lower over the three walls of windows, obstructing the gorgeous views of the water, darkening the room until it's almost pitch black. "If you want to watch a movie during day," she says.

"Or you have a hangover," Brittani pipes up.

Julie raises the shades. "Luc teach you the remote later." She descends two steps into the circular sunken dining room with curved walls of glass that slide open at the touch of another button, bringing the indoors outdoors. "All the doors on the back of the boat open, so you have comfort of the inside with the beauty of the outside."

A large deck with built-in lounge areas extends beyond the dining table into the sun. Julie hits another button and a sunshade stretches out over the deck. "If you have too much sun."

She heads up a stairway that curves around the outside of the boat, and we all follow. Amythest grips my arm, looking down at the sea below us as we ascend. "You okay?" I ask.

She nods. "I just—all this water kinda freaks me out," she admits.

"You're safe." I pat her hand. "See all these rails? They're here to keep you on board."

She laughs nervously but doesn't release my arm.

A blast of bright sun and a gust of warm, salty air greets us as we file onto the top of the boat, squinting at the miles of blue around us. "This is the sundeck," Julie says. "Hot tub." She gestures to a big round hot tub at one end of the deck and then to a deck-wide built-in circular padded lounge area. "And for tanning. Also refrigerator with drinks and snacks." She opens a small refrigerator built into the wall of the bar.

"This'll do," Wendy deadpans.

"Now I show you to your rooms," says Julie.

We thread our way down the outdoor staircase, through the upper deck, and down the spiral staircase, past the main deck, where Summer departs for her room, to the lower deck. It's considerably darker and smaller down here, but still very well appointed, with a thick cream shag rug that makes it feel like a cradle. There are two doors on each side of the short hallway and a door at the end marked CREW.

Julie consults a clipboard as she opens the first door to the right. "Wendy and Claire."

The room is just big enough to accommodate two twin beds with a table between them, a small closet, and a door to a minuscule bathroom. A small round window looks out over the sea. Wendy and Claire spill into the room. "Dibs on first shower," Wendy says.

"Drinks on the upper deck at seven," Julie says, closing their door behind them, then opening the door to an identical room across the hallway. "Brittani and Rhonda."

Brittani bounds into the room, followed by her mother. "See you at seven," Julie reminds them.

Julie opens the door on the same side of the hallway as Brittani and Rhonda's room. "Isabelle and Amy...thest," she says, butchering the pronunciation of Amythest's name.

"It's Amythest, like the stone," Amythest corrects her. "Who's in that room?" She indicates the room across the hall from ours.

Julie references her notebook. "Bernard and Vinny."

Foxes in the henhouse.

"See you at seven." Julie shuts us in our room.

Amythest opens the door. "Wait." Julie turns, her eyebrow arched. "What's the Wi-Fi?"

"No guest Wi-Fi. If you wish use computer, you find two on upper deck."

Oh wow. No Wi-Fi. My brain takes a second to adjust to the news. "No Wi-Fi?" Amythest gasps, looking like she's just been slapped. She waves her purple bejeweled phone. "But we don't have any service out here. How are we supposed to, like, do anything?"

"You have service in port. Or use the computer."

Damn. Okay. Though as controlling as John is, I can't say I'm all that shocked. I nod our thanks and close the door firmly as Julie heads up the stairs.

"Weird," Amythest says. "How am I supposed to brag on social media about the awesome time I'm having if I can't post anything?"

She's looking to me to be as upset as she is, but I shrug. "Think of it as a nice break from constant connection. Plus, you can use your phone in port."

She plops down on the bed under the small round window. "Can I have this one?"

"Sure."

I open the closet to find our dresses hanging, her black ones on the right, my colorful ones on the left, our shoes displayed on the shelf between. Hmmm... Nice not to have to unpack, but I can't help feeling a little violated. Are the superrich so accustomed to everything being done for them that someone going through their belongings is routine, or was this John's way of checking our bags? Good thing I didn't bring my vibrator.

I step into the bathroom and rummage in my toiletries bag for my Dramamine. I'm already starting to feel woozy. I should've taken it before I set foot on the boat, but we never got to lay hands on our luggage.

I down the pill with an entire bottle of water.

"You okay?" Amythest asks.

I nod. "I get motion sick. As you know. But I should be fine in an hour."

"Awesome. You're seasick and I'm scared of water. So a week on a boat should be fun."

I laugh, casting a glance around at our tiny room. "I'm claustrophobic, too."

"Wow. What are you doing here?"

I shrug. "Too good to pass up, right? So how do you and Brittani know each other?"

"She was fucking a guy in my acting class."

"You're in acting class?" I shouldn't be surprised. Every other girl in Los Angeles is an actress.

"Yeah. Check this out."

She rolls onto her side and lifts her shirt, displaying a comedy-tragedy mask tattoo on the side of her rib cage.

"Cool," I say. "What have you been working on?"

I usually avoid asking this question due to my own demons, but I can't help myself. I'm genuinely interested.

"Horror stuff, mostly. I usually play the slutty girl that gets killed. It's hella fun. I've done a bunch of movies." She counts off on her fingers. "*Slasher Hotel 5, Revenge of the Teenage Sluts, Peter Peter Pumpkin Eater, Vampire Girls of Cell Block Six . . .*"

I get the picture. "You've been busy. How long have you been in LA?"

"Oh, I moved down from Oakland as soon as I turned eighteen, like, two years ago? And I've just been working as much as I can ever since." Two years ago—that would make her only twenty. Wow. She pops up to standing, stripping off her clothes. She's not wearing anything underneath. "I'm gonna hop in the shower."

She traipses into the bathroom and plops down on the toilet without closing the door behind her—a level of intimacy I'm not sure we've quite reached.

I lie down on my bed. It's much softer than it looks. My limbs feel like they weigh a million pounds and my brain is cotton candy, the cocktail of jet lag and champagne too strong to resist. I close my eyes.

At 7:00 p.m. sharp, I follow Amythest up the stairs to the upper deck. She's wearing a backless black dress that showcases the intricately shaded angel wings unfurled across the top of her back. I'm still clearing cobwebs from my head, having slept until she woke me ten minutes ago, but I took the fastest shower in the history of showers and somehow managed to pull it together. My wet hair is brushed back in a low ponytail, my face clean of makeup save lipstick in a bright-pink hue to match my pink maxi dress. I won't be nearly as chic as Summer and Wendy,

I'm sure, but what else is new? Anyway, I have to stop comparing myself with them. We have different strengths, I remind myself. And weaknesses.

Dre greets us at the landing with a gilded tray of pink champagne. The crew has changed into black for the evening, the women in cocktail dresses and the men in tuxedos, and he looks even better in a tuxedo. He meets my eye with a sexy smile as I take a glass. I would much rather get to know him than one of John's friends.

Stop it, Belle. Bad idea.

But really, how would anyone know?

I focus on the camera staring at me from behind Dre's head. Right. No hanky-panky with the crew.

Amythest and I join the other girls in the lounge, where golden rays of the setting sun mingle with the chandelier to splinter into a thousand shards of light around us. Everyone looks refreshed. Claire and Wendy have on maxi dresses similar to mine, Brittani wears a surprisingly stylish sundress that I'm guessing was selected by her sister, and Rhonda is in some kind of (also surprisingly stylish) sparkly silver top and white pants. The goons are in suits, their backs to us, looking out over the water in deep conversation, and Summer has not yet appeared.

"I feel like we're inside a disco ball," I say to Wendy as we air-kiss.

She laughs. "I like your dress."

"Thanks." I see no reason to mention I got it for twenty-nine dollars at Target. "Yours is pretty, too."

She tilts her head and assesses me, then unclasps one of her many layered gold necklaces and fastens it around my neck. "There," she says, stepping back to admire her handiwork. "Perfect."

"Thank you." I finger the necklace, convincing myself to be grateful for her generosity instead of nettled by her need to fix me.

"You girls aren't the only ones who are gonna find boyfriends on this trip," Rhonda announces to all of us with a wink.

"Mom, that's gross. You're, like, a million years old," Brittani protests.

"She is not!" Wendy says. "And anyway, she looks amazing for her age."

"Thank you, honey," Rhonda says. She leans in and whispers, "I'm actually ten years younger than John. So is Summer's dad."

"Yeah, but these guys date girls that are, like, our age, obviously." Brittani rolls her eyes. "And even Summer's dad's wife is, like, ten years younger than he is. And he's not even rich."

"Who do you think taught Summer everything she knows?" Rhonda retorts.

I cringe.

"I'm not saying I have to date someone John's age," she goes on slyly. "I'm gonna find me a ninety-nine-year-old in a wheelchair!"

Everyone titters. "Rhonda, you're so funny," Amythest says.

But Rhonda continues, proud of her logic. "I'm serious! Guys that old can't get it up anymore anyway, and girls your age need too much. The oldest men just want someone to cut up their steak and laugh at their jokes till they die. And then you get their estate."

"Or a tenth of it, once you split it with their ex-wives and children," I chime in.

But Rhonda is dead serious. "At ninety-nine, it's a small time you have to work to get the reward." Clearly she has given this some thought.

Amythest nods. "Smart."

I can almost see my sister rolling her eyes. But I have to laugh. Every one of Rhonda's marriages has been shorter and more profitable than the last, and finally her daughter has catapulted her into a world of wealth she never dreamed of. Summer has grown up to become *exactly* who Rhonda hoped she would be. Which, I guess, makes Rhonda a terribly successful mother.

At that moment, Summer herself appears at the top of the stairs, looking appropriately like a shiny trophy in a tight gold Hervé Leger dress that pushes her boobs nearly to her chin. John is close behind her in a navy linen button-down and slacks, his hand on the small of her back, the combination of her jeweled flat sandals and the doubtless lifts in his polished Italian leather conspiring to make them the same height.

Emmanuelle dings a glass, and a hush falls as we turn to face them, like some kind of bridal couple. Summer beams as John raises his glass, and we all do the same. "A toast to Summer. Thank you all for joining us for her birthday voyage."

We all drink to Summer; then Emmanuelle dings her glass again. "We invite you downstairs. Jacques prepare *très bon* dinner for you."

Emmanuelle wears the same black A-line dress as the rest of the female crew, but it fits her lithe body like a glove, revealing curves the day-crew uniform concealed. Summer and John follow her swaying hips down the stairs, and we trail behind.

The table is set with an array of crystal and goldware, adorned with white candles and roses. Jazz music plays softly, and the chandelier over the table sparkles in the low light.

John stands behind a chair at the head of the table, with Summer to his right. Brittani flounces over and plops into a chair across from Summer, and Julie quickly appears behind her, deftly helping her back to standing by her elbow as Brittani makes a face behind her back.

"Rhonda." John gestures to the seat vacated by Brittani. He proceeds to arrange the remainder of us around the table. I'm seated next to Rhonda, across from Summer and Brittani, while Wendy fidgets on my other side. I can tell she's agitated that she's not closer to Summer and John. I'd like nothing more than to give her my seat if I could, but that's obviously out of the question.

As we take our seats, John beckons to Emmanuelle and speaks to her in a low voice. Summer's eyes slide from Emmanuelle's tanned shoulders to her slender waist as she laughs and quickly responds to John. I can't make out the words, but they're speaking French, and Emmanuelle is clearly pleased he shares her mother tongue.

Summer catches my eye across the table. "*Je suis ravi de boire le vin*," she announces, directed at me but loud enough for the entire table to hear.

"*Moi aussi*," I say. I'm not sure what wine she means, but it seems the right response in the moment.

Emmanuelle turns, caught off guard, and Summer gives her an icy smile.

Hugo appears with a bottle of red, some fancy French name I'm sure we're meant to be impressed by, and Emmanuelle evaporates.

"Belle, you're gonna love this mozzarella," Summer gushes as beautifully plated, lush caprese salads are placed before us. "The chef made it fresh."

I cut a bite, thrown by her sudden warmth toward me. "You know how I feel about cheese." The mozzarella is somehow both rich and light at the same time, and melts in my mouth, leaving me immediately craving another forkful.

"Thank you so much for inviting us on this wonderful trip," Wendy pipes up. "I'm so thrilled to be here to celebrate your birthday with you."

Everyone nods and murmurs agreement.

"Tonight," John says, his eyes landing on each of us in turn, "you will all give a toast to Summer, tell us how you met. Rhonda, you start."

Rhonda laughs. "Well, I think we all know how I met Summer. She came out of my hoo-ha!"

Record scratch. Then everyone titters politely. "Please, stand," John says, amused.

Rhonda stands, swaying ever so slightly. "Um, well, my beautiful Summer was born right around this time twenty-seven years ago— you're young enough we can still say your age, right?"

"Until I'm thirty; then it's twenty-nine for life," Summer quips. I wonder when my best friend became such a cliché. But then, I wonder a lot of things about her these days.

"It was a hot night in Texas, so it was just me and my friend Charlene. That was back in the days before people really did epidurals, at least out in the country where we were, so they gave me some Tylenol, but that was it. It was a hard night, but the moment I saw her, it was all worth it. I could tell how beautiful she was from the very beginning, and she's only gotten more beautiful every year."

This is the most earnest I have ever seen Rhonda—she is actually starting to tear up, which makes the rest of us misty-eyed as well. "You'll always be my little girl, and you know I'd do anything for you. I'm so glad you've found such a nice man to take care of you. I always knew you would. Thank you for sharing this trip with your little mama. I love you."

We all raise our glasses, and Summer gives her mom a hug. "I love you, too, Mom."

They both wipe away tears and sit as Brittani stands and looks around. This should be good. "My big sister. She's always been the smart one." No one says anything. "Shit, don't everybody protest at once." She guffaws. "For real, though, good thing I could borrow from her book reports. My teachers always thought it was weird that my book reports were so good but I couldn't actually talk about the book in class. I'm kidding. I would never steal her book reports."

She clearly wants a laugh here, and everyone obliges (though it's hardly a joke: Brittani can't stand to read and would always get Summer to do her homework).

"She's the best sister ever and has been helping me out her whole life. And now, because of her and John, I get to go to an awesome college. So, John, thank you so much for getting me in, and, Summer, thank you for making me go to junior college so that I could 'better myself.' Now I just have to find a husband before I graduate so I don't have to work. I'm just kidding. But not really. Love you."

"Love you, too," Summer says, and blows her a kiss across the table. "And you're smarter than you think you are."

This is sweet but completely untrue. Brittani, God bless her, doesn't have the sense she was born with, and that speech proves it.

John gestures to Vinny, down at the other end of the table. He stands and raises his glass. "To Summer, the most beautiful young woman. Happy birthday."

Now it's my turn. I stand and smile at Summer. "I met Summer when we were freshmen in high school and she moved in next door to me, way down south in Georgia."

"Oh my God." Summer laughs. "Don't remind me."

I ignore this response. "We were best friends from the moment we met, but what I remember the most was the summer before our junior year. We did a lot of trading novels, watching French movies, playing tennis...and sneaking Rhonda's wine coolers that summer."

"I wondered how I was drinking them so fast!" Rhonda exclaims.

Everyone laughs. I take a deep breath and continue. "Summer was truly there for me when I needed her that year, and I'll never forget it. Even after she moved two thousand miles away, we talked as much as if we still lived next door to each other." I don't mention the reason I needed her was that I'd nearly been raped while escorting her to our teacher's apartment, against my better judgment. Nor do I mention that I was a virgin until I was twenty as a result, or that though I've gotten past the fear of sex, the smell of Drakkar Noir can still provoke a panic attack in me. "We've been through lots of ups and downs together, and I look forward to many more years of friendship. Happy birthday!"

"Thank you," Summer says, her hand over her heart. I search her face as I take my seat, trying to see how sincere she is, how sincere she thinks I am. But her eyes are nothing but a shimmering, shallow pool.

Bernard stands and raises his glass. "People think men rule the world, but a beautiful woman can have all those men in the palm of her hand, and you, my dear, deserve it. The smile, the eyes, the body, you have it all. Happy birthday!"

Lecherous old fart. We raise our glasses nonetheless and once again drink to Summer. "That's so sweet. Thank you, Bernie." She bats her eyes. "I'm glad my Spin classes are paying off."

Amythest is next. I wonder what she can possibly say about Summer, having met her yesterday, and I can tell from the slightly amused look on Summer's face that she's thinking the same thing. All eyes turn to Amythest expectantly as she stands, spinning her already empty wineglass between her fingers. "Well, I met Summer yesterday," she starts, "through her awesome little sister, of course." She smiles at Summer. "I always hear such awesome things about you from Brittani, and I can tell they're totally true."

Summer returns her smile. "Aw, thank you."

Amythest continues. "You're someone I totally look up to. I hope I'm just like you when I'm older."

The smile on Summer's face evaporates as Amythest finishes. "Thanks for letting Brittani bring me on this awesome trip. Happy birthday!"

John nods to Claire, who stands nervously and speaks in a rushed, soft voice. "I met Summer through Wendy. You guys have such a wonderful friendship, and I know we don't know each other that well, but you're so sweet, and I'm just so glad to be included, and so happy to be here. Happy birthday."

She raises her glass and sits in one motion, out of breath.

"You're the sweet one, Claire," Summer says. "I'm glad you could come."

Wendy stands and looks around at the table with a smile. "I'm going to break things up a little, and before I give my toast to my best friend, give one to her wonderful boyfriend, John, without whom none of us would be here. John, thank you for being so great to Summer and for taking us all on this fantastic trip."

She raises her glass and everyone chimes in, "Thank you, John!"

John throws Wendy a wide smile, pleased. Wendy's good like that. She always knows when to stroke whose ego and how to strike just the right note so that she doesn't come off as obsequious.

"Now…" Her gaze lands on Summer. "I met Summer through Belle, who I met in college."

"We were all at UCLA together," Summer says.

Not true.

Recognizing the danger in that direction, Wendy seamlessly changes course. "I'll never forget how Summer took care of me after my accident. I broke my leg last year jumping," she explains. "Horses. My parents couldn't come out for my surgery because my father's a senator, and it was right before the election—which he won, thank God." I notice she's failed to mention he's a *state* senator, but no matter. "Summer was there for me, though. She was right beside me in the hospital when I had the pins put in my ankle, holding my hand."

Okay, no, that was me. Missed a callback for a guest-star role on a network show to be there. Summer was supposed to be there, too, but at the last minute she got a date with some guy she was into and bailed.

Wendy casts a glance about the table. Am I imagining it, or is she avoiding my eyes? "She got me such a big arrangement of sunflowers—my favorite—that it barely fit through the door."

I scrutinize Wendy's countenance, looking for any sign as to whether she's totally lost her memory or is intentionally spinning lies. Surely she hasn't forgotten I sent those flowers. She was so overwhelmed she actually sent me a snail-mail thank-you note.

But she has not finished assigning my kindnesses to Summer. "Then, afterward," Wendy rattles on, "Summer was there every night, bringing me home-cooked meals, driving me around to doctor's appointments. I saw what it means to be a real friend during that time, and I'll never forget it."

Okay. Summer has never made a "home-cooked meal" in her life, and she didn't even have a car at that time. She was sleeping on my couch (or rather, in my bed) while she got her life together after the guy she was living with kicked her out when he found out she was cheating on him. Admittedly, I was far from the only one who drove Wendy to doctors' appointments—she has a plethora of friends—but if Summer ever did, in fact, drive her anywhere, which I highly doubt, it was in my car, which she borrowed.

Wendy's poker face is so strong, I can't tell whether she believes her own story or has related it to ingratiate herself with Summer and John, but regardless, it's worked. John pats Summer's hand as she beams at Wendy, saying, "Oh, it was nothing. That's what friends are for!"

I manage to maintain a pleasant demeanor but am quiet the rest of dinner, still flabbergasted by Wendy's convoluted version of events. No one notices my silence, though, as John and his men dominate the conversation with a discussion about the best strategy for convincing some Chinese investors to partner with John's company on what sounds like an incredibly complicated development project. I try to follow along, but all I can gather is that John seems bent on meeting with the men before showing them the property, and Bernard and Vince disagree. John, of course, wins.

When dinner is over, John presents Summer with an emerald set: a necklace, bracelet, and earrings to match. It's gorgeous, if your tastes run toward "Russian matron at the opera."

Afterward, I head to the upper deck and log in to my email on one of the computers under the watchful eye of John's portrait. I send a quick message to Lauren_Carter812:

Hi sis,

Made it to the boat! It's ridiculous. We're somewhere near the border of France and Italy, headed toward Saint-Tropez. Summer's a little removed from all of us, attached to John at the hip, but is at least being nice to me. I'm rooming with a girl named Amythest (yep, you read that right) that Brittani brought. She has eyes to match her name, in case you were wondering. Rhonda's here too...hasn't changed. John has two of his men with him, Bernard and Vinny, who are everything you would imagine in a billionaire's henchmen. There's no cell service and no Wi-Fi on the boat (writing from one of their hardwired computers, remember those?), so tell Mom and Dad not to worry if they can't reach me immediately.

Weather's beautiful, and I'm feeling good, regardless of not sleeping much on the plane. Nothing else to report for now.

Will keep you posted.

Love,
Belle

It's hard to feel totally relaxed sending messages I'm sure are being read, but I remind myself that no matter how creepy his painting, John has no reason to care what's in my emails. No more reason than he does anyone else's, anyway. Given John's concerns about privacy, the hardwired system is probably mainly for his own protection, to prevent hackers from being able to access his servers without physically being on board. Still, it makes me uncomfortable, so I log off without checking social media. A shame, because I bet the pic I posted from the tender got a boatload of likes.

I despise social media, but the sad truth is that it's necessary for my career these days. Some actors even put their followers on the top of their résumé. That would make me *Isabelle Carter: 21.5K Insta, 34K Twitter, 6K YouTube*. Not great, but not horrible. Most of my followers are fans of a cheesy sitcom on the Family Channel that I had a supporting role in a few years ago. I know I should work on growing my following—I could get free stuff for posts, or money. And I need money. But I'm a terrible millennial. I just feel so gross being all, "Hey, look at me!" I didn't get into acting for the fame. I got into it for the art.

I know, what a loser.

I count seven surveillance cameras on the path from the upper deck to my room. Nearly the entire yacht is covered, save the bathrooms and bedrooms. Unless there are hidden cameras... The thought makes me shiver. I wonder who's monitoring them, the little tech guy?

I tell myself I'm just being paranoid. No one's watching me pee.

Back in the room, I'm more tired than I expected after my earlier nap. Definitely too tired to engage with Amythest, who prattles on excitedly about the boat and who we might meet and how awesome it all is. I try to hold my eyes open and nod politely, but they keep closing involuntarily, and after a while she gives up and reads a magazine.

I guess walls on yachts aren't that thick, because as I fall asleep I can hear Rhonda and Brittani talking through the partition between our rooms. It's muffled, but the gist is something about trying to get John to marry Summer so that all their problems will be solved.

* ★ ★

I wake in the middle of the night to a pounding headache and a burning thirst. How much wine did I drink? I've got to be better about hydrating.

I reach for the water bottle on the bedside table, but it's empty. Damn it. Amythest's is empty, too. Going upstairs is the last thing I want to do right now, and I'm tired enough I could probably ignore my thirst and get back to sleep, but I know this will only make my headache worse. I swing my feet off the bed and push myself to standing.

I grip the doorknob and attempt to turn it, but it moves only a fraction of an inch before sticking. I jiggle it and push the door. It doesn't budge. What the...? I throw my shoulder into it, to no avail.

We're locked in.

Amythest stirs, woken by my beating on the door. She looks at me, confused. "What's going on?"

"Nothing," I say, not wanting to worry her. "Sorry. Go back to sleep."

We're fucking locked in.

I refill my water bottle with water from the tap and lie staring at the ceiling. But this time it takes me hours to finally fall asleep.

(two years ago)

Los Angeles

W elcome to Heaven. I'm Belle. I'll be your angel."

Behind my sunglasses I clocked a group of ten in the cabana with a view of Hollywood, seven guys and three girls. They were in their twenties, tanned, and from what I could tell, already well lubricated.

"Our angel!" A bouncy blonde clapped. "I love your wings. I want some!"

I forced a smile. "They're for sale in the gift store." I hated the stupid wings almost as much as I hated the iridescent white bikini top and barely there skirt that made up the rest of my angel uniform. But the money was good and I got to wear sneakers, so I swallowed my pride.

"Just bring her a pair of the damn wings and put it on my tab," instructed a buff guy with mirrored sunglasses, wrapping his arm around my shoulders. His damp underarm hair tickled my skin; I did my best not to recoil.

"Okay." This was a huge pain in the ass, as the gift store was in the lobby and I was working a crowded rooftop pool, but we weren't allowed to say no to the guests. Buff guy's arm slipped from my shoulders to my waist, replacing the tickle of his underarm hair with the feeling of his clammy hand on my stomach. I wasn't sure which was worse. In any other situation, I would've slapped him. But we both knew I needed his tip.

"I'll take a Pilsner," he said. "And a shot of Jack."

"I want a strawberry daiquiri," one of the girls chimed in. "And a chicken salad."

"Cadillac margarita with salt," said another.

"Red Bull vodka," a guy demanded as he pushed past me toward the pool.

"Me too," added another, following him. "And guac and chips."

"Make that three. And a cheeseburger."

"Okay." I maintained my smile. "Is this all on one tab?"

Buff Guy mindlessly stroked my back with his thumb. "I'll take the girls, but the rest of these guys are on their own."

God, I hated my job. "Okay." I wriggled out of his grasp. "Lemme just get this started, and I'll be back for the rest."

I punched in their order on the computer and hefted a tray of draft beers for another table. As I carefully threaded my way through the crowd of wet revelers, I felt a tap on my shoulder and turned to see Summer, her hair swept up in a messy bun, her hot-pink bikini doing an insufficient job of containing her new boobs.

"Hey!" I exclaimed. "What are you doing here?"

"Just lying out. Take a break for a sec. Come hang with me."

"We're not allowed to sit. Or fraternize with guests."

She rolled her eyes. "So stupid. What time are you off?"

"Five."

"Oh good! You have to come with me to this art show. I met the most amazing guy. He's supersmart and so talented, and crazy hot. . . ."

I shifted the tray of beers onto a cocktail table. "Did you break up with Brian?"

"No. I live there! I can't break up with him. But he's barely in town, so it's no big deal. He'll never find out." This seemed like terrible reasoning to me, but Summer's dating habits were so far removed from my own that I knew nothing I could say would matter. "Anyway, I'm meeting the hot guy at this art show, and his brother's gonna be in town for the night, so I thought we should all go out together."

"What's the brother like?"

72

"I don't know, but I saw a picture and he was hot, too. Just come be my wingman. Please? If you don't like him, you don't have to stay."

I shrugged. "Okay."

"Thank you! Thank you!" She hopped up and down, her bouncing boobs drawing stares from every guy in eyeshot. "I swear it's gonna be fun."

Over Summer's shoulder, I spied my boss watching me from the deck. I slid my tray off the cocktail table. "I gotta get back to work."

I'd not taken two steps when a bear of a guy abruptly backed out of the conversation he was having to plow directly into me, drenching us both in Heineken.

"Watch where you're going," he reprimanded me.

I looked up to where my boss stood on the deck to see her shaking her head, her mouth in a hard line. Great. So on top of having to pay for the spilled drinks out of my tips, I was obviously going to be chastised by her as well, if not fired. At least I'd ostensibly be meeting a hot guy later. Good thing. By the end of this day, I was gonna need a diversion.

At six thirty sharp I descended the stairs to the subway, freshly showered and clad in a black dress that I hoped straddled the line between sexy and hip, perfect for an art show. I settled into a window seat as the nearly empty train hurtled into the tunnel, turning my attention to my phone.

It connected to the train's Wi-Fi, and a text from Wendy popped up:

Hey lady do u have that pic of us & Summer from Coachella 2 years ago where we're sitting on a stage? I wanna frame it for her birthday but I can't find it.

I opened the photos app and used the map feature to scroll past this year's Coachella pictures—neither Summer nor I were there; I'd had to work and she'd been in Hawaii with Brian—but Wendy had kept us more than updated with photos of her and the ever-rotating gaggle of gorgeous girls she always traveled with, all hats and feathers and bare midriffs, glazed eyes hidden by sunglasses. Claire was the only one I knew by name, always hovering on the edge of the group looking less like trouble than the other girls. Wendy was invariably at the center, of course, impeccably dressed and perfectly poised, flashing her sparkling smile.

I had to stifle a laugh when I landed on the previous year's Coachella pics—none of which were actually taken at Coachella. Wendy had been working for an event planner in charge of Coachella-adjacent private parties at homes with pools and DJs and had hired Summer and me to sling drinks for inebriated celebrities and their entourages. Wendy's boss ran her ragged while Summer and I were on our feet noon to midnight for a measly three hundred dollars per day (no tips allowed!), wearing see-through burnout crop tops emblazoned with BARTENDER BABES. There was a priceless selfie of the three of us hiding behind the bushes on the side of the party house eating leftover canapés and guzzling vodka Red Bulls in the dark and another of us giggling maniacally while squeezed into a double bed in a house rented by some guy who had a crush on Wendy and let us crash for free.

Finally I reached the pictures from two years ago, the ones Wendy actually wanted. She and I were seniors at UCLA at the time, and someone had gifted her a handful of VIP tickets—an exorbitant gesture of the sort that happened to Wendy on a regular basis. We were relatively new friends, having only met the previous year, so I'd yet to introduce her to Summer.

Truth be told, I hadn't done the best job of keeping up with Summer while I was in college. We'd remained close the last two years of high school, our constant texts and Skype calls serving as a pressure-release valve for my small-town Georgia life, which I was beginning to find suffocating. My freshman year at UCLA we communicated less, though we did have a great time when she came out from Arizona for spring break. But the following year, after she moved with Rhonda and Brittani to the Inland Empire—only an hour away—we only saw each other maybe every few months. It wasn't just the drive; our lives were in such different places—she was working at Hooters and taking cosmetology classes while I was studying and doing plays. When she'd come into LA for the night, she'd want to go out to clubs to meet guys and I'd want to go over to a drama friend's house to smoke pot and listen to obscure records. But I'd always thought that Summer and Wendy would get along, so when one of the other girls from our Coachella group dropped out last-minute, I asked Wendy if I could offer Summer the ticket.

I was right. Maybe too right. From the moment they laid eyes on each other, Summer and Wendy were inseparable. I soon felt like a third wheel trailing behind them, watching their flower crowns catch the afternoon sun as they bent their heads together plotting which stage or bar to hit next. I wasn't surprised that Wendy took to Summer so quickly; she collected pretty friends like charms, and Summer was the most dazzling of them all. It was Summer's instant affinity for Wendy that caught me off guard. Summer had never had many female friends. She didn't need them. In Georgia, I was her sole confidante. In fact, during all the years I'd known her, she'd only introduced me to two girlfriends, neither of whom she'd ever mentioned again. Of course I'd hoped she'd like Wendy, but I never imagined I'd be left in the tent holding our place while they went off to do whatever it was they were whispering about.

The pictures from the trip were reflective of this dynamic. Wendy and Summer dancing, outlined in the blues and pinks of the stage lights; Wendy and Summer peering over identical sunglasses while sipping identical drinks; Wendy with Summer's hair draped over her so that she looked like a blonde. There were a few pics of the three of us mixed in, and I immediately recognized the one Wendy must want. We were backstage—Wendy knew a guy in a band, of course—our ALL ACCESS lanyards layered over our festival beads, perched on the edge of the stage smiling with the sun setting in a blaze of orange behind us. We looked like three sirens just risen from the sea.

I selected the photo and sent it to Wendy with a kissy smiley face emoji. She immediately texted back:

Thx! What u doing 2nite?

I replied:

Hitting art show with Summer. U?

She responded:

Sry I couldn't make it! Have 2 go 2 party my old boss
is throwing. LMK if u guys wanna come by after.

I texted her a thumbs-up, suppressing my irritation that Summer had obviously tried her before me.

Things among the three of us had evened out once Wendy and Summer got through their honeymoon phase after that first Coachella. Wendy and I graduated in May, and buoyed by the first breath of post-college freedom, we lit the town on fire. Summer became a fixture in our lives, rotating between our couches weekend-to-weekend until she finally got a waitressing job at a club in the city and dumped the Inland Empire boyfriend she'd been living with for an investment banker with a sleek apartment in Hollywood, which she added into the crash-pad rotation. She had yet to rent a place of her own; between Wendy, me (definitely more me), and the cast of men in her life, she'd always had a place to stash her stilettos.

We joked that the three of us had navigated the past two years like a tricycle, supporting each other while trying to avoid potholes. Wendy had her interchangeable pack of pretties, Summer had her revolving men, and I had my acting dreams, but more than anything, we had each other.

So in the greater scheme of things, the fact that Summer invited

Wendy first to be her wing tonight was trivial, and I wasn't gonna let it spoil my evening.

When the train pulled into the station, I jogged up the steps and emerged into the concrete jungle, taking out my phone to orient myself. A text from Summer popped up:

Running late, there closer to 7:30!

Great. Really, I should have known, though. Summer was always late.

But I didn't mind. It was a beautiful June evening and Art Walk was in full swing. Light reflected between the tall buildings, bathing the buzzing streets in an otherworldly glow as fashionable connoisseurs and window shoppers spilled out of galleries onto the sidewalk, poorly concealing half-drunk plastic cups of wine.

I strolled through an open door and accepted a cup of warm Pinot Grigio as I perused a wall of golden naked ladies, painted on canvases made of money. On the adjacent wall were primary-color paintings of farm animals with ribbons and price tags around their necks. Interesting juxtaposition.

I checked my phone and found a text from my college roomie Hunter:

Abbey tonight? My doppelgänger is performing!

A series of man-doing-disco emojis followed, along with a champagne bottle, champagne glasses clinking, and confetti. Hunter was never light on emojis. Another text popped up from him, this one a picture of a muscle-bound black guy wearing a thong while dancing on a bar, accompanied by entirely too many men-holding-hands emojis and the message:

See? Totally twinning!

I laughed so hard wine almost came out my nose. It was true; they did favor each other...sort of, if I squinted and used a good dose of imagination. But as much as I adored going dancing with Hunter, I hadn't been so much as kissed in weeks, and tonight I was hoping to meet a guy more interested in my body than my shoes.

> Love to but I'm seeing an art show with Summer

Immediately an eye-popping amount of crying and poop emojis filled my screen, followed by:

> Summer interested in art???
> I must have read that wrong.

I felt momentarily guilty but had to laugh.

> Actually it's the artist she's interested in

He sent a GIF of a drag queen winking.

> Knew there had to be a man involved!
> If she flakes you know where to find me!

As if on cue, a message from Summer popped up:

> Gonna be closer to 8, Brian called. Sorry!

Poor Brian. He'd left his wife for Summer less than a year ago, and here she was already cheating on him. Though I guessed it served him right for having an affair in the first place.

I hadn't known at first that Brian was married. Summer and I had both been so busy last spring that somehow it never came up; I was finishing my bachelor of arts, juggling finals with evening performances of Shakespeare and agent showcases, while she was slinging drinks in a Hollywood club, going home with rock stars and producers. When I finally found out about Brian's wife, I told Summer adultery was bad karma, but she just laughed. She didn't believe in karma. Now I was slinging drinks while she was living the high life in a swanky condo with a view all the way to the ocean. So maybe she was right.

I threaded my way through a couple of abstract exhibitions and a mixed-media show in a bar before I found myself in front of the gallery where I was meeting Summer. I shot her a text and stepped inside.

A jazz band was playing at one end of the airy industrial space, filled with a mostly young, rocker-chic crowd swilling champagne from actual champagne glasses. It was art photography, and I was relieved to find the work was quite good. Not that I was an authority by any means: sure, I'd been to all the major museums in the city and attended my fair share of art shows (mainly those of artist friends from school), but whether I liked something was purely based on whether it spoke to me, not on any knowledge of the art scene or what was *supposed* to be "good." Regardless, I liked these pieces. An aerial photo of a stormy sea beating a sunny shore, a castle built upon a garbage dump, a train station that appeared to be underwater.

I stood in front of a life-size portrait of a naked woman, flowers blooming from her orifices. Eyes, nose, mouth, ears, nipples, vagina all obscured by blooms. She was in black-and-white, and the flowers were in color, giving the work a three-dimensional effect.

"What do you think?" said a deep voice next to me.

My eyes landed on the owner of the voice, and my heart skipped a beat. He was blindingly beautiful, like staring into the sun. Tall and tan with sea-green eyes and a thick head of wavy blond hair pulled back in a messy man bun. He was dressed in ripped black jeans and a T-shirt, tattoos creeping down his arm, and he was looking at me like he could see straight to my soul. Damn.

I caught my breath and glanced back at the image. "I was just wondering if she had flowers coming out of her ass, too."

He laughed so hard he almost spilled his champagne. I hoped my grin didn't give away how inordinately delighted I was he found me funny.

"What about this one?" He gestured to a half woman, half tiger, her head tossed back, fangs exposed.

I momentarily blanked as I gazed at the photo, wanting to keep him laughing. "She's pissed. Can't fuck men, can't fuck tigers; it's a lonely life when you're the only one of your kind."

"Is that how you feel?" he asked, a twinkle in his eye.

A zing went up my spine as I realized I hadn't sounded like a complete ass. "Yes. I lament my inability to fuck tigers every day."

Too far? No. He laughed and lightly steered me to the next work, a lion being devoured by a gazelle. I wanted to turn the questions back to him but couldn't think of what to say, and anyway, I was on a roll now. I studied the picture in front of me. "The victim becomes the victor. Though that's not how a gazelle would kill a lion."

He raised a single eyebrow. "Oh?"

"No," I returned. "Victor and victim are determined only by who wins the race. If the gazelle manages always to stay a step ahead of the lion, eventually she leaves him too malnourished and exhausted to hunt, thereby terminating him through starvation."

He laughed. "Remind me never to chase you."

Buoyed by how easily the conversation flowed between us, I floated along the wall beside him trading witticisms until two pretty girls approached, primed for flirting. "Hiiiii!" they said in unison, then giggled.

I stood by awkwardly sipping my champagne as they took turns giving him hugs, their hands lingering on his chest and biceps as they whispered intimacies in his ear. I slipped away when his back was to me, threading my way to the other side of the gallery. While I had enjoyed our little flirtation, that one was trouble. Too good-looking to date, too charming for a dalliance. Nope. I checked my phone. Summer:

On way now! Sorry!

"Champagne?" I looked up to see him again, offering a fresh glass of champagne.

80

I told myself not to be so pleased as I took it. "Thanks."

He tapped his glass to mine. "Waiting for someone?"

I nodded. "My friend. She's always late."

"I'm going up to the roof," he said. "Come."

And with that, he disappeared around the corner, into the building. I considered not following, but my feet were already moving in the direction he'd gone. No harm in hanging out with him until Summer arrived, anyway.

I found him down a short hallway, holding open the door of the smallest elevator I'd ever seen. I hesitated.

"Claustrophobic?" he asked.

I nodded, embarrassed. "A little."

"I can help." He gestured for me to get in.

Against my better judgment, I stepped inside, and the door closed. I was so close to him I could feel the warmth of his body. He shifted to stand behind me and placed his hands over my eyes with a "May I?" His chest grazed my back. He smelled of wood spice and detergent. "It's not so bad if you can't see the walls," he whispered, though claustrophobia was no longer what I was feeling.

As the elevator climbed slowly upward, I fought a losing battle against the raw desire burning in my veins, hardly breathing. I reminded myself that he had this effect on every girl, including the pretty ones that came in pairs, scattered throughout the gallery below.

"Your shampoo smells good," he said, his voice husky.

Ding! The elevator doors opened, and he released me. A gust of warm wind whipped my hair into my face as I stepped onto the roof. We were about ten stories up in a rooftop garden with sweeping views of downtown. Golden rays from the setting sun flared through the buildings, reflecting in the windows and turning the clouds orange and pink.

I followed him to the edge of the roof, where we stood in silence, listening to the sounds of the city below. Two birds dipped and glided together among the buildings.

"How'd you know to come up here?" I asked.

"I live here." He lit a joint and hopped up on a low wall that ran along the lip of the roof as he blew a line of smoke out at the city.

"Oh, cool. I didn't know there were apartments in this building." Realizing that might sound stupid, I added, "Not that I would have a reason to know whether there are apartments in this building or anything. I've never actually been here before, but...I love the view," I finished lamely.

"Me too," he said, oblivious to my self-consciousness. "I try to come up here every night." I held my breath, watching him walk along the wall. He noticed my apprehension and jumped down. "It's okay. There's a balcony a floor down."

He offered me the joint and I took it. "You're not afraid of heights?" I asked.

He shook his head. "I know how to fall. I rock climb."

"What else do you do?"

"Cook." He gestured to the planters around us. "Garden."

"My mom always says, 'The closer to the earth you eat, the better it tastes.'"

"Better for you, too," he agreed. "It's insane the things they put in our food these days. What about you?"

"I garden, too. On the balcony of my apartment. A couple of herbs and a lone tomato plant. Mostly I like to feel my hands in the dirt."

He held my gaze. "And where is this balcony?"

"Beachwood Canyon."

"I used to live in Beachwood. I shot the series with the women and the flowers there."

The realization hit me like a bag of rocks, and I felt immediately stupid. I combed back through all the supposedly witty comments I'd made downstairs about his work, my cheeks burning. No wonder he was laughing.

"I'm such an ass," I apologized. "I didn't realize—"

He smiled, unfazed. "It's okay. The people downstairs are just kissing my ass in case I end up famous, and I'm kissing theirs so they'll buy my shit."

"I do like your work," I asserted. He smiled at me, amused, so I continued. "I do. There's something really interesting in the way you play with opposites."

His eyes brightened. "Thanks. Most people don't get it. They just think it's fantasy. But to me it goes deeper than that—a marriage of opposites."

"Like life."

He laughed. "Exactly."

Unable to hold his gaze for fear he might read my indecent thoughts, I bent to smell a yellow rose.

"O heavy lightness, serious vanity,
Mis-shapen chaos of well-seeming forms!
Feather of lead, bright smoke . . ."

To my surprise, he completed my sentence, feigning an outsize British accent:

" . . . cold fire, sick health,
Still-waking sleep, that is not what it is!"

We both dissolved into laughter. "How do you know that?" I asked.

"I played Romeo in college."

"I did, too," I exclaimed. "In a production where we reversed the sexes of all the roles."

"Sounds avant-garde."

"Oh, it was. So very avant-garde. So very . . . college."

My phone buzzed. Summer:

I'm here. Where are you?

"Dang," I said. "My friend's here. I've gotta go down."

"I should probably get back, too." He sighed.

The elevator doors opened, and we stepped inside. He placed his hands over my eyes, and I allowed myself to lean into him this time. I could feel his heart beating in his chest, fast like mine. Maybe I was wrong about him. Maybe he was dateable. He knew Shakespeare. Can't judge a book by its cover and all that.

I summoned all my nerve as I sensed the elevator about to hit the ground level, and turned to him, our faces close. "Thanks for the tour."

His eyes traveled down to my lips. "I didn't catch your name."

"Belle."

"Nice to meet you, Belle."

Ding! The elevator doors opened, and the spell was broken. Two men in suits and a fashionable dark-haired woman with black-framed glasses stood in the hallway, as though anticipating our arrival. The woman beckoned to him.

I gave the group a smile and slipped down the hall without looking back.

Day 3

I wake to a soft rapping on the door. Camille, the young crew girl with the long braid, gently pushes it open, holding two steaming cups of coffee emblazoned in gold with THE LION'S DEN.

"Good morning," she says. "Is eight." She sets the tray on the table between our beds. Amythest doesn't budge. "Breakfast on the upper deck in thirty minutes. Wear the gym outfit; you go to town for private..." She spins her hands like they are the pedals of a bike. "You know?"

"Spin class?" I offer.

"Yes, that one."

Amythest snores through this entire exchange. Camille looks down at her, clearly reluctant to wake her.

I shake Amythest's shoulder. She pushes her eye mask up and looks at us, sleepy and confused. "It's eight," I say.

She nods and lets her head fall to the pillow, moaning, "Why am I so tired?"

In the hall, someone calls out to Camille, who closes the door gently as she exits.

"We gotta get up," I say. "We have breakfast, then Spin class."

She sits up, a look of distaste on her face. "Spin class?"

I nod, my sentiments mirroring hers. "Yep."

She flops back down. "You have to be kidding."

"Unfortunately, no. Summer has always been very serious about her Spin class, and apparently she wants to share it with us."

"Ugh. What if we don't want to share?" Amythest pulls the covers over her head. "I'm not done sleeping."

I wiggle into my workout leggings. "Something tells me we don't have much choice in the matter. At least you can use your phone in town."

"Okay." She throws the covers back. "For that I'll get up. What happened last night? You were, like, doing some shit to the door."

I hesitate. "Apparently they lock us in at night."

Her eyes go wide. "What?"

"Yeah. Weird, right?"

"That's so sketchy." She shivers.

I couldn't agree more.

Bernard and Vinny escort us on the tender to the mainland, their black suits incongruous with the bright day. We're quiet as we skim across the glassy sea, too tired to bother raising our voices above the hum of the motor. I want to ask Wendy and Claire if their door was locked, too, but decide that for now it's probably better not to rock the boat. Literally.

The Spin class is up a short path, in an open-air studio under a portico overlooking the sea. The teacher is a ripped Italian guy with an almost impenetrable accent, and I struggle to keep up, feeling like I'm slogging through mud for the first few songs. But the breeze is fresh, the view is incredible, and once I warm up, I'm actually glad I came.

By the time we finish, the day has begun to heat up. We wipe the sweat from our faces with cold, eucalyptus-scented washcloths and thread our way down the hill. As I fall into line behind Summer, I overhear Rhonda telling her what she really needs to do, if she wants to keep John, is to get pregnant. Summer grabs her by the elbow and pulls her aside as the rest of us file into the tiny café near the little dock.

I don't know what Summer says to her, but when they join us in the café, Rhonda's quiet. Summer peers over my shoulder as I shoot a pic of my espresso with the view in the background.

"Nice pic," she says.

I know her friendliness is skin-deep, but I much prefer it to the alternative. "Thanks!"

We perch on a bench in the shade and sip our drinks. "Do you think Emmanuelle is pretty?" Summer asks.

"Which one is she?"

"You know, the short-haired crew girl that was flirting with John last night."

"I mean, yeah. But not nearly as pretty as you."

"You're sweet," she says. "She was throwing herself at him. Girls are always throwing themselves at him right in front of me. It's so rude."

"I don't think she was..."

Brittani slides onto the bench and throws her arm around her big sister. "I'll smack a bitch."

"I don't like her," Summer muses. "I'm gonna have her fired."

"I don't know if that's necessary," I object. "I think she was just trying to do her job."

"What are we talking about?" Wendy asks.

"The crew girl that was flirting with John last night," Summer says.

"Oh, I didn't notice." Wendy cocks her head. "Which one?"

"The hot one with the short hair," Brittani says.

"See? You think she's hot," Summer points out. "It's a problem."

"But you're way prettier than she is," Wendy reassures her. "I mean, look at you. You've just finished a Spin class and you're glowing. You're not even sweating. Do you have pores?"

"I knew I kept you around for a reason." Summer laughs. "But I don't know... She's got that French thing going on. I think I'm gonna have to get rid of her."

It's clear nothing I say is going to change Summer's mind, so I take the opportunity to slip away as the other girls feed her compliments. Not a game I feel like playing, even if we are here at her invitation. I sit on the steps that lead down to the dock and check my phone. Service is spotty, but my signal is strong enough that a message pops up letting me know my phone and watch have finished syncing with the cloud. God only knows what my data roaming charges are going to be, but without Wi-Fi, I have no choice but to use data.

I haven't checked social media in over twenty-four hours, and I have a ton of notifications, mostly from people commenting on the photo of all of us girls on the steps of the jet (2,684 likes), and the photo of the shore from the tender (1,736 likes). I scroll through the comments, then check my in-box. Six new direct messages, but none of them are the one I'm looking for.

I click on Dylan's profile. It's empty, nothing but his first name and a profile picture of a mountain. No other info or pictures. He must be the last person of our generation that refrains from sharing his entire life on social media. Which is cool, but also annoying. Makes him really hard to Internet-stalk.

I click on the direct message icon and write:

Hi stranger! Somewhere off the Ligurian coast, headed to Saint-Tropez. You over here?

Then immediately delete it.

Maybe he hasn't seen the pics I posted yet. He probably doesn't check his feed much, though I know he does at least somewhat regularly, because he often likes my posts. I'll wait one more day, and if he hasn't written, I'll write him.

I'm not unhappy to put it off—my feelings about seeing him are complicated, to say the least. Not to mention, the chances of Summer allowing it to happen are slim.

Regardless, he hasn't contacted me, so no use overthinking it now. I post the pic of my espresso, making sure to geotag it.

I hold my phone in my hand as we're ferried out to the boat, but the only time it buzzes is with a new comment from Hunter:

Espresso? Really? Show us that yacht beotch!

Followed by a shit-ton of boat and champagne emojis. I laugh, missing him acutely, wishing I could confess to him the crazy reality of this picture-perfect trip. But before I can reply, I've lost service.

On the boat platform, Julie hands us each a bottled water and instructs us to shower before our staggered mani-pedis on the lower deck. I wash up quickly, glad to be included in the shift with Summer, Wendy, and Claire.

I'm the first to arrive. A pleasant breeze flutters my sundress as I step onto the lower deck. Emmanuelle greets me with a glass of light-pink champagne, a strawberry balanced on the lip. I thank her and take a sip, the crisp sweetness coating my tongue as I look out toward the sea, sparkling in the sunlight. The yachts belonging to the Russian billionaire have moved on, replaced by the biggest sailboat I've ever seen and a sleek blue vessel about the size of ours. Between them, two Jet Skis cut a line toward the horizon.

Four pedicure baths are laid out in front of the couch that faces the sea, and a white-uniformed manicurist directs me toward one. She taps my watch and motions for me to take it off, but I decline and place my feet into the warm water, still admiring the view. I feel something nick my foot and instinctively jerk my feet out of the water with a gasp, spilling my champagne. I look down to see the water is full of little fish.

"Good for skin," my manicurist says with a smile, making her hand into a little fish and using her fingernails to bite my knee.

I let out a laugh. "They surprised me." I guess I'm more on edge than I realized.

I slide my feet back into the water, and at least fifty tiny fish immediately attach to my skin, gently nibbling. It feels like a ticklish version of the pins and needles you get when your foot has fallen asleep, and I can't help but giggle again. I feel Wendy's nails lightly scratching my shoulder and turn to see her flanked by Summer and Claire, each holding a glass of champagne.

"What are we giggling about?" Summer asks. Her tone is light, but there's a definite acidity to her voice. She relaxes as I gesture down at the fish. "Oh, they're the best." She settles in next to me. "They eat the dead skin right off your feet. Great exfoliation."

"And supposedly they're an aphrodisiac," Claire chimes in, claiming the station on the other side of me.

"No wonder John ordered them for us," Summer remarks. "He's hoping I'll let him do me again against those windows in the bathroom later."

"He sure is horny," Wendy says.

"You have no idea," Summer says flatly. "But hey, a girl's gotta do what a girl's gotta do, amirite?"

I'm the sort of girl who only does who she wants to do, but I giggle with the others nonetheless.

"It's too bad he can't get it up when I'm on top. That would make it more fun." Summer sighs. Okay, I didn't need to visualize that. "But whatever. It doesn't take long."

Wow, her tune certainly has changed since she was with Eric. All she wanted from him was sex. Day and night, she was a fiend. And she kept going back for more, even when she knew it wasn't good for her.

Camille materializes with a beautifully arranged tray of fruit, cheese, yogurt, nuts, and prosciutto and sets it on the table behind our couch. I turn to take a slice of cheese only to find Emmanuelle already whisking the tray away.

"Excuse me," Summer calls. "We'll keep that tray."

"I'm sorry," Emmanuelle says. "Monsieur Lyons doesn't want to ruin your lunch."

No wonder Summer's so skinny.

"Enjoy your last day," Summer mutters under her breath, glaring at Emmanuelle's back as she scampers away with the tray.

Once our nails are lacquered in bright shades of pink and red (I wanted turquoise but it wasn't offered; apparently John is offended by "strange" nail colors), Summer traipses to her room for a massage and facial, and I head up to the sundeck with a script for an audition I have next week.

As I emerge from the stairwell, the glare of the sun on the smooth white boat is so bright that at first I don't see the two people deep in conversation in the hot tub. Their backs are toward me, her long hair twisted in a bun, head angled toward his silver mane as she hangs on his every word. They're so close, I'm worried I've interrupted a romantic interlude and am about to retreat down the stairs when Amythest turns and waves. John swivels his head around and flashes a grin.

"Join us!" Amythest calls blithely, as if their little rendezvous is entirely aboveboard. "John was just telling me about the movie he's producing. It's so exciting."

"That's great," I say, covering my unease. "I was just coming up to try to get some work done, but it's so bright up here, I think I'm gonna head back down. We just finished our mani-pedis, so yours is coming up. You may wanna head down, too."

"Okay." She places her hands on John's shoulders intimately and says something I can't hear over the jets, then emerges like Venus from the water, topless. Thank God for my giant dark sunglasses, because my eyes would betray my astonishment as her perfect DDs float up out of the water all shiny, like some kind of teenage boy's wet dream. She is wearing bikini bottoms, thankfully (though they're a tooth-floss thong), and she struts around to the other side of the Jacuzzi so that she never leaves John's line of sight as she grabs her dress and slips it over her head.

"See ya later," she coos with a little wave, and I follow her down the stairs, speechless. I mean, hell, it's the Riviera and topless sunbathing is de rigueur, but could that tête-à-tête in any way be construed as appropriate? It's a good damn thing it was me who walked up to that deck and not Summer, or Amythest would be on a plane home.

My wits return as we reach the main deck, and I grab her hand. She turns expectantly as I say in a low voice, "Friendly advice. Be careful. With John. Summer can be a little jealous, and you're very young and pretty. Maybe keep your top on when he's around?"

"Oh," she says with an air of innocence, "I'm sorry. I figured it's the South of France. Or, I guess, Italy? Whatever." She giggles.

"If everyone else is doing it, that's one thing. But don't be first. And not when John's around."

She nods somberly. "Thank you. Funny thing, I told John what great taste he had in picking out Summer's canary diamond, and he said it wasn't a diamond. It's a sapphire."

She's searching my face for a response, so I raise my brows. "Oh?"

"I mean, sapphires are nice and everything. It's just, she told us it was a diamond worth, like, two million. So, she lied."

I nod, less than surprised. "Between you and me," I whisper, "she does that a lot."

"Oh!" she exclaims. "And you know how we don't have Wi-Fi?" I nod. "They do. Like, John and his guys, I guess. Probably Summer, too. He was totally getting notifications on his phone the entire time we were in the hot tub and, like, responding to emails and stuff."

I shake my head, once again unsurprised. "Sounds about right."

"Amythest!" Brittani yells from the deck. "Get over here. Your champagne is getting warm!"

Amythest flounces over to the manicure station, and I trudge back up the stairs to the upper deck, where I find Wendy just finishing up a sickeningly sweet Skype call with her boyfriend on one of the computers. I hang back so as not to interrupt as they make kissy noises at each other and profess their undying love before ringing off. Wendy turns to me, her eyes full of tears.

"Sorry. Didn't mean to interrupt," I say.

"It's okay." She shrugs. "We were almost done."

"You really miss him, huh?" I ask in reference to her tears.

"Oh." She wipes away the tears. "No, not at all, actually. That's why I'm—" Her eyes overflow again. I take her hand and sit next to her. "I really wanted him to be the One, you know? But..." She sighs. "He's soooo sweet. It just—it kinda goobs me out TBH—I know that's bad—"

"No it's not," I assure her. "If it doesn't feel right, it's not right."

"And he's terrible in bed," she confesses. "He licks my pussy like he's a kitty lapping a bowl of milk. It's..."

I try to hold back a laugh and it comes out as a snort. I quickly cover my mouth, not wanting to hurt her feelings, but she starts laughing, too, which only makes me laugh harder.

"Like—" She sticks her tongue out and imitates a cat cautiously licking.

Now I'm laughing so hard I'm crying, and her tears have turned to happy ones. "Jesus, Wendy," I say. "Get outa there!"

"But I've wasted a year with him, and I think he'll pop the question soon," she protests.

"Then you better hurry," I say. "Do you honestly wanna *only* sleep with him for the rest of your life?"

She shakes her head vehemently.

"I don't know where you got this shit about needing to be married, but it's not true," I continue. "You're smart, successful, beautiful—you have it all, and you don't need a man. If you find one you can't live without, then awesome, but you don't *need* one just to have one. And you can do better than Wes. I promise."

She nods. "You're right. I have to break up with him." She takes a deep breath. "Not here, though. I'll do it when I get home. I just—I really do want a family."

"And I'm sure you'll have one," I say. "You have lots of time! But how are you gonna meet the man of your dreams if you're with Mr. Pussycat?"

She laughs and gives me a hug. "Thank you."

Once she goes downstairs in search of lunch, I install myself at the computer under the vigilance of John's likeness.

I sneak a glance at the camera positioned behind me, pointed directly at my screen. Of course I don't know how sharp the feed is or whether someone is currently watching, but it makes me uneasy—though I have to assume the computer is being monitored anyway. I also don't want anyone to think I'm up to something because I'm angling the computer away from the camera, so feeling a bit silly, I put on a big show for the phantom watchers, pretending that the reflection of the sun in the monitor is too much. Then I angle the computer away from the watchful eye of the camera and quickly log in to my email before anyone can make me return the screen to its rightful position.

I scroll through my in-box to find only one new email worth opening:

Hey sis,

Glad you're having fun. Your instagram feed is awesome. I'm jealous. It's sunny here too but hot. I need a vacation. Did you figure out how to work that watch LOL?

Saw this and thought of you (may take a min to download, be patient!):

http://tyrlus.grx.au/sdlkvnpq2083r39jfaoijv-84rn82hfpidfn pq9843y-t92nv9 rejfkjsdhf874gpijnv9

Chat soon!
Sis

I click on the link and a pop-up opens with a spinny wheel. After a few seconds, the word "loading" appears under the wheel, and a blue line creeps across the box: 5 percent, 23 percent, 46 percent—it's taking forever.

"What are you downloading?"

I jump about a foot in the air and spin to see Bernard hovering over my shoulder, squinting at my screen. I've been staring so intently at the computer that I didn't notice him enter the room.

"You surprised me," I stammer. "I didn't hear you come in. It's just a link from my sister. We always send each other funny links. It's—why?"

"Let's see it," he says.

I rise to face him, blocking the computer with my body. "I don't— I'm sorry, I'm not comfortable with that." I stumble over my words, my heart racing. "I don't know what it is. It could be personal." He's staring at me like I'm a criminal. "Last week she sent me a pic of an ingrown hair on her bikini line—she would be mortified if you saw something like that," I blurt.

"We don't allow downloads to these computers," he says.

"Okay," I sputter. "I didn't know. I won't do it again."

And with that, he turns on his heel and exits.

Turns out I'm not so paranoid after all. I sink into the chair, my heart hammering, and look up at the computer screen. The pop-up window is gone, and in its place is a GIF showing feather-clad 1920s showgirls dancing in a line, and these words:

All that glitters is not gold;
Often have you heard that told:
Many a man his life hath sold
But my outside to behold:
Gilded tombs do worms enfold.

The Merchant of Venice, of course. I have to laugh, but...much ado about nothing. I don't know what I expected, but if I'd known it was just a silly GIF, I wouldn't have risked angering Bernard to hide it. Too shaken by my interaction with him to reply, I log out of my account, turn the computer back to its original position, and descend the stairs to my room, where I lie down on the bed and breathe, begging my heart to slow down.

(two years ago)

The crowd in the gallery had dissipated when I returned from the roof, and the band had finished. I found Summer swigging champagne in front of a picture of a burning house about to be crushed by an ocean wave. I shifted my gaze to the small white placard underneath. FIRE AND WATER, ERIC THOMAS. Eric Thomas. I tasted the name on my tongue.

"I don't get it," Summer whispered. "None of these pictures makes any sense."

"It's about opposites," I explained. "Like yin and yang. A little bit of white in the black and black in the white."

"Huh. Sorry I was late." She sighed. "After I saw you at the pool, I had to drive all the way to Pomona to give Rhonda money for rent so she and Brittani don't get evicted, then when I was finally ready Brian called and I had to pretend I was staying in."

"Damn. Sorry."

"Yeah, and it's BS because I need to be saving my allowance or I'm never going to be able to move out of Brian's, but I keep having to give it to her."

"Your allowance?"

"He puts money in an account for me, for spending cash when he's out of town or whatever."

So that was how she had money. "I could get you a job at Heaven," I suggested.

"No way." She waved the idea away. "I just got out of that world, and I hated it as much as you do. Oh! There he is."

She grabbed my hand and pulled me across the room, straight toward where Eric was midconversation with a good-looking guy in a suit.

Oh God. *Please let it be the guy in the suit*, I prayed.

"Eric," Summer purred as we approached.

Shit. But then again: of course. I shouldn't have been surprised. It wasn't the first time Summer had staked a claim on a guy I would've liked for myself, and it surely wouldn't be the last. She invariably got her pick of the litter, regardless of whether she was already committed to someone else.

But I wasn't being fair: this time at least, she *had* seen him first.

"Beautiful work," she murmured, draping her arms around his neck and planting a sensuous kiss on his mouth. He tried to catch my eye over her shoulder, but I avoided his gaze. She turned to me. "This is my friend Belle."

His eyes searched mine as we pretended to meet for the first time, but I kept my expression intentionally blank. What else could I do? Regardless of my petty grievances with Summer, it's not like I was gonna choose some guy I just met over our friendship. I watched as he processed my reaction and matched it, finally extending his hand. "Eric." I shook it politely, like the mannered Southern girl I was. "This is my brother, Dylan."

Yep. Summer always got who she wanted, and I always got...the brother. I switched my focus to the brother, taking him in for the first time.

Oh. Perhaps I objected too soon.

They looked nothing, and yet everything, alike. Dylan's hair and eyes were dark where Eric's were light, and he was a little taller and more muscular, but they both had the same square jaw, the same aquiline nose and glint in their eyes. As I took Dylan's hand, I felt as though I'd been struck twice by lightning in the same evening. "Nice to meet you, Belle," he said.

"My brother's only in town for the night," Eric expounded. "And don't be fooled; it's a coincidence he's here for my show."

"Luck," Dylan corrected.

"Where are you in from?" I inquired, ignoring Eric.

"I was in China, but I'm headed back to London tomorrow."

"China, wow. What were you doing over there?"

"Trading his soul for gold," Eric answered.

"That about sums it up," Dylan agreed gamely.

Eric eyed Dylan's dark-gray suit with a smirk. "Nice suit."

"I just had a meeting with the LA arm of the Chinese company we're working with. They're into decorum," Dylan explained.

"That what you're wearing tonight?" Eric prodded.

"I don't have much of a choice. All my stuff's across town at Dad's."

"Let's not call him that," Eric snapped.

"What would you like me to call him, Eric?"

"That Asshole, Monster, Satan... I can think of lots of things." Eric snatched his brother's glass of champagne and knocked it back as Dylan looked on, bemused. "Let's get outa here."

"But it's your party." Summer cast a glance about the room, her gaze landing on a group of girls whispering together, eyeing her and Eric. Pleased, she slid her arm around him and rested her head on his shoulder. I bit my lip to contain a smile; the girl relished nothing more than a healthy dose of envy directed her way, but Eric was noncompliant.

"I've stayed long enough. My dealer can handle it from here." He dismissed the party with a wave of his hand and strode out the door, Summer trailing behind.

Outside, the wind had kicked up and the sky was losing color. Summer leaned into Eric as we waited for the car. "I'm glad I finally got to see your work," she murmured. "I love the way you play with opposites. It's like yin and yang."

"Thanks," he said. I pretended not to see the look he cast in my direction. "That's exactly it, the play of opposites. Most people don't get it."

I wondered how many girls he'd used that line on. I couldn't believe I'd fallen for it—almost fallen for him. Summer could have him. He was exactly what I had initially assumed: a total player, obviously. At least my instincts hadn't failed me. Next time I would listen to my gut. I just hoped he wouldn't say anything about our encounter to Summer.

A black Suburban pulled up to the curb, and the driver opened the door.

"A cab would have been fine," Eric commented as we climbed into the car.

"There are four of us," Dylan replied evenly. "And it's free."

"Nothing in life is free, bro," Eric returned.

Their manner was easygoing, but the barbs were sharp. I was glad Summer was the one who'd get to deal with the dark cloud that had settled over Eric.

In the car, Dylan shed his jacket and tie, loosened his collar, and rolled up his sleeves. "Better?" he asked me with a sly smile.

"Truth be told, I kinda love a man in a suit," I confided.

His laugh was easy, as was our conversation as the Suburban raced down the 10, only to stall on the 405.

"Where are we going?" I asked.

"A party in Bel Air," Dylan replied. "It's hosted by a guy I grew up with—well, I grew up with his little brother, but he would buy us booze and nudie mags when we were in junior high. Now he's some studio bigwig and throws these crazy midsummer's eve parties every year. I've never been able to go, so I wanted to check it out."

"Did you know him, too?" Summer asked Eric.

"No," Eric said. "We didn't exactly grow up together."

"Different moms, same dad," Dylan explained.

"There's that word again," Eric said.

"Who's older?" Summer asked.

Dylan raised his hand.

"By four months." Eric snorted. "Our sperm donor was a stellar guy."

The Suburban rolled through the gates of Bel Air and up the winding streets, coming to a stop in front of an estate hidden by a conflation of trees, shrubbery, and walls. A line of exotic cars waiting for valet service snaked down the long driveway and spilled into the street.

"Probably easier to walk from here if you girls don't mind," Dylan recommended.

"That's fine," I agreed, glad my heels were short. I glanced down at Summer's glitter-covered four-inch stilettos, sparkling in the dark. She wouldn't be happy, but she wouldn't complain, either.

I could hear the music thumping the moment we stepped out of the car. Dylan offered his arm, and I took it as we made our way up the driveway in the glow of the purple lights that illuminated the trees. Around a bend, the house came into view—though "house" was the wrong word. It was a Spanish hacienda the size of a hotel, perched on a hill with a view of all of Los Angeles.

At the gate, a girl dressed in black with a clipboard and headset stood sentry. "Dylan Ross," Dylan said. "Plus three."

The girl checked his name off, then ushered us through a gate made of flowers. "Welcome to Fairyland."

We threaded our way through an enchanted garden lit with twinkling lights and huge animatronic flowers, past a fairy in a swing and nymphs splashing in a fountain that changed colors with the beat of the other-worldly music. Under a rose-covered canopy, a sprite handed us each some kind of glowing purple drink decorated with orchid blooms and tapped our heads with a wand before opening a door in an oversize glimmering tree trunk.

The tree door opened onto the main lawn, where a couple hundred pixies, fairies, and sprites swilled champagne and danced to throbbing house music. China balls made to look like flowers swung from strands of flickering colored lights, fairies in body paint grooved on glowing mushrooms the size of cars, and naked women performed some kind of synchronized swimming in the pool. A number of tents made of patterned and textured fabrics dotted the lawn, each with a different theme.

I stared in wonder at the spectacle. "This is incredible."

"Wish I'd worn my Tinker Bell costume," Summer added.

"Sorry," Dylan said. "Didn't know it was a costume party. At least you're not in a suit."

Eric set his empty glass on a passing waiter's tray and squatted down next to a rosebush, looking up at me with the first smile I'd seen since we left the roof. "Osiria roses."

"They're beautiful," Summer said, leaning between us to smell the blooms.

"White on the inside with colored tips," he explained. "Very rare." He shifted his gaze back to me. "I grow red ones on the roof, but I've never seen purple."

Straightening up, Summer looked from him to me with a flicker of a frown, then took his hand. "Shall we explore?"

"I wanna hit the smoking lounge," Eric said. "I forgot my weed." Again he looked at me. "Anyone wanna come?"

"I'm gonna try to find our host," Dylan said.

I jumped at the opportunity to escape Eric and Summer. "I'll come with you. I wanna check the place out."

As soon as we were out of earshot, Dylan turned to me. "Sorry about my brother. He kinda has a chip on his shoulder about our dad."

"You don't say."

"I try to stay out of it, but he's pissed at me because I just started working for him. Thinks I sold out."

"Ah. Did you?"

"Yes." He thought for a minute. "I just don't have the same need for the world to be a perfect place that Eric does. I'm more of a pragmatist."

"And he's an idealist."

"Yeah."

"Belle!" A high voice cut through the noise of the party, and fingernails lightly scratched my arm.

I turned to see Wendy in full iridescent fairy regalia, her dark skin shimmering with purple glitter. So this must be the party she'd mentioned her old boss was throwing. "Hey!" she exclaimed. "I thought you were going to that art show with Summer."

"It's over," I said.

"Hi. I'm Wendy." She extended her hand to Dylan. "Who are you?"

He took her hand with a smile. "Dylan."

"Just when I thought I knew everyone in LA..."

"I'm only in for the night. My brother's with a friend of hers," Dylan explained.

"Summer," I clarified.

She looked confused for a minute, then widened her eyes in recognition. "Ooooh. You're the brother that's in town for the night."

Dylan laughed. "Yep, that's me."

"Welcome. Come dance," she said. "The DJ's amazing."

"So is your outfit," I complimented her. "You're, like, glowing."

"Literally—watch..." She pressed what must have been a switch hidden in her bodice, and her entire outfit lit up with twinkling violet lights. I finished my drink as the three of us threaded our way through the crowd toward the dance floor. "He's hot," Wendy whispered in my ear. "I figured he'd be a troll. Now I'm pissed I couldn't be his date. Get it, girl."

I laughed and swatted at her as Dylan took my hand and led me onto the pulsating dance floor. Interlocking tiles glowed, emitting colored ripples with every step as the DJ controlled the flow, bringing it up and down deftly while he seamlessly combined songs. The beat was infectious, and before long Dylan and I were moving in sync, dancing like we were part of the music, our bodies an expression of every nuance in the rhythm. Wendy gave me a wink and a thumbs-up over Dylan's shoulder before we lost sight of her.

We danced under the stars until our brows glistened, then hit the bar for another drink before making our way through the crowd, past the pool, and under a tunnel of twinkling lights, emerging at the edge of the lawn, where a series of fountains were lit different colors. A few people were doing key bumps of cocaine around one of the fountains; perched on another was a couple making out. Upon closer inspection, we could see the couple was Summer and Eric.

Dylan took my hand and pulled me toward a path lit with glowing purple tulips that led into what appeared to be a manicured garden forest. A sign nailed to a tree read ENCHANTED FOREST, ENTER AT YOUR OWN RISK. We started down a trail that followed a gurgling brook I suspected was man-made. Tiny lights gleamed in the branches of the trees; the sweet smell of jasmine hung in the air.

"So, what do you do for your dad?" I asked.

"I do mostly future site research and development—figuring out where to build what and the best way to do it."

I nodded as if I understood what that meant. "And what did you do before you started working for your dad?"

"I was a journalist. Spent three years in the Middle East, trying to change the world."

"Ah, so you used to be an idealist," I said.

"Yeah." The corner of his mouth turned down. "Let's just say I learned my lesson." He shrugged it off. "What about you? What do you do?"

"I'm an actress," I admitted. "Just like half the other girls at this party."

"Oh. Am I an idiot for not knowing who you are?"

I laughed. "Not unless you watch the Family Channel or have a knack for remembering one-liners and girls who get killed on TV. I'm currently slinging drinks at a pool bar in Hollywood, if you must know."

"Sounds glamorous. So what's your favorite role that you've played?"

"Hmmm... that's a hard one. I've done a couple of guest-star roles on TV that were great experiences. I mean, those sets run so smoothly, they pay well, and you're working with seasoned actors.... But I think my favorite thing is a web series I'm working on right now, playing a medical school student who gets into heroin and is trying to overcome her addiction while going to school."

"Heavy."

"It's not a big-budget project or anything," I conceded, "but it's my first real lead role, and it's a good one. I can't tell you how sick I am of playing the sidekick, trying to make my handful of expository lines interesting."

"I admire you," he said. "It takes a lot of bravery to put yourself out there like that."

"I love it." I laughed. "When I was a kid I used to make up these extremely complicated and long plays where I would be every character, then perform them in the living room for my poor parents."

"It's funny." He smiles. "I guess when you have a talent for something, you just know. Eric and I used to spend summers with our grandmother in France, and at the end of the summer he'd put on an elaborate art show with all the art he'd made that summer. Had the staff serve canapés and sparkling apple cider in champagne glasses and everything."

"You had a staff?"

"He'd always try to get me to participate, but I don't have an artistic bone in my body."

I couldn't tell if he didn't hear my question or he was ignoring it. Either way, I didn't press. "But you were a journalist. Writing is artistic," I pointed out.

"It's not the same." He shrugged it off. "Anyway, that was a long time ago."

I wanted to know more, but we were interrupted by a loud moan coming from the forest. I quickly spotted the source: a couple in flagrante against a tree just off the path. They were hard not to spot, with the lights of her fairy wings twinkling in the dark and her legs wrapped around him while he plowed her, his pants around his ankles. Dylan noticed them at the same time as me, and the couple clearly saw us but didn't seem to care. If anything, they were only encouraged by our presence, turning the volume on their moans up a notch. Dylan and I hurried down the trail giggling.

"Enchanted Forest—try Fornication Forest," I whispered.

"Show-offs," he agreed with a laugh.

He grabbed my hand and pulled me up an offshoot of the path that led past a view of the shimmering lights of the city into a grotto lit only with floating candles. It was covered in flowering jasmine, and surprisingly deserted.

His hand lingered on my back as we walked along the water's edge in the flickering darkness. "So I've met a girl who's beautiful and smart," he said. "Not to mention a great dancer. And I'm leaving for Europe tomorrow. How's that for luck?"

"Now you're just trying to get in my pants," I teased.

He caught and held my gaze. "Would that be such a bad thing?" His fingertips lightly touched my thigh, lifting my skirt ever so slightly. I looked down at his hand resting on my leg and without warning I was in the elevator again, Eric's breath on my neck.

No, no, no, not Eric. Dylan. Just as hot and not involved with Summer. I looked up to meet his dark eyes, unflinching as his fingers traveled farther up my skirt. What the hell, I figured. He was leaving tomorrow. This was the only chance we'd get. I let him kiss me.

His kiss was surprisingly fervent, his scruff rough against my skin. It was sexy, but I was a little caught off guard by the intensity of his ardor, my heel catching on a stone as he backed me toward the wall, leaving me off balance. He caught me without missing a beat, his biceps hard beneath his shirt, and cradled the back of my head with his hand as he pressed me into the stone. It was the kind of scene that would play as steamy in a movie, but this wasn't a movie, and all of a sudden I was sixteen again, pushed into the corner of a dirty couch by an overgrown frat boy.

Come on, Belle, get it together! You like this guy. Just enjoy it!

I forced the memory back down deep into my psyche, doing my damnedest to stay in the moment. A rock pressed into my spine. I tried to move over, but he was too heavy against me. I gently pushed him back with my hands, and he stopped abruptly. "Is everything okay?"

"Yeah," I said. "I've just got a rock in my back."

He moved us over, feeling the wall for any rogue stones, then went in again for the kiss. His stubble was like sandpaper against my already raw chin. He must've felt me slightly backing away as I tried to reposition my face, because he stopped again, holding my gaze. "You sure you're good?"

"Yes!" I laughed. "It's just your stubble."

"I'm sorry. I'm like a Chia Pet. I swear I shaved this morning."

"Let's just take it a little slower," I suggested.

I leaned in and kissed him slowly, determined not to let my mind get in the way of this lovely evening with an ideal guy. My phone vibrated in my purse, but I ignored it, enjoying the feel of his lips on mine, more relaxed now that he was letting me lead. Before long our bodies were pressed together, our breathing heavy. I could feel him getting hard against my pelvis, but he kept his hands respectfully above my waist and didn't push. I wasn't a sixteen-year-old on a couch. I was twenty-four and turned on. I liked the feeling of being in control, thrilled my mind was finally keeping up with my body.

My phone buzzed again.

"Do you need to get that?" he asked.

"It can wait."

The buzzing stopped as I moved his hand to my thigh and up my dress.

My phone buzzed again.

The sound of laughter and chattering as a group of partiers tripped down the path. Dylan and I froze, waiting for them to pass.

"Look, it's a grotto," one of them called.

"Shit," Dylan muttered.

Footsteps on the path. We quickly readjusted our clothes and leaned against the stone as casually as possible as the group that had been doing cocaine by the fountains stumbled into the cave.

"Wow, this is so cool," a scantily clad chick cooed, her voice echoing.

"Dude, I heard this property was listed at seventy-five million," one of the guys added.

"Is it on the market?" asked another one.

"Properties like this are traded off market, fucktard." The first guy laughed.

Their eyes lit on us. "Hi, guys!" one of the girls said. "Isn't this beautiful? What a beautiful night. It's just magical."

She grabbed another one of the girls by the hand, and they spun around dangerously close to the water's edge until one of them lost her balance and crashed into Dylan. He helped her to her feet and she snuggled up to him, rubbing against him like a cat. "Oh, hey, handsome."

He gave her a perfunctory smile and leaned her against her friend. "We were just headed out. Enjoy."

"No, don't go!" she whined behind us.

As we emerged onto the path, my phone began to buzz again. I took it out of my purse. Wendy.

"Hey," I answered.

She sounded like she was crying. "I've been . . . trying . . . to call . . ." Her words slurred together.

Immediately I was worried: Wendy was never a mess. "Are you okay?"

"No. I feel . . . My drink, I think it . . ."

"Where are you?"

"A tree," she managed. "Behind . . . hookah tent . . ." Her voice trailed off.

"Wendy?"

But she seemed to have dropped the phone.

The party had thinned out as Dylan and I hurried across the lawn in the direction of the hookah tent. We found Wendy slumped against a tree with her eyes closed, her fairy wings twisted beneath her. I gently slapped her cheeks.

"Wendy!"

"Belle." She blinked open her eyes for just a moment and then shut them again.

"Somebody must've spiked her drink," I said. "She never gets this drunk."

"Should I call an ambulance?" Dylan asked.

"No!" Wendy moaned. "No ambu . . . Home."

"If she can talk, we're probably okay to take her home." I jostled her to keep her awake. "I'll just have to stay with her to make sure she doesn't get any worse."

Her chest started to heave. Dylan lifted her and positioned her on her knees, and I held her hair back while she vomited purple liquid into the bushes. *Sorry*, I mouthed to him, patting her back. "That's good . . . You're gonna be okay," I soothed her.

"Let's get her home," he said.

"Not out the front," I insisted. "She'd be mortified."

He nodded, thinking. "I saw a gate at the base of the garden, past the gazebo. We can exit there. I'll have the car meet us."

"I should find Summer," I said.

"Eric texted me a while ago. They left."

Summer always did favor a French exit, especially when there was a man involved. Though I couldn't help but feel a prickle of irritation. What if Dylan had turned out to be a weirdo? Or had taken off and what had happened to Wendy had happened to me? I disentangled Wendy's wings and gathered her shoes and purse while Dylan called the car, then easily lifted her limp form. No one gave us so much as a second glance as he carried her around the edge of the garden and into the woods. We found the gate in no time, the Suburban idling right outside.

In the cocoon of the car, the driver handed us one of those puke bags you normally find on airplanes. "Thanks," I said, impressed.

"Not the first time," he said. "Where to?"

"My dad's place is close if you want to go there," Dylan offered. "It's where I'm staying. He's not there."

Spending the night with Dylan was certainly tempting, but it wasn't in the cards tonight. "I think I better take her back to my place," I said, giving the driver my address.

I rested my head on Dylan's shoulder while Wendy retched into the bag. When she was finished, I folded up the top of the bag and she lay her head in my lap. "Feeling a little better?" I asked.

She grunted.

"What happened?"

"Dunno," she slurred. "I's with Summer and that blond guy; then they lef' and I din' feel good, so I call you."

"Did anyone give you anything? A pill or a mint? Or did you leave your drink unattended?" Dylan asked.

She waggled her finger. "Nope. I's with Summer, on a tuffet like lil' Miss Muffet."

"Was anyone else around? Could someone have passed by and dropped something in your drink?" I pressed.

Again she waggled her finger. "I got up to dance with that guy real quick. Summer din wanna dance."

"With Eric?" I asked.

"Yeah." She closed her eyes.

Dylan and I exchanged glances over her head. *Could Summer...?* Dylan mouthed.

No way, I mouthed back, horrified he'd even suggest it. *They're friends.*

He shrugged. "Sorry. Just a thought."

I squeezed my eyes shut, trying to dislodge the idea he'd planted in my brain. Summer would never.

Surely not.

When we reached my little hillside fourplex, he helped me carry Wendy inside and get her set up on the couch with towels and a bucket while the Suburban idled outside.

I kicked off my heels and gave him a quick tour of my worn but comfortable prewar space, pretending to be a real estate agent. "Built in 1936, this one-bedroom features a living room at the front with French doors leading to a balcony that overlooks the street," I announced with a flourish. He laughed, trailing behind as I led him down the hallway toward my bedroom. "Off of the hallway you'll find a lovely original black-and-white-tiled bathroom on one side and an eat-in kitchen on the other, and here at the end of the hall we have the master."

"I like it," he said. "It's bohemian."

I cast my eyes at the white Christmas lights twinkling in glass jars on either side of the iron bed, the brass Buddha staring down peacefully from atop the dresser, wedged between photos of Bette Davis and Katharine Hepburn.

"Whatever gave you that idea?"

"I wonder how many starlets have lived here, in the shade of the Hollywood sign," he mused.

He was looking at me like he wanted to kiss me again. I turned my face up to his and let him pull me to him. His lips met mine just as the sound of vomit hitting the bucket erupted from the living room.

"Right on cue." I sighed. "Sorry. I gotta see about her."

"I should go anyway," he said. "I have to leave for the airport in two hours."

I left him adjusting himself as I padded into the living room, where I found Wendy leaning over the side of the couch, the bucket beneath her. She groaned. "I feel like crap."

"I know." I wiped her mouth with a towel. "But you're gonna be okay."

Dylan appeared in the doorway, his hard-on still visible through his suit pants. "Wanna come to London tomorrow?"

"I wish." I smiled, averting my eyes from his protruding pants. But I had a job and was trying to have a career, and I wasn't about to pin all my hopes and dreams on some guy I met a few hours ago, regardless of how sweet he seemed. "Wanna stay in LA a few days?"

"I wish."

I walked him to the door, where he kissed me one last time and promised to call next time he was in town. I watched the Suburban drive into the dawn, certain I'd never see him again.

Day 4

The drum of hooves and hot breath as the pack draws near. Dirt clods fly, shadows sharp in the noonday sun, colors so saturated the scene is almost surreal. Green grass, blue sky, blurs of red and white uniforms. Somewhere a stick is raised and a ball flung. Muscles ripple under glossy coats of chestnut, gunmetal, and black, lathering in the heat. Cheers from the small, well-heeled crowd, sipping rosé at picnic tables under the shade trees on the sidelines.

I lean my forearms on the white fence that edges the spectator area and gaze out at the horses, feigning interest in the game to avoid the human buzzards circling our table. Judging by the number of male acquaintances who happened to show up to his match today, word must have gotten out that John is traveling with a harem. I'm reminded that that's what we're here for, after all. "Good for business." I can't keep my eye on the ball to save my life, but the horses are beautiful, as are many of the men riding them. If only it were the strapping Scandinavian-looking one that caught my eye on his last pass who was coming to lunch with us, and not the two old enough to be his father.

I actually got my hopes up when Summer revealed that a few of the polo players would be joining us after the match. My knowledge of polo is limited, but from what I can tell, there are two groups of players, the paid professionals who look like they belong in a Ralph Lauren ad and the rich guys who play to feel young. John and his friends clearly belong in the latter group.

I'm feeling much more myself this morning after finally having had a good night's sleep last night. I'd intended to stay awake to see whether our door was locked during the night again, but I guess I was so worn out from the sun and swimming and Jet Skis that I couldn't keep my eyes open and passed out during the movie we watched after dinner. I'm normally a pretty light sleeper, but apparently it took Vinny five minutes to wake me when it was time for us to go to our rooms, and my limbs were so heavy I could hardly make it down the stairs.

I feel Wendy's nails on my arm and turn to see the others exiting the gate behind her. "We're leaving," she says.

"Why?" I ask, confused. John's still on the field.

"Don't be obvious because she's staring at us, but see that woman over there in the big ugly hat?"

I surreptitiously glance over her shoulder to see a Waspy-looking woman in her forties wearing the biggest, bluest hat I've ever seen.

"Take my arm; let's go," she says. And then, as we walk through the gate, "That's John's wife's best friend. So we have to leave."

"Wait, John's still married? But he was getting a divorce when he and Summer met, what—six, eight months ago?"

Saying it out loud reminds me just how quickly Summer has adapted to her new lifestyle. Wendy wrinkles her brow. "It's been longer than that."

"No," I say. "It was after Christmas when they met."

"Huh. Well, it seems like longer. Anyway, it's complicated. Something about divorce being too expensive right now. So they're still technically married. I mean, she's like his fourth or fifth wife or something, and he only sees her once a month or whatever, and she knows about Summer, but there's an agreement that she and Summer don't share space. And the wife gets priority, or she'll make his life hell. So whenever she or her friends are around, Summer can't be there."

The first of our two black Suburbans peels out of the dirt lot in a cloud of dust as we approach, leaving us covering our faces.

Claire, Wendy, Amythest, and I are all lost in our own worlds as our

Suburban pulls away. I gaze out the window at the brilliant day while we speed along a road that hugs the coast, my thoughts completely out of step with the tranquil setting. I shouldn't be surprised that Summer lied about John's marital status—it's the least of the lies she's spun, and yet somehow I'm thrown by it. When I think of the vicious tactics she's employed to maintain her place... The fact he's still married somehow makes it worse. And that Wendy knew and I didn't? I have to do a better job of paying attention.

I realize I have no idea what I've gotten myself into, agreeing to come on this trip; I probably should have stayed home, gone to see Grannie with Lauren. We'd be doing water aerobics with the biddies right about now, which sounds absolutely wonderful. But it's certainly too late to turn back at this point.

I briefly allow myself a fantasy about what a trip like this would be like if I were here with Lauren and Hunter. There would be more quiet reading time involved (Lauren), and more dancing (Hunter). And certainly no one would tell us where to sit or what to talk about. That's the problem with being on someone else's dime: you serve at their pleasure. At least I'm only here for a week. I can't imagine choosing to live my whole life like this, the way Summer has.

I take out my phone, frustrated that I still have no new messages. But as I'm putting it away I notice the little airplane icon on the top and remember I'd put it in airplane mode to save power since we have no service on the boat. I turn on data roaming and immediately am hit by a flurry of notifications. I scroll through, looking for one in particular. And there it is, a message from @drl1991, sent two hours ago. It's only one line:

Where are you?

I bite my lip. So my posts did their job. But now what? I'm nervous about actually seeing Dylan. It's been so long since we were in the same room, and so much has happened.

Somewhere off the Ligurian coast,
headed to Saint-Tropez. You?

Wendy peers over my shoulder. "Who ya writing?"

I hesitate for a moment before answering her. "Remember Dylan? Eric's brother. We spoke to him on the phone after Eric—Oh! You met him. At the fairy party, like, two years ago."

"Oh my God, the night someone drugged me." She shivers. "I don't really remember him, but I know he saved my ass."

"He's out here for the summer, somewhere near Saint-Tropez, I think."

She raises her eyebrows in surprise. "You guys are still talking?"

"I mean, sort of." I shrug. "He lives in London, so we haven't seen each other or anything, but yeah. I've talked to him a few times, since the news about Eric."

"How's he doing—after everything?" she asks.

"I really don't know. That's why I want to see him."

"That's so sweet of you." She gives me a little hug. "He's been through a lot. I'm sure he could use a friend right now. Wait, he was superhot, wasn't he? And, like, successful? Hmmm." She looks me up and down with a smirk. "No one ever said you weren't smart."

Wow. These friends of mine . . . "Thanks." I laugh. "But I'm not in the man-trapping business. I just wanted to check on him."

"Mmm-hmm." She winks.

Good God.

My phone dings.

In Ramatuelle, just south of Saint-Tropez for the month

I reply:

So close! Not sure I'll be able to get away, but
would love to catch up with you if possible. Any news?

"You know Summer's never gonna let you see him," Wendy says.

"Yeah, I know. But that doesn't mean I can't try."

My phone dings:

> Sorry you're stuck. If we can't connect this trip,
> I'll hit you up next time I'm on the west coast.
> Love to catch up. X.

No acknowledgment of my question. Which I can assume means no new developments surrounding what happened to Eric—or none he's willing to share, anyway. But then, that's not exactly a surprise. I wonder if I saw him face-to-face, would he be more forthcoming?

We bounce along a dusty road, finally parking in front of a restaurant built into the side of a low cliff. As I get out of the car, I can almost taste the salt in the light breeze that blows off the sea, lapping at the rocks below. I instantly forgive myself for saying yes to this trip, no matter how insane the situation might be. I am, after all, allowed to enjoy myself. *Or rather, required to.*

The restaurant is essentially a patio, naturally shaded by the lip of the cliff above. Driftwood tables look out over rocks rounded by the constant pounding of the surf, lit gold in the afternoon sun. The calm sea reflects the luminous sky, and boats bob in the distance.

Summer, Rhonda, Brittani, and the two goons are already seated at a long table on the far side of the patio, and two Chinese businessmen hover close by, sweating in their dress shirts. I slide into the chair next to Summer.

"This place is magical," I say with a smile.

"John's sitting there." Summer doesn't return my smile.

"Of course." I move a seat over.

"Actually, can you sit down there?" She indicates the other end of the table, where Amythest is seated with Bernard and Vinny. "He'll want to sit next to the men who are here to do business with him. They've come all the way from China."

"No problem." So much for that. I move down to the other end of the table and open my menu, ravenous.

"Don't bother looking at the menu," Summer instructs us. "John knows just what to order—he'll take care of it all when he arrives."

Easy for her to say; she probably had a five-course meal on the ride over.

I notice Summer doesn't object when Wendy takes the seat directly across from her and beckons to the Chinese businessmen, one tall and one short. "Come have a seat." She flashes a charming smile. "I want to hear all about China. I've always wanted to go."

The men awkwardly sit next to John's empty seat, and within minutes Wendy has them laughing. I feel a pang of jealousy. This whole trip would be going a lot more smoothly if I had her social skills.

I'm seated too far away from Wendy's one-woman show to participate, and Brittani and Amythest are taking photos of each other in front of the view, so I attempt to strike up a conversation with Bernard and Vinny.

"So, how long you guys been working with John?" I ask.

Neither of them so much as looks at me, and when after a few moments it becomes apparent to each that the other is not going to answer and I'm not going to stop waiting expectantly until they do, Bernard mutters, "Long time."

"How about you, Vinny?" I ask.

"Thirty years," he grumbles.

I let out a low whistle. "So you must know where all the bodies are buried, huh?"

Now I have their attention. Only they're not laughing.

I read a warning in Vinny's bloodshot eyes as he leans in to my ear. "Guests are meant to be seen and not heard," he hisses.

A chill runs down my spine.

Vinny abruptly takes out his phone and begins typing away at the screen as I focus on my breathing, attempting to slow my racing heart. Everyone else carries on with their conversations, oblivious to our tense exchange.

Bernard excuses himself to take a phone call, and as he stands, a pill bottle falls from his pocket, rolling beneath my chair. I bend to pick it up before he realizes what's happened, sneaking a peek at the label as I hand it back to him. Diazepam. It sounds familiar, but I can't place it. He snatches it from my hand without meeting my eye and shoves it in his pocket as he stalks away.

I take out my phone and google "diazepam." Oh right, it's Valium. Bernie's on Valium? I guess that makes sense; it's probably pretty stressful working for John.

I return my focus to my phone and open my email, landing on a new message from Lauren_Carter812:

Hi Sis!

How's the sailing? Hope the weather there is as beautiful as it is here. Did you get my last email?

Love,
Sis

I quickly type:

I got your last email and downloaded the Shakespeare quote—didn't have time to reply—was interrupted by Bernard looking over my shoulder. I got in trouble because apparently we aren't supposed to download anything while using their computers. In other news, they lock us in at night, so that's creepy. This whole trip is kinda bonkers. We're being paraded around like Summer's chorus line, and John is super controlling. Yes, it's beautiful here, and the food's delicious (at a restaurant overlooking the sea currently, entertaining some Chinese businessmen John is working with)—but I wouldn't call it fun. I'm writing more freely b/c I'm on my phone, maybe delete this message when you get it so that it's not in the system next time I log in to the boat computers. Xo

Wendy catches my eye and looks pointedly at my phone and then nods toward my bag. I dutifully put it away, irritated she's taken it upon herself to monitor my behavior.

When at last John and his two Italian polo friends arrive and he orders the long-awaited food, it is every bit as divine as the vista. Plates of prickly sea urchin, salt-crusted sea bass, succulent melon with perfectly cured prosciutto. The rosé from the restaurant's sister vineyard is like sunshine in a glass, so smooth I could drink a bottle on my own without blinking.

I rest my arms on the table and eavesdrop as John and the polo guys schmooze with the Chinese, complimenting them on the success of what sounds like an entire city they built in China, persuading them that what they accomplished there will do even better here. From what I gather, the development John is planning is on the Italian Riviera overlooking the sea, complete with all-new high-end homes, condos, a resort, a spa, shops, restaurants, golf, a marina, and the crown jewel: he's secured a gambling license, apparently a real feat, which the polo guys are somehow involved in.

The womenfolk aren't invited to take part in the conversation, of course, but I'm paying attention nonetheless. Here are the titans of industry in their natural habitat, the delicate balance of power shifting among them as they court one another, vaunting their authority and leverage like birds engaged in a bizarre courtship dance. It's fascinating.

What's even more interesting is the fact that the men seem to have zero regard for the seven women seated at the table—as though it would be impossible for us to hold opinions on anything they're discussing. While there's clearly plenty that's being left unsaid, I'm amazed by how pragmatically they speak about issues like environmental impact and minimum relocation costs—it's all numbers to them; they're not in the least bit concerned about the very real damage to the planet or the disrupted lives of the people forced to relocate to make way for their monster resort.

I don't claim to be well versed in the ins and outs of Italian (or for that matter, American) business regulations, and sure, none of this may be exactly illegal, but their casual entitlement displays an unmistakable moral bankruptcy. Then again, I suppose it's par for the course. It's not like I haven't seen the Russian billionaire keeping a separate yacht for his wife and kids right next door to his boatload of hookers.

After a good hour of smiling vacantly and downing copious amounts of wine in an attempt to drown out my growing ire, I've got a strong enough buzz that I can almost forget the who and why of my situation and simply enjoy the where. But my reverie is interrupted by John, who seems to have remembered that we're here after all.

"Let's talk about our mothers," he instructs us between bites of squid-ink pasta.

Though this edict is directed at the table, it's clearly intended for those of the female persuasion, for the purpose of entertaining the men—which is, in this world, our sole purpose. Our mothers being a safer subject than our fathers, I assume, who are younger than the majority of the men present.

"Wendy, you start," he says, unfurling his Cheshire-cat grin.

"My mom is Sandra, and she's amazing." Wendy smiles broadly at the table. "You know, my dad's a senator in Ohio"—yep, there it is—"so she has a lot of social obligations. She's head of the Cincinnati Country Club Association, the PTA when I was in prep school, and she and I were actually both president of the same sorority. And she has the best taste—I am always raiding her closet when I go home. She's almost as good at tennis as Summer, and she's an amazing cook."

This is all true, though Wendy confessed to me in a moment of weakness facilitated by painkillers after her horse-jumping accident how hurt she was that her mother hadn't come out for her surgery. She admitted that Sandra rarely had time for her and has always been much more interested in her social status than her only child. Apple doesn't fall far from the tree, I guess.

Summer raises her glass. "To Sandra!"

We all raise our glasses. The polo players sit next to Wendy, and I am on the other side, so it falls to me to speak next.

"My mom is Beth, and she's also amazing, but in a different way," I say. "She's a nurse, and even when she's not working, she's always taking care of everyone. When we were little, we would go to this community pool, and any of the kids who couldn't swim, she would teach to swim. If a baby bird fell out of a tree, she was feeding it with a bottle till it could fly. And she loves to garden—she can make anything grow."

"I remember she was always out there with her hands in the dirt," Rhonda chimes in. "Wearing a sombrero and overalls like she fell off the turnip truck." She cackles at her own wit.

Oh. Rhonda is drunk. Drunk and throwing shade at my mom. Great. "Well, we can't all be as fashionable as you, Rhonda," I say dryly. *Oops.* Clearly Rhonda's not the only one who's had a little too much wine. I paint on a smile and soften my voice, grateful for my acting experience, and continue. "I remember when you guys first moved in, my mom baked a lemon meringue pie from the lemons in our lemon tree to welcome you to the neighborhood. You remember, Summer? We ate the whole thing watching *Pretty Woman,* and then we were sick to our stomachs. We've been friends ever since."

For a beat no one speaks, and I wonder if I've said something wrong again, but I'm relieved when Summer smiles. "I could go for some lemon meringue pie right now." She shifts her gaze to John. "Should we order limoncello?"

"That's a great idea," Wendy agrees, and we all nod.

John orders the limoncello, then turns to Amythest. "Amythest, tell us about your mother."

Amythest squirms a little in her chair. "My mom came over from the Philippines with me when I was six. She had a really hard time. I mean, she didn't speak the language or know anybody or anything."

"Tell about your foster moms, though," Brittani interjects. "That's some crazy shit. Amythest had some fucking crazy foster moms after her mom ditched her."

Amythest stares at Brittani, at a loss for what to say, the look on her face a mixture of hurt and surprise. "I don't...She didn't..." Her voice trails off.

"She's an addict. She OD'd and was put in a halfway house," Brittani announces to the table, "and poor Amythest had to go live with just whoever they assigned. It was really fucking shitty. She even got molested. So awful."

It's as though the air has been sucked out of the scene. Everyone is still. Amythest blinks quickly, her face drained of color.

I push my chair back and stand, dropping my napkin on my plate, and glance around the table with an upbeat smile, my gaze landing on Amythest. "I'm going to run to the ladies' room. Does anyone care to join?"

Amythest half nods and shakily stands to her feet while the rest of the table remains still as statues. I take her arm and steer her across the uneven stone toward the bathroom, never once dropping my smile.

Once the bathroom door is safely closed behind us, I glance under the two stalls, ensuring we're the only ones inside. Amythest leans against the wall, staring out the small open window that looks over the sea, her fingers absently pulling at a piece of hair from the back of her head.

"She's drunk," I say.

She nods, tugging at her hair until strands come loose and flutter one at a time to the white marble floor, leaving a pattern of tangled black lines.

"Careful." I gently pull her hand away from her hair.

She looks at her reflection in the mirror over the sink and spies the canister of cigarettes sitting next to the peppermints and perfume on the counter. She strikes a match from a box marked with the name of the restaurant and lights a cigarette, inhaling deeply.

"God, I've been wanting a cigarette for days." She exhales.

I light one in solidarity and inhale, then cough. This happens every time I try to smoke cigarettes. It always seems like a good idea in the moment, and then I'm sorry.

We lean against the wall on either side of the window, blowing smoke out at the sea. She drums her bedazzled bloodred nails on the windowsill.

"How'd you get that?" I ask, pointing my chin at her nails. "We were on strict orders, red or pink, no decorations."

She titters. "I bring my own bling. Just in case."

She looks out at the view and sucks her cigarette deeply, then exhales smoke through her nose. "I'm pretty strong, but some things just . . . I never tell people about my shitty life. I trusted her."

"You guys are pretty good friends, right?"

"I mean, yeah, we party together. We have fun." She shrugs. "I just don't understand why she's being such a bitch."

"Sometimes people behave differently in different situations. Especially around money."

She nods. "But then, like, why the fuck did she invite me here?"

It strikes me that perhaps Brittani invited her here expressly for the purpose of fucking with Summer, her golden sister. But I'm not about to say that. "If it makes you feel any better," I say with sympathy, "I've been wondering the same thing about Summer."

"Well. If she wants to play games, I can play games."

She grinds her stripper heel into her cigarette butt and marches out of the bathroom. I stub mine out as well and follow.

We emerge from the ladies' room to find the rest of the girls posing in front of the view while one of the polo players snaps photos on a phone and the other directs them with cries of "Show us *Charlie's Angels*! Now *Blue Steel*!" I catch myself before anyone sees me rolling my eyes for the umpteenth time.

John sits at the table with the rest of the men, clearly in the midst of a serious discussion.

I casually peruse the wall of framed photographs featuring famous people visiting the restaurant while covertly tuning in to John's conversation. They're speaking French now, and I was right—what they're discussing hardly sounds legal.

The taller Chinese guy is speaking in tones low enough that I can only hear part of what he's saying and some of the words I can't understand, but I'm able to translate "...end of week the tariff on steel imports will...Good time to adjust your position before..."

"Helpful...connections," John replies. "...last development...able to cut building costs...materials that wouldn't have been approved for anyone else. But...no problem."

I pretend to drop my gold ring in the shape of California on the ground beneath a neighboring table and inch closer to their table as I reach my arm out to retrieve it. The shorter Chinese guy clears his throat, and I worry for a moment he's seen me. But they're leaning in toward each other, oblivious. "We like to keep the cost low," he says, "but not sacrifice safety."

The men go silent. Finally John speaks, switching to English. "I understand your concern, but it's unnecessary. The collapse was tragic, but it was the fault of the contractor, who altered the plans after they had been approved. Lionshare was cleared of any wrongdoing."

From where I'm crouched next to a chair retrieving my ring I sneak a glance up to see solemn nods around the table.

"What are you doing?" Wendy says from right behind me. I start, knocking my head on the table, and she laughs. "Sorry. I didn't mean to scare you."

She's holding my bag, Claire at her side, the photo shoot over. "I dropped my ring," I say, displaying the ring on my finger, "but I found it."

Wendy hands me my purse. "Did you hear? John has a surprise for all of us!"

"It's in town," Claire offers.

"Great!" I hope for the best as we make our way toward the Suburbans.

The polo players triple-kiss us all goodbye before climbing into their white Lamborghini and roaring off in a cloud of dust, and for once John's men stay with him and the execs, leaving us girls nearly unaccompanied, save our drivers. A minor miracle.

★　　★　　★

Rhonda has a headache (no mystery there) and Amythest claims one as well, so the two of them head back to the boat in the first Suburban while the rest of us pile into the second. After all the rosé and limoncello consumed at lunch, everyone is in a good mood, squealing like preschoolers as we jostle down the bumpy road. "Papa Don't Preach" comes on the radio, and Summer calls out, "Turn it up!"

Before long, we're all singing along, dancing in our seats.

"I feel like I'm at a bachelorette party!" Wendy cries.

"Too bad we don't have a stripper," Claire pipes up, laughing.

Spiciest thing I've ever heard her say. She must've had as much limoncello as I did. I grin at her, trying to get back into the spirit of things.

"Hopefully soon!" Summer answers.

"You got us a stripper?" Wendy jokes. Brittani hoots in celebration.

"No, dumb-dumbs. Hopefully there will be a wedding soon!" Summer laughs.

"Yeah, all we gotta do is get him to leave the old hag!" Brittani chimes in. "Maybe she'll just die. Wouldn't that be great?"

"Brittani!" Summer chides her sister with a playful swat. "I was talking about Wendy! Mine's gonna take a little more time."

"*Petit à petit, l'oiseau fait son nid*," I tease.

"What's that mean?" Wendy asks.

"Little by little, the bird makes its nest," I translate, proud I was able to come up with a French proverb suitable to the moment.

"What are you trying to say?" Summer fixes me with a not-altogether-friendly smile.

I jab my finger in the air. "*Paris ne s'est pas fait en un jour!*"

"Paris wasn't built in a day." Summer rolls her eyes. "Why are you speaking in French mottoes?"

"I thought they applied," I say, taken aback. "And we're in France," I add lamely.

"We're all friends here." She pats my knee. "You don't need to prove how smart you are."

Her tone is affable, but her words are combative. Regardless of the fact that she herself was speaking in French proverbs the day before yesterday, my intelligence is one of the reasons she's always liked me, or so she said. I guess I should be grateful for this window into how she sees me now.

"I'm sorry, I wasn't trying to . . ." I don't know how to complete that sentence. Make conversation? Re-create our former camaraderie? Pretend I'm not nauseated by the superficiality of my erstwhile friends?

"Next thing we know, you'll be quoting Shakespeare," she gibes.

I would challenge you to a battle of wits, but I see you are unarmed. I catch myself before my laugh escapes, biting my tongue so hard I taste blood. It's only afterward that it occurs to me to wonder if she meant anything more with that gibe. Has Summer been reading my emails? No, surely not. It must have just been a lucky shot.

Before the convivial mood in the car can sour, we pull up to a storefront on a cobblestone street. The driver opens our door and hands us down one at a time.

We stand in front of a small boutique with a selection of bohemian beachwear hanging in the window and a sign that reads LE REVE, and in smaller print underneath, MAILLOTS DE BAIN.

"Swimsuits," I say automatically, then immediately regret it, lest the others think I'm showing off. Though any idiot could gather that the shop sells swimsuits by the window display. Oh my God, maybe I am insufferable. I resolve to keep my trap shut for the rest of the day.

A pretty French girl about our age opens the door of the shop and says, "*Entrez, mademoiselles,*" with a smile. "*Aidez-vous à faire du champagne.*"

I do not translate, but do take a glass of champagne from the tray on the faded teal table next to the door as we all file into the shop, and the other girls follow suit.

Everything in the store is flawlessly shabby chic, in shades of distressed beach colors—white, sand, seafoam, turquoise. The racks are made of driftwood and display a collection of tiny bikinis with exquisite detailing: embroidery over a floral pattern, well-placed transparent lace; some even have elements of leather. A rack to one side has a sign that says PRÊT À PORTER, VENTE! €500. "Ready-to-wear, sale! Five hundred euros." I can only assume John is paying for this surprise, because certainly none of the rest of us is.

A well-tanned Frenchwoman of indeterminate age who is clearly the shop owner stands in the middle of the cozy space dressed in flowing gray linen, her arms crossed, unabashedly looking us up and down as we enter. As her assistant locks the door behind us, she finally bestows on us a smile.

"Welcome," she says in heavily accented English. "I am *très* happy you are petite. Some Americans, they are . . ." She makes a gesture with her arms that clearly demonstrates her distaste for well-fed tourists. "But you, *très belle*. Make my job easy."

Apparently she didn't get the memo that fat-shaming is no longer *très cool*. Regardless, we accept her compliments perhaps too eagerly with a chorus of "*Merci*," still unsure what exactly is going on.

The pretty girl who greeted us gestures to a row of chairs against the back wall and says, "*Asseyez-vous s'il vous plaît.*"

I take a seat on the end next to Summer, and the shop owner stands before us. "You choose style; you choose fabrics; you choose *embellissements*. We measure, we make."

The five of us exchange murmurs of excitement. She claps her hands twice, and a willowy model prances from behind a door, dressed in a skimpy black bikini.

"Here you see the shapes; they are black, but you choose fabric you desire."

The model spins, and the assistant hands us all little notepads and pencils so that we can take notes.

While the model is getting changed into her next bikini, Summer bends her head toward mine with a conspiratorial grin and whispers, "I always think of Ryan—or shall I say Monsieur Stokes—when I speak French. Remember?"

"How could I forget?"

"Too bad I had to get him fired." She sighs.

I look at her in shock. "That was you?"

She nods. "After what his friend did to you? I couldn't let you sit in his class the rest of the summer."

If she'd told me this a few months ago, I would have believed her, would have been touched by her revelation. But a lot can happen in a few months. Nevertheless, I bring my hand to my heart and open my eyes wide. "You did that for me?"

"That's what friends are for, right? Having each other's back. And I was moving anyway. It's not like they could reprimand me."

"Wow. Thank you."

"You would have done the same for me," she says lightly.

I watch the model prance about in another suit, confounded by Summer's timing. Why is she telling me this now?

Not that it makes a difference. Even if she did have my back ten years ago, it wouldn't change what she's done. We've never discussed it, but she's not stupid. She may not realize the extent of what I know, but she has to recognize that I'm aware she's less than a loyal friend to me.

And yet she invited me on this trip, and I'm here. Is she trying to buy me?

"That cut would look great on you." I indicate the suit on the model.

"Yeah, it's my favorite so far, I think. Maybe in green to match my eyes."

Back in the Suburban on the way to the tender, I check my phone:

Hey sis,

Just because you're on a yacht doesn't mean you can't be miserable. All that glitters is not gold, LOL. And don't worry, I wasn't planning to

127

send you any more illicit attachments. Sounds like your host has a lot of paranoia, but remember: it has nothing to do with you. You're just a bystander. So you're locked in at night...OK, yeah, that's weird but it's only a week, right? Try to keep your head up and not get caught up in Summer's mind games. You'll be home before you know it, and you never have to see her again if you don't want to. Breathe. Soak up some sun. Everything's gonna be ok!

I've been friends with Summer for so long that it's hard to imagine my life without her in it, but I have to admit that the idea of never seeing her again fills me with euphoria. This could be my final few days with her, ever. Yes...freedom lies in wait just around the bend, if I can only make it through this week and not let her get to me. Still, something tells me she won't let me go easily.

By the time we get back to the boat, we have less than an hour to freshen up and get ready for dinner, but Amythest is occupying the shower in our room, so I get my outfit ready, selecting a pale-green maxi dress and silver sandals. When I open my jewelry travel bag, one of my earrings tumbles to the floor and rolls under Amythest's bed.

I drop to my hands and knees and use the flashlight on my phone to sweep the plush carpet beneath the bed. I see a flash of silver and reach for the earring, but my fingers brush something else as I grab it. I jump, conditioned to think all surprise objects in dark places must be rodents, but when I shine my phone in that direction, I see not a pair of eyes glaring back at me, but a pair of sunglasses.

I take them out and look at them in the light. They're men's black Oliver Peoples wraparound glasses that look familiar, but I can't place where I've seen them. I set them on the bedside table as Amythest emerges from the shower wrapped in a towel. Her eyes dart to the glasses.

"I found them under the bed," I say. "Probably from whoever stayed in this room last, but I figured I'd ask at dinner."

She makes a move toward the glasses, then stops herself. "Uh, yeah, probably."

But as I step into the bathroom and turn to pull the door closed behind me, I see her stuff them in her purse. Here I was feeling bad for the girl that she didn't get to design a ridiculously expensive bikini today, when clearly she's had a far more interesting afternoon than I have.

At eight sharp, Amythest and I make our way up the spiral staircase to join the others for hors d'oeuvres on the main deck, but when we reach the landing, we're diverted by a commotion in Summer and John's room. Summer's voice rises above another female voice, both upset, while Claire, Wendy, and Brittani hover in the doorway, looking on. Peering over their shoulders, I see Summer at the foot of the bed, the emerald necklace John gave her dangling from her fist. Rhonda's arm is around Summer, and Julie has a steadying hand on the back of a tearful Emmanuelle.

"Apparently Emmanuelle tried to steal Summer's necklace," Brittani explains under her breath.

Julie and Emmanuelle confer in French too quickly and quietly for me to catch the exact words, but I can tell that Emmanuelle is vehemently denying the charge.

"I saw you put it in your pocket!" Summer maintains.

I feel a heavy hand on my shoulder and turn to see Vinny, with John on his heels. We step aside, and the two men enter the room. Summer clings to John. "Oh, thank God you're here. I caught her"—she points at Emmanuelle—"trying to steal the beautiful necklace you gave me."

"It's not true!" Emmanuelle protests. "I put the necklace in the box." She indicates Summer's gold jewelry box. "That is all. I promise."

"Liar," Summer snaps.

John looks between the two women, weary.

"Emmanuelle is an honest person," Julie pipes up. "I have worked with her for three years and never had trouble. I believe it is a simple misunderstanding."

"You're just covering for her," Summer accuses. "We should call the police."

"Okay," John says. "Emmanuelle, Julie, come to my office." He turns his attention to Summer. "Our guests have just arrived. Please take your friends and go entertain them until I return. And not a word about this. Understand?"

She nods. John and Vinny exit with Julie and Emmanuelle trailing behind like scolded dogs. Rhonda hugs Summer as the rest of us pile into the room and gather around her.

"Are you okay?" Wendy rubs Summer's back as Rhonda and Brittani hug her.

Summer nods, taking a deep breath to calm herself. "I just feel so violated, you know?"

Am I the only one who remembers that just yesterday Summer told us all she was going to get this girl fired? I can't understand why she's even bothering to pretend now that John's left the room. I contort my face into a mask of sympathy to match the others, but I don't for a second believe that Emmanuelle was trying to steal her gaudy necklace. Summer's wanted Emmanuelle off the boat since dinner the first night and has doubtless been stalking her since, waiting for the right moment to strike. The poor girl never had a chance.

Over Rhonda's shoulder, Summer catches my eye and winks. Then, in a flash, the tears return.

(one year ago)

Los Angeles

On a suffocating Tuesday afternoon in late August, I lay prostrate on my couch sipping an iced coffee and half watching *Arctic Worlds* in an effort to cool down. Even with the curtains closed against the sun and the window unit in my bedroom chugging away, the heat remained thick as fleece.

Hunter stood at the window, peering through the drapes at the outside world. "There goes another one," he announced as a man jogged by. "Shirt off. My God, look at that six-pack! That's five so far today. Eight if you count the short ones."

"This is why you should move back from New York and take the empty apartment on the first floor. It would be like old times." Hunter had moved to New York for a part in a musical eight months ago and was now recording an album there as well, so I no longer got to see nearly as much of him as I'd have liked.

"But I get to stay for free on your couch," he reasoned. "And this way you have a place to stay in New York, too. It's like we're bicoastal. Oh. My. God. Another one!"

"It's the hiking trail at the end of the street. It draws them like flies."

"We should get a baby pool and sit in the front yard," he suggested.

"So you can out-six-pack them with your rock-hard abs?" I giggled.

"Yes." He grabbed my hand and pulled me up to sitting. "We have to get out of this apartment. I'm dying."

I groaned as he peered through the slit in the curtains.

"Speaking of dying, your plants don't look so good, either," he said. "Come on, let's water them. It's not like it's any cooler in here. We can put up the umbrella, catch a breeze..."

Clearly he was not going to be deterred, so I filled the watering can and followed him onto the balcony, where he promptly stripped off his shirt, revealing rippling muscles under smooth dark skin. Two girls walking by caught sight of him, and one almost walked into a street sign. He waved.

"Too bad you're playing for the other team." I laughed.

I watered my poor shriveled plants while he leaned on the railing posing like Adonis awaiting his Prince Charming. I couldn't help myself. I had to pour the water on him. He swatted at me, which only made me splash more on him. "I'm just adding to your allure," I teased.

"Whatever," he returned. "It feels good."

An Uber pulled up to the curb outside my building, and a blond head emerged from the back. "Is that who I think it is?" He peered over the top of his sunglasses.

We watched as the driver helped Summer heft two huge bags from the trunk. "No way is that tramp getting my spot on the couch," he said through his teeth as he waved to her with a bright smile.

"Oh, come on. You know you're gonna pick up one of these hikers this afternoon and I won't see you again for months."

"You mean until you drive my ass back to LAX next week. 'Cause you know you ain't getting out of that, girl."

I laughed. Despite his bravado, Hunter was a gentleman, and he bounded down the stairs to help Summer with her bags.

She dragged herself through the door and flopped on the couch, looking the worse for wear.

"What happened?" I asked.

"Ugh." She sighed. "Brian found out about Eric and kicked me out." Finally. I'd been wondering how long that would take.

"How did he find out?" I asked.

"A freakin' condom."

I stared at her, incredulous. "You did it in his apartment?"

"But the good news is, you were using protection," Hunter chimed in.

"So stupid, I know," she admitted. "But I've hardly seen him, I swear! He wanted to shoot pictures of me for this series he's doing, and the view there is so amazing, and then, you know how it is . . . We got carried away."

"So what are you gonna do?" I asked, as though the answer weren't obvious.

"Can I stay here for a sec? Just until I get a job. I may die if I have to stay with Rhonda in the Inland Empire again. Pretty please?"

"You'll have to duke it out with Hunter," I said. "He has dibs on the couch."

"I can just sleep in your bed with you." She must've seen the hesitation on my face, because she added, "For just a little while, I swear." She threw her arms around my neck and gave me a kiss on the cheek. "Thank you for having my back."

"You don't wanna stay with your new boyfriend?" Hunter asked.

She shook her head. "He lives in his art studio downtown, and he's traveling a lot right now. I wouldn't want to be there alone."

For the past year I had mostly avoided discussing Eric with Summer for fear she might sniff out my sensitivity surrounding the subject and become suspicious. But finally the question begged to be asked. "What's the deal with you guys, anyway?"

"I mean, he totally wants to be with me," Summer said. "But he's, like, broke. So I don't know if it can go anywhere."

"But he's a successful artist," I said. "He doesn't make any money from that?"

"I guess he does." She shrugged. "He's super weird about money. He never spends anything—he doesn't even have a car. But he owns that entire building his art gallery is in. Apparently his family is, like, superrich, and I guess he has a trust fund and everything that he won't even touch."

"I can help him with that," Hunter offered.

"Believe me," Summer said, "if I can't get him to spend money, no one can."

★   ★   ★

Besides her nasty habit of stealing the sheets, Summer wasn't a terrible roommate. It was nice to have someone to chat with over a glass of wine in the evening, and she was a neat freak, which meant she did the dishes and cleaned the place before I could even think about it.

Much to my relief, Eric never came around. Though I wouldn't in a million years have admitted it to anyone, I'd been unable to ever totally let go of the time we spent together on the roof. I knew it was foolish—my logical mind recognized that he was a player and, even without Summer in the picture, he'd likely never have been with me— but my heart still curdled at the idea of the two of them together. In the beginning I'd tried to replace any errant thoughts of Eric with Dylan, but it hadn't worked. Sure, I'd liked Dylan—and I imagined I would've been far more into him if I hadn't met his brother first—but it wasn't Dylan who turned up in my dreams. My obscenely sexy, stubbornly recurrent dreams.

Luckily, my dreams were the only place Eric turned up. He rarely seemed to be in town, and when he was, Summer preferred to stay at his place unless they were fighting, which they did regularly. I gathered both of them were incredibly jealous, but neither was particularly faithful. She threatened never to see him again over nudes he'd shot of other women or amorous text messages in foreign languages. He broke it off with her over dates she went on or new Jimmy Choos bought by a suitor. I could hardly keep up.

The theatrics were unusual for Summer; normally she had her guy wrapped around her little finger, and when she crooked it, he bought her baubles—or she dumped him for another man who would. But Eric had staying power regardless—or perhaps because—of his failure to bow before her. She was obviously more smitten with him than she cared to confess, and I daresay (in spite of her claims to the contrary) he was less with her, which drove her nuts. I had no doubt that if he actually wanted her to be his girlfriend, she'd have turned down the French Laundry with millionaires in Lamborghinis to eat ramen and ride the subway with him. For once in her life, the tables were turned. And this, I was ashamed to acknowledge, made me more than a tiny bit gratified.

One Saturday evening I arrived home bone-tired from a long day slinging drinks at the pool to find the door to my bedroom closed. I'd had to get up at the crack of dawn to drive Wendy to a physical therapy session for her broken leg, and was badly in need of a nap. But I didn't want to nap with Summer. I wanted to nap alone.

Annoyed, I pushed the door open to find Summer fully nude on my white down comforter, posing seductively while Eric snapped pictures. I froze, rooted in place.

Making no attempt to cover herself, she calmly rolled onto her side. "Hey. We're just doing a photo shoot. We'll be finished soon."

I blinked. Eric lowered the camera. "I'm doing a series on female erotica."

"On my bed." My voice sounded high and strange.

"It's a good bed," Eric said. "I like the iron; it photographs well."

How the hell did neither of them realize this was totally weird? Having no idea what else to say, I backed out of the room, avoiding looking at Summer as I shut the door behind me, and walked blindly into the kitchen, where I poured myself a shot of tequila. I knocked it back, the booze burning my throat.

Had they fucked in my bed?

I knew I shouldn't care. I'd stayed in hotel beds a million times, where God only knows how many people had done God only knows what. But it was *my* bed.

And why was I so turned on by the idea of Eric fucking in my bed?

Aaaah! I squeezed my eyes shut, trying to erase the thought, and when I opened them, Eric was standing in the doorway, gazing at me. "I like your garden."

"Thanks," I managed.

"Have you heard from my brother?"

"He invited me to London," I said.

This wasn't exactly true, of course. He'd thrown it out there the night I met him, a full year ago, but he hadn't mentioned it the handful of times we'd emailed since, and if he had, it was doubtful I would have gone.

"Are you going to go?"

I shrugged. "Maybe."

"I'd love to shoot you sometime," he said.

I pictured Summer nude on my bed. "No thanks."

He glanced toward my bedroom. "Not like that. I've been looking for a queen for a series I'm doing. Your face, your attitude—you'd be perfect."

Over his shoulder, I noticed Summer lingering in the hallway, now wearing a sundress. She draped her arms around him from behind and nuzzled his ear. "What are you guys talking about?"

"Belle modeling for me," Eric said, not taking his eyes off mine.

I wanted to slap some sense into him, but all I could do was stand there gaping like an idiot.

Summer slipped past him and slid her arm around me, giving me a little squeeze. "She is pretty, isn't she?" she asked, stroking my hair. And then lightly: "But you lay a hand on her and I'll fucking kill you."

Day 5

Wednesday morning—Saint-Tropez, France

John's portrait looms above me, dark despite the bright day. Uncomfortable under his shifting gaze, I once again angle the computer screen away from the unblinking eye of the security camera and type quickly:

Hey Sis,

Sorry for the delayed response, we've been kept busy helping John entertain some foreign executives he's trying to get to invest in a resort on the Italian coast. It's a gorgeous day here and we're on the boat near Saint-Tropez, going for lunch somewhere fancy with some rich people later.

In other news, Summer got one of the crew girls fired last night because she didn't like the way the poor girl looked. So that was dramatic. Meanwhile I'm trying to just be nice and get along, as you suggested. Hoping I can make it through the trip without being fired myself, haha.

How are you? Everything good?

Love,
Sis

I realize I'll come off as ungrateful if anyone is monitoring my emails, but at this point I just don't care. I grab my latte and laptop and pad over to one of the couches looking out toward the shining sea.

The entire back of the boat is open to the morning light reflecting off the water, and the other girls are splayed out in the sun on loungers, half reading beauty and gossip magazines as the boat rocks gently back and forth. We've been given a blissful break from our packed schedule by John's urgent need to see some land he intends to buy, and Summer has gone with him, leaving the rest of us to our own devices. This, at last, feels like paradise.

I open my computer and pop in my earbuds, then pump up some Jimmy Buffett. We are at the beach, after all.

After the drama with Emmanuelle, last night's dinner on the boat was mostly uneventful, largely because the combination of jet lag, sun, and alcohol had left us all so tired we could hardly see straight. Even Brittani was subdued. The investors from China joined us again, and the ladies were expected to keep quiet so that the men could discuss matters Summer assured us were of the utmost importance.

Though once again they mentioned nothing exactly illegal in range of our delicate lady ears, at this point it's clear that John pairs a take-no-prisoners approach to enterprise with a practice of doing everything as cheaply as humanly possible, regardless of pesky rules or environmental ramifications. To summarize: no surprise, he's a real motherfucker and it's made him very, very rich.

It makes my blood boil. So many good people suffer through their lives trying to make ends meet while he sits on his throne counting his gold, believing he deserves every ounce of it. For he is a lion, hear him roar! I took a zoology class in college, because why not? And what I remember most vividly about the exalted rulers of the animal kingdom speaks more to their cunning than their courage: in a drought, the king of beasts drives the lesser creatures from the watering hole while he drinks, then falls upon their weakened bodies with triumph, devouring their parched flesh before they've even expired.

You can't blame a lion for being a lion. An animal has no wickedness; it knows only how to survive. But a man who fancies himself a lion to excuse his depravity? Well, he's no more than a predator.

But, of course, no one's asking my opinion.

After John's associates left, he and Summer withdrew to their room and I climbed up to the roof deck for a nightcap with Wendy and Claire. None of us needed another drink, but there was half a bottle of Dom left, and it felt wasteful to abandon it. The evening was beautiful and clear, the moon yet to rise. A dazzling array of twinkling stars lit up the sky as the boat bobbed gently in the tide, but I could hardly keep my eyes open to enjoy the display. Claire leaned on Wendy's shoulder, and Wendy leaned on mine, all of us so drowsy that the trek back to our rooms seemed almost insurmountable. "I don't think I've been this sleepy since I was on painkillers after my accident," Wendy commented, yawning.

"I feel drugged," Claire agreed, matching her yawn. "It must be all the sun."

"And champagne," Wendy added, taking a slug from the bottle.

Suddenly I remembered the Valium in Bernard's pocket. I thought about how strangely tired I'd been every night, how deeply I'd slept, the floating sensation I couldn't seem to shake. *Could they be drugging us?*

No, surely not. But the idea wasn't ill founded. I considered whether to broach the subject with Wendy and Claire. I didn't want to alarm them, but I was curious whether they'd noticed the same things I had. "You guys"—I lowered my voice, pretending to be more drunk than I was—"what if they're, like, drugging us?"

Claire sat up, her eyes wide in the starlight. "What?"

Wendy laughed. "Oh my God, of course they're not *drugging* us. That's insane."

"Yeah," I whispered conspiratorially, "but just go with me here—we're sooo tired at night, and there's cameras everywhere, no Wi-Fi...Doesn't it seem like something *shady* could be going on?"

Wendy rolled her eyes. "Ohmygod, stop being dramatic. This isn't one of your horror movies."

I laughed, taking the bottle from her. "I have been in waaay too many horror movies." Bubbles fizzed and popped in my mouth.

"This is our best friend we're talking about," she continued quietly, "and it's super nice of her to invite us here. Let's just be grateful, k?"

It was no surprise that ever-diplomatic Wendy preferred us to stay in our lanes. I should have known better than to bring it up with her. I sighed, passing the champagne to Claire. "Okay, Mom."

A star shot across the sky. I pointed, glad for the diversion. "Did you see that?"

"Make a wish," Wendy said.

Claire squealed and wiped her mouth with her hand. "I got so excited I spilled champagne all over myself."

I lifted the seat cushion next to me, revealing rows upon rows of neatly stacked navy-and-white towels beneath. "You get a towel." I tossed Claire a towel. "And you get a towel." I tossed Wendy a towel. "And I get a towel! Everybody gets a towel!"

We laughed together and curled up beneath our plush towels, our eyes fixed on the diamond-studded sky.

Once we retired to our rooms around midnight, I forced myself to lie awake quietly listening until I heard the click of the lock in the door. Amythest slumbered while I stealthily got out of bed and tried the handle, confirming we were indeed locked in. So I wasn't crazy. Claustrophobia wound around me like a python. I squeezed my eyes shut and controlled my breath in an effort to pry it loose.

It couldn't be one of the crew locking us in; there's no way that could be safe. If the ship were to go down, we'd have no way out.

So it must be Bernard and Vinny, our hall monitors. But why?

Regardless of how tired I was, sleep eluded me. After what must have been more than an hour of tossing and turning, trying to convince my feverish mind to sleep, I heard a motor out on the water, close by. I carefully climbed over Amythest and pushed up the shade on the small round window above her bed. In the silvery moonlight, I could just make out the back of a tender idling by the landing at the stern of our boat. Two men were in the process of boarding the *Lion's Den*, though whether others had gone before them, I couldn't tell. Nor could I tell anything about their identity, other than that they were dressed in white robes and wearing headpieces of the type favored by royalty from certain Middle Eastern countries.

Whoever these men are, they must be shadow associates of the variety a high-profile American businessman fraternizes with only in private. Was this the sole reason for our being locked in at night? Or was there something more? I wondered what Summer was privy to and how much control John exerted over her evening hours, beyond his seemingly unquenchable thirst for sex. And what of the crew? Did they know about this, or were they confined to their quarters during certain hours as well?

Leaving the shade partially open, I crept back to my bed, where I remained vigilant in the hope of possibly getting a better look at the visitors when they departed. But I never heard the motor fire up again, and at some point I must have given in to sleep, because the next thing I knew, Camille was rousing us this morning at dawn with instructions to report to the dining room dressed for Spin class. We sat around the table for an hour before Summer showed up to inform us that Spin class was canceled because she and John were going to look at land. She was in an exceptionally cheerful mood and even gave me one of her Dramamine pills when I discovered I'd misplaced my own. I suppose I could've gone back to bed after she and John departed, but I was so wired from all the coffee I'd consumed, I figured I'd try to get some work done.

So here I sit, trying to read a television script I have an audition for next week, but my stomach hasn't felt right all morning and I'm distracted. Summer's vicious elimination of Emmanuelle has me on edge, especially coupled with her unusual friendliness toward me this morning. I feel like I'm playing a game of increasing stakes with ever-changing rules.

Of course I knew intellectually going into this trip that Summer was no longer the girl I'd always shared secrets with, but seeing her without the rose-colored glasses of years of friendship, I hardly recognize her. And I feel stupid for not seeing her more clearly before.

I realize it should be a simple trick to not get caught up in her machinations, but I don't seem to be able to disentangle myself and can't help but wonder at her intentions for bringing me here when she so clearly despises me. Granted, things were different between us when she first extended the invitation—God, was it only six weeks ago? This is the first time we've spent any quality time together since what happened to Eric.

Eric. Regardless of my promise to myself that I wasn't going to think about him this week, my heart tugs at the idea of him.

But I'm here now, so I have to keep up the act, pretend everything's great and I'm having a wonderful time. It's the most exhausting role I've ever played, and the whole thing makes me nauseated. I take a sip of my coffee. My stomach roils. I put the coffee down. Maybe no more coffee this morning. Hopefully this is just a case of too much coffee on an empty stomach and not something worse. I look out at the horizon in an attempt to still my thoughts and my churning stomach.

Camille appears in my line of sight, speaking words I can't hear. I rip the earbuds from my ears. "Sorry. I had it up loud."

"Not a problem," she says. "The tender will leave at noon."

"Oh!" I glance at my watch. It's 11:43 a.m. "I didn't realize we were leaving so soon."

She nods. "Madame Lyons would like everyone there early."

"She's not Madame Lyons, you know," I say tersely. "She's his mistress."

Camille looks at me wide-eyed, unsure how to respond. As I snap my laptop closed, I notice Dre and Hugo collecting towels and magazines from the deserted sundeck. Camille follows my gaze and apologizes. "They went down thirty minutes ago. I didn't see you here. I'm sorry."

My stomach lurches as I stand. Oh no.

I scurry down the stairs to our room, where Amythest is already perfectly made up and curling her hair in front of the mirror wearing a shiny purple bikini. I enter the bathroom, waving her out. "You can have it back, but I need it for a minute."

"Can't you just pee in front of me?"

"I don't need to—"

And just like that, I'm on my knees, hurling my morning coffee and croissant into the toilet.

"Shit." Amythest drops the curling iron and pulls my hair back in one motion.

After I finish, she wets a washcloth and hands it to me. "You okay?"

I nod. "Better now."

"Did you forget to take your Dramamine this morning?" she asks, concerned.

I shake my head. "I couldn't find my pill bottle, but Summer gave me one of hers."

Amythest narrows her eyes. "Are you sure it was Dramamine?"

"No." I bite my lip, realizing. I'd recognized the goons might be drugging us with their Valium, but it hadn't occurred to me that Summer would drug me. How could I have been so stupid? "She said it was a different brand that did the same thing." Amythest raises an eyebrow. I take a deep breath and let it out. "But why? Why on earth would she want me to be sick? I coulda hurled all over her precious boat!"

She shrugs. "She doesn't like you. It's pretty obvious."

"Thanks."

"Oh, come on. Like you don't know."

She's right. I know.

"Maybe you should skip lunch," she suggests.

I shake my head, wobbling to my feet. "And let her think she won? No way."

I wash my mouth out and brush my teeth, noting my ghostly appearance in the mirror. Amythest is right. I should probably skip lunch, but that's not happening. I focus on the horizon through the window above Amythest's bed in an effort to quell my nausea while she looks on, amused.

"Well," she says, "it's a beach club. So, like, bring a bikini so we can lay out or whatever after lunch. If you can keep it down."

She gives me a wry smile and turns back to the mirror.

Beach club. That means I don't have to shower, right? I forgo the shower in favor of a spray of perfume and a layer of deodorant, and throw on a simple white bikini under a red sundress. A layer of mascara, a little stain on my lips, and I'm done in just enough time to scour our room once more for my bottle of Dramamine, but turn up nothing. Odd. Or maybe, all things considered, it's not so odd.

I grab my bag and slip out the door, thankful to escape the cloud of Amythest's hair spray and perfume. We exchange compliments with Wendy and Claire in the hallway before heading up to the main deck to wait for the tender.

Brittani and Rhonda are already reclining on the loungers sipping champagne when we arrive. Camille offers us a tray, but I decline, instead requesting Dramamine. Camille scurries off in search of it.

"Party pooper!" Brittani declares.

"I'm feeling a little woozy," I explain.

Claire gives me a side hug. "Sorry. All this rocking's not great for me, either."

"You okay to go to lunch?" Wendy asks.

I nod. "It'll do me good to get off the boat."

Curiously, Camille is unable to find a single pill or patch for motion sickness anywhere on the boat, but I am not to be deterred. I steel my resolve and board the tender, praying I don't throw up on the choppy ride to the beach club.

Vinny slides onto the bench seat next to me, watching me like a hawk. The vibration of the motor is almost worse than the bumping up and down, but if I lean slightly over the side and trail my fingers in the water just so, focusing on the coolness of the sea, I can hold on. Vinny leans into me, sweating in his black blazer. The stench of his perspiration singes my nostrils and tugs at the bile in my throat. He keeps his gaze trained on the horizon as he murmurs, "You should know, Emmanuelle was fired because she stole a necklace, not because she was pretty."

Every nerve in my body jolts to attention. I steal a glance at him, thankful my big dark glasses hide my eyes. But his lumpy countenance is inscrutable, his eyes also hidden behind a pair of shades. On the other side of him, Bernard mutters something I can't hear over the alarm bells ringing in my head, and Vinny turns his attention to him, leaving me wondering whether I imagined the entire exchange.

No. I may be nauseous, but I'm not crazy. It was a warning: he's reading my emails. Jesus. In my mind I thumb back through every email I've sent and received from the hardwired computers. Nothing too nefarious, I think. I've been careful. But still...

We lurch onto the shore, and Dre and Hugo drag the boat out of the surf and hand us down onto the sand. I'm so unsettled, I hardly notice the transparent turquoise water and golden beach. I can't take in the perfect temperature of the breeze or the laughter of vacationers playing in the sand and water.

My sandals in hand, I take a few steps into the sea, soaking my feet in the refreshing water, my focus on the skyline. If Vinny's reading my emails, who else is? John? Summer? How stupid of me. I should have known. And now I do. No more emails from the hardwired computers, clearly.

"Come on, Belle." Wendy's damn fingernails on my arm. I recoil.

"Sorry," I say. "Not feeling well."

I want to strip off my dress, dive under the water, and let it consume me. Let the surf wash away my memory, forget I ever met Summer, forget this fucked-up trip, forget Eric, forget everything. Instead I reluctantly turn and follow Wendy across the sand, through the maze of blue and white umbrellas and loungers, past the heavy tables in the shade, into the indoor reception area that feels strangely like a hunting lodge, and straight out the front door, where we're dumped into a dusty parking lot.

The sun beats down mercilessly, the breeze that was so cooling on the beach side nowhere to be found. Vinny's revelation on the tender has just made my seasickness worse. How long can it last? Surely the rocking will stop now that we're on land. I'd google it, but I can't imagine focusing on my phone.

Vinny and Bernard indicate that we should sit on a bench in front of the restaurant, and we exchange confused glances. "But there's a bar inside, and I think I saw a ninety-nine-year-old in a wheelchair!" Rhonda exclaims.

Everyone but me titters. I'm too busy trying to stop the ground from moving before my eyes to pretend to think this is funny.

"Mom!" Brittani cries. "That's impossible. You can't have a wheel-chair in the sand!"

"Okay, maybe it was a walker. I can't be sure."

"You need to stay together," Bernard instructs us. Or is it Vinny? I can't determine the difference in their voices while staring at the sandy shale.

"We can stay together at the bar," Wendy offers him with a wink. "Aren't you thirsty? I'll buy ya a drink."

"Mr. Lyons said wait here, so we wait here," he says. "You can sit on the bench."

The slick green wood of the bench is hot to the touch, but sit-ting at least grounds me somewhat. We wait in sweltering silence as chauffeured cars deposit occupants armed with beach bags, hats, and sunglasses. I wish I'd brought a freaking hat. Even Wendy can't hide her annoyance.

"This is ridiculous," she whispers to me, shading her face with one hand and gathering her hair off her neck with the other. "I'm sweating, and I don't need any more sun. I'm getting darker than my foundation."

"I have to pee," Brittani says.

Vinny sighs. "Okay. You can go two at a time. But come right back. We need to all be together when they arrive."

Brittani grabs her mother's hand, and they dash inside. My insides rumble. Oh God. This is not the place to be sick. In the event Brittani and Rhonda ever return (which I highly doubt), I know the bathroom will be full of old ladies powdering their noses and socialites doing cocaine, so I scan the area for a better option. To my left is the beach—no good. But to my right...Who knows what lurks around the ther side of the building, but it has to be better than my other options.

Amythest sees me searching and whispers, "I got ya," as she helps me to my feet.

"She doesn't feel well," she says as we stumble past Bernard and Vinny.

Bernard blocks our path with his hulking frame. "Wait for the others to return and you can go next."

Amythest looks up at him without fear, clearly someone who has had her fair share of encounters with bouncers. "Move or she's gonna spew on you." She pushes past him, dragging me with her.

The thirty feet between us and the corner of the building are the Sahara. I grip her hand like it's a life raft and let her guide me to what I can only hope is a puking oasis. We round the corner of the building to find a false green wall that hides the trash. The smell pushes me over the top, and I dive behind the nearest bin and retch.

"Oh God," Amythest says. "I'm sorry...I can't...the smell."

After she leaves, I proceed to empty what is left of the contents of my stomach into the dirt behind the rotting waste of the rich. At one point a young busboy throws a bag into the bin and spies me there on my knees, but he doesn't say anything. Nor, apparently, does he alert anyone, because I am left to vomit in peace.

When I have sufficiently drained the swamp, I dust myself off and hobble around to the other side of the trash bins in an attempt to find somewhere more pleasant to sit and pull myself together before return-ing to my crystal cage. The dirt driveway empties into a delivery area with a ramp up to a loading dock, where the busboy leans against the wall, smoking a cigarette. He sees me emerge and extracts a fresh bottle of water from his back pocket, holding it out to me. I gratefully take it from him and wash my mouth out, afraid to swallow the water for fear of waking the beast in my stomach. "*Merci*," I say.

"*Un moment.*" He disappears through a cracked door, returning after a few moments with an ice-cold towel.

He finishes his cigarette as I thoroughly wipe myself down and hand it back to him. "*Merci beaucoup.*"

He takes a pack of cigarettes from his back pocket and offers me one, but I decline. "*Tu es mon sauveur,*" I say.

He nods and goes inside, and I return to the bench, wishing I had a toothbrush but otherwise feeling better. Rhonda and Brittani have not returned and Vinny is gone, but the rest of the group is still there, wilting in the sun. They look up at me expectantly.

"You okay?" Wendy ventures, handing me a piece of spearmint gum, which I gratefully put in my mouth.

I nod. "I'm just seasick. Yay."

Claire pats my arm, and I take a seat between her and Amythest.

"What time is it?" I ask.

"Almost two," Wendy says.

"They're an hour late," Amythest adds.

"They will be here any minute," Bernard says.

As if on cue, a silver convertible Ferrari pulls up in a cloud of dust, and Bernard waves us all to our feet.

Amythest remains sitting, doing something on her phone. Bernard grabs her by the arm and jerks her to her feet, causing her to drop her bejeweled phone on the ground. She wrests her arm away from him, and I pick up the phone and hand it to her.

Summer emerges from the car looking fresh in a white sundress and giant sunglasses and unties the blue flowered scarf from her hair while she waits for John to come around to her side and take her hand. He's in a linen suit and sunglasses, and as they come toward us, I recognize the glasses he's wearing. They're the pair I found under Amythest's bed yesterday.

Realization washes over me like a cold shower. If I were a loyal friend,

I would be outraged, but it's all I can do to keep from laughing. Here's Summer, acting like she's to the manor born and we're her ladies-in-waiting, when right under her nose, a younger woman has easily seduced her sugar daddy. But then, what can she possibly expect? The man who sleeps with a woman thirty-six years younger behind his wife's back will sleep with one forty-three years younger behind his mistress's.

And then Summer's air-kissing me and we are filing inside, the dark of the vestibule such a contrast to the bright sun that I can hardly see two feet in front of me. As I step out onto the shaded dining patio, the sea breeze caresses my skin and leaves me feeling instantly ten times better. Chill lounge music thrums under the sound of the waves, and waiters in green polo shirts bustle between tables crowded with a dizzying array of well-to-do French families on vacation, Russian billionaires and their entourages, Greek shipping magnates conducting business meetings—just a usual August afternoon on the Riviera.

We have a corner table with a view of the sea, our dining companions apparently the richest people in some country I've heard of but couldn't place on a map. Latvia? Lithuania? I don't know, and I really don't care. Looking at them, you'd think they were perhaps a Midwestern high school football coach and his wife. They're middle-aged, average white people you could meet five times and still not remember. Alas, I will never know anything else about them, as they are seated with Summer and John at the better end of the table, and I am seated at the opposite end with their two teenage sons, bodyguard, and nanny.

One of the sons is probably sixteen, and I never get a clear look at him before he dashes for the beach with friends whose parents are installed at a neighboring table. The younger son, who I'm guessing is the painful age of thirteen, sits next to his nanny on my left and gives me a weak smile before permanently turning his acne-pocked cheek toward his gaming device. To my right is their bodyguard, a large man in a black suit who I am told does not speak English. It seems to me that he should be closer to his employers and facing the action to be worth a damn in a crisis, but I guess this is not an area of high alert.

Regardless, I'm glad I don't have to worry about making conversation with either of them. All I want is to make it through lunch with as little interaction as possible and get back to the boat, where I can take a nap. I could seriously put my face down on the table and snooze right now. I can't fathom eating.

Brittani and Rhonda have been husband-hunting at the bar for the past hour, and when Vinny escorts them back to the table, they are already on the downhill of a slippery slope, giggling all the way. Their jovial state does not escape Summer, who deftly steers them down to my end of the table, as far away from the Latvians as possible. I steel myself for an hours-long installment of "Brittani and Rhonda Do Europe" as Amythest takes the seat across from me.

Amythest, my violet-eyed best friend. And to think I was initially annoyed I had to room with her. Now I am thrilled I don't have to room with anyone else.

The waitress sets a shot of vodka in front of each of us, a gift from our dining companions. The man says something about how they drink it in their country for good fortune and that this bottle is two hundred years old. That can't be right. I'm probably seated too far away to hear properly. At any rate, everyone, including the thirteen-year-old, takes the shot. I need a shot of vodka like I need a shot to the head, but I see Summer's eyes slide to me and I toss it back, just to prove to her that I'm totally fine, regardless of whatever the hell kind of pill she gave me this morning.

My stomach immediately revolts, but my mind smooths out nicely. Mind over matter. Mind over matter. Mind over... Nope.

I stand, my eyes scanning the back of the restaurant for the exit to the bathroom. Amythest starts around the table to escort me, but Wendy steps in and grabs my hand, leading me across the restaurant. The din of conversation, plates, music, and waves all grows to an unbearable roar in my ears; my head spins. *Keep it together, Belle! Keep it together.*

I put one foot in front of the other, forcing myself to breathe deeply, all the while tightly gripping Wendy's hand as she leads me through the strangely dark bar and out the back door, down a shrub-walled path covered by a trellis. Why did I drink that vodka? What was I thinking? Stupid. Stupid. Stupid.

"Are the bathrooms on the moon?" I grumble.

"They're really locker rooms. They serve the people using the beach club, too," Wendy explains, pushing open the door.

It's all cool white marble inside, and somehow miraculously I'm not throwing up. I feel like I might, but I'm not. I lean against the wall in the handicapped stall, my head in my hands, breathing slowly, while Wendy strokes my head.

"I'm sorry," I say. "I shouldn't have taken that shot."

"Yeah, that was dumb," she says with a little laugh. "It's okay. It's not your fault. Once we get you some Dramamine, you'll be a lot better."

"I have Dramamine!" comes a high, British-accented voice from the adjoining stall. "I'm sorry for eavesdropping, but I turn green at the sight of a boat. It's the absolute worst!"

"You're an angel!" I say.

A pale hand with perfectly manicured bright-blue nails appears under the stall with what looks like a little round Band-Aid.

"It's a patch," she says. "Just put it on your neck; it'll fix you right up."

"Thank you so much," Wendy says, taking the patch.

She opens it and hands it to me. Too sick to turn down drugs from random strangers in bathrooms right now, I place it on my neck. The toilet next to us flushes. "Good luck," the voice says.

"Bless you!" I call after her.

"You think you're gonna be okay now?" Wendy asks. "We should get back to the table before Summer thinks we've run off."

I nod. "I figure her thinking we've run off is probably better than me hurling all over the table."

"I had no idea you got so nauseous," she says.

"Me neither. But then, I've never spent a week on a boat before."

"Those things are supposed to work wonders, though."

I don't know if it's psychosomatic, but even as she says it, I am starting to feel better. The walls have stopped shifting. I can feel my feet on the floor. I step out of the stall, and the world doesn't crumble.

I splash my face with cold water and blot it dry with a hand towel while Wendy touches up her face and fixes her hair. Once she's satisfied with her own appearance, she turns her attention to me. "We've gotta get some color back into you."

She fishes in her makeup bag, coming up with five different lipsticks, none of which she deems appropriate for my skin tone, then finally locates a translucent rose stain she says will have to do. I obediently dab my lips and cheeks with it. "Not bad," she says, spritzing me with perfume.

I pop a mint in my mouth as we exit the ladies' room, grateful I'm finally beginning to crave a piece of the fresh-baked bread I saw at other people's tables.

"You know who that was that saved your ass?" Wendy whispers as we stride arm in arm up the pathway that connects the restrooms to the restaurant. "Tamara von Klein. Duchess of Austria? I think it's Austria. But she was raised in England, clearly."

"How on earth did you know that?"

"I know these things."

"But we didn't even see her."

She shrugs. "I saw her go in the bathroom ahead of us and noticed her nails."

I push open the heavy door to the bar, blinking as my eyes adjust to the dimness of the wood-paneled room. Velvet drapes block most of the light, and lurid oil paintings of wild animals tearing one another to shreds hang on the dark-green wallpaper. "Why is it so dark in here?" I ask.

I meant it as a rhetorical question, but of course Wendy knows the answer. "This restaurant has been here a hundred years, and the bar has always been the same. It's famous."

My eyes land on John, standing at the elaborately carved mahogany bar, in conversation with a tall, dark-haired man. Both have their backs to us.

As we approach, John slaps the man on the back and walks away without spotting us. The man turns. My heart stops.

It's Dylan.

I haven't seen him in more than a year, but he looks just the same: rakishly handsome in an impeccably wrinkled white button-down and faded red shorts, his skin sun-kissed, his dark hair tousled. He gives the air of belonging in this place and seems relaxed—far more relaxed than I'd have assumed someone who'd just lost his brother might be.

Neither of us moves for a moment, both caught off guard. And then he breaks into a smile and approaches, his arms outstretched. He wraps me up in a hug as Wendy looks on, amused.

"I didn't think I was going to get to see you," he says as we separate.

"Yeah. Small world," I agree, my surprise robbing me of anything more interesting to say. "This is Dylan," I explain to Wendy.

"I remember." She smiles. "Sort of. Thank you for rescuing me at that fairy party."

"No problem."

"What brings you here?" I ask.

A wry smile plays around his lips. "Same thing as you, I suppose."

"Lunch!" Wendy interjects brightly.

He seems less excited to see me than I might have expected, the easy rapport we had last time we met now strained. But then, he's been through hell since the last time I saw him.

"How do you know John?" Wendy asks him.

He shifts his weight and runs his fingers through his hair, clearing his throat. "We—uh, we work together."

Interesting. His eyes flicker toward me to gauge my reaction, but Wendy plows ahead. "And what do you do, Dylan?" she pipes up.

He glances over his shoulder as though looking for someone. "Future site research and development."

"That sounds cool," she says, laying a hand lightly on his biceps. "What does it mean?"

He crosses his arms, his eyes scanning the restaurant behind us. "I create viability reports on potential locations for commercial development."

Why is he acting so odd?

"Cool," she says. "Summer mentioned John's building a resort around here—are you working on that with him?"

He furrows his brow, but before he can answer, a waiter approaches and bows slightly to Dylan, who looks decidedly relieved by his appearance. "*Monsieur, votre compagnon est arrivé.*"

His companion, ah. He's on a date. Of course. So that explains it.

He nods. "*Merci.*"

The waiter continues to hover. I force a smile, wishing I had more time with him and that Wendy weren't beside me. "Don't let us keep you."

"I'm sorry," he says. "It's my grandmother. She's ninety-one. I don't want to keep her waiting."

"Of course," I say. "It was good to see you."

"I'm so sorry about your brother," Wendy says with sincerity.

He nods, his countenance for the first time showing signs of melancholy. "Thank you."

I see my opportunity and speak up. "Is there any news?"

He quickly shakes his head. "Please do call me if you get a few hours while you're here," he says. "I'd love to catch up properly."

He leans in and plants a dry kiss on my cheek, then follows the waiter from the room.

Wendy sighs as she watches him leave. "So sad."

I nod. "Yeah."

She squeezes my hand and smiles. "I forgot he's such an eyeful."

"Yeah."

"Seems to like you, too," she adds.

"I don't know. I didn't really get that feeling."

"I'm sure he was just surprised to see you, and after everything with Eric, he can't feel great knowing Summer's around...would just be so hard..."

"Yeah," I agree, unsettled.

"And he knows John…He must know about him and Summer, then," she prattles on. "I wonder if he's upset about it. I mean, he's probably upset, right? To see her here all happy with John when his brother was, like, crazy in love with her and now he's—God, it's so awful. Poor Summer…" Her voice trails off as our eyes land on Vinny, who has appeared in the doorway that leads to the restaurant.

"Girls." He beckons to us. We scuttle over to him like well-trained dogs. "No more taking off."

Summer's unsmiling eyes track us as he guides us to the table with a hand on each of our backs.

I take my seat, ignoring the fish on my plate, staring up at me with empty eyes. Brittani, Rhonda, and Amythest are tittering somewhat quietly together while Summer, Wendy, Claire, and the rest of the table listen with rapt attention to the rich woman we're dining with prattling on about a castle they've bought for the rock-bottom price of twenty-five million. It's uninhabitable, of course. They're going to have to put another twenty in to make it livable.

I let my gaze wander about the restaurant, scanning in vain for Dylan and his grandmother. As I survey the tables, I realize that my earlier assessment was incorrect: not all of the patrons are titans and celebrities. There's the security guard seated across from me, and at the table next door, an au pair trying to gently maintain control of a wound-up toddler. Various assistants and entourage members are scattered about the tables, often indistinguishable from their hosts until they hop to do whatever is asked of them. And then there are the few tourists lucky enough to secure a reservation, overdressed and sneaking vertical videos with their cell phones despite the signs indicating that cameras aren't allowed, before flipping over their menus in search of the unlisted prices.

The restaurant is its own ecosystem, really, with its own food chain.

My mouth is dry as the desert, and I feel a headache coming on. I'm probably dehydrated from all the puking. I flag a passing waiter. "*Excusez moi, un verre d'eau, s'il vous plaît?*"

He nods and scurries away. When I look up, I find Summer inexplicably staring daggers at me. She whispers something to Bernard, who gets up and makes his way down to my end of the table, sitting heavily into the chair vacated by the teenage son of the rich people. "John does the ordering," he growls into my ear.

"It's okay. I just needed a glass of water." My voice sounds maddeningly meek to my own ear, but I want him to know that I am trying to play by the rules.

"Don't be disrespectful," he spits just as the waiter appears with my glass of water.

Bernard shakes his head at him before he can place it before me, and to my disbelief, the waiter whisks it away. My blood boils. I want to wrap my hands around Summer's neck and squeeze until her eyes bulge. But I simply nod and fix my gaze on the ocean, ever placid beyond the chaos of the restaurant.

How quickly the line between guest and prisoner crumbles, like a sand castle swept away by the sea. But the tide always turns.

(nine months ago)

Los Angeles

On a particularly gloomy morning in November, I emerged from an audition at an office downtown to find the temperature had plummeted and rain was pouring down in sheets. Of course I was dressed as a homewrecker at eleven in the morning, wearing my most expensive four-inch stilettos and a slinky green silk cocktail dress, and my car was parked three blocks away in the cheapest lot I could find.

I had no umbrella and the building had no lobby—only a small vestibule with banks of elevators—so I stood looking out at the rain, willing it to stop. The street outside was industrial, no shops or restaurants, but a few doors down I recognized the back entrance to the flower market I'd visited a few months ago to buy Wendy sunflowers after her horse-jumping accident. Though it was in the opposite direction from my car, I figured anything was better than standing where I was, so I made a mad dash for it, holding the script from my audition over my head as a makeshift umbrella.

Ten steps outside I knew it had been a terrible idea, but I was drenched already, so I kept running. I burst through the entrance to the flower market looking like a drowned cat, my shoes and dress ruined. The polished concrete floor inside the door was so slick with rain that I immediately lost my footing in my stupidly high heels, and arms flailing, landed hard on my ass, flashing everyone in the checkout line my fuchsia panties.

Awesome.

The cashiers and patrons looked on with concern as the security guard rushed over to help me to my feet, lifting me by my elbow. "Are you okay?"

I nodded, mortified. At least I'd never see any of these people again. I looked down at my dress and noticed I'd split the hem on the left side clear up to my hip. Fantastic.

"Belle," said a deep voice.

Oh God. Who was this going to be?

I turned to see Eric, a large bunch of pale-pink roses in his arms, his brow wrinkled with worry. Great. Exactly who I wanted to see me like this.

"Are you okay?" Eric asked. "This floor is unforgiving. You hit your tailbone pretty hard."

"Oh, hi." I tried to shrug it off like I was cool. "Yeah, I'm fine."

The security guard nodded to Eric and walked away, leaving me with him. I rubbed my throbbing ass. "I live in the next building. You want to come up and dry off?" he offered. "Maybe borrow some pants?"

I cinched the side of my dress together in my fist. Considering that Summer, whose jealous streak had been particularly pronounced of late, was still living with me and seeing Eric, I knew going home with him was a terrible idea. Not to mention my hurt pride and ass. But it was still pouring rain outside, my dress was ruined, and one of my heels was broken. "Okay," I said. "Thanks."

He shifted the flowers into one arm and offered me the other. I had no choice but to take it, limping along on my broken heel. "Do you want to get on my back?" he asked.

"I'm heavier than I look."

"I'm stronger than I look. You just have to hold the flowers, and I'll hold you."

"Everyone will see my ass," I protested.

"Lucky them. Come on."

I stuffed my shoes in my bag and grabbed the flowers, then hopped up on his back. He easily carried me through the flower market, pointing out different varieties of blooms like we were just on a normal stroll as we traversed the aisles to the door on the other side of the warehouse. The rain was still coming down hard outside. He sprinted through the alley with me on his back, both of us laughing, and came to an abrupt halt at a door in the back of the building. "My keys are in my left pocket. Can you get them?"

I reached into his pocket. The fabric inside was thin and wet. I could feel the warmth of his skin through it, and something else. Oh. He didn't seem to be wearing underwear.

The keys, Belle. Get the keys.

I extracted the keys from his pocket and handed them to him. He opened the door, and we tumbled inside, dripping wet. I hopped down from his back. "Thank you."

"My pleasure." He punched the call button of the elevator.

I cast a glance up and down the hall, orienting myself. "I didn't realize your building was so close."

"Downtown's confusing."

The elevator door slid open, and he gestured for me to step into the dim interior. I hesitated, and he smiled. "I remember. You're claustrophobic."

I nodded. "It's an incredibly small elevator," I pointed out.

"I'll cover your eyes, like last time," he offered.

Last time. Before I knew he belonged to Summer.

Seeing no other choice, I stepped onto the elevator. He followed, his arms full of roses. The door slid shut. "I don't want to stick you with these thorns," he said. "Turn this way."

I turned toward him, our faces inches apart in the confined space, my heart pounding in my chest. The sweet scent of the flowers filled the elevator.

"Close your eyes and put your face on my chest." He moved the roses out of the way.

It wasn't necessary. I could've just closed my eyes and the walls wouldn't have seemed so close. But like a fool, I rested my forehead on his chest. And there it was again, the smell of spice and detergent, the warmth of his skin through his wet shirt. He bent his head ever so slightly toward mine.

The elevator dinged and the doors slid open. We didn't move for a fraction of a second. I ripped myself away from him and spilled into his loft, flushed.

It was just chemistry. A stupid attraction to an inappropriate man. Not the first, and I was sure not the last.

I reminded myself of all the reasons I didn't actually want him as I looked around his light-filled loft. I'd seen his art gallery and the roof the night I met him, of course, but I'd never been in his personal living space. It felt oddly intimate to be in his home, surrounded by his things.

The loft was huge; it took up the entire floor of the building and was 180 degrees from what I was expecting from Summer's description, which had it sounding like a dingy bachelor pad.

I could sense him watching me as I took it in.

He was Summer's. I had no claims. He wasn't what I wanted, and I wasn't what he wanted. He was just a flirt, a playboy. And I wasn't about to stab Summer in the back to become one of his conquests.

"This place is amazing," I said.

"Thanks. I like it."

Even on this gloomy day, light poured through floor-to-ceiling windows in every direction, reflecting off floors of brushed concrete. Brightly colored exotic rugs and midcentury modern furniture were clustered in different areas across the open floor plan—a living area featuring an impressive record and book collection, a dining area with a Sputnik chandelier dangling from the soaring ceiling, an art area, canvases in different stages of completion, and in the corner, a chef's kitchen with Carrara marble countertops and an industrial oven. And plants. Everywhere, plants.

It was my dream home.

He was a womanizer. He was moody. He had a chip on his shoulder.

I found myself standing in his art studio, wandering among the paintings. They were all different styles—abstract, mixed media, dream-like renderings stolen from some of his photographs—but something tied them together. Wild whimsy, controlled chaos, that same play of opposites that infused his photographs.

I heard the click of a camera and turned to see him with a film Nikon raised to his eye. He quickly fired again before I could cover my face. "Oh my God, what are you doing? I must look a mess," I said, ducking.

"A beautiful mess," he returned. "Angle your face toward the light."

"No, Eric, seriously."

"Please?"

Those sea-green eyes. I looked toward the light.

I allowed him only a few shots before I turned my back on him. "Okay. I'm freezing. How 'bout those sweats?"

He beckoned for me to follow him through a doorway into his room. It was fairly orderly for a bachelor not expecting guests, and dark with the blackout shades drawn, his platform bed unmade.

A vision of us tumbling into it, ripping the wet clothes off each other, flashed before my eyes. I blinked it away.

He rummaged in a chest of drawers and produced a black long-sleeved T-shirt and a pair of women's leggings.

I held up the navy-blue leggings. "Are these Summer's?"

"No. You can have them, though; she won't be coming back for them."

I had to laugh. "Gotcha."

"I know Summer's your friend, and I respect that." He found and held my gaze. "I don't know what she's told you, but we're not together. I've been very honest with her about that."

I bit my lip. "Why?"

He shrugged. "We're not compatible."

I knew it wasn't my business and I should probably have left it there, but after months of hearing it from her side, I was interested to hear his. "What do you mean?"

"How can I put this without sounding like a total dick?" He sighed. "She's obsessed with money. Status. I understand it: she didn't grow up with it; she's looking for security. But that's not what I'm looking for. I'm the opposite—my childhood was the casualty of a horribly greedy father. I've spent most of my twenties thinking money is responsible for all the evil in the world. But, of course, that's not true, either."

"So why do you still see her?"

"I don't know. I don't want to hurt her. And I enjoy her company. Like you do, I'm guessing. In small doses. She knows we're never going to be serious, and she's okay with it."

I was shocked that he could be so perceptive about her and yet so blind. "Eric," I laughed. "She's not okay with it."

"She says she is," he protested. "I really am honest with her."

I furrowed my brow. "Trust me," I said, "she's not. Summer's used to getting what she wants. And she wants you. Once she realizes she's not going to have you—well, you'll know."

He nodded slowly, but I could tell he still didn't understand. "I'm moving to New York in a few weeks anyway, so that should put an end to it."

I felt an unexpected twinge of disappointment. "Permanently?"

He shrugged. "I don't know. I'll keep the place here, and I'm sure I'll be back and forth some, but I need a change."

He flicked on the light in the bamboo-and-slate bathroom, and I heard the water turn on. "A shower will warm you up," he said as he left, gently shutting the door behind him. Our conversation echoed in my head while I warmed my shivering body under the hot water. How on earth could he believe that Summer was okay with their not being together? She must put on quite an act.

I emerged from his bedroom freshly showered and cozy to find him in the kitchen arranging the roses in a vase. He looked up and smiled. "Feel better?"

I nodded. "Beautiful flowers."

"It's my mom's birthday," he explained. "Tea?"

"Sure." He filled a mug and handed it to me. "She lives here? Your mom?"

He shook his head. "She died when I was eleven."

"Oh," I said. "I'm so sorry."

"Thanks. She's the one who got me into gardening—she loved roses, so every year on her birthday, I buy them."

"That's so sweet." I wanted to ask how she died, but knew it wasn't polite. "Did your dad raise you after she passed?"

His face clouded. "No. My grandmother."

"I'm sorry. I didn't mean to pry."

"It's okay," he said. "You know how I feel about my father."

"He's really horrible, huh?"

His eyes met mine, and suddenly I saw a lost little boy.

I set my mug on the counter and wrapped my arms around his waist, laying my head on his chest. "I'm so sorry."

He hugged me tightly, burying his face in my wet hair. We stayed like that for a long time, our bodies pressed close together. I heard his heartbeat as his chest rose and fell.

When we finally separated, his eyes were wet with tears. He wiped them with his sleeve. "I'm sorry. It's hard for me to talk about it. Especially today."

"It's okay." I wanted to say more, wanted to know more. But that way lay danger. And outside, the rain had cleared. "I should go."

"Let me get your car for you."

While he was gone, I perused his collection of records and books. We had crossover in our taste, though his skewed darker than mine. I wanted to ask him about his thoughts on *Siddhartha* and *Heart of Darkness*, wanted to know which was his favorite Rumi poem. But I'd have to leave that to Summer.

Summer, shit.

When he returned, the first words out of my mouth were "Let's not tell Summer I was here."

He nodded. "I wasn't going to. Sure you don't want to stay for lunch?"

I'd have loved nothing more. "I can't."

Even if he stopped seeing Summer altogether, if she married someone else and was totally happy, I'd still never be able to go anywhere near Eric without being ready to permanently end my friendship with her.

I knew this. Yet in the elevator, we stood face-to-face. His eyes rested on mine. An electric current coursed through my body, pulling me toward him with a force I couldn't describe. Was it just me? A reaction to his blinding beauty? Or did he feel the same current? I reminded myself once again he was a rake, a trust-fund kid with the privilege to "reject money" who was moving to New York in a few weeks.

Don't fall for it, Belle.

And then, without warning, as though the magnetic force was too strong to resist, his lips were on mine. The heat of a thousand suns burned between us, our arms wound around each other, his pelvis pressing into mine. And there the blaze burned even brighter.

Ding! The elevator doors slid open, and light poured in. I pulled away. "Eric," I cautioned.

"Belle." His voice was rough with desire.

He reached for me.

"We can't," I said. "This didn't happen." And without a backward glance, I was out the elevator door and running down the hallway toward my car.

The following week I was on my bed memorizing lines when Summer arrived home from her private-airline steward training class. She flopped down on the duvet, sending pages fluttering. "Hey," I protested. "I was using those."

"Sorry, I'm just so tired." She groaned. "I've been on my feet all day. I need a nap." She crawled under the covers next to me. "Can you maybe do that in the other room?"

"Summer—" I pressed the palms of my hands into my eyes in frustration. She'd been living with me three months and had yet to donate a cent in rent. But we both knew I didn't have the balls to ask her for it. I got up and started straightening the room, throwing discarded piles of clothes into the hamper.

"What's up? You're mad. I can tell you're mad," she said.

I sorted through a pile of books and magazines stacked on the bedside table. "My sister's looking at USC Law School for next fall—"

"That's great!"

"...so my parents are coming out with her during the holidays."

"Nice. Where are they staying?"

"Here," I said. "In my bed. Lauren and I'll share the pullout couch. Paying for a hotel for a week in LA is too expensive, and I want to spend time with them. Anyway, you'll have another apartment by then, right?"

She sat up on her elbows. "Oh. So that's what you're mad about."

"I'm not *mad*, I just... can't afford to support you forever."

She sighed dramatically and flopped back on the pillow. "It's not forever. I told you, it's just for a few months..."

"You said a few weeks."

She looked at me, hurt. "Are you kicking me out?"

Now I felt like an asshole. "No. I'm not kicking you out, I'm just... wondering when you might get your own place."

"I don't know. I mean, I'm done with training next week, but I've gotta get a job, and I'll need a security deposit, a car.... It's a lot. You're lucky—you have parents that help you out, but I don't."

"You know my parents don't help me," I said flatly.

"Yeah, but, like, they would if you needed them to."

I shook my head. The kind of help my parents provided was unconditional love and a hundred dollars at Christmas. They couldn't afford anything else, and I'd never ask. Sure, I guessed I could always go home to my childhood bedroom and figure out some kind of job in Georgia if I totally couldn't make it on my own, but I'd never seen that as an option. "I love you. You know I love you. But it's been three months, and I'm struggling myself. If you're gonna live here, it would really help if you could at least pay some rent."

Her eyes widened. "I'm sorry. I didn't realize things were so bad for you."

I looked at her like she was crazy. "How do you possibly not know things are bad for me? Do you think I eat pasta every night because I love it?" I grabbed the scuffed-up pair of heels I broke at the flower market. "My stilettos are worn down to the nail. I busted my ass wearing these in the rain last week." I chucked them into the closet.

"I'm broke, too," she said. I picked up a pair of Prada booties she came home with last week and raised an eyebrow. "I didn't buy them," she protested.

I sighed. "Can you just contribute something? My rent is eighteen hundred. I'm not asking you to pay half. Anything helps."

She nodded. "Yeah, yeah, of course... Dad's coming into town next week. I can ask him."

It took me a minute to remember that "Dad" was Three, Rhonda's third husband and Summer's recent baffling choice of father figure, who now lived in a gaudy mansion in Vegas with a bride just ten years our senior. I guessed he was the best (or richest, anyway) of Rhonda's erstwhile husbands, but he'd been sleazy ten years ago, and I couldn't imagine that had changed. Summer had despised him when we were in high school, but now that he periodically sent her money, she'd changed her tune. These days she referred to him as "Dad" and waxed on about looking up to him for being able to "capitalize on opportunity," whatever that meant.

"Or you could just get a job," I suggested. But she was already shaking her head. "If you were at Heaven, you'd make at least a couple hundred a night."

"I told you, I'm not doing that again."

I gathered my script pages from the bed and the floor, irritated. She had no problem with me working in a club to pay for the apartment she crashed in, but she was too good to do it herself. And yet I was too freaking nice to kick her out.

"I'm gonna get some rent money. I swear!" she promised to my back as I stomped down the hallway to finish my work in the living room.

A few days later I came home early from a soul-crushing Tinder date with a handsy wannabe director to find the door to my bedroom closed, sex sounds coming from within. The blood rushed in my ears. I wanted to scream.

After the afternoon I'd shared with Eric, he had the audacity to fuck her in my bed not two weeks after? And she was yet to give me a dime of the rent she'd promised. Screw them. I had half a mind to throw open the door and kick them out. I stood with my hand poised above the doorknob, listening to the grunting as my headboard slammed against the wall. It was all male. I heard nothing coming from Summer. And it didn't sound like Eric. Not that I knew what his sex noises sounded like.

I quietly backed away from the door, unsure what to do. I wanted to leave, but it was 10:00 p.m., and besides the fact that it felt wrong to vacate my own apartment so that Summer could soil my bed, I didn't have anywhere to go. But I also didn't want to be sitting in the living room when she and whomever she was screwing emerged from their tryst. *Especially* if it was Eric.

The porch would have to do. I'd have a clear shot of the walkway below, so I'd see him when he left and know when the coast was clear to return to my apartment and rip Summer a new asshole. I grabbed a hoodie from the hall closet and stepped onto the balcony, leaving the curtains drawn across the French doors so that I wouldn't be visible from the living room. God, I hoped they'd finish up quickly; it was freaking freezing outside. I sat in the uncomfortable iron chair hunched over my e-reader, but I couldn't concentrate and kept having to reread pages of the novel that had been so gripping until now.

Eventually, after what seemed like eons but according to the clock in the corner of my device was only ten minutes, I heard footsteps in the living room, then on the stairwell, and finally spied a man emerge from the building. It wasn't Eric. This man was tall and balding, wearing a sport coat, and there was something familiar about him. I sat up and watched while he loped down the walkway with the carefree gait of a man who'd just bedded a hot blonde, toward a town car idling at the curb. As he climbed into the backseat, he cast a glance toward the building, his face illuminated by the streetlight.

It was Three.

Immediately I ducked, praying he hadn't seen me. Summer was fucking Three. My God. What the hell?

When I heard the car pull away from the curb, I emerged from under the table and slid open the door to the apartment. I stepped through the curtains to find Summer curled on the couch, staring at me with red eyes. "Was that Three?" I asked, though I knew the answer.

She nodded, then burst into tears. I sat next to her and wrapped my arm around her shoulders. "What happened?"

"He said if he was going to be paying the rent, he wanted to come see the place." She suppressed a sob. "So he came up, and when we got in the bedroom, he shut the door and he...he..." She broke down.

"It's okay." I hugged her. "Did you tell him no?"

"At first. But..." She wiped away tears. "I didn't know what to do. I needed the money, and he..." She buried her face in her hands. "He made me call him *Daddy*."

My heart plummeted. "Oh God." I stroked her hair as she cried into my sweatshirt. "I'm so sorry. That is so fucked up. I'm so, so sorry, Summer. If I'd had any inkling this might happen, I would never have asked you for rent..."

"It's not just you." She pulled away. "I'm out of money, and my mom hasn't been working. She's staying with a guy she's been seeing who treats her like crap..." She shot to her feet abruptly, cutting off the tears. "I need a shower."

"Wait. You shouldn't take a shower before we go to the police," I said.

She emitted a short bark of a laugh. "I'm not going to the police."

"But he raped you—"

"So? What good is going to the police gonna do except to stop him from sending me the five grand he promised?"

"But, Summer, he—"

"It's my decision," she snapped. "At least he paid for it. I've been sleeping with Eric for over a year and he won't give me a dime." She slowly moved down the hallway, but paused when she reached the bathroom door and turned. "I'm not gonna live my life like this."

"No," I said, going to her. "You deserve so much more."

She met my gaze with steely resolve. "Let's never talk about it again."

Day 5

Wednesday evening—Golfe de Saint-Tropez, France

The monstrous boat looms above us, silhouetted against the bright-blue sky. This one's got to be twice the size of ours, and she does have a helipad. We bob in the cool of her shadow, her shiny black exterior so close I can see our reflection as our tender slowly makes its way around the back of the yacht into the full glare of the low sun, where TYGER is etched in gold script across her stern.

A ladder lowers, and we shade our eyes and gather bags as two crewmen in crisp white uniforms help us up one at a time. A crew woman offers a tray of champagne, and I gladly accept a glass, briefly wondering what percentage of the world's champagne is consumed on the Riviera in August. A photographer appears and snaps photos as we toast for the camera.

We're all looking fresh in the blue hi-lo dresses gifted to us by John. They're each a slightly different shade of blue, but all the same cut: gauzy fit-and-flare spaghetti-strap with a crisscross low back, save Rhonda's, which is less revealing—a fact I overheard her complaining to Brittani about through the paper-thin walls on the boat, but as far as I know she has not shared her displeasure with Summer. We look like a bunch of bridesmaids for Summer, who's dressed in a similar-cut dress by the same designer, in white.

They're beautiful dresses, and very expensive, I'm sure, but the whole thing is just weird. And blue has never been my color, especially the shade of dusky blue my particular dress is made from. I wouldn't be surprised if Summer selected it for that purpose. Wendy's shade would have looked much better on me and mine on her, but Summer wouldn't let us switch, pointing out that since I was taller, Wendy's would be much too short on me, and mine too long on her.

Summer notices me check my watch. "I thought I told you not to wear that," she says.

I meet her glare with a smile. "Sorry. Forgot."

We both know I didn't forget.

"You can put it in my purse," she says.

"No, that's okay." I swig my champagne. "I like it."

I can tell she wants to rip it off my arm, but she is stopped by John, who takes her by the hand.

It's true; she told me not to wear it when she came down to our quarters to see us in our dresses earlier. Which, of course, was never going to stop me. She was eating something out of a jar with a mother-of-pearl spoon.

"What is that?" I asked, knowing full well what it was.

"Mmm...It's caviar. So good. I'm starving, and this was the only thing in the fridge in our room. Go figure." She didn't offer me any, and I didn't ask.

She reviewed our jewelry selections and made suggestions as to whether we curl or straighten our hair. "I mean, we need to look our best. You know who Marlena Falgione is, right?"

When we all shook our heads, confirming our ignorance, she gleefully informed us, "She's only one of the premier artists on the scene right now. Everybody is crazy for her work. John bought a painting of hers last month for one-point-two, which was a steal. And she's a designer as well, super stylish. The dresses are from her summer line. And her husband, Charles Bricknell—well, you know who he is. He owns one of the biggest tech companies in the world, and John is trying to secure him as an investor for this huge development he's working on. So, everybody, best behavior tonight. That means you, too, Brittani."

"Don't worry, honey. I'll keep her in check." Rhonda winked.

Rhonda keeping Brittani in check is like a bear keeping a wolf from mauling anyone, but it seemed to satisfy Summer.

"Why you gotta pick on me?" Brittani said. "Belle was the one hurling behind the restaurant earlier today."

Summer feigned surprise. "What?"

"From seasickness, not alcohol," I clarified. "I guess the pill you gave me didn't work."

She didn't flinch. "Are you okay now? Because you can't be doing that tonight."

I nodded and displayed the patch on my neck. "I got a patch. I'm fine."

After Summer had spritzed us each with her signature Chanel No. 5 and departed for her own quarters, Amythest tried to change back into the predictably short, black dress she had originally selected for herself, but I managed to convince her otherwise. Nothing was to be done about the violet contacts, though. Summer had tried to talk her out of wearing them, but Amythest insisted they're prescription and she's blind without them.

As Amythest turns toward me now with the glare of the low sun in her eyes, the rim of her almost black irises is visible around the violet. The effect is startling and a bit unsettling, as though she's a member of the undead. "Who I gotta screw to get a room on this boat instead?" she whispers.

A stocky crewman leads us up a set of stairs onto the lower deck, with its sleek built-in loungers and tables open to a sunken living room that features an ostentatious chandelier, a grand piano, and a giant fish tank. But he doesn't stop there, ushering us up a wide exterior spiral staircase that leads to the main deck, where a table for twenty is being set by white-uniformed staff and a couple of musicians are testing their sound equipment.

"Everyone is on the upper deck for the sunset," he informs us as we follow him into a game room lined with huge TVs, past a pool table, poker table, foosball table, and a bar that wouldn't look out of place in a restaurant. We ascend another wide spiral staircase, this one carpeted in white shag, with a light sculpture made of crystal orbs running up its center, and emerge onto the open upper deck.

It's nirvana on the Mediterranean. A long-haired flamenco guitarist picks a melody with his eyes closed, the notes drifting on a gentle breeze that lifts the heat of the day as waiters pass hors d'oeuvres to a handful of elegantly dressed guests scattered across the deck. The shimmering sea is speckled with ships suspended in the tide, and green hills rise from the water, dappled with villas whose windows are lit fiery orange by a setting sun that bathes the entire scene in golden light.

I accept a sliver of grilled octopus, which melts on my tongue, and follow it with crisp champagne, amplifying the nutty flavor. A striking woman who looks to be in her late forties approaches us, smiling. Her dark hair is short in the back and longer in the front, streaked with a dramatic blue that accents her slate eyes, her tanned face clean of makeup save a bright-red lipstick. She is dressed in a cream modified leisure suit, which sounds awful but looks incredibly stylish on her slim frame.

Summer lights up at her approach, clearly pleased when the woman takes her hands and air-kisses her cheeks three times before looking her in the eye and saying in Italian-accented English, "Summer, so lovely to see you. And John, of course, always a pleasure." She turns to the rest of us. "I am Marlena."

As we introduce ourselves, she grasps each of our hands in turn, meeting our eyes with interest.

"Thank you so much for inviting us," Summer croons when the introductions are over. "And for letting my friends come, too."

Marlena envelops us in her radiant smile. "Welcome aboard *Tyger*."

"'Tyger, Tyger burning bright'?" I venture, ignoring the sharp glance from Summer.

"'In the forests of the night,'" she confirms.

The other girls look at us blankly.

"I noticed the spelling when we boarded," I explain. "May I ask why?"

"It is between my husband and me a—how do you say—private funny?"

"Inside joke?" I suggest.

"That's the one. Thirty years I am married to an Englishman, and still the words escape me." She takes my elbow and steers me toward the bar. "You must come and meet my husband and my son."

Marlena beckons for the others to follow, looping her arm through mine as we traverse the deck. Trailing behind us, the girls fan out around John like the petals of a flower.

"It's such a beautiful evening," I remark.

"Isn't it?" Marlena agrees. "It never becomes old. Every night I am here, absorbing this beauty. It is so important to be in life, don't you think?"

"Absolutely." I like this woman.

She slips her arm around a wiry, intelligent-looking man about her age and gives him a kiss that leaves a lipstick stain on his cheek. His curly hair falls in front of his glasses as he turns to us with a lopsided smile. "This is my husband, Charles."

"Hello, ladies," he says. "And John. I'm glad you could make it on such short notice."

"Impromptu parties are the best parties." Marlena taps the shoulder of a young man in a seersucker suit who is deep in conversation with the bartender. "Darling, I hate to interrupt, but you must meet our guests." And then to the bartender. "And, Emelio, I'd love a martini."

"Mother doesn't drink champagne," the young man says, turning toward us with his father's lopsided smile. "I'm Michael."

Michael is about our age, good-looking and coiffed beyond metrosexuality. A paisley silk pocket square adorns his seersucker, and underneath he wears a pink button-down, open deep enough to show his hairless chest. He raises his champagne glass to us, and we reciprocate. "Cheers," he says.

The photographer snaps more pictures as we sip our champagne and gaze at the sunset, mesmerized by the view. Summer hangs on John's arm while he chats with Charles, her eyes sliding helplessly toward Marlena. But Marlena is far less interested in idle chitchat with Summer than in telling bawdy jokes with her son and the bartender, who appears to be his boyfriend.

A few additional guests filter in, but it's an intimate gathering, and our group of ten will likely take up half of the dining table. Claire is confiding in me about how much she misses her boyfriend when I notice Wendy talking with an unusually tall man on the other side of the deck. Their backs are to us, but I can tell she's in flirt mode as she smooths her glossy black tresses over one shoulder and places her hand lightly on his arm, hanging on his every word.

"Wendy seems to have found a friend," I say.

Claire follows my gaze. "Yeah, she said she knew him from somewhere, but I can't remember where. I think Summer knows him, too."

Wendy leans her back against the rail and meets my eye. She beckons for us to come over, and he turns as we move toward them, flashing a smile. He looks familiar, but I can't place him.

Wendy's face is lit with delight as we approach. "Belle, Claire, this is Leo Martin."

My hand swims in his paw. He must be six foot six, but he's not gangly; he's well proportioned, fit, and sharply dressed.

"My pleasure," he says.

"You remember Gianni?" Wendy asks.

Gianni, the Italian designer Summer dated in the small pocket of time between when Eric moved to New York and she met John. He wasn't around long. I only met him once or twice. It ended badly, but I can't quite remember the details.

"And remember Gianni's birthday party," she continues, "at that beautiful home down in Newport Beach, when everybody jumped in the pool at the end of the night?"

Ah, yes.

"That was Leo's house! He's friends with Gianni. He was throwing the party for him."

It's all coming back to me now. Leo's rich. Like, John rich. A count or a baron or something, far richer than Gianni, and better-looking, too.

Summer got uncharacteristically sloshed at the party and threw herself at Leo, who rebuffed her in deference to his friend.

"What a small world," I say. "We met briefly at the party. It's nice to see you. How is Gianni?"

"He's well. I was just with him at his home in Sardinia," Leo replies. "He is there for the month, with his children and his girlfriend."

"Have you said hello to Summer yet?" I ask with a big smile. "I'm sure she'll be thrilled to see you."

I should keep my mouth shut. But I'm on my second glass of champagne, and I'm sick of being treated like the help. I want to see her squirm. Anyway, it's a party of twenty people; it's not like they're going to be able to avoid each other all evening.

As if on cue, Summer turns to see all of us staring at her, a flicker of recognition playing across her face as she notices Leo. She releases John's arm and slips away, striding toward us with a smile plastered on her face.

"Hiiiii," she says as she approaches.

Leo bends to give her kisses on her flushed cheeks. "You remember Leo," Wendy says.

"Of course," Summer intones without dropping her smile. "How are you?"

"I'm well. Just saw our mutual friend in Sardinia."

"Ooohhh." She watches him carefully. "That's nice. I'm here with my boyfriend, John."

"Yes, Wendy said," Leo returns. "I know John. He is a lucky man to have you beautiful girls with him."

Summer relaxes a little. "Yeah, I brought my friends to celebrate my birthday. I guess Marlena and I have birthdays a day apart."

"Happy birthday." Leo smiles.

"Thanks."

"It's crazy," I say to Summer. "I mean, you told us that everyone who's anyone is on the Riviera in August, but I didn't think I would know so many people. Leo—"

"Mmm-hmm." Her eyes slide past me toward John, who is still engrossed in conversation with Charles.

I shouldn't poke the bear, I know. But I simply can't help it. "And I ran into Dylan at the restaurant earlier," I continue, watching for her reaction. "Did you know he and John work together?"

I think I see her smile falter, but maybe I'm imagining it.

"How strange." She glances over her shoulder at John. "I better get back. Good to see you," she says to Leo, and heads for John like a homing pigeon.

Once the sun has set, the stocky steward rings a bell and invites us all down to the main deck for dinner. Wendy hasn't left Leo's side. I'm glad she's warmed to the idea of finding someone better than Mr. Pussycat, but a little surprised that she would be so obvious about her interest in Leo in front of Summer after what happened between them. Wendy is generally an incredibly loyal friend, but I guess Leo is an even better catch.

As we head down to dinner, I watch Summer's eyes travel to Leo's hand on Wendy's bare lower back while Leo explains to John that he and Summer met through mutual friends. No specifics or insinuations, no ego boosters to spoil any story Summer might spin for John. A gentleman used to covering his tracks.

I wonder if Summer is having second thoughts about her commitment to John, considering whether she could have done better. But she's made her bed.

The table is lined with white roses, set with silver and crystal that reflect and splinter the flickering candlelight. A quartet plays what I can only describe as Mediterranean jazz as the sky loses its color, and we exchange our champagne glasses for wineglasses. I locate my place card, thrilled to find I'm seated at the opposite end of the table from Brittani and Rhonda, next to Michael.

Marlena is in the midst of an impassioned discussion with one of the men as she makes her way down to her seat at the table. "No, I am happy to pay the taxes," she's saying. "If we humans cannot take care of one another, then we are all doomed, because there is no one else."

"But you're paying more." The man's accent is American, his watch worth more than my car. "If it were a flat tax, you would still be paying your share, and it would still be more because you earn more, but you wouldn't be penalized for earning more."

"Oh! You poor man, *penalized* for earning more." She dismisses the idea with a wave of her hand. "I am a lucky woman. There are many artists better than me who are not so lucky. Now the people like my paintings. They think I am a good artist. I have them fooled. Tomorrow, who knows, they don't like my paintings. I am out of favor."

"You're too modest," the bejeweled wife of the man chimes in. "Your paintings are brilliant."

Again, the dismissive wave of her hand. "It is all in the eye of the beholder. The mistake is to believe we deserve the things we have."

"You deserve it all, Marlena," says the man lightly.

"Do I like this boat? Of course I like this boat," Marlena continues. "I love this boat, but I do not deserve this boat. I do not need this boat. I was happy before I had this boat."

"That's because you'd never had the boat," the man says.

Everyone laughs.

"Mother, for the last time, please don't give away the boat," Michael implores.

"Okay, we keep the boat." She smiles. "For now."

"A toast." Charles raises his glass from the head of the table. Everyone quiets down and raises their glass. "To my beautiful wife on her..."

He looks to her across the long table for confirmation he may reveal the number, and she rolls her eyes. "*Cinquantaquattro!* Fifty-four! And glad of every year!"

"On her fifty-fourth birthday," Charles finishes.

She blows him kisses and we all drink. "*Grazie mille.*" She raises her glass to us. "And to all of you, for making it a party. I do love a party."

We drink again, then take our seats. Immediately, as if in one motion, the staff places our plates in front of us. The steward announces, "Bresaola, arugula, Grana Padano, and fresh lemon."

I lose count of the perfectly timed number of plates, each small enough not to be intimidating and big enough that I am full before we're halfway through but keep going nonetheless, unable to turn down the experience of each delectable dish.

This is the first dinner I've had on this trip during which the conversation is not moderated by our patron, and it's lovely. There is actually an exchange of ideas, witty repartee.

But like Victorian children, John's girls are meant to be seen and not heard, to speak only when spoken to. I've been trained by the conditions of the past few days (was it only a week ago that I was in the bohemian cocoon of my apartment, packing for this trip?), and I know better than to make waves.

This, of course, does not stop me from engaging in conversation with my new friend Michael, who, it turns out, is a big fan of Hunter's music and is ecstatic when he finds out I'm friends with him.

"I love Hunter Rogers!" he enthuses. "He's so dapper, and his voice is sweet and smooth, like molasses. And he's gorgeous."

"He would be thrilled to hear you say that." I laugh.

The best way I can describe Hunter's music is Cole Porter goes to Ibiza. Original songs in a jazz standard format, set to dance music. He's not hugely famous, but he does have a loyal following among Broadway fans and dance music lovers. So, mainly gay men. Which, of course, suits him just fine.

"You have to introduce us," Michael begs. "Maybe he's my soul mate. We could have a wedding right here on the boat. You could be our maid of honor. But I'm getting ahead of myself. How did you guys become friends?"

"We met doing a musical in college. *Grease.* I was Sandy and he was Danny. Then we lived together till he had to move to New York for his first Broadway show."

"I live in New York! Where does he live? Not that I'm gonna stalk him or anything, of course." He winks.

"He has a loft in the Meatpacking District."

"I'm in SoHo! Seriously, you have to call me next time you're there. We can all hang out. I swear I won't be weird." He lowers his voice. "I'm gonna go smoke some hash before dessert. Wanna come?"

I glance down the table to where Summer is sitting. She's engrossed in conversation with the bejeweled wife of the American that Marlena was debating taxes with earlier, her back to us. John wouldn't notice if I fell off the boat, and Wendy is across the table to my left, but she's so captivated by Leo that she hasn't glanced at me since we sat down. Claire is their third wheel. Brittani, Rhonda, and Amythest are doing shots of limoncello, and Bernard and Vinny are nowhere to be seen.

I turn my attention back to Michael and grin. "Sure."

Indeed, the only person who notices as we push our chairs back and exit down the spiral staircase behind the table is Marlena, who meets Michael's eye and nods.

On the lower deck, Michael sinks into one of the couches and lights the spliff. "Your friend Wendy is in for a disappointment if she's looking for more than a night of fun. Leo's a trophy hunter." He inhales.

"She has a boyfriend at home anyway," I say, suddenly defensive of poor Wendy, so desperate to start a family.

"Don't they all?" He blows smoke rings as he exhales.

"Neat trick."

He passes me the joint, and I inhale the taste of tar and tobacco. Hash is a different beast than California Kush, and while I personally prefer the green stuff, I'll take what I can get.

"My mom taught me," he says.

I laugh. "Your mom's pretty cool."

"When I was younger, I was super annoyed that she wasn't like the other moms. But then I figured out that I wasn't like the other boys, and we've been tight ever since. I mean, she always encouraged me to be whoever I wanted to be, but she was secretly so relieved to have a gay son. She abhors all the traditionally male things, like sports and cars and hunting..."

"Hunting? Who in New York City hunts? That's where you grew up, right?"

He nods. "In all the traditional places, there's always the head of some poor beast staring down from on high while you eat his brothers. A reminder to all the men they are kings of the jungle."

"I'm surprised your mom goes to those places."

"Oh, she avoids them like the plague. My dad drags me along every so often. He went there with his dad...he likes tradition. I have no idea how the two of them work, but they do."

"They probably balance each other out. It's nice to see a couple who actually love each other in this environment. Most of the other romantic situations seem so overly...complicated."

He raises his eyebrows. "Like your friend?"

I snort. "My friend."

"Lemme guess. She's totally smitten with her sugar daddy. It's true love."

"Let's just say she'd do anything for him."

"Full disclosure, my mom can't stand her," he whispers. "Or John. She's philosophically opposed to gold-digging as a career choice."

I haven't so much as said a bad word about Summer this entire trip, but the wine and the spliff have loosened my tongue, and I'm thrilled to have someone to confide in. "I swear she wasn't always like this. Or maybe she was. I don't know. Money does strange things to people. That, or I'm a terrible judge of character."

"Money doesn't change people," he reflects. "It only magnifies the qualities that were already there."

I nod, thinking about the Summer I used to know. She always found her validation in men, even when we were sixteen. "That makes sense."

"I've seen it over and over with the owners of the companies my dad buys," he expounds. "Money allows them to be who they truly are, without restriction. Someone generous becomes super generous; someone with insecurity becomes a super dick."

"You're very observant."

"I've been watching people court my parents my whole life. Your friend's sugar daddy is really only here to get money out of my dad. They're not friends; their ideals are diametrically opposed. And my dad's never gonna invest in the project he's proposing."

"How do you know?"

"John's already burned him once, and now he wants to completely destroy a town that's hundreds of years old, upending the lives of all the people who have lived there for generations, to make way for an incorporated luxury town and resort for the superrich. My parents have spent my life teaching me the importance of strengthening and giving back to communities, not destroying them. Not to mention you'd have to consider the environmental impact of a development of that scale. The ecosystem of this area is very delicately balanced."

Sounds familiar. "I think I've heard him discussing that project the past few days."

"He's already bought most of the town at ludicrously low prices and run the rest out with threats of imprisonment for withholding property and all kinds of other made-up charges."

"How can he do that, legally?" I ask.

"You can do anything with enough money."

I think of Summer and what she's gotten away with.

"Wait." He jumps to his feet. "You said earlier you were Sandy in *Grease*. So do you sing?"

I nod. "When I'm drunk enough."

"I play the piano. I can play anything. Like, anything. Come on."

My body tingles from the hash as he pulls me to my feet and across the sunken living room to the grand piano. I'm on a yacht in the Mediterranean and life is good. Tonight has finally felt like a vacation. I curl my toes in the plush carpet as Michael lifts the shiny black top of the piano and takes a seat on the bench. "A grand on a boat," he says, playing arpeggios. "What a terrible extravagance. So much damage from the salt air, you have to pitch them overboard every couple of years."

"Is that true?"

He shrugs. "I don't know. Makes for a good story, though, doesn't it? You know this one?"

He starts into "Fly Me to the Moon." I spin, my arms outstretched like wings. "A few steps higher."

He scales up, and I start in, singing as much of the song as I know, which is more than I realized.

"*Bellissimo!*" He claps. "What do you like to sing? Throw it at me."

"'God Bless the Child'?"

He throws his head back in laughter as he plays the opening notes. "What are you trying to say?"

I join him, and before long Marlena wanders in with the Italian couple who were seated across from her. She lights up to see us playing. "I knew I gave you piano lessons for a reason. You have?" She raises two fingers to her mouth in the international mime for joint.

He extracts the spliff from his pocket with one hand, the other never leaving the keys, and the Italian man lights it for Marlena. Michael and I are warmed up now—flying, in perfect sync. He seamlessly flows into "Summer Nights," and I squeal with delight. We camp it up as Sandy and Danny as the other dinner guests begin to file in.

Wendy dances coquettishly with Leo while Brittani and Amythest become our backup dancers. The Italian couple joins Leo and Wendy, and the others drape themselves across the furniture or lounge on pillows on the floor, incapable of supporting themselves after the generosity of our hosts. John and the goons are missing, but I notice Summer on the couch with Claire, her platinum hair looking yellow in the lamplight, the rocks in her ears and the big stupid not-a-diamond on her finger glittering as she mechanically nods her head to the music. She has a lipstick stain on her perfect white teeth, and there's something sour about her smile.

The crew brings in tiramisu that looks divine, but I'm having too much fun singing to take a break to eat. Brittani dances like a bull in a china shop, while Amythest gyrates in the light, clearly not wearing any undergarments beneath her dress. The thin pale-blue fabric pulls in such a way that it looks like it wants to slip right off her—which I don't think anyone would mind, except Summer, of course, who stares daggers at her.

We're doing "The Girl from Ipanema" when I notice that John has returned. He's leaning in the doorway, watching Amythest with X-ray vision. After a moment, Summer spies him. She swallows and readjusts herself on the couch, breathing shallowly, then looks back at John, trying unsuccessfully to get his attention. At the same moment, Amythest notices John watching her and gives him a wink.

Summer rises from her seat and starts for John, but Bernard taps him on the shoulder and he disappears into the hallway, leaving Summer unmoored in the middle of the room. I grab her hand and make an effort to dance with her, but she jerks it away and gives me the evil eye before stalking out onto the back deck, Rhonda scuttling after her.

After the next song, I hand the mic to one of Marlena's Italian friends and wander into the hall in search of a bathroom. The closest bathroom is occupied, so I wind up the thick-carpeted wide spiral stairs looking for another one. Funny, now that I'm not dancing, I can feel the boat rocking. Or is that me? I grip the railing as I go around, still managing to step on the hem of my dress and nearly bust my ass. I sit down right in the middle of the staircase and try to focus on the large abstract painting staring at me from the wall, but the colors all want to blend together. I feel my phone buzz in my clutch and extract it, noticing I'm connected to Wi-Fi. I guess not all rich people are crazy paranoid. I scroll through my email, the messages swimming before me.

Sis,

Beautiful day here too! Though nothing like floating around on the Mediterranean, I'm sure. I'm great, everything awesome. Sorry you're having such a rough time out there. At least the food is good. Have you tried any sea urchin? I hear it's delicious. I hope you don't get voted off the island LOL. Keep me posted. Thinking of you. Xoxo

I immediately reply:

Heeeeeey sis whats up we're on ths crazy boat and I just smoked a spliff so excuse my typos hahahhahaaa. Spent the morning puking z cuz my dramamine disappeared nad Summer gaveme something she said was but wasn't. Aaaaand found out from vinny tht my emails are def being read on the boat so I wont be emailing from there anymore. So aslo u'll never guess who I ranin to at lunch?? Dylan. Yep. was there with grannie who ai didn't meet tho but was talking to john when I saw him. He told me to clall him lol. think I should??

Haven't triee any sea urchin yet

I think threre r some rough seas ahead.

Rough seas I tell u. STORMW!!1!

Oh and Amythest! Is fucking JOhn!! HA!

I press send without rereading it and totter to my feet. Sheesh. I'm kinda wasted, it turns out. Good thing you don't have to wear shoes on boats because heels would not be my friend right now. Okay. Where was I going? I have to pee. Upstairs. I was going upstairs to pee.

At the top of the stairs, I pause to pull myself together and scan for the bathroom. The place is deserted, but I hear men's voices coming from behind a partially closed door. I know I'm drunk and probably not very quiet, but it's too good an opportunity to snoop to turn down. I linger in the shadows as one of the voices rises above the others. The accent is British; it must be Charles.

"...is not a matter of the return, which I'm sure you are right about. It's the principle. You couldn't get this past your own board last time we spoke."

"There's no problem with the board," John says flatly.

Charles standing up to John: this I have to hear. Out of sight between the office and the bathroom, I brace myself against the wall, listening. This should be good....

Charles says something unintelligible, to which another voice replies something also unintelligible.

I strain to hear Charles sigh before returning, in a somber voice, "You may have the ability to circumvent the laws, as you did on our last venture, but that doesn't mean you should. We have a responsibility to set a precedent, to safeguard the communities and land for future generations, not to pillage and destroy, take advantage of every business opportunity that arises."

I inch closer to the door.

"I should think," John warns, "after your part in our last venture, you would want to remain in the family."

"I was nothing but a financier. I had no knowledge you were using substandard materials until the accident," Charles spits.

"And you didn't report it, even then," John returns.

"Are you threatening me?" Charles asks.

"I'm sure you understand what damage—" John is interrupted by laughter ringing up the stairwell as guests climb the stairs, and the door immediately shuts. I quickly step into the bathroom and close the door behind me, too loudly. Shit. But I don't think anyone heard. They were all in that office.

Michael was right about his father. At least someone in this gilded world has a moral compass. I bet John got Charles tangled up in that shopping center collapse the guys were talking about at lunch the other day. John is a *bad* man. A *really, really* bad man. But then, I knew that.

I pee for about six years, then splash water on my face in a vain attempt to sober up, and retouch my makeup. By the time I return from the bathroom, Bernard and Vinny are herding our blue-dressed harem back to the tender, where John and Summer are already waiting.

We're a hot mess. Amythest's dress is ripped. Brittani's mascara is running. Even Claire nearly tumbles into the ocean as she's handed down into the tender. But Wendy is the standout, her lipstick smeared and her chin chafed, her eyes a haze of longing for Leo as she wishes him goodbye.

Summer sits in the back of the tender next to John, her eyes fixed on the sea as we push away, but the rest of us are jovial. Brittani starts a reprise of "Summer Nights," and everyone joins in until John has Vinny silence us.

The twinkling lights of the boat recede on the horizon and the music grows ever farther away, until all that's left is the throbbing of the tender motor and the slap of the waves as we skate over the water.

(seven months ago)

Los Angeles

It was sometime after we ate the mushrooms that I noticed the hole in the sky. A distinct black pinhole in the powder blue, like someone pricked it. How had I never seen it before? Maybe it was only a satellite. Or maybe it was the drugs. Was it moving? Watching us? I tried to sit up, but couldn't coordinate the muscles required to do so. "There's a hole," I said, but it just sounded like *galumph, galumph*, like everything else.

Galumph, galumph, galumph, galumph. Why did everything sound the same? Maybe the sound of the universe wasn't *Om*, but *galumph*.

I could feel the top of Hunter's head touching mine, like we were conjoined twins who shared a brain. I endeavored to send him a message. "*Galumph, galumph*," he said.

We both collapsed in giggles. When our laughter subsided, the sky had darkened, and the palm trees were lit from below by the streetlights.

"It looks like a movie set," I said, glad my words were coming out like words.

"We're the stars of the movie," he agreed.

A scuffling drew our attention to the hatch that led down to my apartment, and a blond head emerged. Summer climbed out onto the roof, no easy feat while wearing her private-jet stewardess outfit—a tight, collared navy-blue dress with the gold logo of the company she worked for pinned above her heart, a silk Burberry scarf around her neck. "What are you guys doing up here?" she asked.

"Shroomies." Hunter waved the bag of iridescent fungi in her direction. "Want some?"

"No thanks."

She turned to go back inside, but I noticed that she was holding a bottle of water, and I desperately needed a sip. "Wait," I called, pointing urgently at her water. "I need a sip."

She traversed the distance and handed me the bottle. I stared at it, unsure what to do with it. She sighed and opened the top for me. "Do you need me to pour it down your throat, too?"

I grabbed the bottle and guzzled it until Hunter snatched it from me and finished it off. "I thought you weren't coming back until tomorrow," I managed, proud of my ability to string together a coherent sentence.

"Trip got shortened." She sat in one of the folding chairs Hunter had dragged up, kicked off her shoes, and began massaging her feet. "But I got a job offer from the client."

"Good!" I said. I was finding it incredibly difficult to focus on what she was saying, but I knew I should be pleased. I searched for the next logical question. "Who?"

"His name is John Lyons, and he owns this huge company that invests in everything from real estate to movies. He sold his jet and has been waiting for his new one to be finished, which is why he was flying with JetSafe. But he wants me to come on this trip with him to Japan, Singapore, and Bali, and then we'll figure out the contract if it's a fit."

I wondered if this meant that she would finally move off my couch, or rather, out of my bed, but was unable to formulate the question in any intelligible way, so simply nodded and smiled in what I hoped was a supportive manner.

"The Benjamins!" Hunter exclaimed. Summer looked at him like he'd lost his damn mind. "The Benjamins?" He carefully changed his inflection, turning the statement to a question, and I understood he clearly wanted to know how much the job paid, but she wasn't getting it.

"How much does it pay?" I interpreted.

She shrugged. "We haven't worked out the details, but his assistant told me that he pays really well, and he'd give me a signing bonus after our first trip."

I could feel her sobriety rubbing off on me, erasing the effects of the shrooms. A little annoying considering how difficult it had been to obtain them. Perhaps I could just take a break, flip to the serious channel, and match Summer's vibration to converse with her. Surely it would take only five minutes of intense concentration before she'd go back downstairs and I could return to the movie Hunter and I were starring in, which was obviously a stoner comedy with no role for Serious Summer.

Focus. "Did you see Eric while you were in New York?" I asked like a totally sober adult.

Though she'd never admit it, I knew Eric had broken her heart when he moved to New York a few weeks ago, effectively ending whatever was left of their relationship. She'd quickly rebounded with an Italian clothing designer, but that had also fizzled quickly, leaving her truly single for the first time in years. Eric's departure, combined with the horrible thing that happened with Three, had changed her. Sharpened her somehow.

She nodded. "He wants me to move there and live with him, of course, but it's not happening."

I could see the lie hanging in the air between us like a black cloud, so thick I could almost reach out and touch it. Why did she feel the need to lie to me? It was so stupid. Then, of course, she wasn't aware I could see her lie; also, she knew nothing of my afternoon with Eric or our budding friendship. His fault, not mine. I never planned to talk to him again after our kiss, but it wasn't like I was gonna unfollow him on social. What was the harm? His accounts were mostly art stuff, and he had thousands of followers, so it was easy to lurk without engaging. I noticed he started following me back after that day in his loft. Likes here and there followed—totally public, nothing illicit, and anyway, Summer wasn't on social media. Then he started direct messaging me, and it would have been rude not to reply, right? I may be many things, but rude is not one of them. And it was mainly just about stupid stuff like a movie he saw or a book I read or a meme that reminded one of us of the other. It was foolish, I knew. Extremely foolish. Sure, we were "just friends," but if Summer ever found out, she'd straight-up kill me. She'd said it herself. The thought brought me crashing back down to the roof, where Summer was now lying to Hunter.

"His lifestyle isn't really what I see for myself long-term," she was saying.

"He's broke," Hunter recalled. "I remember. I think we had this conversation last time I was in town."

"He's not, though," I objected. "His..." I was about to say something about his loft being gorgeous, but mercifully stopped myself in time, finishing, "...art sells for a lot."

"It's like he wants to be broke, though," Summer insisted. "It's so weird. You know he has a stake in his family's company he won't even acknowledge?"

"A steak?" I asked.

"I love steak," Hunter said.

We snickered, and she ignored us. "A board seat, tons of stock, his name on trusts, buildings...and he wears T-shirts with holes in them and gives all his money to his skeezy Burning Man friends. He's got some Turkish hacktivist staying with him right now."

Travis. And he was Syrian. So she did see Eric after all, and he didn't mention it to me. The snake of disappointment uncoiled inside me. No. This snake wasn't disappointment; it was jealousy—and that pang I felt was its fangs, sunk into my heart. Oh dear. If Summer didn't go downstairs soon, this trip was going to take a dark turn.

"Did he tell you all this?" Hunter asked.

"God no," she said. "He won't talk about it, won't so much as mention his family's name, and the Internet gives me nothing but puff pieces on his art and pictures of models hanging all over him. I found mail on his desk months ago, asking for his signature to increase shares in a holding company, a trust deed to a building in Manhattan with his name on it—all just buried under sketches and junk mail. I asked him about it, and he lost it. He has such a big chip on his shoulder, it's ridiculous."

"I'm sure he has his reasons," I said, thinking of what he'd told me about his father that afternoon in his loft.

"Yeah." Summer scoffed. "Anyway, Hunter, I heard your song at a party this weekend. People were really loving it."

Hunter and I went to give each other a high five and totally missed, then crumpled into a heap of giggles. With a sigh, Summer got up to leave. "Wait!" I called out. "I need you to order pizza from my phone. We can't see the buttons."

She held her hand out, and I gave her my phone.

"The code is, uh . . . It's—"

"I know your code," Summer said as she typed it into the phone. "It's the same for everything."

Two weeks later, I pulled into the driveway of my fourplex to find a white Mercedes with dealer tags in my parking spot. It was past midnight, and I was worn out from a fourteen-hour day being chased barefoot through a scalding parking lot on an ultra-low-budget movie that paid pennies. But the money from the commercial I'd had running over the holidays was drying up, leaving me desperate for acting work so that I wouldn't have to go back to slinging drinks. I was already seriously doubting my life choices; the Mercedes was the last straw.

Street parking in my neighborhood was a nightmare, so I drove in circles for a full twenty minutes, cursing the asshole driver of the Mercedes, before I finally found a spot. It was only when I got out of the car that I saw the sign that read NO PARKING SATURDAY 8A.M. TO 10A.M. Street cleaning on a Saturday? Seriously? It was all I could do not to scream.

I pushed open the front door to find all the lights on and Summer's suitcase open in the middle of the living room. So I guessed she'd made it home from her big trip to Asia. "Summer?" I called out.

No answer. I opened the bedroom door to find her sprawled across my bed, snoring. I shoved her over and crawled into bed. I clearly needed to talk to her again about finding her own apartment.

But when my alarm went off at the ungodly hour of seven so that I could move my car, Summer was gone. Thankfully, so was the white Mercedes. I parked my car where it belonged, making a mental note to put up a RESERVED sign. But as I turned toward the apartment, I spied the Mercedes coming up the driveway.

I stood there in my glasses and pajamas with my hands on my hips, an intimidating presence I was sure, staring at the car as it slowly pulled toward me. I prepared to give the driver a piece of my mind as the window rolled down.

A manicured hand emerged holding a Starbucks latte, and then I recognized the blond hair. "Hey," Summer said brightly. "I was up early so I picked up coffee."

I stared at her. "Whose car is that?"

"It's mine!" She beamed. "John got it for me as a signing bonus. He knew I didn't have a car. Wasn't that sweet? I have so much to tell you. But can you move your car so I can park in the spot? I don't wanna leave it on the street. It's brand-new."

I grabbed the coffee and walked toward the door. "I'm sure it's insured." The door slammed behind me.

I'd finished my coffee and gotten ahold of myself by the time she entered ten minutes later, carrying a bag of croissants. "God, parking in this neighborhood is a nightmare."

"Tell me about it," I agreed. "It took me half an hour to find parking at midnight."

"Oh, sorry about that. I figured you were gone for the night." She put the croissants in the oven to heat and sat across from me at the breakfast table. "So. I have to tell you about my trip."

"You slept with him."

She smiled confirmation. "How did you know?"

"Um, he bought you a Mercedes? Your pussy must be made of solid gold, because I've never had a man buy me a Mercedes after one week. Or ever, actually."

"It was two weeks, and they were the most insane weeks of my life," she raved, her cheeks flushed. "I mean, I've seen wealth, but nothing like this. He owns, like, half the world. He knows all these powerful people. It's like they're in a club—princes and prime ministers and CEOs and movie stars. Insane. A Mercedes is nothing to him. I could have asked for a Bentley and he would have bought it, but I didn't because I don't want him to think I'm in it for the money, you know?"

"Yeah," I said dryly. "Wouldn't want him to think that. Wait. Didn't you say he was married?"

"Yeah, his third wife. But they live separate lives—I'm not the first affair he's had, obviously, but he says he's never felt the way he feels with me—and anyway, she's, like, fifteen years older than me. They're getting divorced in the next couple of months. It's just too expensive right now."

"Does he have kids?"

"Yeah but they're grown and he totally wants to have more with me."

"I thought you didn't want kids."

"I mean, I never have before." She shrugged. "But with him it would be different. I would have, like, a nanny for each kid. They would have the best of everything, and I could just be there for the good parts."

She didn't seem to be kidding. "Sounds healthy. How old is he?"

"He's sixty. Well, sixty-three. But, like, a young sixty-three. He plays polo, he swims, he does mountain climbing—he's super well rounded."

"Isn't that weird? I mean, you're twenty-six. Do you even know any of the same cultural references?"

"It doesn't matter. We talk about art, and business, and wine...."

I laughed.

"What?" she said. "I really like him. I do. And you should see the clothes he bought me. We went shopping in Singapore—the shopping there is insane; it's the best in the world—and they shut down an entire floor of a luxury department store so that I could shop. He's so sweet!"

Amazingly, she sounded serious. Or maybe she'd convinced herself of how much she liked him in order to take advantage of all a relationship with him stood to offer. Regardless, her complete devotion either to the man or to the lie she was telling herself was pretty impressive.

"Oh, he got me these, too." She stroked the giant diamond studs in her ears. "And when I got back, that car was waiting for me."

"And how was the sex?"

"It was good!" she said. "I mean, not like Eric good, but nothing is going to be Eric good." She shivered. "And Eric didn't buy me a car. He never bought me a damn thing. And anyway, I'm not thinking about him anymore. He's not worth my time."

She'd always raved about how great Eric was in bed, obviously dying to dish the dirty details, but I never bit, Summer and Eric's sex life being about the last thing in the entire world I wanted to discuss. I much preferred to hear about her not-so-sexy tryst with some old dude. "So saggy-old-man balls are a myth?" I teased.

She sighed, not amused. "I just... I've been through a lot in the past few months." She looked at me pointedly, and I knew she was referring to the incident with Three that we'd agreed not to mention. "I'm doing the best I can with what I've got, and this could be really good for me..." She took a deep breath, and I saw she was holding back tears.

I reached out and grabbed her hand, realizing I was being insensitive. "I'm sorry, Summer. I wasn't thinking."

She nodded, and a tear slid down her cheek. "I just..." Her voice shook. "I need you to be supportive of me, okay?"

"I'm so sorry. I didn't mean to upset you." I pulled her in for a hug. "I totally support you in whoever you want to date."

"Thanks." She grabbed a Starbucks napkin and wiped away her tears.

"So, are you still gonna work for him, or...?"

"He's gonna keep paying me a salary and benefits, so I'll technically be working for him, but I'm not actually gonna be working. And you don't need to worry because I'm never gonna be here. He travels all the time and wants me to come with him."

"That's great!" As much as my heart went out to her for what had happened with Three, feigned enthusiasm was about as much as I could muster for her salaried-girlfriend position. I hoped this meant he'd get her an apartment of her own as well, but I kept my mouth shut on that front, not wanting to come off as even more callous.

A rapping at the front door stopped our conversation short. "Who is it?" I called out.

"Eric," came the voice on the other side.

I choked on my coffee.

Summer buried her face in her hands. "I totally forgot he was coming today. He has a show in Beverly Hills. I asked him to pick me up here."

"One second," I called. My heart fluttered like a bird caught in the rafters. Despite our slew of emails, I hadn't actually seen him since our kiss in his elevator. "I thought you weren't seeing him anymore," I whispered.

"I'm not!" she insisted. "I made these plans before I met John."

"Do you want me to get rid of him?"

She bit her lip. "No. It'll be fine."

I stood and pointed my feet in the direction of the living room, reminding myself with every step to act nonchalant in front of Summer. I swung open the door to find Eric dressed in his usual black, the morning sun lighting his green eyes. He smiled, and any annoyance I'd had at him for turning up on my doorstep to collect Summer dissipated. "Hi." He leaned in to give me a lingering kiss on the cheek. My pulse quickened. "Good to see you. Hey, I finally saw your web series where you're a junkie in med school. Awesome work. You were so raw. It was—I was blown away. Really."

I raised my brows, taken aback. "Wow, you actually watched it. Thank you." Then, remembering why he was here, "Summer's—"

I turned to see her lingering in the doorway to the kitchen, eyeing us. "Did you see her web series?" he asked Summer. "This girl's a real leading lady."

"Not yet. But I'm sure it's great."

"You guys ready?" he asked. "The gallery gave me a driver." He gestured in the general direction of the street. "He's waiting."

"Belle's not coming," Summer said.

"Oh." He turned to me. "Why not?"

I raised my hands. "I don't know what's going on. I hadn't heard you were in town."

He looked between us, confused. "We were all going to my hotel to hang out by the pool and then go to the show tonight."

"Sorry." Summer smiled. "I just got back from Asia last night. Things have been kinda crazy. I totally forgot. Lemme just grab a couple things."

She strode down the hallway to the bedroom, and Eric moved deeper into the living room, out of her line of sight. "Did you not get my DM?" he whispered.

I shook my head. "Sorry."

"Fuck." He actually seemed upset. "You can't come?"

Was he crazy? Or did he have some fucked-up idea we were going to have a threesome or something? I laughed. "No way am I hanging out with the two of you and whatever's going on there."

We were silenced by the sound of Summer's stride in the hallway. She appeared looking like a million bucks in heels and a sundress, a new Louis Vuitton overnight bag slung over her shoulder. I'd never in my life wanted to sock her as badly as I did in that moment. "Okay." She beamed. "Ready."

"Have fun, guys!" I buried my resentment under a bright smile, fully aware I had no right to be resentful in the first place. He was, after all, *her* ex . . . or whatever.

Eric turned to me. "Belle, you really should come, too. It'll be fun—"

I was saved from coming up with an excuse by Summer, who clearly didn't want me along, either. "Belle has other things to do."

"I gotta go work on something." I excused myself, beelining for the hallway.

But before I could reach my room, Eric called out, "You should at least come to the show tomorrow night. It's all about botany. I think you'd like it."

"I'd love to," I said, "but I'm shooting tomorrow night."

"Oh, what are you working on?" Eric asked.

"Low-budget thriller. But at least I don't die in this one. Have a good show."

"Thanks," he said. "Stay alive."

"Same to ya."

I closed the door to my bedroom, turned on the music, and balled my fists so tightly my nails left crescents in my palms.

Day 6

'm never drinking again. My head is throbbing, my mouth is dry, and I've sweated through the sheets; all I want to do is hide in the dark, cool cabin until the cloud lifts, but someone is knocking at the damn door.

Amythest continues to snore, dead to the world. I wish I could sleep like that.

"Yes?" I call when I realize the knocking is not going to stop on its own.

There it is again. I groan and throw the covers off, pull on a T-shirt, and open the door.

Camille stands in the hallway with a tray of coffee and red, puffy eyes. "Sorry. I must make sure you get out of bed. You go shopping today. We dock at ten."

"Are you okay?" I ask.

She nods quickly, but the tears that spring to her dark eyes betray her. She tries to hand me the tray so she can leave, but instead I motion her inside, closing the door behind her as she sets the tray on the bed and furtively dries her eyes. I don't want to pry, but the girl is clearly upset, and I'm worried she's the latest victim of Summer's displeasure. "Is there something I can help you with?" I ask gently.

This elicits a fresh round of tears, which she tries in vain to dam. "*Dé-désolé*," she stammers.

"It's okay," I say, handing her one of the napkins off the tray. "You're safe here. This is *entre nous*."

We both look over at Amythest, sleeping like the dead.

"*C'est...ma mère,*" she says. "I send to her *mon chèque, habituellement par* Western Union. She depend on it. She is sick. *Mais maintenant* Emmanuelle go, I must stay here on the boat to do her work. I cannot *poster le chèque.*" She chokes back a sob. "*Désolé, je suis très fatigué.* I do not want *problèmes.*"

"It's okay," I say. "I'll go to Western Union for you."

She looks up at me in disbelief. "*Vraiment?*"

"Yes, it's no problem," I say. "I understand. They're working you too hard. You know, I have a job a lot like yours back home."

She eyes me sideways, incredulous. "*Vous? Une serveuse?*"

I nod. "*Je suis une serveuse.*" I mime holding a tray. "A waitress and a bartender."

She pats her face with the napkin, laughing in disbelief. "I know," I say. "The stranger thing is that I'm here." I nod to Amythest. "I'll wake her up. You go get the money, and I'll send it in Saint-Tropez today."

"*Merci,*" she says, quickly running her fingers beneath her eyes and smoothing her hair. "*Merci beaucoup.*"

"*De rien.*" I smile.

Camille slips out the door, and I shake Amythest's shoulder until she surfaces from dreamland, staring at me like I'm evil. "What's happening?"

"We have to wake up," I say. She sighs and closes her eyes. I grab a cup of coffee from the tray and wave it under her nose until she sits up. "We're going shopping today."

"I don't want to go shopping," Amythest grumbles. "I have no fucking money." She flops back on her pillow and pulls the covers up over her head.

I check my watch. "We have thirty minutes to get ready."

"Didn't you guys fucking go shopping yesterday?"

I shrug. Was the bikini shop only yesterday? The days are all beginning to blend together. Through the wall we share with Brittani and Rhonda, I can hear Brittani singing a Beyoncé song, terribly off key. I shove the cup of coffee into Amythest's hands, gulp down a cup myself, and hurl my aching body into the shower.

Summer has still not appeared as the boat pulls into the Saint-Tropez harbor, but the rest of us are all miraculously dressed and I have Camille's envelope in my purse, ready to be posted. We stuff our faces with croissants and fruit on the deck while we slowly make our way through the port. Julie, seemingly fully recovered from the loss of Emmanuelle, cheerfully points out boats belonging to princes and movie stars as the rest of the crew busily readies the boat to dock, then carefully guides it into a front-row slip facing the shops and restaurants of the town.

Vacationers stroll by on the promenade an arm's length away, craning their necks to see who we might be. "These are the best slips," Julie says.

Summer arrives looking like death warmed over just in time to give us our marching orders before the crew lowers the plank. She's not coming with us, she explains, because she and John need some alone time. She sweeps her gaze across each of us, poison in her eyes. "He was very disappointed in the way you behaved last night. Especially you." Her manicured finger points at me.

"Me?"

"Oh, don't act stupid," she scolds. "Prancing around singing, drawing attention to yourself, doing drugs."

"It was just hash! Marlena was smoking it, too," I protest.

"Don't act like she's your friend. You never would have been there without me."

"None of us would be here without you," Wendy pipes up.

"And you." Summer swings around to Wendy. "Throwing yourself at Leo Martin, making out with him in front of everybody. I'm disgusted."

Wendy looks like a bucket of ice has been thrown in her face. "I'm sorry," she splutters. "I got carried away."

"You're supposed to be my friends," Summer reprimands, "and yet none of you gave any thought to how bad you were making me look.

This isn't Hollywood. You can't just act like tramps. Our behavior reflects on John."

A solitary tear rolls down Claire's cheek.

"We're sorry, honey," Rhonda says, patting Summer on the back. Summer recoils from her touch.

"Yeah, sorry," Brittani says.

"Sorry," the rest of us mutter.

"I apologize," Wendy says. "It was thoughtless of me."

"I'm this close to sending you all home." Summer opens her fingers a centimeter. "After all we've done for you. So disrespectful." She turns on her heel and stalks back to her room, leaving us all staring after her, traumatized.

Julie clears her throat, and we collectively shift our dumbfounded gaze to her. "Everybody stick with your roommate and be back at noon," she instructs us, her voice stubbornly cheery.

We gather our purses and deboard in silence, our eyes downcast. Once we've joined the throngs of tourists that stroll along the boardwalk, I catch Wendy by the arm. "You okay?"

"Yeah," she says, stricken. "She's right. We should have behaved better."

I roll my eyes. "We were fine. She's just pissed because Leo turned her down and he went for you."

"You think he likes me?" she asks hopefully.

"Obviously. Though I wouldn't hold my breath. According to Michael, he has a reputation as a bit of a playboy."

She looks out at the floating palaces lined up in the sun. "Yeah, I know," she admits. "But a lot of men are playboys until they meet the right girl."

Seeing no reason to murder any more of her dreams this morning, I switch subjects. "Anything in particular you're shopping for today?"

"I want a pair of those lace-up sandals everyone's wearing, and I need, like, SPF100 sunscreen. I'm so done getting sun. How about you?"

"I need a dress for the Webby Awards."

She looks at me blankly.

"It's the awards for web series. One I had a part in is nominated. I told you about it—*Junk*?"

She nods. "Oh yeah." But it's clear she has no idea what I'm talking about.

"We're getting souvenirs," Rhonda says.

"Who knows when we'll be in France again." Brittani snorts. "We're probably too embarrassing to get invited on another trip."

"Souvenirs!" Rhonda steers her daughter by the elbow toward a tchotchke shop. Brittani gestures to Amythest to join them, but Amythest pretends not to see, turning stone-faced to stare out at the sea. Brittani sticks her tongue out and flips the bird at Amythest's back before following her mom into the store.

Wendy, Claire, and I exchange a weighted glance. *Good luck*, Wendy mouths, cutting her eyes at Amythest. Then, at full volume, "Okay, we'll see you in a bit."

Claire gives a little wave and follows her toward a shoe shop. I feel a burden lift from my shoulders as they disappear from view. This is the first break from the herd and the least amount of supervision I've had since we started this trip. I turn to Amythest, leaning over the railing and looking out at the boats, big black sunglasses hiding her eyes. "You okay?"

"Fine," she says flatly.

"If you wanna just sit in a restaurant or something and chill while I go find this dress, it's totally cool," I offer.

"Nah. Let's go."

We cut across the road, and I consult the maps app on my phone to find the nearest Western Union, which is luckily only a few blocks away. "I just have to run to Western Union first to send this money for Camille," I say. "She's not allowed off the boat, and her mom needs the cash."

Still lost in her own world, Amythest nods vaguely and follows me up a cobblestone street lined with charming boutiques. She sits on a bench outside the storefront fiddling with her phone while I wait in the long line to send Camille's money. By the time I emerge, her mood seems to have improved.

"That's pretty awesome your web series was nominated," she says as we make our way up the sidewalk among shoppers laden with bags. "What was it?"

"It was called *Junk*. I played a junkie medical school student trying to go straight. And failing."

"Sounds intense. So, like, what do they pay for that?"

"Exactly zero dollars," I divulge. "But it was an awesome experience. I learned so much and really got to stretch as an actor, as cheesy as that may sound."

"No, it's cool. I wish I could do something like that."

I stop in front of a boutique with a deep-purple strapless dress displayed in the front window.

"You know how I feel about purple," Amythest says.

We enter the store and I peruse the racks, nonchalantly turning over the first price tag I see. Five thousand euros. I turn over another one. Six thousand. I catch Amythest's eye and casually stroll out.

"How much?" she asks.

"Six grand." I sigh. "I'm looking for more like five hundred, which to me is still a lot to spend on a dress that I'll maybe wear a handful of times ever."

She laughs. "Good luck."

We make quick work of it from there, but have a hell of a time finding anything that fits my budget. There are stores that sell cheaper clothing, but they don't have formal dresses. Along the way, Amythest picks up a big floppy hat, and I grab a necklace for my mom and a pair of earrings for Lauren.

We're already short on time from the length of the line at Western Union, and I've just about given up when I see the most beautiful emerald-green empire-waist dress in the window of a consignment store. I check my watch. It's eleven thirty.

"That would be sick on you," Amythest says.

"Okay, we just have to be quick. The boat is still a ten-minute walk."

The dress is 460 euros, which translates to a little more than the five hundred dollars I intended to spend. But after the other dresses today, it seems like a steal, and when I try it on, it's absolutely perfect in every way. Amythest claps as I spin in front of the mirror. "Hot." She whistles. "Hella hot."

As the shopgirls are wrapping it up for me, Amythest goes through a rack of clearance items in the back. "Ooh," she exclaims. "What about this?"

It's a gold vintage shift cocktail dress from the sixties that is probably the most stylish thing she's ever picked out in her life, and I wish I'd seen it first.

"Yes." I check my watch again. "But we have to be walking in ten minutes, so snap, snap."

She scurries to the dressing room and emerges transformed. The dress fits her perfectly, turning her from death-metal stripper to stylish gamine.

"Yes," I say immediately. "A hundred percent."

"I don't know if I can afford it, though."

"How much?" I ask the shopgirl.

"*Très belle*," she says. "And on final sale, *alors* . . . forty-five."

"Okay, can I put it on a card?" Amythest asks.

"No Amex, but Visa is okay."

"Great. I'll do it." Amythest smiles. She rummages in her purse and hands the shopgirl her credit card. "Can you ring it up while I change?"

The shopgirl runs the card through her machine while Amythest changes back into her black cutoff jean shorts and tank top. We still have fifteen minutes to make it back to the boat, which should be plenty. I text Wendy:

Headed back now. You find the shoes?

She replies immediately:

Yes!! See you soon x

I glance over at the shopgirl, who is still looking at her machine. "Is there a problem?"

"*Pas de problème.* The machine always slow."

The machine beeps, and she sighs.

"What happened?" Amythest asks.

"It was connect but now is not. I don't know if it go through."

"We're kind of in a hurry," I say. "Is there any way to speed it up?"

"It will work," she says, looking at the machine. "I call."

The minutes are ticking. "Could you take another card?" I ask.

"*Le problème* not the card. *C'est la machine.*"

"What about cash?" I ask. "I could pull some cash out if there's an ATM nearby."

"You don't have to," Amythest protests. "And we don't have time. Go ahead. I can catch up."

"No. I'm not leaving you."

The shopgirl dials a number on the shop phone and speaks to someone in French. She seems to be following their instructions as she punches buttons on the machine. Finally, after what seems to be a decade, the machine beeps.

"Oh! It go through." She hands Amythest the receipt.

Amythest signs and we dash out of the store. I text Wendy and Summer as we rush down the street, scampering around shoppers:

There in 3 min!

We're not gonna make it by twelve. There's no way. But we'll only be a few minutes late. My sandals are rubbing blisters in my feet as we make it onto the promenade. Boats bob in their slips, glinting in the bright sun. I spy the *Lion's Den* a hundred yards away.

"Thank God." I pant. "Boat's still there."

But as we draw closer, I see two of the crew guys lifting the gangplank. They're in shouting distance, so I yell, "Hey! We're here!"

Hugo and the burly one whose name I can't remember look up and wave, then prepare to put the gangplank back in place.

We're twenty feet away now, and I can see Wendy and Brittani, shopping bags in hand, on the deck with Summer, watching us approach. I look at my watch as we reach the railing. It's 12:03.

"Sorry we're late," I call. "Credit card machine issue. We ran all the way."

Summer gives an instruction to the crew guys that I can't hear over the thrum of the engine, then walks inside without a backward glance. The crew guys pause with the gangplank in the air, speaking to each other in low tones, then begin putting it away. They're going to leave us.

"Brittani!" Amythest shouts. But Brittani turns her back and goes inside.

Hugo catches my eye. "Sorry. Return at five."

I look to Wendy. "Seriously?"

"Sorry." I can't see her expression for the shadow cast by her giant hat, but Wendy gives a *nothing I can do* shrug and follows Summer and Brittani as the boat pulls away.

Amythest and I watch with dread as the boat chugs steadily into the bright day. Adrenaline surges through my veins. A friend's knife is always sharpest, but double betrayal is a special torment. I text Wendy:

What just happened?

"I can't believe this shit," Amythest says.

"Yeah, ditto," I fume. "Well, to hell with those bitches. I'm hungry."

I march across the street to a restaurant that faces the harbor and take a seat at an outdoor table. Amythest slumps into the chair opposite mine, flipping up her menu. "You've gotta be kidding me. The cheapest drink on here is twenty euros."

"My treat," I say, mentally tallying the small amount of money I have left.

"That fucking cunt," she seethes, twisting her hair madly around her finger.

"Look, I'm just as pissed as you are right now, but honestly, I'm also kinda stoked we don't have to hang out with them today."

Tears roll out from under her big black glasses. I flag down the waitress and order us each a hair-of-the-dog glass of rosé.

"Listen." I pat her hand. "Let's just tell them that it's my fault about being late, okay? I'll tell them what happened, just that it happened to me instead of you. Sound good?"

She chews her lip, her gaze trained on the boats bobbing in their slips. I quickly text Summer:

> Sorry we were late. Was my fault,
> was trying to buy a dress and the credit card
> machine froze, so I couldn't leave with the dress,
> and couldn't leave without it. Again, sorry!

I don't know what else to say. My phone has autoconnected to the restaurant Wi-Fi, and messages are pouring in. As I scroll through my in-box, my eyes land on my message chain with Dylan.

I briefly consider calling him, but decide the better of it. Summer's pissed enough at me as it is—the last thing I need to do is make it worse.

Our rosé arrives, and Amythest chugs hers like it's a keg at a frat party, then sets the glass down with a resounding clank.

"Thirsty much?" I tease.

"Screw Brittani. I'm that bitch's only friend. No one else can stand her."

"I'm sorry she's treating you like this. If it makes you feel any better, her sister is doing the same to me," I sympathize.

"I don't give a shit if she's loud and she's rude," Amythest says. "At least she's straight up about who she is. But ever since we got here, all she does is lick her sister's asshole. Like it's so special she's fucking some old rich guy. Ha!"

She juts her chin out as she speaks, a hardness in her manner. She reaches across the table and takes a slug of my wine. "Joke's on her. I'm fucking him, too."

Here's the dirt. "Yeah," I say carefully. "I saw him wearing the sunglasses I found under your bed, so I kinda figured."

"Wasn't even hard," she boasts. "Well, I mean, like it wasn't hard to fuck him, but his dick wasn't exactly hard, either. And he is *kinky*. Dirty." She shivers. "He wanted me to—"

But I have no interest in hearing the filthy details of Amythest and John's tryst. "Girl, you need to be careful," I cut in. "As big of a bitch as Summer may be, we're here as her guests, and . . ."

"What goes around comes around." She snorts. "If she would've been nice to me, I would've given her respect, you know? But you treat me like I'm a whore, I'll show you who's a whore."

"I get it. But Summer's—" I have to stop here. I can't tell her the full truth about what I know, but I need to tell her something. "You know the real reason Emmanuelle's no longer on the boat is Summer thought she was flirting with John, right? She set her up for stealing that necklace."

"Yeah, duh," Amythest says.

"It's not the first time she's done something like that," I say, casting around for an example. "Back when Summer was waitressing, she didn't like this one girl she was working with who would always take the good tables. So she set the girl up to look like she was stealing and got her fired."

"Too late." Amythest shrugs, unimpressed. "'Cause I left my panties in his jacket pocket after he finger-banged me under the table at that party last night."

Jesus Christ. "Wow," I say.

She takes another slug of my wine. "All these rich people think they're so special, but they're just like everybody else. Everybody fucking everybody and nobody happy."

"I'd venture to say there may be slightly more fucking among the rich."

I flag down the waitress and order us each another glass of wine, as well as a caprese salad and prosciutto sandwich to share. Amythest chews her cheek and twirls her hair, turning her attention to her phone, so I take mine back out as well. My gaze lands on a reply to my incoherent message last night:

How you feeling this morning, party girl? Crazy news about Amythest and John. But not surprising. You may want to make it your mission that Summer doesn't find out—she's so jealous, God only knows what she'd do. What did she give you instead of Dramamine? Are you okay? Please be careful. Clearly you can't trust her. And no more emailing from that boat! Again, wish I could say I was surprised. Crazy you ran into Dylan. Maybe better not to call him, sounds like there's enough going on out there. Is it storming yet? Beautiful here, but hot. So damn hot. You only have a few days left then you'll be home, but you don't have to stick it out, you can bail early if you need to. Keep me posted...

I hit reply:

Yeah I totally drunk messaged you, sorry! We were all pretty wasted last night—Summer was not amused, chewed us out this morning. Having lunch in St. T with Amythest now, the boat left us b/c we were 3 minutes late after shopping. Apparently they'll be back at 5. I'm glad for the time off. Bailing is tempting, but I'm broke and it's only a few more days, I think I can make it. Sunny enough today, but may storm tonight I think. Don't forget to delete these messages. Not planning to email from boat but if I need to, obvs don't want anyone reading.

I wince as I sign the check, noticing I've spent nearly a hundred euros, but I'm too buzzed to worry about it for long. "Let's go for a walk," I suggest.

Swinging our shopping bags, we sail out of the restaurant on a cloud of rosé and turn inland up the first street we come to, if you can call it that. The lane is wide enough only for scooters, the distance between the buildings on either side so narrow that the sidewalks remain shaded with the sun high in the sky. Most of the shops are shuttered for lunch, and the crowds have thinned, leaving a soothing quiet in their wake.

We stop at an ATM and I pull fifty euros out of my rapidly shrinking bank account so that I at least have some pocket cash. "Why are you friends with Summer?" Amythest asks as we resume our stroll. "You're so nice, and she's such a bitch."

I laugh. "We met when we were fifteen," I say. "And she wasn't always such a bitch. She's been through some things. . . ."

"Like what?"

I sigh, unsure why some part of me still feels the need to protect her, after everything. "Her mom's husbands, for one. All four of them. The last one was a cop who beat the crap out of Rhonda and gave Summer a black eye when she tried to intervene. And the one before that, number three . . . did some horrible shit, too."

Amythest pauses in front of a display window featuring impossibly thin mannequins dressed in resort wear, and places her hand on the glass, transfixed. "If I were rich," she muses, "do you think I'd wear clothes like that?"

I laugh. "Not all rich people wear caftans and gladiators."

She wipes a tear that rolls from under her glasses. "Ugh." She groans. "This kind of shit doesn't usually upset me. But this week I just feel so . . . small. So fucking lame."

"I know what you mean," I say. "If it makes you feel any better, Summer only got here by opening her legs." This isn't true. She's done far more than that to secure a place at John's side, but I want to cheer Amythest up.

She snickers. "You say it like it's a bad thing. From where I'm sitting, it looks pretty good. Except the fact that John's doing me behind her back, of course."

She spins as though she's made her point and strides up the sidewalk. I hasten after her. I want to stop her in her tracks, to shake her and open her eyes to just who she's messing with, but I worry revealing anything more to her than I already have would only backfire.

After a few turns up farther narrow streets lined with tawny shops and faded blue shutters, the maze abruptly ends. To our left is the changeable blue sea, backed by mountains; to our right, a grassy hill with a citadel on top. I stare up at the fortress, shading my eyes. "I think I read that's some kind of museum now. Wanna check it out?"

She shakes her head, the purple streaks in her hair glinting in the sun. "It's so nice out. Let's walk along the water."

The sun is strong as we hike along the path by the ocean and I wish I had a hat, but the view is to die for and the breeze keeps us cool enough. After a couple hundred yards, we come to a parking lot and an arched gate. An investigation reveals it to be, improbably, a cemetery.

Rows upon rows of closely stacked marble graves, most of which resemble legless twin beds with cross-engraved headboards, sit upon sandy shale, the waves of the bay crashing on the rocks only yards below. Amythest stares in wonder. "How cool."

We wander through the cemetery contemplating the names and years, and I do my best to translate the epitaphs. "'Do not mourn my death, but celebrate my life,'" I read. "'Gone too soon. Loving mother and grandmother.' Oh, this one's Shakespeare: 'Like as the waves make towards the pebbl'd shore, so do our minutes hasten to their end.'"

"Heavy," she says.

"How about this one: '*Danser au paradis*'—'dancing in heaven.'"

She laughs. "I like that. Emille Broulet Marchand, 1903–1923, she was just my age." She stares down at the grave. "You know, my real name's not really Amythest; it's Jessica. I changed it because...I don't know, I guess it made me feel special."

"But you are special," I say.

She gives me a shy smile, then shifts her gaze to the horizon. "I wouldn't want to be buried by the sea." She shudders. "All that water. I know I'd be dead, but..."

"You've gotta learn to swim," I say. "When we get back to LA, you can come over to Wendy's and—"

She snorts. "As if Wendy would ever invite me over."

"She's really not—"

"I don't care," she cuts in, holding up a hand. "After this week, you're the only one of these bitches I ever want to see again."

My phone dings, and I fish it from the bottom of my purse. It's a text from Summer. My pulse quickens as I read:

> This is John's boat and it leaves when he says it does. It is not your boat u r a guest here and on our schedule. I can't believe how rude u r. After all we have done for u. Be there at 5. U have a mtg with John, and u can apologize to him for how ungrateful u r.

"What is it?" she asks.

"Summer." I hand her the phone. "Fuck her. After all she's done for me? I let that bitch sleep in my bed for I don't even know how many months for free! I've picked up the pieces after every one of her relationships fell apart. I've given her clothes, gotten her jobs..."

I'm seething. I want to throw the phone in the ocean and never go back to that floating prison. If I had any more money, I would jump ship and get a flight back. I wonder if... No. I can stick it out. It's only a few more days.

"Shit," Amythest says, returning the phone to me.

"We should head back to the boat." I drop the phone into my bag and march out of the cemetery, fuming.

Amythest scampers after me, peppering me with questions I can't answer as we hurry along the sea path, then weave through town. "If you guys were such good friends, why does she hate you now? How long has she been like this? Did you do something to her? Why did you come on this trip?"

Sweat runs down my back; my sandals chafe. Finally, somewhere in the midst of the maze, I have to stop her. "Amythest," I pant. "If I could tell you more, I would. Please, please, let it go. Let's both just keep our heads down and get back to the States without any more drama, okay?"

She must see the desperation in my eyes because she nods, her violet eyes serious. "Okay."

(twenty-six days ago)

Los Angeles

I was driving home from yoga one sunny morning in July when my phone dinged with a text from Summer.

I'm back, where are you?

I couldn't remember where she'd gone—it had become hard to keep up with where in the world she and John were hopscotching to. She'd breeze in for a day here or there, dropping nuggets of her new life: a Cartier watch on the bathroom sink, a story about dinner with a famously conservative senator and his "ladyboy" girlfriend in Bangkok, a VIP security pass for the palace of an oil-rich dictator not known for his human rights record. Every time I was tempted to feel envious, I reminded myself of the part of herself she'd traded for a seat on that jet.

I was more than a little vexed that she was yet to officially move out of my apartment, but after what happened with Three—which both of us still felt was at least somewhat my fault—I didn't feel like I could be too pushy. I'd seen very little of her over the past few months, anyway—and though she still wasn't paying rent, she was very generous with her loot, gifting me designer clothes John didn't like and even a little round Gucci bag I absolutely adored. She mostly stayed with John in Beverly Hills when they weren't jet-setting, and I'd been busy bartending at a new bar and hustling acting jobs—whatever came my way—trying to eke out a living.

I'd met John twice. The first time was just in passing while lying by the pool with Summer at his Beverly Hills mansion, but the second was a month or so ago at an awkward dinner with Summer, Wendy, and Claire that none of us besides Summer knew he'd be attending. He showed up after we'd ordered and sat with us for a torturous thirty minutes, during which he interviewed us like job candidates while one of his goons lingered at the bar behind us, before dropping his card and decamping. When I'd asked Summer about it, she'd demurred. "Oh, he's heard so much about you guys; he just wanted to meet you."

The following week she sent the three of us a photo of herself sunning on his yacht:

Who wants to join me here for my birthday?

An official invitation to Summer's birthday trip arrived a few days later, in the form of an email from John's travel coordinator, coupled with a request for our passport information. It turned out John actually *had* been interviewing us at that dinner—apparently we'd passed. "I told him you guys were beautiful and amazing," Summer confided the next time I saw her, "but he's super particular about his image, so he had to see for himself. My mom and sis are coming, but between us, I have to buy them all new outfits for the trip."

Though I was still having trouble getting on board with Summer's May–December romance, I'd be a liar if I said I wasn't thrilled by the idea of an all-expenses-paid trip to the Mediterranean aboard a yacht. Sure, it was her sugar daddy's yacht, and I realized the trip wouldn't likely be exactly what I would imagine for myself...but still, a yacht. The Riviera. Hell yes.

When I got home from yoga, I found my door partially open and Summer in the living room, throwing things into a new, oversize Louis Vuitton suitcase that matched her overnight bag. "Hi!" she said brightly. "I texted you."

"I was driving. What's up?"

"John has to work in the Middle East the next few weeks, and I can't accompany him, so he got me a beach house in Malibu." Hallelujah, she'd finally gotten her own place. It was all I could do not to break into song. "Wanna come out for the night? Or the weekend?"

A beach house, a yacht trip...I had to admit there were definitely perks to having a rich friend. "You know, I think my schedule just cleared up." I smiled.

"Great!" She clapped her hands. "Because the house is ridiculous. And it comes with a wine cellar that he had an assistant stock. Only thing is, you'll have to drive because my car's at the garage."

We sped up the coast with the windows down, singing along at top volume to blaring nineties pop songs the entire way. It had been a while since we'd had that much fun together, and it felt good—like old times, almost. When we pulled up to the house, Wendy's SUV was already parked outside. "What up, sluts?" she said. "This place looks incredible."

"I thought you had to work tonight," Summer goaded.

"Yeah, I did until I pulled up pictures of this place," Wendy divulged. "Also, AssPlay is going to be there, and I really don't want to see him."

"Remind me who is AssPlay?" Summer whispered as we pulled into the garage.

"Who do you think? The guy she dated last year that was so into playing with her ass. You met him. She brought him to my birthday party."

Summer snorted. "Must not have been memorable."

The house was a large modern affair, made almost completely of glass and situated directly on the beach. Every room had wall-to-wall views of the ocean, and sliding glass doors stretched across the front of the house. We immediately pushed them open, letting in the ocean air and the sound of the crashing waves.

"How long do you have this place?" I asked. "Because I figure you've stayed with me what, a year? So I can move in at least that long, right?"

She laughed. "I have it for the rest of the summer. But I don't know...maybe I'll keep it. Although it might get kinda lonely in the winter. And you can stay here as much as you want, as long as John's not in town."

"And you guys clearly need me to keep you company," Wendy chimed in. "This house would feel empty with just the two of you."

Summer opened the refrigerator, which was stocked with neatly organized rows of water, fruit, wine, snacks, and prepackaged meals from Whole Foods.

"There's a person who comes and cleans and stocks the fridge and takes my dry cleaning and everything," Summer dished. "Wine? What should we drink, Chardonnay, Pinot Gris, or rosé?"

"Rosé!" Wendy and I answered in unison.

Summer collected the glasses and Wendy poured while I prepared us a plate of cheese, crackers, and fruit. Summer's phone buzzed on the counter. "Ugh. Eric." She silenced it.

I knew he was currently in town for a show—he'd invited me, but I'd turned him down. I'd stonewalled him for a couple of weeks after that awkward morning when he showed up at my apartment, but once I understood how serious John and Summer were, I relaxed my stance and gradually resumed communication. He'd been in town a few times since, but I had yet to see him. It was much easier not to be attracted to him when he wasn't in front of me.

"He won't leave me alone," Summer complained. "This is the thirteenth time he's called this week. I tried to tell him it was over last time I saw him, but he wouldn't listen."

Funny, he'd told me just the opposite. But then, why was he calling her?

"He may not have taken you seriously if you were telling him while having sex with him," Wendy teased.

"Have you told Eric there's someone else?" I asked.

"No," Summer admitted. "I was kinda hoping I wouldn't have to."

"You gotta tell him," Wendy said. "You don't want John finding out."

Eric already knew. I'd accidentally told him months ago, not realizing it was a secret—a fact I didn't share with Summer for obvious reasons. He'd been relieved to hear that Summer was in a serious relationship, but that had been the extent of our conversation about it. We didn't discuss details, and in fact, we hadn't talked about Summer since— and Summer hadn't said a word about Eric to me, either. So while I'd assumed the two of them had stopped seeing each other, I now realized I could be totally wrong.

"I didn't know you guys were still seeing each other," I said casually.

"Yeah," she said. "I mean, it's been a while 'cause I've been so busy with John, but he's never given up. He's always begging me to come out to New York for the weekend."

Okay, clearly one of them was lying. I just couldn't understand why. I was dying to ask more, but didn't want to raise Summer's suspicions, so I backed off.

Later that night, Summer, Wendy, and I were curled up on leather recliners in the velvet-curtained movie theater watching *The Great Gatsby* when Summer's phone rang again. She groaned. "It's Eric."

"Answer," Wendy said.

"You guys can keep watching. I've seen this a million times." She answered the phone as she exited the room, shutting the door behind her.

The movie had ended by the time she returned, her mascara streaked and her face puffy. "How'd it go?" Wendy asked.

"Not good. He already knew, and even knew who John was. That's why he's been calling nonstop—"

"Wait. How did he know who John was?" I asked, confused. I was certain I hadn't told him.

"Have you guys been photographed together or something? Or was he one of Eric's buyers?" Wendy guessed.

"No," Summer said, pacing in circles around the furniture. "But it's not like we haven't gone out in public, to restaurants or whatever."

"So someone who knows Eric saw you with John and told him?" I asked. The idea seemed a bit far-fetched. The world of the rich might be small, but John and Eric didn't exactly travel in the same circles.

Summer waved the question away, clearly annoyed at my pursuit of this line of questioning. "I don't know. . . . He wouldn't say exactly. Anyway, what does it matter? The important—"

"I'd wanna know—"

"Belle!" She spun to face me. "Can you just listen instead of interrupting me all the time with stupid questions?"

Suddenly it hit me: she knew perfectly well who'd told Eric. She just didn't want us to know. Which of course only piqued my curiosity. But in the interest of preserving the peace, I raised my palms. "Sorry."

"Anyway"—Summer paused as if trying to remember what she'd been saying—"the point is, he was *very* upset." She sank into a chair. "He kept saying how I betrayed him and I'm just into John for the money and he hates me. He threatened to tell John everything."

Wendy's hand flew to her mouth. "Oh my God."

It was hard to know how much of Summer's story to believe. Even if she and Eric had still been seeing each other regularly, I'd have had a hard time buying him losing his mind over her dating someone else, and now that they weren't in any way together, it just seemed bizarre.

"But what can he say to John?" Wendy asked. "You had only just met him last time you saw Eric, and you haven't been with Eric since things became serious."

"John's jealous as it is," Summer moaned. "He'll dump me on my ass and cut my salary, take back my car, make my life a living hell." She bit her lip. "Also, I did see Eric again, in New York a few months ago."

I wondered if that was the time I knew about or yet another incident. Maybe I didn't know Eric as well as I thought. "But how is Eric going to get in touch with John, and what is he going to tell him that proves you've seen him while you were together?" I asked.

"He's smart. I'm sure he can get in touch with him if he wants to. And there are emails, text messages, pictures. . . . God I'm so stupid! How could I be so stupid! What am I gonna do?"

A desperation I hadn't heard before had crept into her voice. And yet still I was not entirely convinced by her story. "How did you leave it with Eric?"

She sighed. "We were yelling at each other, and he hung up on me. Then he called back, but I didn't answer."

"Oh man," Wendy said. "This is bad."

Wendy and Summer spent the rest of the evening analyzing the situation from every angle while I did my best to participate in the conversation amiably, all the while unable to shake the feeling that Summer was at best omitting details. Even if my gut instincts about Eric were wrong and he had in fact freaked out on her for dating John, it was still obvious she was covering something up. But what—and why? We were her friends, who could surely help her better if she'd tell us the truth.

I finally crashed around two in the morning, my mind made up to call Eric the next day and hear his side of the story. I knew it was a betrayal of Summer's trust, but then, what trust? If she trusted me, she'd have told me what was actually going on. Maybe I'd find she was, in fact, telling the truth, and then I'd have to face that reality—but I could no longer pretend to have blind faith in Summer.

In the morning I woke to the sound of my bedroom door opening. Summer was silhouetted in the doorway wearing black Lulus, her hair pulled into a ponytail under a baseball cap.

"You going hiking?" I asked, rubbing the sleep from my eyes.

"I'm going to the desert to stay with Rhonda for a few days," she replied. "Eric won't be able to find me there."

"Okay." I fumbled for my phone on the bedside table, but it wasn't there. I must have left it downstairs last night. "What time is it?"

"Eight," she said, approaching the bed. As she drew closer, I noticed her normally rosy cheeks were pale, her eyes rimmed by dark circles.

"Are you okay?" I asked.

"I need your car. Please, you know Wendy will never let me borrow hers."

"But I need my car," I protested, pushing myself up to sitting.

Her hand trembled as she placed a set of keys on the bedside table. "You can use mine till I'm back. I texted you the address of the garage and the code to get in. It's way nicer than yours anyway. You'll like driving it. And Wendy can drop you. It's near her place."

Too tired to fight, I acquiesced. "Okay. Just don't wreck it."

"You should hope I do. I'd make John buy you something better." She jingled my keys. "Thank you. You're the best. Love you, babe."

She blew me a kiss and quietly closed the door behind her.

When I woke again, it was to blinding brightness as the automated blackout shades slowly rose, letting in the glaring sun and pounding surf. I buried my head under a pillow, only to have it removed by Wendy.

"You sadist," I grumbled.

"Rise and shine," she chirped. "I gotta get back."

"I need a ride."

"I know," she said. "I'm gonna shower up. Can you be ready in thirty?"

I was unable to reach Eric when I called him later that afternoon, and he didn't respond to my messages, either. Summer was unreachable, too, and as unlikely as it seemed, I couldn't help but wonder if the two of them had reconciled and run off together.

When we still hadn't heard from Summer by the next day, Wendy and I were both a little worried. We'd left messages, texted, and emailed, but she hadn't replied to either of us, so finally I called Rhonda.

"Hi, Rhonda, it's Belle," I said when she answered. "Is Summer there?"

"Hi, Belle!" she said brightly. "Yeah, Summer's here."

"Oh, good!"

"Yeah, she's been here since lunch yesterday." Rhonda continued before I could say anything more. "We don't get great cell service out here, so she probably didn't get your messages."

"Is she around?"

"She's down at the pool right now, but I'll tell her you called."

"Can you tell her to call me back?"

But she'd already hung up.

The next day, Wendy and I were waiting in the shade of a cabana by her deserted rooftop pool when Summer arrived. She was wearing big sunglasses and a wide-brimmed hat, and I could tell immediately that her energy was off. She started to undo the ties that held the curtains on the pool side of the cabana open, muttering something about wanting privacy.

"Come on, it's hot. We need the breeze," Wendy protested. "And anyway, we're the only people crazy enough to be up here in this heat wave."

Summer looked over her shoulder, sighed, and sat on the edge of my lounger. "Can I get a sip of your water?"

I noticed she was shaking as I handed her the bottle, her normally manicured nails ragged. "What is going on?"

She took a long swill of water. "It's Eric."

"What happened?" Wendy asked.

"He was acting crazy, so I just told him I needed time to think and went to my mom's and turned off my phone." Her words came out too quickly, tumbling over one another. "Then, when I turn it back on this morning, I get this email he'd sent day before yesterday, saying goodbye."

Wendy furrowed her brow. "Goodbye?"

Summer picked at her cuticles intently. "That if he can't be with me, life isn't worth living."

"Wait, *what*?" I gasped.

Unable to sit still, she pushed herself to standing and paced back and forth, cracking her knuckles. "Like, he was gonna kill himself." Her voice shook. "And now I can't get in touch with him. His phone goes straight to voice mail, and the text messages are going through green instead of blue—like his phone is turned off or he's out of range."

No. This couldn't be real. Eric wouldn't kill himself. And certainly not over Summer. I knew he wouldn't.

Or did I? He'd done a lot of things I couldn't necessarily explain. But *this*?

"Oh my God," Wendy said.

"Have you called the authorities?" I asked.

She nodded. "Yeah, I did a couple of hours ago, but it's not a missing persons case until twenty-four hours."

"Can they track his phone or something?" I asked. I was desperate to call him again myself, but of course I couldn't do that in front of Summer.

"It doesn't seem like his phone's on," she said, continuing to pace.

The pressure was building in my chest, constricting my lungs and making it hard to breathe.

"And of course John is flying in from Dubai this weekend just to see me, and I have to act like everything is *fine!*" She choked back a sob, collapsing onto a lounger with her arm over her face. "This is so bad."

My brain simply couldn't accept the idea of Eric committing suicide. It didn't make sense. Unless . . . unless he was the one who had been lying this whole time, and Summer was telling the truth about his protestations of love. "You don't think he really killed himself? I mean, he never struck me as suicidal. He seems too egotistical to kill himself."

Summer sat up. "Are you kidding? Killing yourself is pretty much the most egotistical thing you can do."

No, it couldn't be. A flash of memory—his lips on mine. With a herculean effort, I blinked away my tears and turned my attention to Summer, praying she wouldn't read how upset I was.

"Are you okay?" My voice cracked. "Sorry, I know you're not. This is really upsetting."

Summer wrung her hands. "I feel sick."

"Breathe." My instruction was directed at Summer, but clearly I needed it as badly as she did. "Just breathe. I should call Dylan."

"Have you talked to him recently?" Summer asked.

I shook my head. "We've emailed some. He reached out last time he was in town, but I was in Georgia visiting my parents."

She handed me my phone. "Can you do it now?"

I balked at the phone, watching as my hand reached out to take it from her. My heart was in my throat as I found Dylan's number and pressed call. I heard the double ring of a foreign line and secretly hoped he wouldn't answer so that I could prepare myself better before talking to him. But no such luck.

"Belle." There was a smile in his voice. My stomach tied itself in knots. "How are you?"

"I'm good," I replied robotically. I reached for words, falling back on social custom. "How are you?"

"I'm in France for the next few months, working. I'm sorry I didn't get to see you last time I was in town."

"Me too."

Summer signed for me to get to the point.

"Um, listen." I swallowed. "Have you heard from your brother?"

"We talked last week."

"Did he seem okay?"

"We were fighting." He sighed. "As usual. Ever since I took this job, all we do is fight. But I guess you know that. Why? What's going on?"

"It's just, Summer got a disturbing email from him a few days ago, and now she can't reach him."

"What was it?" he asked.

"I'll let her tell you," I said, afraid my emotions would betray me.

I switched the phone to speaker, and Summer sat next to me and relayed the sequence of events. I peered over her shoulder as she read from the email Eric sent her on July 22 at 2:04 p.m. The messages he'd sent me were almost poetic—all lowercase and full of line breaks and ellipses—but this one was oddly formal, capitalized and punctuated like a term paper. Strange. When she finished, Dylan was silent.

"Dylan?" I asked.

"Yeah, I'm here."

"Do you think he would do it?" Again, he was quiet long enough that I wondered whether the call had dropped. "You still there?"

"Yeah, sorry." He sounded tired. "No. It just doesn't sound like...I can't...But I don't know. I mean, he has an artist's temperament. He's up and down..." Another long pause. "His mom committed suicide. I don't think he ever really got over it."

Suicide. My heart ached for young Eric, eleven and suddenly mother-less. I couldn't read Summer's reaction with the hat and sunglasses obscuring her face, but if she was surprised, she hid it well. Had he shared this tragedy with her? Perhaps their relationship was indeed deeper than he'd made it out to be. I leaned closer to the phone. "Do you think you could help find him?"

"Of course," Dylan said, pulling himself together. "I'm sure there's an explanation for this. Let me see what I can do. Forward that email to me. I'll get back to you."

As I hung up the phone, I felt a prickling sensation at the base of my spine. Something just didn't add up.

Day 6

Thursday evening—Saint-Tropez, France

It's ten to five when we get back to the port. The day is still torrid, and when the boat has not arrived by five thirty, we trudge across the street and take a seat at the restaurant where we had a glass of wine earlier. I guzzle a fizzy water and blot my face with the napkin. I am not looking forward to my "meeting" with John—or seeing Summer, or Wendy, or any of it. If all my stuff weren't on the boat, I'd be more than tempted to just bail, regardless of everything else. But for now I'm stuck. I don't even have my passport.

I'm so distracted by my thoughts that I don't see the *Lion's Den* pull into port. Amythest grabs my arm. "Let's go. We don't want to get left again."

The knot in my stomach tightens as we board the boat. The deck is deserted aside from Dre, who helps me down from the gangplank, whispering, "Sorry about this afternoon. All the crew wanted to wait, but they say no."

I nod. "Thanks. Where is everyone?"

"In their rooms, dressing for dinner."

"I thought we were supposed to be going to drinks with John's friends here at five."

"Change of plans," he says. "Dinner on the boat while we go to Italy. Monsieur Lyons has a meeting there in the morning."

He reels in the gangplank and the boat is moving.

When I reach the room, Amythest is sitting on her bed, phone in hand, giggling.

"What is it?" I ask.

"Just John."

"Seriously?"

She titters. "That bitch thinks she's better than us because she has all this, but it's not hers; it's his. She thinks she has him wrapped around her finger, but it could be me inviting you to come on this trip next year. And I would—I'd invite you. None of the rest of these hoes, but you've been good to me."

"Amythest. You literally just promised me you'd keep your head down and go home without any more drama."

"It's not drama if she doesn't know about it."

I pop my knuckles in frustration. "Just...please be careful," I plead. "You really don't want her to find out. I know you're pissed, but just maybe hold off till we get home. Let's try to make it through the next two days without it becoming a soap opera." Who am I kidding? It's already a soap opera.

"More like a skin flick." She winks.

In the shower, I try to psych myself up for my meeting with John, going over what I plan to say to him. My mind keeps cycling to what I'd actually like to ask him, but I know he wouldn't answer and I'd only jeopardize my own safety. Beyond that, I'm divided about whether I want to get kicked off the boat or stick out the rest of the trip. I have no desire to be here anymore, obviously, but getting fired isn't exactly ideal, either. Surely they would at least give me a plane ticket back if they exiled me?

While I'm washing the conditioner from my hair, Amythest slides open the shower door, already naked. "Camille came by. You have a meeting with John at six thirty."

I wring out my hair. "Fun."

"You should bring me with you."

I reach past her for a towel, and she takes my place in the shower. "I don't want to get you kicked off the boat, too."

"If I get kicked off, I'll get kicked off in style. Don't think I haven't recorded my sessions with John."

"You're kidding." I'm hit with a tidal wave of both horror and pride. Didn't know the girl had it in her.

"Nope," she says proudly. "I recorded everything with my phone. You never know when something like that might be useful. I'm sure he doesn't want the world to know how much trouble he has getting it up. And how nasty he is. I look great, though, so I don't mind. Check it out—my phone's on the bed. My password's 6969."

Of course it is. Do I even want to see this? But I have to know. I can only imagine what John and his goons would do—or worse, Summer. I scroll through her videos folder and click on one featuring an askew angle of the bed I'm sitting on right now. There's something hanging down in the foreground...a purse strap. She'd set up the phone in her purse so John wouldn't suspect. Smart. I cringe to see John's junk on camera.

Amythest strokes him with her bejeweled nails, trying her best to get him hard. She blows him and gets him up to half-mast, then pushes him back on the bed, stuffs him up inside her, and bounces up and down with zeal. After a minute, they have to stop because he can't keep it up.

"How do you want me?" she asks, coquettish.

"Have you ever done a golden shower?" he asks.

My jaw drops. This is too good to believe.

"No," she says.

"It really turns me on," he says. "And girls who turn me on get rewarded nicely."

I can't help but snort with laughter. This is exactly how I would've expected John to talk in bed.

She looks him, at the bed, considering. "But the bed—"

"I'll have someone clean it up."

"Okay." She positions herself above him. "Where do you want me to—"

"On my cock," he says. "I want you to piss all over my cock."

Oh my God. I don't want to see, but my eyes are glued to the screen. *And there it is.*

Wow. I don't want to be the type of person to judge other people's sexual proclivities, but...gross. Does Summer do this, too? I shudder and throw the phone on the bed. There's a good deal more of the video, but I've seen enough. I'm not going to be able to unsee it. Though I do wonder what use it might be.

Amythest may be some kind of nympho, but she's not stupid.

I throw on a dress and run a brush through my hair. Fourteen minutes until the meeting. I realize my nerves must be the effect of my ego, bracing for a hit. But a needy ego is no reason to stay here. So it's decided: I'm done with this charade. I've played my part; I'm ready to take a bow and go home. I'm gonna go up there and politely ask for my passport and a plane ticket. No hard feelings, just goodbye.

I step across the hall and knock on Wendy and Claire's door. Claire answers, wearing a paper face mask made to look like a cat. "Hey," she says, her eyes sympathetic. Then, remembering the mask, she laughs. "Oh. Wendy's making me moisturize."

Wendy's sitting on the bed behind her in a matching face mask, her hair piled on top of her head amid some kind of deep-conditioning treatment. She looks up from the magazine she's reading and waves as though nothing is amiss.

"I'm sorry you got left," Claire says.

"Yeah, me too," I agree, glancing at Wendy, who doesn't meet my eyes. "How did your day go?"

"It was great!" Wendy chirps without looking up from the magazine. "We went to this cove that was absolutely beautiful and swam off the back of the boat and rode Jet Skis." She gestures to her hair. "Ruined my hair though, so I had to wash it. So annoying. What'd you do?"

What the hell is wrong with her? "Nothing much," I say. "Just had lunch, walked around. Did Summer mention anything about having left us?"

Wendy shrugs. "No. She was just having fun."

"It was kinda weird to just leave you in port, then not say anything all day, like nothing happened," Claire says.

"Yeah, she sent me a text telling me how ungrateful I was," I divulge. "I have a meeting with John in a minute. I'm sure I'll get my ass handed to me."

Wendy flips a page in her magazine and continues to read.

"I'm sorry," Claire sympathizes. "I know you didn't mean to be late."

"No. We ran all the way. I texted, but...it seems like Summer has a bigger problem with me. Like she thinks I was intentionally rude or something."

"For what it's worth, I don't think you've been rude," Claire says sweetly. "This whole trip has been different than we expected."

Wendy still doesn't look up from her magazine. "Wendy, has she said anything to you?" I ask.

Wendy shakes her head and gives me a perfunctory smile. What is going on with her? I try a different tactic. "Did she say anything more to you about Leo?"

Again she shakes her head. Clearly, for whatever reason, I won't be getting anything out of her. "Okay, I gotta go meet John. Wish me luck."

"Good luck," Claire says.

Wendy calmly flips to yet another page of celebrity gossip as I back out of the cabin.

The living room is empty when I arrive at exactly six thirty. I fiddle with my watch while I wait for John to arrive, then try to ground myself by taking a deep breath and feeling it all the way down to my feet, like I learned in yoga class. This meeting is nothing I should be afraid of. *Just ask for your passport and a ticket home.* Out the windows, I watch as dark clouds close in, obscuring the evening sun.

When John hasn't arrived by six forty-five, I take a seat in front of the computer and fire up my email. I've been careful to delete every message after I've sent it, so I'm not too worried about Vinny or whoever else poking around in my in-box. I'll just have to watch what I say.

> Writing from the boat—I'm in trouble for returning late after shopping, awaiting the opportunity to apologize to John, which Summer so thoughtfully arranged. Looks like rain tonight. I'm sure rocking seas will do wonders for my seasickness. Heard there may be sea urchin for dinner though, if I'm still

"Isabelle."

I jump and turn to see John, freshly showered and flashing his most disarming smile, designed to throw me off balance, I'm sure.

I hit send without finishing the sentence I was typing and log out of my email as fast as humanly possible, then vault to my feet as he approaches and shake his hand like I'm interviewing for a job. "I apologize for being late today."

He nods coolly, and I follow him to the formal sitting area, where I perch on an uncomfortable chair across from him, hastily explaining what happened with the credit card, substituting myself for Amythest. "I'm so sorry," I conclude, hating myself for groveling. "I didn't mean to be ungrateful or disrespectful. It was an honest mistake."

Strangely, he pats my hand. And then, without addressing anything I have just said, "Summer's always spoken so highly of you. I know you've been friends for a long time, and it can be hard when a friend is taken away by a new relationship. Especially when that friend has been letting you live with her for free."

My brain shorts. Did Summer tell him I was crashing with her and not the other way around? "I'm sorry?"

"You must have a lot of anger toward her, toward me. It's understandable. But Summer invited you here to have fun, and you're not having fun. So maybe it would be best if you went home. I know your sister misses you."

Nothing about him reads as angry or vindictive, but I'm sure I've never mentioned my sister in front of him, which means he wants me to know he's been reading my emails. I stare at him, unsure what to say. A voice in the back of my head reminds me that it doesn't matter, that he's right and it's okay for me to leave now, but I'm too shocked to respond immediately. My ego takes advantage of my hesitation to jump in, wanting to save itself from criticism and make everything okay. "I'm having fun!" I lie.

No, no, this isn't how this is supposed to go! I don't need to please this horrid man. I conjure up the image of his flaccid penis.

Still smiling enigmatically, he again pats my hand. I resist the urge to jerk it away and yell at him not to touch me. "You should ask for her forgiveness, not mine," he says. No part of me wants to eat humble pie for that bitch. "You can do that now."

I slowly rise to my feet, reminding myself of why I'm here. Even if I'm gonna jump ship, I should do so on good terms. "Is she in her room?"

"Go to your room and call her."

I'm kicking myself as I climb down the stairs to my room. What just happened? Why was I so obsequious? What a waste. It was supposed to be my decision to leave. And I didn't ask him for my passport. I totally disregarded my plan. I failed.

"What happened?" Amythest asks when I get back to the room.

"I'm supposed to call Summer to apologize now."

"Lame." She rolls her eyes.

I pick up the handset on the bedside table and hit the button for her room. I'll ask for forgiveness, then tell her I think it's best if I take off, blame it on feeling sick. I've stayed long enough; I don't need to be here anymore. She answers on the first ring. "Hi," I say. "I was just calling to apologize...."

"You don't sound like you're sorry," she charges.

"Honestly," I insist, reminding myself to be nice, to get my passport back. "I didn't mean any disrespect...."

"This is John's boat, and it leaves when he says it does—"

"I got that. Look, I don't know what I did to upset you, but..."

"You've been a nightmare this entire trip," she chides. "You haven't noticed that I've been acting different toward you the past few days?"

"Yeah," I counter, slowly coming back to my senses, "but you've been acting different this entire trip."

"You should have come to me and asked me why I was mad at you."

I take a deep breath. I know it does me no good to blow up at her, but I'm having trouble maintaining my composure. "I didn't know you were mad," I say evenly. "I can't read your mind."

"Maybe if you weren't so wrapped up in yourself, you would have noticed," she snaps. "How am I supposed to feel? I invited you here to have a good time, and you were sulking at lunch yesterday—"

It's like a fun-house version of the conversation I just had with John, only nothing about it is fun. The details of my supposed transgressions on this trip are so petty, so trivial in the face of the bigger picture. Yet my ego wants to argue with her, to convince her that she's the awful one. And then there's the part of me that wants to talk this whole thing out with her, my onetime best friend, to make sense of what has happened between us—not just over the course of this trip, but before. What did I do to make her hate me so?

But it doesn't matter. She's changed, and I have, too. We're no longer compatible as friends; I knew that going into this trip. Riding on jets and yachts may be fun and all, but I can't begin to fathom believing this lifestyle to be worth the sacrifices she's made to obtain it. So I simply apologize, noting that I was sick to my stomach yesterday. But she's not finished cataloging my sins.

"I don't believe you. And you've been hanging out with that whore my sister brought—"

"She's my roommate, who you assigned to me and required I hang with," I return, exasperated.

"And then, last night, singing, drawing attention to yourself—"

"Oh my God." I clench my jaw. "I was having fun, which you literally just said you wanted me to have." I am so tempted to come clean, to tell her everything I know, to torch the house of lies she's built to the ground. But that would only compromise my position. I ball my fists and control my voice. "Look, I'm sorry if I offended you. I didn't mean to. Our friendship has meant a lot to me over—"

"I don't believe you," she interrupts. "I think you should just go home."

"Okay." I must get off the phone before I say anything I'll regret. "I'll just need my passport."

"You can go back upstairs now." She hangs up on me.

Amythest stares at me expectantly. "I'm being sent home," I say.

"Lucky bitch. Hopefully I'm next. What did she say about me?"

"She called you a whore."

She laughs. "Maybe she found the panties."

"I think you'll know if she finds the panties."

I wonder how Amythest will fare on her own once I'm gone, but then I remember the sex tape. She'll be just fine.

When I get back upstairs, Vinny is sitting at the dining room table, scowling at me. My chest is tight as I take a seat across from him.

"You leave tomorrow," he growls. "Out of Genoa. You'll have dinner in your room tonight. A car will pick you up in port tomorrow morning at eight."

I take a breath. At least they're paying for my ticket home. "My passport?"

"Your driver will give it to you with your ticket when you reach the airport tomorrow."

"Why can't I have it now?" I ask, suspicious.

"We hold on to it until you leave."

Now I'm getting freaked out. "I'd like my passport back immediately," I demand as forcefully as I can muster, wiping my sweating palms on my dress.

"No," he refuses. "That's final. Now go to your room."

Blood rushes in my ears. I should keep my trap shut and do as he says, but what the hell. I'm going home tomorrow anyway, and I'm done with being treated like an imbecile and a child. I push myself to standing and fold my arms across my chest, my breath shallow. "You know"—I narrow my eyes, trying to keep my voice steady—"John should be more careful about what he discusses at the dinner table. Not all women are purely ornamental."

Vinny rises to his feet, his movements startlingly sudden. "Don't be stupid. I've warned you once: mind your own business."

"Or what?" I challenge.

He grabs my arm just above the elbow, compressing the flow of blood to my hand. "He sees and hears everything," he hisses in my ear. My eyes slide to the camera just behind his head. "Everything. You know that already. Keep your fucking mouth shut and go to your room."

He drops my arm forcibly, his eyes boring holes into me. My instinct is to resist, but something about the intensity of his admonishment stops me. I could almost imagine it's not a threat at all, but a warning. Which is, of course, all the more alarming. "*Go*," he orders, pointing at the stairwell.

I have no power here. There's nothing for me to do in this moment but comply. Again I descend the stairs to my quarters, my legs jelly.

Back in the room, I'm trembling as I shut and lock the door. Amythest eyes me from her post at the bathroom sink, concerned. "Are you okay? You look like you just saw a ghost."

"It's just Vinny."

She runs a brush through her hair. "He's hella scary."

"Yeah. He——" But I decide the better of recounting his warning. After all, maybe it was nothing. And telling her might bring up questions I don't want to answer. So instead I change the subject. "I'm so glad you bought that dress. It's gorgeous on you." She's decked out in her new mod dress without the purple contacts. Her makeup is toned down, and she really does look fantastic. "I like your natural eye color, too."

She laughs. "It's so *weird*, suddenly my vision is like new. So? What happened up there?"

"Officially canned."

"I can't believe they canned you and not me. I figured she would have found the panties by now and kicked me off the boat. Or killed me." She laughs.

"Not funny. Vinny wouldn't give me my ticket or my passport. Says I'll get it when they drop me at the airport in the morning."

Her eyes go wide. "Damn, that's some gangster shit. I bet Vinny's mafia. These guys are all connected. John was telling me how he's friends with that Italian politician that's always having affairs and is so obviously shady it's like a joke? I can't pronounce his name, but you know the one. He, like, basically owns the country."

"I think I know who you're talking about."

She smears a red stain across her mouth. "Okay." She rubs her lips together. "Time to go poke the bear. What do you think she'll do if there's lipstick on his collar?"

"Amythest." I shake my head. "You just said yourself that he's con-nected to gangsters."

"Yeah, he is. Not her. And he likes me. I'm younger, fresher pussy." She snickers.

"I just think, if it's a rich guy you want, there are plenty of them, and I'm sure you could have any one you want," I implore. "Maybe a younger, richer one even."

I'm not sure exactly why I'm trying to talk her out of it. At this point, I would love for her to steal John from Summer. It would be the ultimate revenge, and Summer sure as hell deserves it. But the whole thing makes me uneasy for Amythest.

"I woulda let it go if she'd been cool, but she's not, and she needs to learn her lesson." She checks the time on her phone. "I gotta go. Dinner's in five. I'll come down after to give you the report." She breezes out the door.

I open the closet and throw my suitcase on the bed, my limbs still viscous from the draining adrenaline. What a colossal mistake coming on this trip turned out to be. At least I'll be home tomorrow. I never want to see Summer again.

(twenty-two days ago)

Los Angeles

The day after Summer returned from Rhonda's, I accompanied her to the Sheriff's Department to make a report. We'd both spent the night at Wendy's and hadn't slept a wink for searching desperately online for clues, coming up with alternatives to what might have happened to Eric. I'd taken the task of sweeping his social media, stealthily deleting all the comments and likes between us, though I did leave our WhatsApp thread, knowing it was encrypted. I messaged him again and again through it, hoping against hope that he'd respond to me. But as the hours wore on, my hope evaporated and guilt for having doubted Summer began to creep in.

At the precinct, I let her do the talking. I tried my best to act like a normal supportive friend, but my facade was gossamer-thin, the tears I couldn't shed in front of her threatening to breach the flimsy barrier at any moment. Given how gutted I felt, I had to accept I'd cared more about Eric than I'd ever allowed myself to understand. But I pushed the thoughts away. It was too late now. Anyway, if nothing else, the events of the past few days had made it painfully clear it was Summer he'd loved after all. I was a fool for ever believing otherwise.

We sat uneasily in the antiseptic pale-green-and-gray lobby with the other unfortunates who found themselves in the waiting room of a police station on a Tuesday afternoon. A woman in the corner wouldn't stop muttering to herself about God and the laws of karma, the chairs were uncomfortable, and I felt like my heart was made of lead. After what seemed like an eternity, the desk agent called Summer's name, and I waited for another eternity while she made her report to an officer in a room down the hall.

By the time Summer emerged puffy-eyed, it was getting dark.

"Can you stay with me at the beach house?" she implored. "John doesn't come back until Friday, and I don't want to be alone."

I did want to be alone. But she needed me, and after everything, I felt I owed it to her. Plus, maybe it would be good to have to hide the depths of my distress for a few more days. "Of course," I agreed.

She'd picked me up on the way to the station, but after making the report, she was tired and asked me to drive the convertible Porsche she'd borrowed from John's garage out to Malibu. She put the top down and leaned her head back, letting the wind whip her hair as we cruised through the canyon and up the coast to the house. When we arrived, she withdrew to her room immediately and closed the door behind her. So much for needing my company.

I trudged up the stairs to the guest room, where I finally undammed the tears I'd been holding back for twenty-four hours. I couldn't imagine the pain Eric must have been in to do what he did, but I still didn't believe that pain had anything to do with his relationship with Summer, regardless of what he may or may not have told her about his mother's suicide. So, what then? Was he suffering from depression? Or had he been diagnosed with some terrible disease I didn't know about? I kept thinking that if I'd known what he was dealing with, I could have done something. I couldn't wrap my mind around it. I wanted to press rewind, go back and save him somehow—but that was impossible.

When I finally slept, my dreams were disrupted by horrific images of Eric killing himself in violent ways: a shotgun under his chin, brains splattered on the shower wall; a silent fall from the Golden Gate Bridge, his imperceptible splash into the frigid water beneath; a handful of pills and a bottle of Jack, vomit foaming from his mouth.

I woke panting and lay staring at the ceiling, wishing the past few days had only been a dream. I revisited the hour we spent together on the roof the night I first met him, then the rainy winter day in his loft, remembering the light in his eyes, imagining different outcomes. If Summer had never come into the picture, what might have happened? Would he still be alive?

Again I cried myself to sleep, plunging into nightmares that he was drowning while I swam after him in the ocean, pulled farther and farther out to sea by the riptide. Summer waved at us from the shore, then turned her back and walked away.

The next morning, I woke up late to find a voice mail from Dylan saying to call him as soon as possible. My throat was tight as I dialed the number, but it only rang and rang. Downstairs, I poured myself a cup of coffee and joined Summer out on the deck.

The day was still, the sea like glass. She stood at the railing, staring out at the waves lapping at the shore, oddly calm. "I really like it here," she said.

"It's beautiful," I agreed.

She turned to me, and I saw she was as hollowed out as I was, her emotions exhausted. "I've cried so much I don't have any tears left."

Me too, I wanted to say. "It's okay." I squeezed her hand. "I understand."

"No you don't," she muttered. And then quickly, "I'm sorry. I'm just emotional. Thank you for being so supportive."

"I'm here for you."

"My mom's gonna come out today," she continued. "I'd like to spend some time with her before John gets here Friday. I ordered a car to take you back to the city."

"Okay." I didn't mind the dismissal, relieved to be able to go home without making up an excuse. "When will it be here?"

"It's here," she said. "Waiting in front. I didn't want to wake you."

In the car, I gazed out the window at the sea, unsettled. I was upset about Eric, yes, horribly. But underneath it all was the sense that something still didn't feel right about all of this. I couldn't put my finger on it, but it all seemed a little too easy. Too . . . anticlimactic or something.

Probably just a symptom of my anguish. Disbelief. Wasn't that one of the stages of grief?

I tried to reach Dylan again, to no avail.

When I got home, I took a hot shower to clear my head, letting the almost scalding water run down my body, breathing in the steam. I made myself another cup of coffee and settled at the table in my cheery yellow kitchen, looking out at the palm trees and the mountains, then opened my laptop and typed "missing persons California."

A website popped up that listed all of the missing persons in California, with their photographs and information, organized by date. Two yesterday, one three days ago, one four days ago, two six days ago, all from different counties. I was astounded by the number of missing people, but none of them was Eric.

So I looked up the coroner's office, did a search with his name and age. Nothing. But then, maybe he wasn't in the system yet. We had only reported it yesterday.

I dialed Dylan's number again. This time he answered, his voice hoarse.

"Belle, I'm sorry, I'll have to make it quick. I'm getting on a plane."

"Okay," I said.

He took a deep breath. "They found his rental car at a park in Ventura. They're searching the park now."

My heart sank. "Oh." Then, "Was there anything in it? His personal stuff? A note?"

"No note," Dylan said. "No wallet or phone."

"Do you really think he killed himself?" I asked.

He paused. "Maybe."

"What makes you unsure?" I asked, hopeful.

He sighed. "That email. It wasn't the way he writes." So I wasn't crazy. He'd picked up on it, too. "And no offense to your friend. I'm sure she's a lovely girl—"

"Summer," I said.

"Yeah, Summer—but he wasn't in love with her. Sure, he and I hadn't talked much recently, but still—I've seen him in love before. This is not what it looks like." I stifled the impulse to ask what it did look like. "So it's really fucking hard to imagine he would kill himself over her," he concluded.

"I know," I agreed. "I didn't know him nearly as well as you obviously, but their relationship always seemed—casual. On his end, anyway."

"But I don't like any of the alternatives, either."

"What alternatives?" I asked.

"There were things—he may have gotten mixed up in...." He paused, catching himself. "I don't know. I'm trying to find out as much as I can."

Mixed up in? Again I was reminded of how little I actually knew of Eric. "Like what?" I asked.

"I can't...I'm sorry. It's probably nothing. Forget I said anything."

"I thought the email was strange, too," I said. "If you need help—"

"No," he cut in. "I don't want you anywhere near this. And like I said, it's probably nothing. I just wish I knew better what was going on with him. If he hadn't been so damn stubborn about our dad..."

"But that's just him, right? Full of ideals, principles—"

"Yeah," he scoffed. "And I've always been the one in the real world."

I floundered for words, taken aback by his cynicism. But of course he was feeling bad; he'd just lost his brother. His brother, who was nothing if not defined by his ideals and principles. My instinct was to defend Eric, but I knew that would do no good. And so I simply said, "I'm sorry you're going through this, Dylan."

I heard voices in the background. "Yeah," he said. "Me too. I have to go. I'll let you know when I hear anything."

"Okay. Thank you."

I hung up the phone, suddenly feeling very alone. The kitchen darkened; I looked out the window to see thunderheads converging above the mountains, blocking the sun. I knew the fact that Dylan was suspicious, too, should make me feel better about my own doubts, but it only aggravated my sense of helplessness. What could he have meant by Eric getting mixed up in something? Drugs? But Eric wasn't a druggie, and he didn't seem to be in need of the money he might make dealing them. I wondered if Summer had knowledge of whatever it was. . . . Perhaps this thing he was mixed up in was what she'd been hiding at the beach house when she was fighting with him. A part of me wanted to call her and tell her what Dylan said, perhaps give her a reason to hope, too. But I still didn't trust her. Whatever was going on, she already knew more than she was letting on, and she'd chosen not to share it with me.

I swallowed the lump in my throat, slathered a piece of bread in peanut butter, and placed it in the toaster oven, watching through the glass door as it bubbled. But when the oven dinged, I found I had no appetite.

I could almost see Eric lingering in my doorway, the morning sun in his eyes, not two months ago. He was so full of life.

I blinked away the vision and forced myself to eat the damn toast. Casting about for a distraction, I addressed the heap of mail on my kitchen table. Circulars, bills, political mailers, a wedding invitation . . . and a parking ticket. Strange. I hadn't gotten a parking ticket lately, at least that I was aware of. After once getting the boot on my car for failing to pay a pile of tickets during college, I'd become a meticulous sign reader.

I opened the envelope and read the citation: ninety-seven dollars for failure to display a valid parking pass at California State Park number 24476 on July 22 at 1:42 p.m.

It had to be a mistake. I hadn't been to any state parks lately. But the license plate and car description matched mine.

I opened my laptop and entered the park number. A map popped up, showing a park about two miles inland from the beach in Ventura County. My heart dropped.

July 22. I had a sinking feeling about what day that was, but pulled up my calendar to be sure. I was right: July 22 was this past Saturday. The day Summer borrowed my car to go to her mother's house in the desert, the opposite direction of Ventura. The day Eric went missing.

Day 6

Thursday night—somewhere off the coast of Italy

I'm nearly finished packing when there's a knock on my cabin door. I open it to Camille, who holds a dinner tray, a sympathetic look in her eyes. I tuck my hair behind my ear, trying to look less rattled than I feel. "I guess I'm the one stuck here this time," I joke. She doesn't seem to catch my meaning right away, though, so I add, more seriously, "I sent the money."

She sets the tray on my bed as I rifle through my wallet for the receipt and hand it to her.

"*Merci beaucoup,*" she says, her eyes reddening again. She takes a breath. "I'm sorry you eat in your room. If you want, there is *un petit* crew deck, opposite the upper deck. Guests not allowed, but no one will see. We serve tonight. If you go there, you will be alone."

"Wow, thank you," I say. "That sounds a lot better than being stuck in here all night. My seasickness isn't great down here, even with medicine."

She smiles, indicating the door at the end of the hallway. "The crew door is open. Take the stairs to the top."

"I will. That is so kind of you."

After she leaves, I sit on my bed to eat my dinner, ruminating about what I could have done differently this week, but I can't come up with anything that would have made a difference. Regardless of whether I'd remained completely sober at Marlena's birthday party and been three minutes earlier to meet the boat today, I have a

245

feeling Summer would've just come up with another reason to find fault with me.

I'm almost finished with dinner when Amythest opens the door and slips inside, checking that no one is in the hallway before closing the door behind her. "Hey." She's on edge, whispering, her teeth stained purple with wine.

"How'd dinner go?"

"Well, first off, Brittani cornered me on the way up the stairs and chewed me out for the way I've been acting, said I was ungrateful and had embarrassed her and she wished she'd never brought me here."

Brittani, embarrassed? "Why was she mad at you?"

"Because her sister's giving her shit for bringing me, I'm sure."

"But what is she saying you've done wrong? Brittani doesn't know about John, does she?"

"She does now." Amythest smirks.

I'm incredulous. "You *told* her?"

She laughs. "She thinks she's better than me just because her sister's screwing a billionaire? Well, I am, too, so fuck her."

Oh God. "And then what happened?" I ask, fearing the worst.

"I mean, dinner was pretty uneventful. John wasn't there. Summer was trying to act like everything was normal, but everybody was real quiet. It was weird that you weren't there. Then Brittani made some comment about how if Summer was going to banish you, she should banish me, too. I'm sure she was saying it just to try to get back on Summer's good side, but Summer got upset and said she makes her own decisions and not to tell her what to do."

"Brittani used the word 'banish'? I'm impressed."

She nods. "All right in front of me, like I wasn't there. Then, after we finished dinner, I saw Brittani whispering with Summer. Everybody was going to the front of the boat to watch the sunset, but I snuck away to come down here. Summer followed me down the stairs and grabbed my arm so hard it's bleeding." She displays her arm.

I inspect the little red half-moons around her elbow. "Damn."

"And she said to 'stay away from my man, you little whore,' and I said 'Or what?' and she said 'You don't wanna mess with me,' and then she went upstairs."

I press the heels of my hands into my eyes. This whole trip has been like *The Real Housewives* on a boat, only there's no television crew to mediate, and I have a terrible feeling it's not going to turn out however Amythest thinks it is.

She paces the small room like it's a cell. "I need a fucking cigarette so fucking bad right now."

I sit on the bed. "So Summer knows."

"Oh yeah, she knows."

I rub my temples, my head suddenly throbbing. "Amythest, I'm sorry, but what the hell were you thinking? You need to go right back and say it was a bad joke or something."

"Are you fucking kidding me?" She snorts.

"I guess you'll be coming home with me tomorrow." If she's lucky. This is not good. I have to say something. But can I trust her to keep her mouth shut?

"Doubt it. He wants me to meet him in his office later so we can fuck. He sure is horny for someone who can't get it up without a pill."

"It's a power thing for him," I say. "Everything's about power with him."

"Anyway, I don't think she's said anything to him about me yet."

"I doubt she's gonna say anything to him," I venture. "She wants to hold on to her position. She doesn't want to sink the ship."

I watch Amythest prowl back and forth in the small space like a caged animal. She's spoiling for a fight, but there's no way this ends well for her. "Why don't you just chill with me tonight?" I suggest. "Camille told me there's a hidden crew deck. I was gonna go up there and hang out. And I bet if you told Brittani that you wanted to go home, she'd make the case to Summer, which would give her an excuse to get John to get you a ticket to go back tomorrow without having to confront him about hooking up with you."

She considers. "No. I'm gonna go back up there."

"Why? What do you think is going to happen?"

She shrugs. "She thinks she's better than me, but she's not. I want to make her as uncomfortable as she's made me."

I try a different tactic. "You know you're in the wrong here," I point out. "You're sleeping with her boyfriend on a trip she invited you on."

"She didn't invite me. Brittani did. And he's married to someone else, so what the shit did she expect?" she scoffs. "Like I said, if she woulda been nice, I woulda left it alone. But she wasn't, so this is what she gets."

And here we are again. I bite my lip. It's now or never. "Here's the thing," I say. "You know how Summer's ex committed suicide?"

She nods. "I didn't know it was a suicide."

I take a deep breath. "That's just it.... It wasn't." I exhale.

Her dark eyes go wide. "Are you saying she killed him?"

"Something like that," I say quietly.

"What?" She stares at me, unglued. "Oh my God. How do you know—does she know you know?"

I shake my head. "I don't know. It's not—" I'm already regretting telling her. "Please don't say anything to her."

"This is insane. She's insane." She's pacing again. "Wait—why are you—"

"Amythest," I cut in. "I've already said too much."

"But you can't just drop that. You have to tell me—"

"I can't," I say. Suddenly my head is throbbing, swimming with images of microphones planted throughout the room. Please God, let me only be being paranoid. "I really can't. You just have to trust me. And no one knows about this—not Wendy, not anybody. So please—please, don't say anything to anyone. Promise me."

She squeezes my hand. "Okay, okay! I promise I won't say anything. But I can't promise I won't bug you for more info later tonight. And I can't promise I won't see John."

My heart sinks. She rises and smooths her hair in the mirror, her gold earrings glinting in the light. I wish I had some way to protect her from Summer, and from herself. I suddenly have an idea. I slip the gold watch from my wrist for the first time on this whole trip and hold it out to her. "It'll look perfect with your dress," I offer. "And it's a *fuck you* to Summer from me. She wanted to try it on, but I wouldn't let her. This way she'll know I've got your back."

She slides it over her wrist with a smile. "Thank you." She blows me a kiss and slams the door behind her. As soon as she's left, I notice her cell phone lying on her bed. I quickly grab it and poke my head into the hall. "Amythest!"

Nothing. I start up the stairs. "Amythest? Your phone!"

No reply. I don't want to go any farther for fear of running into Summer or one of the goons, so I turn around and nearly collide with Bernard, coming out of his room. I instinctually hide the phone behind my back and move to the side of the hallway to let him pass, lowering my eyes. He points to my quarters, and I dutifully step inside, praying he doesn't lock my door. I give him a minute to ascend the stairs, then slip out of my room and through the door to the crew area.

The hallway on the staff side is tighter than the hallway on our side, and the rooms are packed closely together. I poke my head into the laundry room, where Camille is ironing sheets, and she looks up and smiles. Across the hall, Hugo and Dre are having a laugh over dinner in the tiny crew kitchen.

I take the stairs at the end of the corridor two at a time, all the way up, up, up to the door at the top, and push it open, stepping onto a deck about the size of my apartment balcony. We must have started the trip to Italy, because we're moving faster than usual. Or maybe it just feels that way from up here. The sky is wild and red with the setting sun, the ocean breeze refreshing as the boat cuts through the sea.

I lean over the railing and peer below. I'm on the front side of the sundeck directly above the upper deck. I can barely hear the other girls' voices above the noise of the engine and water. I try to pick out the tone of the group, but it all blends with the sound of the motor and the water into a kind of contented, soothing murmur. I wish I could see, but I would have to lean out farther than I'm comfortable doing at this speed to spy on them.

I turn and gasp when I see Camille behind me with a glass of wine. "Sorry," I say. "You startled me." I take the glass, considering whether one of the goons could have somehow spiked it. "This may sound odd, but did you pour this yourself?" I ask.

She nods. "You need anything else?" she asks.

"This is perfect, thank you. Just let me know if they come looking for me."

She nods and goes back inside. I sink into the lounger and take a tentative sniff of my wine. The wine smells fine—great, even—but I still decide the better of drinking it, just in case, and set it on the table next to my chair.

Golden cliffs rise dramatically from the sea, their peaks crowned with little villages that must have been there hundreds of years, though I can't imagine how some of them were built. I'm not sure how long we've been moving at this clip, or whether we've reached Italy, but the coast is less crowded wherever we are. We pass a few yachts and cruise ships, but nothing like the traffic around Saint-Tropez. I lay my head back and watch the sky slowly darken.

I wake with a start to the sound of arguing. It's dark and I'm disoriented, unsettled by a vivid dream of falling into deep water, unable to reach the surface. How long have I been asleep? I look at my empty wrist, remembering Amythest has my watch—but her phone is still in my pocket. I check the time—nearly eleven We're still moving at a good clip, and there's a chill on the wind. I could use a sweater.

The moonless night is lit only by the stars; I can't see the line where the sky meets the sea. There are no boats or towns on the horizon, but I can feel the ocean heaving beneath us as we plow through the water. We must be farther out than usual, still moving quickly toward Italy.

A spike in the conversation below. Two female voices. I can only imagine it's Amythest and...someone. Brittani or Summer, most likely. I've never once heard Claire raise her voice, and Wendy's not one to argue. It could be Rhonda, but the voices sound younger. I try to make out what they're saying, but the words are drowned out by the sound of the boat.

I edge over to the railing, straining to see below without leaning out too far. The boat pitches over the rolling sea, and I brace myself, holding tightly to the railing.

A third voice rises above the wind.

"*Summer!*" That, I think, is Rhonda. "Leave...not worth..." The rest is lost.

The voices quiet down. I struggle to catch another phrase or even a word, but it's all too muffled. They must have moved to the other side of the boat. I might as well go back to the room and finish packing. I'm sure Amythest will fill me in later.

Before I can open the door, a scream rips into the silence. Just one scream, bloodcurdling. A thump, the sound of something hitting the boat, and the scream stops abruptly. I listen for anything further, but all I hear is the sound of the boat cutting through the water.

I fling open the door and dash down the stairs two at a time until I reach the crew quarters. I burst into the kitchen, where most of the crew is eating dinner.

"I heard a scream," I cry. "I think it was on the bow side of the upper deck. And I thought I heard something hitting the boat."

Immediately all crew members are on their feet and pushing past me, dinner abandoned. I follow on their heels, my orders to stay in my room forgotten.

"There was arguing," I add as we cut through the empty living room, "but I'm not sure who it was."

Half the crew splits off toward the bridge, and the rest of us race out the doors, up the spiral stairs, and around the side of the boat to the bow of the upper deck. As we come around the corner, I see a pool of dark-red liquid on the deck and gasp before I notice the remains of a shattered wineglass rolling with the pitch of the boat. It's only red wine.

Summer, Rhonda, Brittani, Wendy, and Claire are huddled against the wall looking shell-shocked. Claire is sobbing softly into Wendy's shoulder, while Brittani and Rhonda have their arms around Summer, crying tearlessly into her wine.

Amythest is missing.

The boat lurches forward as it slows suddenly, sending us all scrambling for something to brace against. The exterior lights go on, illuminating the inky depths below.

"What happened?" Julie asks.

The other women look at each other in stunned silence before anyone speaks.

"Amythest...she...just fell in," Rhonda finally says.

Julie speaks into her headset. "Man overboard." Then, urgently to Rhonda, "Where? How long ago?"

Rhonda points at the railing just past us. "It just happened."

Julie speaks into her headset. "Man overboard, starboard bow, deck two. Man overboard. One to two minutes."

"She can't swim," I say.

Everyone looks at me.

"She told me on the plane over here."

I hear a tender splash into the water behind the boat, followed by another two splashes in rapid succession. Then the engines of the tender and Jet Skis fire up and speed off. The boat begins to slowly turn. I follow Camille to the railing where Amythest fell and look over.

We both see the streak of deep red smeared down the side of the boat at the same time. My hand flies to my mouth. This streak is not wine. My heart sinks like a stone.

Julie leans over and looks, then speaks into her headset. "PIW injured, most likely unconscious."

I see something glint and kneel down next to where Amythest went overboard. Half of a bedazzled red nail rests on a fresh deep scratch in the wood. I feel the eyes of the other girls on me as I point it out to Camille and Julie.

"What happened?" Julie asks.

"She was drunk." Summer folds her arms across her chest. "She just fell over. None of us could get to her in time. It happened so fast."

Julie studies the railing. "What was she doing before she fell? It's a high railing to fall over."

Wendy and Claire huddle together against the wall in stunned silence with their arms around each other, watching the exchange.

"She was playing on it," Summer says. "We told her not to, but she did it anyway, and she fell."

"Which way did she fall?" Julie asks.

"Over," Brittani snaps, choking on her tears. "Can you just fucking go get her?"

"Brittani—" Rhonda warns, grabbing her arm.

"Frontward or backward?" Julie asks. She's trying desperately to maintain an air of composure, but I notice her hands are shaking.

"I don't know!" Summer retorts. "She's in the water, and you should be saving her, but you're just standing here asking stupid questions. It's gonna be your fault if she dies." She buries her head in her hands, and Rhonda puts her arms around her.

"Don't worry, ma'am. We're trained for this sort of thing," Julie says evenly. "Let's get you all inside while we wait for the Coast Guard."

"Where's John?" Summer asks. "He knows people. He can get the best people out here."

In the living room, we find John and Vinny waiting for us with a couple of the other crew members. Summer rushes into John's arms, crying, "Oh, it's just terrible! I saw her go over, and I couldn't do anything!"

Wendy and Claire huddle together on one couch; Rhonda and Brittani cluster on the other. I take a seat next to Wendy and give her a little hug. She's trembling.

"Are you okay?" I ask.

She nods. "Shock, I think."

I reach across her and pat Claire's knee. She looks at me and bursts into a fresh round of tears.

Brittani pops up and paces between the two couches, cracking her knuckles. "Fuck, fuck, fuck, fuck, fuck..." she repeats over and over.

"Brittani, sit down," Summer orders. "You're making it worse."

Brittani drops onto the couch beside her mother, continuing to wring her hands. Rhonda rubs her back, whispering something in her ear, then flags down Hugo. "Can we get some more of that panna cotta?" she asks. "I think everyone could use a distraction."

Hugo blinks, as though unsure he's heard correctly. "Let me see what I can do."

Summer's gaze darts about the room, landing briefly on each of the other girls as though clocking their emotional state.

"And coffee," Rhonda adds. "I bet we're gonna be up awhile, and I could fall asleep sitting up right now."

"That's a good idea," Summer says. "I'll take a double vanilla latte with almond milk and only half the amount of vanilla you usually put in. And a sprinkle of cinnamon."

"Anyone else?" Hugo asks.

"Bring a pot of coffee," John instructs, "and the rest of the panna cotta."

Summer excuses herself to change into something more comfortable, and as she moves past me, I notice the strap of her dress is ripped, holding on by a thread. On her shoulder is a long scratch, raised and red, the lower end dotted with fresh blood. John follows her back to their room, leaving the rest of us to sit staring at one another.

Brittani hops back up and resumes pacing while muttering expletives, her mother looking on nervously. Wendy strokes a still silently sobbing Claire's hair, her eyes downcast.

Out on the water, a siren grows closer.

"That must be the Coast Guard," I remark.

Brittani narrows her eyes at me. "I thought you were supposed to be in your room. What are you doing up here?"

"I heard the scream and was worried," I say, exasperated.

Brittani cocks her head, unconvinced. "You heard the scream all the way from your room?"

Anger simmers in my chest. "Why do you even care right now?" I retort. "Your friend is literally dying somewhere under this boat."

Brittani bursts into tears and runs toward the back of the boat.

"Brittani—" I chase after her, catching her arm before she can push open the sliding glass doors to the deck. "I'm sorry. I'm just upset."

She wrests her arm away from me, her clumpy black mascara streaked down her face. "No you're not. She was *my* friend. I'm so glad my sister is sending you home tomorrow. You're such a selfish bitch."

Before I can come up with a reply, the deck doors slide open and two men in Italian Coast Guard uniforms enter, almost on top of us.

Brittani and I step out of the way. "Did you guys find her?" Brittani asks immediately. "Is she dead?"

Rhonda rushes over and puts her arm around Brittani. "I'm sorry. We're all worried. Do you have any news?"

They look at us, nonplussed. "No English," one of them says.

"*Italiano?*" the other offers.

Everyone stares at them blankly.

"*Uno . . . minuto.*" I'm sure I'm butchering the Italian, but I hold up a finger to demonstrate my meaning.

I head for the bridge to find a crew member who speaks Italian, but run headlong into Summer coming back from her room, dressed in white jeans and a light cashmere sweater, her shoulders covered, her face freshly washed.

"Where are you going?" she demands.

"To get someone who can speak Italian," I reply. I have no time for her bullshit right now.

"John can speak Italian," she snaps. "Go back and sit down."

I stand my ground, glaring at her. "Can you get him now? Time is of the essence, no?"

Just then, the wiry technical engineer comes around the corner. "Luc," I say. "Do you speak Italian?"

He nods. "A little."

"Can you please come translate for the Coast Guard?"

Summer bores into me with her death stare, but I ignore her. She grabs his arm. "No," she says. "She is not your master. I am, and I say—"

"No one is his *master*, Summer! What the fuck is wrong with you?"

John comes around the corner and immediately assesses the situation.

"Isabelle, go back to your quarters," he says. "You weren't there. You don't have any information the Coast Guard needs. Summer, come with me."

He steers her back toward their room as I exit in the direction of the stairs, but instead of turning to descend, I proceed past the stairwell to where the others wait in the living area, confirming that Luc is behind me as I enter. Rhonda and Brittani now sit on the couch with Claire and Wendy, all of them obviously exhausted, the Coast Guard officers hovering above them. Everyone looks at me warily.

"I've been told to go back to my room," I announce to the Coast Guard men, "but I'd like to make a statement." Then to Luc. "Translate, please."

My heart hammers in my chest while Luc translates and the men confer in rapid Italian. Finally Luc nods. "They say tomorrow."

I can tell I am about to be dismissed, so I decide to just play my cards. "There are cameras everywhere." I point out the cameras in the room. I know the feed is likely already deleted, but someone should at least be looking. "You should check them."

I turn my back and march down the stairs. I'm shaking as I push open the door to my room and almost jump out of my skin when I see Bernard there, going through Amythest's stuff. He's holding a black canvas bag and throwing things into it.

"What are you doing?" I stammer.

"We need to find her phone to notify next of kin."

Bullshit. We filled out contact info for next of kin on the NDAs we signed on the plane. I have her phone in my back pocket, but I'm not about to tell him that. "She probably had it on her," I say, trying to sound nonchalant. "She always had it on her."

He grunts and leaves. It's not until after he's walked out that I notice *my* phone is missing from the bedside table. Motherfucker.

I dart out the door and up the stairs, catching him on the landing of the upper deck with the black bag slung over his shoulder. Everyone turns to look at us. I register that John and the Coast Guard aren't in the room as I hold my hand out to him. "I think you accidentally took my phone."

He doesn't budge.

"The phone you took is mine, not Amythest's," I insist, keeping my voice steady but loud enough for everyone to hear. "It's in that bag and I need it back, please."

He holds his hands up. "I didn't take any phone."

I turn to the others, watching me wordlessly with guarded eyes. "He was in my room looking for Amythest's phone, and I think he accidentally took mine instead," I assert. "Unless one of you has it? Because it's gone."

No one replies.

"You probably misplaced it, Isabelle," Summer says icily. "We've all been through something very traumatic tonight. Can you please take this drama about your phone elsewhere?"

I want to rip the diamonds from her ears, knock her out, and mop the floor with her overprocessed hair, but I bury my rage and stomp down the stairs to my cell, angry with myself for acting like a child.

I lock the door and stand in the middle of the room, unmoored. I know I should be doing something right now, but I don't know what. My phone is gone, my watch is at the bottom of the sea with poor Amythest—God, I hope that wasn't the cause of her argument with Summer. I should never have given it to her. I need to think clearly, be smart. But I feel the walls closing in, and I'm starting to panic.

(twenty-one days ago)

Los Angeles

I lay in the bath, submerged in hot water, staring into the flame of a serenity-scented candle while rain drummed steadily on the roof of my apartment. It was past midnight and the bubbles were all gone, yet my mind was still miles from the tranquility required for sleep.

I hadn't breathed a word to a soul about the parking ticket I'd received in the mail that morning and was yet to come up with any explanation for it that didn't point to Summer's lying about going to her mom's house and instead heading to Ventura, where Eric's car had been found. But why? What was she doing in Ventura?

Did she kill Eric?

It was a leap—but not an implausible one. Though why would she do such a thing? Would she go so far as to take his life simply to prevent him from revealing their involvement to John? I couldn't wrap my head around it. Still, the Summer I'd known had died the night Three raped her. Her loss of integrity had of course already been an ongoing affair by that point, but he'd pounded the last bit of humanity out of her and now I could believe her capable... of anything, really.

So let's say she *did* kill him, and that she'd done it at the park. What proof was there? It was my car that was linked to the scene of the crime. And I had no alibi. At 1:42 p.m. on July 22, I was home alone, talking to no one, doing nothing that would have been recorded.

I couldn't shake the feeling that Summer had known what she was doing, borrowing my car. And that she wanted me to know the danger I would be putting myself in if I raised any questions about Eric's death.

Above the sound of the rain I heard a thumping. I sat up in the tub, listening. A branch on the roof? But it was more like a knocking. Maybe it was the neighbors downstairs. But there it was again over the low rumble of thunder, louder. Someone was knocking on my door.

Who on earth? I launched out of the tub and quickly dried myself, pulled on a bathrobe, and tiptoed into the living room, where the rapping continued. I crept to the door and put my eye to the hole.

A charge scorched through my veins. A man stood outside, backlit and wearing a black hoodie, his body contorted in what looked like pain. Or he could be hiding a gun. Regardless, I wasn't opening the door.

"Belle," he called, his voice hoarse and low.

So it was a man who knew me, or knew where I lived, anyway.

"I know you're there," he whispered.

"Go away," I said. "I'm calling the police."

"Please open the door. Please."

His voice was muffled but familiar, though I couldn't quite place it.

"Who is it?"

"Eric," he said.

My heart stopped. Was this guy messing with me? Did someone know my car was in that park in Ventura?

I put my eye to the hole. "Push back your hoodie."

"My face is fucked." He pushed back the hoodie, revealing shorn blond hair, but he was still so backlit that I couldn't see him well.

"Step into the light."

He stepped into the glow of the porch light. His face was swollen and covered in scratches, his head shaved. But it was Eric.

Eric was alive.

I opened the door. He limped past me into the apartment, then with great effort reached over me to shut the door and bolt it. I stood staring at him as he stumbled to the windows and pulled all the curtains shut, dripping all over the rug.

"I thought you were dead." I blinked away tears, trembling.

He shivered. "Almost."

Finally he turned to me, revealing the full damage to his face. His jaw was swollen, both of his eyes were black, and his nose was probably broken; blood seeped through the flimsy Band-Aids that held together the deep gash in his right cheek.

I moved toward him cautiously. "Take that off. You're soaking wet."

He flinched as I unzipped his hoodie. "I think my collarbone is broken. And some ribs."

"Okay, we'll go slow."

He winced as I gently pulled the sleeve of his sweatshirt over his swollen hand. "Probably broke my hand, too."

"Have you been to the doctor?"

"No."

I eased the sweatshirt over his distended shoulder, revealing gashes on his arms that bisected his tattoos. "We need to get you to a doctor ASAP." I cast a glance around for my cell phone. "I'm calling an ambulance."

"No."

"Eric, you're in bad shape. These wounds could get infected. Your bones won't heal properly if they're not set...."

He swayed, unsteady. I helped him onto the couch, and he crumpled like a paper bag. "You can help me."

"Eric, don't be insane."

"Please," he begged. "You have to help me."

I bent and unlaced his muddy boots, noticing one of his ankles was enlarged. "What happened to you?"

"Your message." He closed his eyes. "I went. She was there.... She..."

"Summer was there?" I inferred. "Where? What did she do?"

He raised his feet up onto the couch with a groan. "I'll tell you everything in the morning."

So I was right. But what message? It took every ounce of my

willpower not to question him further, but he looked so pitiful. "You can sleep in my bed," I said, backing off. "I'll take the couch."

"Don't wanna move anymore," he mumbled.

I gave him a Percocet left over from when I sprained my ankle, cleaned and rebandaged his face wound, then covered him with a blanket. He was fast asleep before I could even turn out the light.

Day 7

Friday early morning—somewhere off the coast of Italy

I pace my tiny room in a cold sweat, heart hammering in my chest. I'm nearly certain Amythest is dead. The speed we were going, the blood on the side of the boat, her inability to swim—each fact a nail in her coffin.

But Summer's explanation that she was drunk and playing on the railing? That feels patently false. She wasn't drunk when I saw her an hour before, and she was deathly afraid of the water since she couldn't swim, so I highly doubt she would do something to put her in danger of accidentally falling in.

Besides, there's the arguing I heard beforehand. Who else could it have been but Summer and Amythest? I guess it could have been Brittani and Amythest, but it's unlikely. Brittani's not smart enough to have lengthy arguments. She'd leave it at "you're a whore" and think she'd won.

And that scream. Bloodcurdling. I can't get it out of my mind. It was a call for help. And it failed.

Chills run down my spine.

Summer pushed Amythest. I know it in my bones. With her history . . .

Through the open bathroom door, I catch my reflection in the mirror above the sink. I look unhinged: eyes haunted, jaw clenched, hair wild. It's probably a good thing I wasn't allowed to give a statement tonight. No one would have believed a word I said. Of course, I have to face the reality that they may not believe me regardless of how credibly I present myself.

But the cameras... The cameras will have captured it all. I wonder how quickly the footage can be destroyed. And who will do that? Bernard? The IT guy? John himself? Ultimately, how much does John know? How much bad behavior will he tolerate from his mistresses? And what of the other girls? They were there. They must have seen the whole thing. And they're keeping silent.

Maybe they're waiting to tell the police in private. Surely there will be an investigation. We'll pull into the nearest marina, and the police will interview everyone, collect evidence. She can't get away with it. You can't just murder someone in front of five people and expect to walk free.

Or maybe, on John's boat, you can.

At least I still have Amythest's phone. I extract it from my pocket and punch in her passcode, checking that the videos of her and John are still there. If only there were Wi-Fi on this damn boat, I could email them to myself.

But I can plug her phone into my computer and at least back them up. I reach into the bag next to the bed where I keep my computer, but come up empty-handed. I pull the bag into my lap and open it. My books are there, my earbuds, my wallet, but my computer is gone.

I tear the bed apart. I turn the room upside down. Nothing. Bernard must've taken my computer, too.

I step across the hall and knock on Wendy and Claire's door. Wendy opens it a crack and peers at me expectantly.

"Hey," I say. "How are you guys?"

Over her shoulder, I see Claire curled up in a ball on top of her bed.

"Really shaken up," Wendy says without opening the door any farther. But amazingly, she doesn't look that shaken up. She's in yellow silk pajamas, her face washed, her hair neatly wrapped in a matching silk scarf. Her eyes aren't even puffy. But then, Wendy's eyes are never puffy.

"Can I come in?"

"Aren't you supposed to stay in your room?"

I furrow my brow. "C'mon, Wen. I know I wasn't there, but I'm also shaken up. I probably spent more time with her than any of you, and now she's dead."

"We don't know she's dead," Wendy says, crossing her arms.

"Okay. So what do we know? What's the Coast Guard doing?"

"There's a search-and-rescue team looking for her."

"And are the men still upstairs?" I ask.

"They left so we could get some sleep. They'll be back tomorrow to brief us."

"We're not, like, stopping at a port so they can investigate?"

Wendy wrinkles her nose. "Investigate what? She fell. Listen, Belle, I'm upset, too, but—"

"So, did they interview everyone about what happened, or...?"

She sighs, growing impatient. "John talked to them and told them what happened. He's the only one who speaks Italian."

"But he wasn't even there," I protest. "Didn't you want to talk to them?"

"Belle, it was an accident," she insists. "She fell in. She's in the water. They'll find her or they won't, but me talking to the Coast Guard isn't going to do anything. Look, we're really tired and upset. Can we talk in the morning?"

I squint at her, trying to work out where she's coming from. "I'm sorry," I say with as much patience as I can muster. "I'm just trying to understand what's going on. Are you sure she just fell in? You saw it happen?"

"Yes." Wendy eyes me carefully. "Why are you asking so many questions?"

Why are you not? I stifle a scream. "I thought I heard arguing," I admit, watching her just as closely. "Before she fell."

She shakes her head emphatically. "If you heard arguing, it was all of us telling her to get off the railing, that she was going to fall in, and her refusing to."

I hold my hands up. "Okay."

"Now I really do have to get to sleep. Good night."

"Good night," I say. But she's already closed the door.

Back in my room, I stare at Amythest's empty bed, wondering what to do. My gaze lands on a pair of earrings on the bedside table, and suddenly I have an idea. I rummage in my jewelry bag and come up with an earring, the size and shape of which allows me to jam the lock on the door so that I can't be locked in—one of the many tricks I learned acting in the kind of second-rate horror movies where girls get locked in rooms, a tool I never expected to have to use in my real life.

I perch on the edge of the bed, my head spinning. Wendy certainly doesn't seem like she's secretly waiting to tell the cops that she saw Summer shove Amythest into the water.

Which means either it didn't happen and I'm just being paranoid, or she and all of the other girls are covering for Summer.

Rhonda would cover for Summer in a heartbeat. Summer's her daughter and also her meal ticket, so it's a no-brainer. Brittani has a big mouth, but she also has no moral compass and, despite her shit-talking, she worships the ground her sister walks on. Also, John got her into college and she's clearly banking on him paying for it, so she would definitely cover for her sister.

Wendy and Claire are the wild cards.

Wendy may be a flake, but I don't think she's a bad person. Sure, she's out for herself, but at the end of the day, aren't we all? And the fact that she won't go out of her way for anyone leads me to believe that she wouldn't cover up a murder for someone. I check myself. It's not true that Wendy won't go out of her way for anyone; she won't go out of her way for me, but I have nothing to offer her. I have no jet. I have no yacht. I have no key that opens doors to the rich and famous. Summer does. Nevertheless, Wendy's never been cold to me until today, which makes me think Summer must've said something to her in my absence, perhaps forced her to choose a side. And the way Wendy acted toward me just now would seem to suggest that she's chosen her side and has every intention of covering for Summer.

Claire, on the other hand, is a good girl, a wilting flower. She goes to church and doesn't make waves. She's not interested in being a part of this world...but she's loyal to Wendy. She does have a moral compass and I think she'd want to do the right thing, but would she have the balls to speak up if no one else did? Doubtful.

I'm slowly coming to the terrible conclusion that if I don't come up with some kind of evidence to support my theory before I leave this boat, there will be no investigation into Amythest's death. It will be swept under the rug the same way Eric's was.

Oh, Amythest, why did you have to be so hardheaded?

Maybe there is something I missed on the deck where she fell, some proof of what really happened. I close my eyes and picture the scene: the shattered glass, the spilled wine, Amythest's broken nail...*the nail.* Summer had that scratch on her shoulder. Could the shred of red nail I saw on the deck have Summer's DNA on it? Damn it, I should have picked it up, but maybe it's still there.

I know I'm not supposed to leave my room, but what's the worst they can do to me if they catch me? I don't think they'll risk killing off two of us in one night, and I'm being sent home tomorrow morning anyway.

But first...First I need to contact the outside world. Let someone not on this boat know what's going on. In case something happens to me. Oh God, I can't think like that.

I'll have to sneak upstairs to use the hardwired computer, which of course means my email will be read, so I can't say too much. Just enough to cast doubt if anything were to...

I take a deep breath and quietly poke my head into the empty hallway. Before I have time to second-guess myself, I slip out and press open the entry to the crew quarters. To my relief, the doors to all their bedrooms are shut and no one is out. It occurs to me to wonder if they get locked in, too. Surely not? But I can't risk checking.

I quickly move down the hall and up the stairs, all the way to the second landing, where I press my ear to the door marked UPPER DECK. I can't hear anything. I push it open a crack. Silence.

I edge into the darkened hallway and press my body against the wall, my breath shallow. A light shines through the crack beneath the door to the bridge. I look up to see a camera directly over my head. I have to bank on the assumption that either the cameras have been disconnected to cover up tonight's events, or at this hour no one's watching.

The living room is lit only by the starlight through the windows and the glowing green of the EXIT signs above the doors. I tiptoe past John's portrait and take a seat at the computer. When I click the mouse, the screen comes to life with blinding brilliance. I quickly turn the brightness down to its lowest setting and log in to my email.

I have new messages, but I don't dare open them in case someone is watching my screen. I compose a new message at the speed of light, hyperaware that at any moment someone could walk in:

Hi Sis,

Amythest has gone overboard, probably dead. Summer says it was an accident, that she fell in. Coast guard came briefly but left after speaking to John. She was wearing my watch, and my computer and phone are gone so I'm writing from the boat computer. I was being sent home tomorrow, not sure if that will change now. In other news, I had the sea urchin tonight, and it was everything you said it would be.

X. Sis

I hit send, log out of my email, and turn off the monitor, then stumble across the shadowy living room, slipping out the side door to the narrow exterior deck. The wind hits me as I open it, and I have to use both hands to keep it from slamming shut behind me. It's nearing four in the morning, but the skies remain dark and we're still moving at a steady clip, the boat keeling as she moves through the water. We didn't even stick around overnight to look for Amythest, which only makes me all the more sure of my theory about her fall. I grab the railing to steady myself and make my way toward the front of the boat, ducking as I pass the windows to Summer and John's room.

My heart in my throat, I ascend the stairs warily, straining to hear anyone above, but all is quiet. As I emerge onto the deck, my eyes dart from shadow to shadow until I'm satisfied that I'm alone. I steal across the freshly scrubbed and brushed wood planks. I'm grateful that the deck lights are dimmed, but the darkness makes the task at hand more difficult. I kneel by the railing, looking for something, anything that doesn't fit the story of the accident. The telltale signs are all cleaned up but forever imprinted on my mind: the glittering broken nail, the shards of glass, the horrifying smudge of blood. I fish Amythest's phone from my pocket and lean out over the railing, shining the flashlight down the side of the boat. Someone has washed the blood away, but a discolored stain remains in its place.

A light goes on somewhere behind me. I freeze.

"What are you doing out here?" Summer calls out.

I switch off the flashlight on Amythest's phone as I pull myself to standing and activate the video camera. Maybe I'll get some usable audio. I hit record and stealthily slip the phone into my back pocket as I turn to face her.

Silhouetted in the open doorway, she watches me, her face inscrutable in the darkness. Both of us are still, the sea and sky around us an inky black void.

I release my grip on the railing, edging toward the center of the deck just as the boat pitches forward, throwing me off balance. I scramble to catch my footing, and an overlooked shard of fine glass slices into the soft flesh between my toes. I stumble to my knees.

She laughs.

Fuck. I shouldn't be here. I've made a terrible mistake. I should have stayed in my room and kept my mouth shut like the others.

But I'm through keeping my mouth shut.

Backlit, she is all blond hair and diamonds and glimmering teeth, her eyes in shadow as she advances toward me.

I desperately wish I were wrong about her, that it was only an accident. But the smile that plays around her lips is not one of goodwill. She towers above me, well oiled with power and champagne, a lion considering wounded prey.

And I know I am not wrong.

I extract the bloodied glass from my foot and rise to meet her, grateful for my height. She's cool, so close I can smell her Chanel No. 5. Adrenaline pumps through my veins.

"What did you do?" I ask.

She feigns innocence, her eyes wide. "It was an accident."

"You can stop the lies. I know it wasn't an accident."

She drops the act. "You've always been so unsupportive," she complains.

"You just fucking killed someone."

"Me?" She eyes me pointedly.

"The Coast Guard has already come," I say, reading her implication. "Everyone knows I wasn't there."

"Everyone is going to say whatever I tell them to say." Her smile curdles my blood. "Including the Coast Guard. And so should you, if you know what's good for you."

"Or what? You'll kill me, too? Or just set me up, the way you tried to for Eric's death?"

She smirks. "I was wondering when you'd finally ask me about that. I knew you must've paid the parking ticket, but you kept your mouth shut, which at this point makes you an accessory, even if anyone could prove that it was me there in your car."

"So you did kill him."

She sighs as though I'm slow on the uptake. "You know I did. You told Amythest."

The blood freezes in my veins. "What did she say to you?"

"So it's your fault she's dead," she sneers. "And Eric, too."

My heart hammers erratically in my chest. I feel like I'm going to throw up. *Breathe.* I can't let her get into my head. "Why? Why frame me for Eric's death, when you'd already set it up as a suicide?"

"Always have a backup plan." She smiles. "And you deserved it."

"But I was never anything but good to you," I protest, bewildered.

"Ha!" She snorts. "I read the messages, Belle."

"What?"

"I have your passcode, you dumb slut. You thought you were being so smart using whatever apps, but I've seen them all, read every witty, pretentious line."

"We were just friends—"

"Oh, come on. You stopped having my back the minute you met him. I saw the way you guys looked at each other and talked over my head, always quoting obscure movies and showing him your stupid plants. He wouldn't shut up about how you were sooo smart, sooo talented, and such a *natural* beauty. And then I found the picture in the drawer of his bedside table."

The wind whips my hair into my face, and I gather it into a ponytail, holding it back with one hand. "What picture?"

"Of you. *In his loft.*"

In the rain the day he kissed me. He must have printed the picture. And kept it. Next to his bed.

I'm so stunned that I can hardly formulate words. But I can't let this end here. "Why did you invite me on this trip if you felt that way?"

"To keep an eye on you."

"To manipulate me, you mean. But it hasn't turned out quite the way you thought it would, has it?"

She raises her chin in defiance. "Things are gonna turn out fine for me."

"Really? How does all this end? How many younger, prettier girls are you going to have to murder to keep your position?"

"I don't give a damn who he screws once we're married." She laughs. "I loved Eric."

I clench my jaw. "You killed him and then cried on my shoulder over his death."

"I was upset," she insists. "It's upsetting to lose a man you loved. But sometimes you have to make sacrifices to get what you want."

The use of refrigerator-magnet philosophy to justify murder would be mind-boggling if it weren't coming from Summer's glossy lips. "Is that what Amythest was? Another sacrifice at the altar of your vanity?"

"That bitch deserved what she got." She snickers. "So let me tell you how this is going to go." She places a manicured nail on my sternum.

I bat her hand away. "Don't touch me."

She crosses her arms. "This conversation never happened. In the morning, you'll apologize to everyone for being so upset. She was your roommate, after all. It's understandable. Everything will be peachy between us. Then you'll go home and we'll never see each other again. And if you care about your family, or your freedom, you'll never speak to anyone about anything that happened here, or with Eric."

"That's your plan? How can you be so sure that no one will find out what really happened?"

She rolls her eyes. "You still don't understand how the world works, do you? Everything has a price, and I can afford it."

I shake my head. "John can. Not you."

"It's in his best interest to protect me," she says calmly. "He has too much to lose. And now he knows that if I go down, I'm crazy enough to take him with me."

And with that, she spins and strides back to the open door, calling out to Vinny. He appears, and she says something to him that sends him over to grab me by the arm. I try to wrench away, but his grip is like steel as he steers me by the elbow down the exterior stairs.

"You know she pushed Amythest off the railing?" I say.

He grunts.

"She *killed* her."

He shoves me inside the main deck and prods me down the staircase. "What'd I fucking tell you? You gotta learn to keep your mouth shut."

He throws me into my room. I hear a key turn in the lock, and when I turn the handle, it won't budge. So much for the earring trick.

My legs weak, I sit on my bed. I'm sickened by the thought that Amythest's death is partially my fault. If I hadn't told her about Eric...But no. I can't go there. I told her to protect her. Summer wants me to feel responsible; she's framing it so I do.

I extract Amythest's phone from my pocket and press play on the video, turning the volume all the way up. Our voices are muffled, nearly drowned out by the sea and the wind, but I can make out words here and there. And I bet the cops have voice-enhancing software that will make it clear as day.

My hand shakes as I put the phone down. I'm unnerved by the encounter with Summer, but also exhilarated. I can't believe it. She played right into my hands. Thank God I had Amythest's phone. Now all I have to do is hold on to it, keep my head down, and get to a police station. That, and stay alive.

I think back to when Eric "committed suicide," how Summer was beside herself. I never even thought to question her whereabouts until I got that parking ticket in the mail, because why would I suspect my best friend had killed her boyfriend?

In the next room, I hear Brittani and Rhonda talking in low tones. Unable to make out what they're saying, I press my ear to the wall and catch Brittani asking for Ambien.

"It's too late," Rhonda hisses. "...be loopy tomorrow...keep your big mouth shut."

Brittani's naturally loud voice is easier to make out than Rhonda's. "Yeah, well, you try keeping your mouth shut next time Jeffrey Dahmer kills one of your friends right in front of you," she says. "I always knew she'd snap one day."

"Shhhh!" Rhonda says. "...not funny..."

"Oh my God, Mom. Give me a little fucking credit. I'm not as dumb as you think I am." I hear a pop, then, "Ow! What the shit? This is child abuse."

"*Shut up*, Brittani. You're the one...bring that tramp on this trip, so...all your fault."

"Really, Mom? Really?" Brittani's technically whispering now, but she might as well be using a megaphone. "She was my friend, and she may have been a whore, but she didn't deserve to fucking die. So forgive me if I'm a little fucked up about it."

"...thin ice. One wrong move...over. Over. Jail...life. You understand?"

"Jesus, okay! Can you let go? Your nails are digging into me."

"Promise me."

"Okay, I promise! Shit!"

The clock on the bedside table reads 4:34 a.m. Amythest's phone has 38 percent battery power, and Bernard must've taken our chargers because they're both missing. I turn off the phone and store it under my pillow for safekeeping.

Eric had a picture of me in his bedside table. Does that mean what I think it does?

I'm physically tired, and I know I need to get some sleep so that I can be on point tomorrow, but I'm not in the least bit sleepy. My gears are cranking. I'm amped. My mind is speeding a million miles an hour. I need to get my passport back, my computer and my phone. I need to get to the police in the morning.

Eric had a picture of me in his bedside table.

Breathe.

Should I give Wendy and Claire a warning so that they can save themselves? If they haven't been interviewed yet, they haven't lied. As hurt as I am by Wendy, I don't want her to go to jail. And certainly not poor Claire.

I tried cocaine once and never did it again because it made me feel exactly how I feel right now: unable to hold on to thoughts speeding by too fast to articulate, a sense of impending dread, an anxiety I couldn't pinpoint. Though now I can pinpoint it.

I repeat the same mantra now that I used that night—*Everything is going to be okay, everything is going to be okay, everything is going to be okay—* over and over and over, ad infinitum. But it's hard to believe.

I check the clock. 4:56. Okay, that's good. Time is passing. Just two more hours until I can get up and shower.

Eric kept a picture of me in his bedside table.

(twenty days ago)

Los Angeles

In the morning, a leaf blower aroused me from fitful sleep.

Eric is alive and on my couch.

My eyes flew open. I jerked myself out of bed and padded quietly into the living room, where Eric was still sleeping soundly. He didn't look good. His skin was pale and his brow glistened with sweat.

Should I wake him and drag him to the emergency room immediately?

No. Sleep was probably the best thing for him.

I gazed out the kitchen window as my coffee percolated, watching the wind ripple the fingers of the palm trees. The day was bright and clear, the world fresh from last night's rain.

What was he doing here?

It dawned on me that I should call Dylan. I palmed my phone and scrolled through my contacts for his number, but hesitated, my thumb hovering over the call button. Though Dylan had given me no reason not to trust him, calling him somehow felt like a betrayal of Eric, who had come to me, not his brother. A little voice in the back of my mind whispered that perhaps I should wait to find out why before I contacted anyone.

I put the phone down. Maybe I'd find when Eric woke that he'd already contacted Dylan and my caution was unnecessary. Regardless, Eric would be up soon—I could delay calling anyone until I talked to him. The fact that Eric had shown up on my doorstep demonstrated some level of trust in me, and I felt obligated to at least honor that faith until he'd had the chance to relate what had happened to him.

But why come to me?

My head throbbed. I'd had less than four hours' rest, but was afraid that Eric would leave if I fell asleep again, so I poured my coffee and trudged back to the living room, where I curled up in a chair to wait for him to wake and promptly nodded off myself.

My neck was cramped from napping in the chair and my leg was asleep by the time his moaning woke me. His eyes fluttered, his skin clammy in the light through the curtains. Pins and needles shot through my foot as I limped to the bathroom, returning with a thermometer. I slipped it into his mouth, and he opened his eyes with a start. "It's okay," I said as calmly as I could muster. "I'm just taking your temperature."

He closed his eyes while I watched the numbers on the digital screen escalate. The thermometer beeped and flashed red: 104.3.

Shit, that was high. I dredged the depths of my mind for the medical knowledge I'd garnered while playing a med student. If I remembered correctly, 105 was hospital zone.

I googled it to confirm, then ran a cool bath, as the Internet suggested. I returned with Tylenol and a glass of water, but he waved it away.

"Just wanna sleep," he murmured.

"Eric, your temp is really high," I insisted. "You need to take this Tylenol and drink this entire glass of water, then come get in the bath, or I'm calling 911."

He raised his head, and I placed the Tylenol on his tongue and held the glass while he gulped most of the water before diving back to the pillow.

"Okay, now the bath," I instructed. He didn't move. "Eric, I'm serious. I can't lift you myself, and I'm not sure where all you're injured, so you have to help me."

I assisted him up to sitting, and he swung his feet to the ground. I slipped my right arm around his waist, placed his left around my shoulders. "Okay, on three. One, two, three."

And we were standing. Unsteadily, but standing. We shuffled the short distance to the bathroom, where I closed the lid to the toilet and sat him on it, then helped him out of his T-shirt. His torso was covered in scratches and bruises; a bandage on the outside of one of his biceps was soaked in blood. Even beaten to a pulp, he was still beautiful. His chest was lean and toned, like someone who did yoga and free weights, and his abs were hard.

But I couldn't be looking at his body. I had to get him into the bath. Naked. Right. I'd glossed over that part of the operation when I'd come up with it. He must've had the same thought, because he gave me a half smile. "I always wondered what it would be like for you to undress me."

How he had it in him to flirt right now, I had no idea. But I felt the heat rise in my cheeks and turned away to check the water temperature. "It's cool," I said without turning around, "but not cold, so it shouldn't be too much of a shock."

I'd just put him in the bath in his underwear; that would solve the problem. Without meeting his eyes, I reached for the bandage on his arm, and he instinctively jerked away. "Sorry. That one's the worst. Maybe we should leave it."

"We need to clean it and rebandage it."

"Separately," he insisted.

I acquiesced as he used the sink to push up to standing and undid the button to his jeans. Should I leave? I didn't want him to fall asleep and drown. I could wait in the kitchen, where I could see him through the open door but still give him space.

"Do you need help?" I asked, turning to face him.

He unzipped his pants and let them fall without a hint of self-consciousness. He wasn't wearing any underwear. So much for modesty. I kept my gaze lifted as he stepped into the bath and slowly sank into the water.

"Okay, I'm gonna go make some tea in the kitchen. I'll be right there if you need me," I said, indicating the kitchen.

"Stay." He laid his head back and closed his eyes.

I perched on the toilet lid. The faucet dripped. Neither of us spoke for a long time. Outside, two birds chirped back and forth.

"Maybe it's a love song." He referenced the birds without opening his eyes.

"Maybe."

"Do you have any coffee?"

"Yeah. But you gotta drink it iced."

I kept an eye on him through the open door while I made his coffee, and brought him a banana as well. He didn't want the banana, but I made him eat it.

I prepped a fresh washcloth with warm water and soap as he sipped the coffee. "Do you mind?" I asked. He shook his head. "Lean forward a bit."

I lightly washed the wounds on his back, then his arms, all the while studiously avoiding looking at any other part of his body. He opened his eyes as I moved to gently wash his chest, and I looked down to notice my boobs were right at eye level, straining against my thin spaghetti-strap nightshirt. I straightened up and handed him the washcloth. "You can finish the rest of your body," I said, turning away.

"Belle." I felt his eyes on me and met his gaze. "Thank you."

I nodded. "You still owe me an explanation."

"I know."

After thirty minutes, he was looking a little better. I helped him out of the bath and wrapped him in a towel, once again averting my eyes from his naked body. The clothes he'd been wearing were filthy, pieces of mud crusted around the bottom of his jeans.

"My friend keeps some things here," I said. "You guys are about the same size. Let me see what I can find."

"Boyfriend?" he asked too quickly.

I laughed. "No."

He followed me to the bedroom and watched while I rummaged through Hunter's drawer, coming up with a pair of gray sweatpants and a dark-green T-shirt. "They're not black," I said, "but they're comfortable."

He took the clothes, and I turned back to the drawers to rummage around for nothing while he pulled on the pants. He started to put on the T-shirt, but I stopped him. "Wait. We need to deal with your wounds."

I sat him on the bed facing the windows and opened the curtains so that the morning sun streamed in. He squinted into the light. "Is that the Hollywood sign?"

"Yeah. The—wood, anyway."

I placed the thermometer in his mouth while I gathered the bandages and first-aid ointment. The thermometer beeped and flashed red: 102.2. I showed him. "You're still hot, but you're moving in the right direction."

"You think I'm hot?" he joked.

"I'm glad you're feeling well enough to joke, but we do need to get you to a doctor." I rubbed ointment into the wounds on his chest and inspected the laceration on his forearm. "This is deep." I filled the wound with antibacterial ointment and closed it with three butterfly bandages. "And your cheek, the bones..."

"We need to go to Mexico," he said.

"You're in no shape to be traveling."

"I want you to take me," he entreated. "Please. I'll see a doctor there."

"Eric, I...I can't just go to Mexico. I have responsibilities. I have to be at work in three hours. I have..."

"I'm sorry," he apologized. "I'm asking a lot without telling you anything. What do you want to know?"

He winced as I peeled the bloodied bandage from his biceps, uncovering a deep gash. I inhaled sharply. I had no idea how to clean a wound so serious, but I knew it needed to be tended to immediately.

"I told you it was bad," he said.

"What happened to you?"

"Summer pushed me off a cliff."

I froze, my breath caught in my throat. Well, there it was, then. She was capable of it after all. As soon as I could speak again, the questions came. "How? Why? Does anybody else know you're alive?"

"No. When I got your message, I went out to the park to meet you. I saw your car in the lot, but when I got to the lookout point, Summer was there."

"What message?" I asked, confused. "The only one I sent you was the evening you disappeared, asking you what was going on with Summer. And then a bunch in the days afterward, wondering what had happened to you."

He wrinkled his brow, processing. "Of course. I'm so stupid. It must have been her. I got a message from you early the morning after Summer and I fought, saying that you needed to talk to me about something important but that no one could know, so to meet you at this lookout point at a park in Ventura...."

I grabbed my phone and opened our message thread, showing him there was no such message. "Not me," I said.

"Could she have gotten into your account?" he asked. "She could have deleted the message on your end after she sent it, leaving it on my end."

"Yeah." I smacked myself in the forehead. "She knows my passcode. I spent the night with her in Malibu last Friday and left my phone downstairs when I went to bed. Do you have your phone?"

He shook his head. "You back up messages to the cloud?"

"I don't know."

I handed him my phone, and he thumbed through a few screens. "Here we go."

He hit the button to restore my messages. Luckily, there weren't many, so we had to wait only a few excruciating seconds while they loaded. When the screen refreshed, sure enough, there was a message from me to Eric, sent at 5:42 a.m. on July 22, begging him to meet me at a park in Ventura. And his reply, agreeing.

"Jesus." I stared at the screen.

"She must've banked on the fact that you wouldn't check your deleted messages."

"Or she didn't care if I knew." I tried to put myself in her shoes. "And she'd want them to still be traceable by police if necessary." I knew at this point I shouldn't be surprised by her duplicity, but the betrayal still stung. My best friend had tried to frame me for murder. It was incomprehensible. A flame of anger flickered to life inside of me. "What happened when you got there?" I asked.

"It was foggy, and your car was the only other one in the lot. I didn't run into anyone on the trail. When I got to the lookout point, Summer was there waiting for me. I asked her where you were, and she started yelling at me, accusing me of cheating on her with you. She demanded to see my phone, so I unlocked it and handed it to her. She went over to the edge with it and was saying all this shit about how I wouldn't care if she just jumped. She was freaking me out, so I went to her, and when I got to her, she attacked me. We were tussling—I thought she might try to jump, so I was holding her as tight as I could, and then she kneed me in the balls and pushed me over the edge. The next thing I knew, I was waking up in a tree at the bottom of the cliff."

"Oh my God."

"I got unbelievably lucky I landed in that tree," he said. "I know how to fall from rock climbing, but no one survives a fall from that height."

"She tried to murder you."

He nodded. "I should have left when I saw it was her waiting for me instead of you, but...I underestimated her."

"We have to go to the cops."

"No," he refused. "No one can know where I am."

"Why?" I asked.

"My father."

"What does Summer trying to kill you have to do with your dad?" Then, remembering, "We have to call your brother—"

"No!" He grabbed my wrist, his grip gentle but firm.

"My brother can*not* know I'm alive. Do you understand?"

"But he—"

"He's working for our dad. I can't trust him."

I would've been exasperated if he didn't look so dreadful. "What does any of this have to do with your dad?"

"You don't know," he said, realizing.

"Know what?"

"But how would you? I have my mother's last name, and Dylan uses his middle name instead of his last."

"What are you talking about?"

His eyes met mine. "John," he said. "John Lyons—is our father."

I stared at him slack-jawed, my mind unable to knit the two worlds together. "What?"

"The man Summer's dating is—"

"I heard you. But—how?" It was too big of a coincidence. The world just didn't work that way. "Does Summer know?"

"Yes. It's why she went after him. I didn't find out until recently."

"Wait—" I had so many questions, I didn't know where to begin. "So, does John know about the two of you?"

"He knows we dated a while ago—he has to; he does his due diligence on anyone in his orbit and he has eyes everywhere—it's probably one of the reasons he chose her, to spite me—but there's no way he knows we'd seen each other since the two of them got together. If he did, he would have dumped her—or worse. But that wasn't—"

"And you threatened to tell him when you found out, so she tried to kill you?" This much, at least, I could gather from what Summer had related of her phone conversation with him when we were in Malibu—though the very fact that he'd threatened to tell John bothered me.

"It's more complicated than that." He sighed. "My father is a bad man. I didn't want to be with Summer anymore, but I still didn't want her caught up in his world. I mean, was I angry that she'd gone through my personal things and tracked down my father so that she could throw herself at him? Sure. But that wasn't why I called her. I was worried she was in over her head with him and was trying to warn her off getting involved any deeper than she already had—but she wouldn't listen. My threats to tell John about us were empty and aimed at getting her away from him for her own good. Shit, there are a million other rich old men out there that aren't monsters, who I'm sure would be happy to give her what she wants."

I watched him carefully as he spoke, weighing whether to believe him. It was his word against hers, and I recognized now more than ever that I didn't know him well at all. But I knew her. And she was at this point officially the person I trusted the least in the world, which meant that, comparatively, I trusted him more. "So much for saving her," I said dryly.

He nodded. "But I have far more to fear from my father than I do from her."

Was this real? I was beginning to feel like I was in a telenovela. I closed my eyes and pinched my nose. "What do you mean?"

He grabbed my hands, his eyes clear. "I promise I'll tell you everything. But can we please get out of here? They're looking for me, and I don't want to put you in danger."

My head swam with questions: Who were "they"? Why were they looking for him? What had I gotten myself involved in?

The sun caught in his shorn golden hair, giving him a halo that framed his beaten face. He needed a doctor worse than I needed answers. I would put my trust in him, at least for now.

Day 7

I'm up at first light, showered and completely packed before I finally hear the lock turn in my door.

"Who is it?" I call out.

"Julie."

I open the door to Julie, who hands me a cup of coffee. "Thanks." I glance into the hallway to see Bernard disappearing up the stairs. "Where's Camille?"

"She's no longer assigned to you."

"Is she okay?" I ask, worried that I've gotten her in trouble for allowing me to go up to the deck last night.

Julie gives me a tight-lipped smile. "She's fine."

Obviously I'm not going to get any more out of her on that score. "Any news?"

"Nothing yet."

"Are they coming back this morning to take our statements?"

She shakes her head. "We dock in an hour. You all go to town while John has a meeting, then to Monte Carlo for the night."

I'm dumbfounded. "So they're just acting like nothing happened?"

She shrugs apologetically. "It is an accident. Nothing to do."

"So I'm still leaving for the airport, right?"

"No," she says. "You stay here."

Oh no. No, no, no.

"What? But I don't want to stay," I protest. "I want to go."

"I'm sorry," she replies on her way out the door. "They are waiting for you at breakfast."

Shit. How do I get the phone to the cops with John's henchmen watching? And how do I keep it safe in the meantime?

I stall, racking my brain for a plan. But it's useless. I have no idea what I'm walking into today. Nothing to do but arrange my features into some semblance of good spirits, stuff the phone in the Gucci crossbody purse Summer gave me what seems like a lifetime ago, and head up the stairs, my apprehension growing with every step.

I find everyone installed at the outdoor table on the upper deck, quietly drinking cappuccinos and eating pastries. The day is brilliantly clear, as though the sea and sky are competing for the most vivid shade of blue. We're moving slowly along a coastline peppered with colorful homes built into sand-colored cliffs, and a pleasant breeze blows off the water.

My breath is shallow, my palms sweaty as I approach the table. Summer looks up and smiles. She's wearing sunglasses, as is everyone else, but she appears to be smiling at me. Unless there's someone behind me. I turn around. Nope, no one behind me. I wish I'd remembered my sunglasses.

"Good morning, Belle!" Summer says brightly. "Oh, I gave you that purse, didn't I? Gucci's a bit loud for me, but it looks great on you."

"Any news about Amythest?" I ask, ignoring her backhanded compliment.

Somber head shakes all around.

"We're hoping someone picked her up," Wendy says glumly.

Brittani slams her coffee mug to the table. "Can we all just stop bullshitting to make ourselves feel better? No one picked her up. She's dead."

Summer clenches her jaw. Rhonda lays her hand on top of Brittani's. "Honey, we're all upset."

"No you're not," Brittani retorts. "None of you even liked her. She was my friend."

Claire and Wendy look on silently, clearly wishing they were any-where but here. I take the empty seat next to Claire, and she passes me the basket of pastries with a halfhearted smile.

"So, I'm not leaving today?" I ask, trying to maintain a friendly tone as I butter the croissant I'm not in the least bit hungry for.

"No need," Summer says. "I think last night put everything into perspective, right? Silly for you to leave two days early and miss the rest of the trip." She turns her attention to a picturesque arrangement of yellow, pink, and orange homes spilling down a bluff to the turquoise sea. "Oh, look how pretty!"

Wendy listlessly palms her phone and drifts to the railing, snapping pictures of the coastline.

"Let's take a picture of us," Summer says, rising to join her at the railing. "Mom, will you take it?"

Rhonda holds the camera with a synthetic smile, and Wendy puts on her happy face to mug with Summer for the picture. Summer must be dead confident there will never be a court case over Amythest's death, because this cheery photo would be positively damning if there were.

"Now all of us together!" Summer cries.

Brittani and Claire reluctantly get up to flank the two of them, but I hang back. This is all too weird, and no part of me wants to be next to Summer by a railing.

"Come on, Belle! Get in the picture." Summer waves me over.

I slide in next to Claire, scowling at the camera.

After we're all seated back at the table, Summer dings her glass with her fork, and everyone gives her their attention. "I am so lucky to have my best friends with me here on the Riviera," she says, her hand over her heart. "I'm so, so sorry you've all had to go through the trauma of last night. But I've got another surprise for you all today that I think you'll really like. So go get ready for our excursion, and I'll see you back up here at nine so we can go into port."

Everyone rises and files down the stairs like a good little girl. I trail behind, stuffing the rest of my croissant into my mouth. But before I can reach the stairs, Summer grabs me lightly by the elbow. Out of the corner of my eye, I notice Vinny and Bernard watching us as I turn to face her, trying to maintain a calm countenance.

"We're all good, right?" she says with a guarded smile. It's a statement, not a question.

I choke on my croissant. "Yeah." I cough. "All good."

It seems like the best answer for the circumstance. The circumstance being that I want to make it off this boat alive.

"Good." She pulls me into a hug.

Once she releases me, I scurry down the stairs straight to Wendy and Claire's room and knock.

Wendy opens the door a crack and eyes me warily.

I push past her into the room, shutting the door behind me.

Claire is sitting crisscross on the bed, her face puffy. She's clearly having a much harder time with being an accessory to murder than anyone else.

"Hey, guys?" I say, making sure I have their eyes before continuing. "Whatever happened last night, the truth is going to come out eventually, so you wanna make sure you're on the right side of it."

I can almost see Wendy's anxiety bubbling up between the cracks of her composed facade. "Belle," she says carefully, "you know how much I love you. But we were there last night. Amythest fell in. That's it. It was awful, and you're not making it any better." So I was right; Wendy has clearly chosen her side. "Right, Claire?"

Tears well in Claire's eyes as she nods.

"Okay." I raise both my palms. "I'm just making sure you know you have options." I look directly at Claire. "I would hate to see you pay for someone else's crime."

"Don't be so dramatic." Wendy pats my back, ushering me to the door. "I don't know what you're trying to imply, but it was an accident. A terrible, tragic accident. Coast Guard is looking for her. There's nothing we can do—we have to get ready."

Well, I tried. I hear the lock click into place behind me. I stand motionless, listening for their voices, but I can't hear anything.

The boat has docked by the time we meet upstairs. I'm not sure exactly where we are, but it's a small port with red-roofed buildings perched on green hills that slope down to the inexplicably deserted marina where we're moored. No colorful umbrellas dot the strip of sand that borders the port. No lively vendors peddle souvenirs. The faded paint on the buildings is peeling, the windows dark or boarded up. The only movement comes from the ravens that circle overhead, calling to one another.

The gangplank is down and the other girls are gathered in the shade of the upper deck, staring out at the forlorn town. I can only assume this is the village John's acquired, the site of his big new development.

"Good. You're here; we can go now," Brittani says as I approach.

Everyone gathers their things, and Vinny leads the way across the gangplank.

The town is situated on an inlet protected from the wind, and while I imagine that the cliffs provide shade earlier or later in the day, the sun is high now and there's no place to hide from its wrath.

"This place better fucking have air-conditioning," Brittani gripes to Summer as Vinny helps her down to the brick promenade that rings the harbor.

Summer wraps her manicured fingers around Brittani's elbow and hisses something in her ear. Brittani jerks her arm away. "I know, God!" Brittani mutters.

Visible heat waves rise from the blacktop road between us and the village, the streets eerily empty of the summer tourists that have crowded every other city we've visited. My eyes are peeled for police, my mind working overtime to formulate some sort of plan to get to the authorities, but I see no evidence of any form of law enforcement.

But what am I thinking? If John owns this town, surely he owns the police as well. My heart sinks. I have to come up with something else. I'm dying to check whether Amythest's phone has service, but I don't dare take it out of my purse lest anyone notice it, since I'm not supposed to have a phone at all anymore. But if I can just connect to Wi-Fi, I can upload the video of Summer's confession to the cloud, where it will be safe no matter what happens to the phone.

The sidewalk is under construction, lined with an orange plastic fence that forces us to walk down the blacktop for a block before turning up a narrow road. The buildings are all shades of weathered terra-cotta and appear to slope with the incline. Most of the stores and restaurants are shuttered. I can't tell whether it's due to the time of day or year or whether they're closed permanently.

A scrawny black cat cuts across our path and scurries into an open window. "Bad luck," Claire whispers.

"How far is this place?" Summer asks, impatient. "Maybe we should have taken a car."

"Not far," Vinny grumbles.

The narrow road empties onto a wider street, and we turn left in single file, trying to stay in the small strip of shadow that hugs the wall. This street is lined with what must be vacant office buildings, though they are in keeping with the general appearance of the rest of the town. Here and there more of the orange barriers block streets and wrap around buildings, though no construction is evident.

As we cross the street, I spy a handful of parked Vespas ahead, all white and bright sky blue. A few blocks away, a lone white car with a stripe that same distinctive shade of blue slowly moves up the road toward us. Is it a police car? I strain to see better without making it obvious that I'm looking, but I have to rush to catch everyone as they turn up another street. I look back as the car passes, and sure enough, it says POLIZIA MUNICIPALE on the side.

Vinny stops beneath a green sign with a picture of a watch, and we all gather in the small patch of shade created by the awning.

Summer turns to us, beaming. "I wanted to do something special for my girls. It took John's assistants all night to find what I wanted, but here we are. I hope you like it!"

Vinny opens the door, and we all file into the small store. It's dark and cool inside, and the walls are lined with glass cases full of watches, lit from below. There are no price tags and I don't know anything about watches, but these look expensive. A wiry gray-haired man in his seventies stands in the center of the shop, smiling at us tentatively.

He silently gestures to one of the cases. A velvet display box is open on top of it, showcasing six identical Rolex watches. They're lady-size, with silver bands and mother-of-pearl faces.

Rhonda places one on her wrist. "Oh, Summer, they're beautiful!" she says with strained enthusiasm. "How sweet of you."

"So beautiful," Wendy agrees, putting on a smile. "You are so thoughtful. Thank you so much."

Is she really trying to buy our silence with Rolexes?

The shop owner passes out the watches, and we each slip one on.

"I picked them out myself," Summer says, pleased. Her eyes land on me. "I figured you could all use new ones."

So she did notice Amythest wearing mine last night.

Brittani's scowl dissipates as she studies the watch on her arm. "Thanks, sis," she says.

"Thank you. It's gorgeous," Claire adds breathlessly, unable to meet Summer's eye.

"Oh, you're so welcome," Summer says. "Gotta take care of my girls!"

The shop owner says something in Italian to Vinny, who relays to us, "Okay, now he's gonna fit the watches to your wrists."

A tiny old woman who must be the shop owner's wife appears from the back with a tray of glasses and a pitcher of water. The tray trembles as she carries it across the room and carefully sets it on top of a display case, then proceeds to painstakingly pour and hand each of us a glass of water while her husband measures our wrists and takes notes with a little stub of a pencil and a yellow notepad that looks like it's been around since he was a boy.

As she hands Summer the glass of water, she says very carefully, "We hope Signor Lyons keep our store. We sell best watches to *turisti*."

Summer nods. "Yes, I will send your regards."

The embassy. Why didn't I think of it before? I can call the American embassy, tell them what happened. They should be able to help me, right? I have to get out of here, and this is probably the best chance I'm going to get. I hand my watch over to the shop owner and lean in to Wendy.

"I think my Dramamine patch is wearing off," I whisper. "I'm not feeling well. I need to find a restroom and a pharmacy where I can get another one. Seems like this would be a good time to do that."

Wendy considers me carefully. "Yeah, you definitely don't want to throw up here."

"I'll be right back," I say, holding my stomach as though I feel sick. "Will you please tell Summer? I really have to go."

I slip out the door without giving her the chance to deny me and dart in the direction from which we came.

My sandals slap the knobby cobblestones of the deserted road, reverberating between the crumbling buildings as I run. I round the first corner without incident and pull the phone from my purse. No service. Crap. I make a mad dash to the next intersection, where I see the motorbikes I spied earlier a block ahead of me.

Surely the police station has Wi-Fi. Or a phone I can use. A pay phone—do those exist anymore? They don't know who I am. I can tell them I lost my passport, that I need to call the embassy to make an appointment to get a new one.

I hurry up the street, again checking Amythest's phone for wireless connectivity. Nothing.

A wide set of stone steps leads to an ornate concrete building with POLIZIA MUNICIPALE TERRALIONE spelled out in block letters over the double doors. It's an imposing building for such a small town, and I am acutely aware of the fact that I am going to be lying to them as I climb the steps two at a time. I take a deep breath and put my hand on the heavy door. It suddenly swings in, opened by a burly guard in uniform.

I manage some version of "no Italian" that produces a nod and a gesture toward the metal detector. It goes off the first time I try to walk through, and I realize I'm still wearing my purse across my body. I hand it to the guard, who rifles through it while I walk through the metal detector again, this time successfully.

"Wi-Fi?" I ask when he returns my purse.

He shakes his head and points to an empty desk at the end of the hallway.

"Phone?" I ask hopefully, making my hand into a phone.

Again he shakes his head and points.

The wide tile corridor is lined with doors that I imagine lead to offices, but the only sounds are the slap of my sandals on the floor and the hum of the air conditioner. The hallway dead-ends into an identical perpendicular hallway, where rows of mismatched plastic folding chairs line the walls, empty.

At the intersection sits an unmanned big black desk, in the center of which is an old-school black push-button phone.

I stand at the desk, unsure what to do. "Hello?" I call.

No one answers. I probably have ten minutes before anyone realizes my story about needing a Dramamine patch was a lie. I need to make the call before then, or Vinny's liable to find me and drag me back to the boat and...

I reach for the handset, glancing up and down the hall as I put it to my ear. No dial tone. I start pressing buttons, but none of them light up or produce any sign of life.

A uniformed woman emerges from one of the doors and moves down the hallway toward me. I drop the phone into its cradle, firing up my smile. "*Mi scusi*," I say. "*Inglese?*"

She looks bemused, as though I'm the first person ever to come into the police station in whatever town this is.

"*Un po'*," she says quizzically.

"I need to make a call," I say. She doesn't seem to understand. I make a logical guess, gesturing to the telephone. "*Telefono?*"

"*Quello non funziona*," she replies, sizing me up. "*Mi segua, signora*."

I follow her down the hallway and through a door that leads to another waiting room. Another unmanned black desk, two doors behind it.

"*Aspetti un momento*," she says, and disappears through one of the doors.

The only sound to cut the silence is the hum of the fluorescent lights overhead. I lean against the desk while I wait, again checking Amythest's phone for service. Nothing, and battery power is running low.

God, I'm tired. My body is buzzing with adrenaline, but the accumulated lack of sleep is catching up with me. My brain is frayed, my muscles weak, and my heart is galloping like a racehorse in the last turn.

It's been ten minutes. They're going to be wondering where I am. I need to make this call and get out of here before anyone knows better.

Finally an officer who looks like he's barely out of high school emerges from the door that the woman disappeared into. He's skinny with acne, and he shifts his weight from one foot to the other. "You the lady want make call?"

"Yes, sir," I say.

He cocks his head and narrows his eyes at me. "Who you want call?"

"I need to call the American embassy. I've lost my passport," I say, trying to sound as normal as possible.

He turns, beckoning for me to follow. I hurry after him, through a door and into a windowless room with a desk and a number of closed folding chairs leaning against the wall. There is no phone in the room.

This was a bad idea.

I think fast. "Actually...can I use the restroom first?" I ask. "I'm sorry. I really have to go."

"Okay. Down the hall."

"Thanks."

I scurry out the door and hasten down the empty hallway as quickly as I can while still maintaining some semblance of nonchalance. I see no other way out of the building than back the way I came, so I retrace my steps, push open the double doors to the main entrance hall, and run headlong into Vinny.

He stands under the fluorescent lights, the bulk of his body blocking the hallway. His brow is bathed in sweat, his jacket rumpled. "What the fuck were you thinking?" he snarls.

I look right and left. Nothing but closed doors. This building is designed to allow only one entrance and exit point. I could sprint around him, but I'd only be stopped by the security guard in front. I stall. "I went to look for a bathroom."

"Don't lie!" he snaps.

"I'm not—"

He considers me, unblinking. "Thought you'd sell your friend out, huh?"

I break for the door, but he grabs my arm before I can get away. "Ouch," I yelp.

I try to wrench free, but his grip is unyielding as he shoves me down the hall.

I change my tactic. "You know she killed her. You've seen the security tapes," I reason. "It's going to come out. You may have bought off the cops here, but with that many witnesses, and the boat crew, too, there's no way to keep it quiet forever."

"Shut up, Belle."

The metal detector beeps and flashes red as he hustles me through. The security guard averts his eyes. Vinny pushes us out the double doors into the heat of the glaring sun, so bright that I recoil, my hand flying to shade my eyes.

Something bulges under his jacket. Is it a gun tucked into the back of his waistband? That must have been what set off the metal detector. His grip on my arm is so tight, I'm losing feeling in my fingers.

"You can let go now," I say. "I'm coming."

He flings my arm at me. I rub the red skin where he gripped me and switch tactics again. "Vinny, look. I know you're loyal to John. But Summer's a liability. He should cut his losses and get rid of her. He's still clean. He wasn't there. He's only reported what Summer told—"

"Stop talking!" he snarls. "You don't understand."

This is good. At least he's communicating with me. "What don't I understand?"

He leans in close, his breath sour. I force myself not to back away as a drop of sweat runs down his brow and splashes onto my shoulder. "This is nothing, a blip on his radar. He will not change his plans for this. Maybe he gets rid of Summer, maybe not. But on his time. It's not your fight. Stay out of it."

His sweat trickles down my arm. "You know he was sleeping with Amythest," I say.

"So?" He throws his arm wide at the town. "He takes what he wants. This town, he owns it. It will be destroyed next month. And he will build a resort, a port—billions of dollars. That is what this trip is about. Not this...girl drama."

"It's not drama," I say. "It's murder." I don't know why I'm trying, since he's clearly never going to see it my way. We're operating from two completely different rule books, and his trumps mine.

"Accusations can go both ways," he warns.

He wheels around and marches down the wide stone steps. The glare of the sun on the white stone is so bright, I can hardly look at the ground in front of me as I hurry after him. "Are you threatening me?"

"Your sister's on her way to your grandmother's," he growls.

What? How does he know that? "Please leave Lauren out of this," I beg, remembering all the emails.

"Don't be stupid." He turns to face me. "Remember why you're here."

I'm trying to figure out what he means when I notice the gun in his hand, glinting in the sunlight, and my mind blanks. The breath goes out of me. Instinctively, I raise my hands. "Vinny, please."

He comes around behind me and buries the barrel of the gun just above my tailbone. Suddenly the heat of the day is gone. I'm cold with terror, every nerve in my body focused on the hard point of metal thrust into my back. "Walk," he orders.

I put one foot in front of the other, my mind speeding. I think of Lauren, my parents, Grannie, Eric. I have to get away. It can't end here. "Please don't kill me," I plead. "I'll keep my mouth shut. I swear."

"I'm not gonna kill you," he hisses into my hair. "I'm helping you."

Wait, what?

I twist around to see if he's fucking with me, and he prods me with the gun. "Keep walking."

He pushes me up a deserted street that doesn't look familiar. The cobblestones are uneven, all the shops shuttered. Is he just pretending he's helping me so I'll comply while he walks me to my death?

Apprehension thrums under my skin. "Helping me do what?"

"Get the fuck out of here. Against my orders."

"Why?"

"I've done terrible things for him," he confesses grimly. "But I don't believe in hurting women and children."

My mind spins. *Could* he actually be trying to help me? "How do I know I can trust you?"

"You don't." He prods me forward. "There's a string of towns just over the hill up there." He points ahead of us. "Find the train. Come to 12 Chemin de la Pommière in La Quessine at nine tonight. I'll get you out."

"But how? I have no money, no passport. . . ."

He reaches in his pocket and hands me a few folded bills. "Twelve Chemin de la Pommière, in La Quessine. At nine."

I wrench around to see his face. "Where is that?"

His brow is furrowed, his eyes dark. "Near Saint-Tropez."

"But—"

"Now go," he barks. "I'll tell them you got away."

Gripping the cash in my sweaty palm, I take off up the hill, fear propelling me forward at a speed I have not run since high school track. As I reach the first intersecting street, I glance over my shoulder to see

Vinny standing silhouetted by the sun where I left him, the gun dangling from his hand. I break around the corner and sprint into the shade created by the height of the buildings, pushing myself harder, faster up the desolate road, turning again at the next fork to continue up the hill.

Twelve Chemin de la Pommière in La Quessine.

I catapult over an orange construction barrier and leap over an open trench, my sandal folding as I land, sending me to all fours on the uneven pavement. The cash scatters onto the street and I scramble to scoop it up before it blows away, stuffing it into my purse in a clump. One of my knees is bloodied and pain shoots through my ankle, but I brush myself off and push on.

The road narrows as it climbs up the mountain toward the edge of town. My breath ragged, I hurtle up the incline, right and left and right until a sharp twinge in my side doubles me over in the boarded doorway of an abandoned home.

My breath comes hot and fast. I watch a sticky line of blood cut through the dust on my leg. Is that a siren in the distance? I have to keep going. My tongue feels like cotton, but all I can do is continue up the hill.

Twelve Chemin de la Pommière in La Quessine.

Right, left, up a set of stairs, right again, tripping up the bumpy road. I wipe the sweat from my brow, panting, and slow just enough to maintain my pace.

As I climb higher, I feel the beginnings of a slight breeze. I'm relieved I must be reaching a break in the maze. I need to find a lookout site to reorient myself and determine whether I'm still headed in the direction Vinny indicated.

Jesus. *Vinny.* Who would have thought...? But I can't wrap my head around any of that right now. I spot a narrow stairwell leading up to a terrace and take the terra-cotta steps two at a time, my legs wobbly from overexertion.

A rush of fresh air hits me as I ascend the last steps to find myself standing in the full glare of the sun, high above the town. Uneven rooftops tumble down the colorful crescent slope to the sea, where the *Lion's Den* bobs alone in the cove. I instinctively flatten my back against the wall, but I'm likely too far away to be seen.

I take Amythest's phone from my purse and key in the address before I forget it, then count the wad of cash Vinny gave me, my hands trembling. It's eighty euros. Not a lot, but better than the less than forty I have left. The phone still has no signal, so I carefully lean out over the railing to orient myself. I'm a good way toward the east side of the crescent, near where the town fades into the terrain. I can't see the cliffs from this vantage point, but I can tell that I'm close.

I clamber back down the stairs and continue up the street until it dead-ends into a stone retaining wall with a blur of green above it. It's about seven feet to the top, too high for me to pull myself up unassisted, but the rocks are big enough that I should be able to get a pretty good grip with bare feet.

I unstrap my sandals and stuff them halfway in my bag, then place my less-injured foot on a big stone about two feet off the ground and push off, simultaneously reaching up with my opposite hand to grab the upper lip of the wall. With my fingers firmly grasping the grooves of the rocks on top, it's easy enough to scale the rest of the wall. I scramble to standing.

The slope of the hill beyond is steep, but not insurmountable, and it appears to level out about a hundred or so yards up. The terrain is not unlike California: rocky and blanketed in a fine dry dust, scattered with shrublike bushes and wildflowers that should camouflage me as I climb.

I wish I had hiking shoes, but my flimsy sandals will have to do. I slip them back on and grab the stem of a scrawny tree to hoist myself up. Branch by branch, rock by rock, I slowly but surely ascend, ignoring my unbearable thirst. Somewhere near the top, I stumble upon a hiking trail and have to stifle a shriek of glee at my good fortune. I follow the path to the crest of the bluff, where I can see Terralione arranged around the little port way down below.

The *Lion's Den* is gone.

I scan the blue sea for that one particular white dot and spot her sailing west toward France. She cuts through the water easily, a vision of grace and style. Anyone watching her sleek shape pass would aspire to view the shore from her wide deck, to be rocked gently to sleep in her cool embrace.

The yacht's departure is cold comfort at this point. But as she slips away, one of the tightly strung threads inside me loosens ever so slightly. Vinny kept his word.

(twenty days ago)

Los Angeles

The Prius twitched through traffic beneath a procession of swaying palm trees arched toward the sun. I shouldn't have been driving—I hadn't slept. I was too wound up, too distracted. My hands were clammy, even with the AC blasting. But we were on our way downtown to meet Eric's art dealer, George, who'd arranged a passport and a place for him to stay in Mexico.

"So, your father—John—" A small shake of my head. I still couldn't quite get used to this. "Why are you afraid of him? Is it because of Summer?"

"God, no." He laughed. "Summer's just a fly...a diversion. The irony that after everything, *she'd* be the one to nearly succeed in killing me..." He laughed in disbelief.

Irritation prickled my spine. He was asking a lot of me and had given me almost nothing, promising to tell me everything once we were on the road. I yanked the wheel and gassed it into a faster-moving lane. "So, what then?"

"Do you remember last year, a shopping center in Colombia collapsed while it was being built, killing four people and injuring dozens?"

I accelerated through a yellow light. "No."

"It was pretty big news, but it wasn't in the States, so it didn't stay in the cycle for long. Anyway, it was my dad's company that was building the mall. There were a million corners he cut that resulted in the collapse—the concrete they were using was substandard and not suited to hold that amount of weight; there weren't enough steel-reinforcement bars; the plans were changed once the permits had been obtained—common practices for him. He, of course, denied any wrongdoing. There was an investigation afterward, but he managed to bribe his way out of it, and eventually the blame was placed on the contractor."

"Jesus, that's . . . beyond horrifying." I stole a glance at him just as the car in front of me suddenly stopped. I jammed on the brakes, coming to rest inches from its bumper. I took a deep breath and looked over at Eric, who was wincing in pain from the seat belt. "Sorry."

"It's okay." He took a deep breath. "I learned the truth only because the families of the men who died wanted some kind of reparation and had hired lawyers who were working their way through the different names and companies associated with Lionshare, which is how they found their way to me. They showed me the amount of evidence they had amassed—it was staggering. I went to my father and asked him to make it right with them, but he refused. He said that admitting any involvement in the collapse would be catastrophic for Lionshare and tried to convince me of how much I had to lose if the company went under. When he saw that line of reasoning wasn't going to work with me, he warned me to let it go—for their sake and for my own."

"What did you do?"

"I didn't let it go. I went to Dylan to try to get him to help me investigate—he used to be a journalist, and he had access to records because of his position at Lionshare—but he stonewalled me. He thought I was out of my mind for risking my life for these people I'd never met, when there was no way I was going to win."

"So that's why you guys had been fighting."

"The latest reason anyway—and the worst. But I didn't give up. I found a guy with a conscience who worked for the committee tasked with investigating the collapse. He felt so guilty about the whole thing that, against his better judgment, he was willing to go on record and provide proof of the crimes and bribes my father and his men had ordered." He pointed. "Turn here."

I made a right onto a one-way street that stretched past city hall into the heart of downtown.

"I flew down there two weeks ago to collect the evidence and interview the guy myself before finding a journalist to write the story; then I stored everything in my place here and went to my show in San Francisco. When I got home, my loft had been ransacked, and all my evidence and the interview tapes were gone." He pointed at an alley up ahead. "Left there."

He took the jeans he'd been wearing last night out of the backpack I'd loaned him and rifled through the pockets as I gunned it through a break in the traffic across three lanes, into the neatly swept alley. Tall buildings towered above us, casting deep shadows that kept the narrow passage cool. "Stop here," Eric indicated.

I brought the Prius to a halt in front of an unmarked steel door, and he handed me a folded picture. "They left this."

I unfolded it and gasped. It was a photo of a dead man, his white button-down stained red by the blood from bullet holes in his chest. "Oh my God," I said. "Who is this?"

"My informant."

"Jesus," I breathed. So this was the trouble Eric had gotten himself caught up in, and it was far worse than anything I could have imagined. I returned the photo to him, and he carefully placed it in the pocket of his jeans. "This was John's doing?"

"Has to be. But I'm not letting it go. It's only a matter of time before something like that collapse happens again. Summer actually did me a favor pushing me off that cliff. She gave me a chance to disappear until I can figure out a better plan to bring him down."

"But how did he know you were talking to this informant?"

"I don't know. Initially I assumed Dylan had told him of my intention, but he didn't know the specifics. John could have been in my email or tapped my phone—he has the capability I'm sure—

though I was careful. Or it could be as simple as someone on my informant's end who learned he was working with me and ratted him out."

I tried to recall whether Eric and I had ever emailed or talked on the phone—I didn't think we had. We'd used apps mostly, which even with my limited knowledge of such things I knew were harder to hack than email. Not, I reminded myself, that anyone besides Summer had reason to be suspicious of our interaction. "Does Summer have your phone?" I asked.

"Yes."

"Which means if anyone becomes suspicious there was foul play involved in your disappearance, she'll find a way to turn it in, implicating me." The realization hit me like a bus. "Fuck. You're gonna have to figure this shit out before I get thrown in jail for your murder."

"I'm not gonna let that happen." He grabbed my hand, forcing me to meet his eye. "I promise."

The steel door in the wall opened and a striking Latina in a black tunic dress emerged, a messenger bag slung across her shoulder. Her long dark hair was swept up in a messy bun, her lips stained red. She smiled and waved.

"That's George?" I asked, surprised.

"The one and only," he confirmed.

She peered into the car, her eyes going wide behind her black-framed glasses as she saw Eric.

"*Dios mío*," she said, getting into the backseat. "You look terrible."

"Thank you," he said dryly. "You sure you weren't followed?"

"Yes. I did just what you said. What happened to you?"

"Summer pushed me off a cliff."

Her jaw dropped.

"My sentiments exactly," he said. "But that's the least of my problems. My father wants me dead, too."

"Welcome to the club. My father ever escapes from prison, I am—" She drew a finger across her throat.

It was disconcerting yet grimly charming, how lightly she alluded to her own demise. I extended my hand through the center divide. "I'm Belle."

She flashed a somber smile. "Thank you for taking care of my friend. I'm sorry I can't go with you. Mexico is still too dangerous for me, even with my new name."

"George isn't your real name?" I asked.

She laughed. "I was Maria in a past life."

"George and I met here," Eric explained. "But later figured out our illustrious fathers had collaborated on a development in Mexico many years ago—"

"That drained a marshland and displaced an entire village," she elaborated.

"Small world," I commented.

"Yes," she agreed. "At the top, all the most powerful men are in each other's pockets, though they are always claiming otherwise."

"And now she somehow miraculously convinces suckers to pay far more for my art than it's worth," he finished.

She passed him the messenger bag. "One hundred thousand. You have a couple of pieces pending, so there should be more soon. The passport and the key to my friend's place in Rosarito are in the front pocket. He understands the need for confidentiality."

"I can't thank you enough," Eric said.

"You've done more for me." She waved his gratitude away. "I had a weird message from your brother yesterday. I haven't called him back."

"Did you save it?" Eric asked.

She brought up Dylan's voice mail on her phone and hit play. Dylan's voice was tinny over the speakerphone. "Hi, George. It's Dylan. Please call me back as soon as possible. It's important."

"Can you call him now?" Eric asked. "I want to hear what he has to say."

She hit call back. As the other end rang, Eric mouthed, *You haven't seen me. You know nothing.*

"Dylan, it's George Ramirez, returning," George said into the phone.

"Right." Dylan cleared his throat. "Hi, George. Thanks for calling me back. I'm sorry to—"

"What's going on?" George asked, feigning concern.

"It's Eric. He—" Dylan stopped himself, taking a breath. "You haven't heard from him recently, have you?"

"No," she said. "Not since his show last week."

"And how did he seem, at his show?"

"Fine. Normal," George replied. "Why, Dylan? What's up?"

"He . . . They're saying he may have killed himself."

"Oh God," George cried. Eric signaled for her to find out more. "When did this—what happened?"

"A few days ago," Dylan said. "He sent a suicide email to his ex-girlfriend and then he disappeared."

Eric and I exchanged a glance.

"Disappeared?" George asked.

"They found his car in a park in Ventura. They're treating it as a missing persons case right now, but—"

"So he could be alive," George interjected.

"We have people looking for him," he said somberly. "It's unbelievable, really. I can't imagine he'd do something like this, but . . . I know how close you guys were. I should have called sooner. I was hoping I wouldn't have to—"

"*Mierda,*" George said. "Do you need my help with anything?"

"My dad's out there right now, dealing with everything," Dylan said, glum. "He's trying to retrace his steps. He asked me to tell you to please hold on to any money that comes in from his art. We'll figure out what to do with it when we have time."

"Okay. I'm so sorry, Dylan. Please keep me posted."

Voices in the background. "I have to go," he said. "Take care."

The line went dead, and George looked up at us expectantly. "He sounded upset."

Eric nodded slowly. "Doesn't mean I can trust him."

"You guys should hit the road if you wanna make it down by sunset," George said. "I'll let you know if I hear anything."

"I'll text you from the burner when I get it," Eric replied.

George kissed him on both cheeks. "Take care."

I watched her disappear into the building before pulling away from the curb. "Dylan doesn't believe the suicide story," I said. "Yesterday when I spoke to him, he mentioned something about it feeling off and being afraid you'd gotten caught up in something."

"I didn't think he would," Eric said. "He knows me too well. And he knew what I'd gotten into with my dad. But I'm surprised he said anything to you."

"He didn't mention specifics. Did you tell him about what happened to the informant?"

"Not yet. I wanted to confront him over it, but I didn't get a chance before Summer tried to off me."

"It sounded like he was attempting to warn you through George that your father's looking for you," I ventured. "Maybe you should give him a chance to help you."

"That's a stretch." He shook his head. "Anyway, it's too much of a risk. Even if he didn't go running to John, he's likely being monitored by him. Without a body, I doubt John believes the suicide story, either— probably thinks I tried to fake it. There's no question he's got people looking for me."

I replayed the phone call with Dylan in my head as we wove through downtown traffic. He'd sounded distressed, concerned for his brother. And here I was, driving Eric to Mexico without any evidence that his crazy story was true. My instinct was to believe him, and I was pressing on with the expectation that he was sincere, but somewhere in the recesses of my mind, a nagging voice kept reminding me that he was involved with Summer. Could this all be some elaborate plan by the two of them to bilk John out of his money? I couldn't quite come up with what that plan might be or how I fit in, but...

If I wanted to back out, this was my chance. Eric had his money now. I could leave him at the Metro station and try to forget this ever happened. I'd slowly phase Summer out of my life. Get new friends, normal friends. Friends whose fathers weren't criminal billionaires, friends who didn't try to kill their ex-boyfriends.

This was probably what I should do.

But I knew I wouldn't.

I believed him. I couldn't explain why, and I hoped it wasn't just because of those sea-green eyes, but I wanted to help him.

"You're quiet," Eric observed.

"It's a lot to process," I said. I accelerated onto the freeway, only to find it crawling at a glacial pace. "How did Summer know John was your father?"

He sighed. "A number of his properties and subcompanies are owned through family trusts, so I get a constant stream of documents in the mail that have to do with Lionshare, most of which I ignore. But one morning, probably a year ago, I woke up to find Summer sitting at my desk, going through a pile of papers that had accumulated there—property deeds, stock info, signature requests, one of which was for the purchase of a new jet—things that had his name and info on them. I asked her what she was doing, and she said she was looking for a menu. She never again mentioned anything about it, and I didn't think about it until last week, when Dylan called with the news that Summer was dating our father."

"Weird. I talked to Dylan a bunch of times in the past week and he never once mentioned about Summer dating your dad to me."

He shrugged and threw me a glance as if to say, *See?*

"At least he told you when he found out," I pointed out. "She claimed to me that she met John when he randomly flew JetSafe."

He frowned. "It wasn't random. I did a little sleuthing after I found out they were dating. She applied for a job on his new jet and had one of his travel coordinators that she'd worked with at JetSafe call on her behalf and arrange for her to work a flight he was on."

"So you do care."

He stared out at the palm trees that peered over the top of the freeway wall. "No one likes to be used. Or lied to."

"The funny thing—if any of this is funny—is that they truly are perfect for each other," I said. "They're both monsters."

Day 7

Friday afternoon—Ligurian coast, Italy

The wildflowers are resplendent in the afternoon sun as I hasten down the dusty path toward a colorful village built into the bluff above the sea, but I've got no time to stop and appreciate the view.

My legs are wasted from the climb, my throat parched. A couple of sunburned hikers talking excitedly in German stall as I hurtle past them down the trail; I can only imagine what I must look like: dirty, sweaty, bloody, probably sunburned and wholly improperly dressed. But it's all downhill from here. I'm ten minutes from water—and, I'm hoping, cell service.

The path empties out onto a cobblestone street that winds through the quaint town toward the port. I follow it past a bed-and-breakfast with all its windows open, under laundry flapping in the breeze, past a restaurant with a sign in the window that says they will return at four...and then, like a mirage in the desert, I spy a small café.

My focus narrows. I beeline into the dark interior, to the refrigerator, and grab the biggest bottle of water they have. My mouth salivates as I peruse the premade sandwiches displayed in the case, pointing to one with what appears to be salami. The owner eyes me curiously, but takes my money without argument, and the next thing I know, I'm sitting on the curb, guzzling cold, refreshing, delicious water. I've never been so thirsty. I drink all of it but the last inch or so, which I use to splash my face and wash my hands. When I'm finished, I make quick work of the sandwich, hardly noticing the spicy, perfectly cured meat, earthy olive oil, and soft focaccia.

I could lie down and take a nap right here, but I know that's a bad idea.

I toss my trash and fish Amythest's phone from my purse. It's completely dead. Damn it. Can't I catch a break?

I head back into the café and show the man behind the counter the phone. "Charger?" I ask.

He shakes his head and says something in Italian that I don't understand.

"*Telefono?*" I beg. I dig a five-euro note from my purse, show it to him, and point to his phone. "*Un minuto.*" I make prayer hands.

"*Tutto bene, signorina?*" he asks, eyeing my disheveled appearance.

I nod and smile, having no idea what he said. He shrugs and slides his phone across the counter.

"*Grazie mille.*"

I scoop up the phone, google the number for the American embassy, and hit dial. Immediately a recording clicks on, informing me that walk-in embassy hours for emergencies are Monday through Friday, 8:30 a.m. to 12:00 p.m. Appointments for nonemergencies may also be made within those same hours.

It's 1:46.

The shop owner raises his eyebrows at me, and I give him my most winning smile. "*Un momento,*" I promise again as I keep googling, finally coming up with an emergency number for American victims of crime abroad.

I key through the automated menu until the line finally rings on the other end. "American Consulate Emergency Line, what's your emergency?" a woman answers.

"Thank God." I exhale. I urgently outline the events surrounding Amythest's death while she listens quietly. When I've finished, I ask if there's someone who can help me.

"I'm sorry, Miss Carter, I can't help you with investigation of a crime. It's out of our jurisdiction," she says politely. "But I can make a passport appointment for you on Monday if you like?"

My brain shorts. "But an American citizen was murdered," I object.

"And it will be investigated by the Italian or maritime authorities, depending on the exact location. We can't interfere in the justice system of foreign entities. We provide support for victims of crime. Have you been the victim of a crime?"

"I witnessed a murder," I say. "My passport, phone, and computer were stolen. I'm afraid for my life. What am I supposed to do?"

"If you're afraid for your life, you should report to the nearest police station. I can give you the address for the closest branch if you give me your location?"

Oh my God.

"Is this how you help victims of crime? You tell them to go to the police?"

"We provide options for resolution, and your best option is—"

"Is there nowhere else I can go? Somewhere American?" I interrupt.

"Walk-ins are accepted at the embassy Monday through—"

"I know," I cut in. "Anywhere else? I really need help."

"I'm sorry," she says. "The embassy has closed for the day. I advise you to go to the local police. Do you want that passport appointment for Monday?"

"Sure," I say.

Once the woman's taken my personal details for the passport appointment I'll never make it to, I hand the man his phone and return to the sidewalk to count my cash.

I have thirty-seven euros left of the fifty that I pulled out of an ATM in Saint-Tropez yesterday, plus the eighty Vince gave me. Not enough to make it to Monday unless I want to sleep on a park bench for three nights. I assume a wire transfer would take at least that long as well. I know I have another hundred or so in my bank account, but I don't want to use my debit card if I can avoid it. I haven't forgotten Vinny's warning that accusations can go both ways. For all I know, Summer may have told the authorities that I killed Amythest; if I show up at a station, they could consider me a murder suspect. Or John could be using his nefarious connections to keep tabs on me for his own purposes. I need to get back to the relative safety of the States as quickly as I can.

At least I still have the evidence on Amythest's phone. I desperately wish the damn thing had power—but truthfully, I have no useful phone numbers memorized anyway, and I'm afraid to communicate by email because I stupidly didn't have a password on my computer, so my emails are completely accessible to John and Bernard. I have to pin my hopes on Vinny's help and find the address he gave me by tonight. If La Quessine is near Saint-Tropez, I'm guessing it's about four or five hours by train, which means I can make it, if the train schedule is favorable.

I march back into the café for what I hope will be the last time. "*Treno?*" I ask.

The man points east. "*Nel prossimo paese.*"

I can gather that *prossimo* means "close," or "next." I don't know *paese*, but I hope one of the water taxi operators will be able to clarify. I trek down to the water, where a dock stretches into the waves, a handwritten sign in Italian and English advertising boat rides for ten euros. A swarthy, round man in his fifties sees me eyeing the sign and approaches with a grin.

"Boat ride. *Bellissimo.* You like, I take you."

I look over at the boats, little blue and green motorized dinghies, half the size of our tender. Getting in a boat that small with a man this large is counterintuitive, but he must do it every day, and he seems friendly enough.

I quote the man in the café, pointing east. "*Nel prossimo paese?*"

"You want, I take you," he says amiably. "You want watch the town, I wait."

"Is there a train station there?" I ask.

"*Sí, signorina.* Ten euro, good price."

"Is five okay?" I plead. "I'm really low on cash."

He shrugs. "For you, okay."

"*Grazie.*" I give him a five-euro note, and he hops into the boat. The dinghy rocks under his weight as he hands me down and helps me to sit on the bench. I see him register the scratches on my arms and dirt clinging to my torn dress as he releases me, but before he can comment, I give him my best smile. "Beautiful day," I say, sweeping my arm at the coastline.

"*Sí.*" My cheer must convince him I'm fine because he fires up the engine, and we're off. I gaze at the picturesque town as we bump across the surf, the sea spray cool on my burned skin. I feel like I can breathe for the first time since I slipped out of the jewelry shop. I've been in survival mode, able to think only of the next steps, but now Amythest's face comes back to me, and I'm racked with grief for the girl I'd just begun to know...and guilt. I should never have told her the truth about Summer, should never have given her my watch. Her words just yesterday about not wanting to be buried near the sea haunt me, an eerie foreshadowing of her watery death. Somewhere beneath the waves, her lifeless body undulates with the tide. She'll wash up on shore swollen with seawater in a few days or weeks, only to be discovered by some unsuspecting passerby, who will be forever scarred by the sight of her unrecognizable corpse. I stifle tears.

Around an outcropping of rocks, another village comes into view, probably twice the size of Terralione. This one is full of life. A narrow strip of sandy shore speckled with blue umbrellas is ringed by yellow and terra-cotta buildings that climb up the green hills. At the far end of the harbor, a small port curls into the azure water like a fishhook.

Sunbathers have spread towels on the biggest boulders, and the water is so clear that I can see little fish flitting in and out of the shadows cast by the rocks on the seafloor. We dock next to a row of boats no bigger than ours, and the driver hands me up to the cobblestone promenade.

(t w e n t y d a y s a g o)

Mexico

It was late afternoon by the time we reached the border. I fingered my passport, nervous. I'd never driven into Mexico before and didn't know what to expect, but Eric had assured me there was very little likelihood of anyone stopping us. Of course, if they did, they'd find a very beat-up guy with a fake passport and a bag of a hundred thousand dollars in cash.

I glanced at him as he finished off the In-N-Out burger he'd insisted we pick up when I'd revealed I'd never had one. He was looking better than he had this morning, but I was glad we'd finally be seeing a doctor tomorrow. I couldn't imagine how he'd made it through the past few days with all those injuries. "What?" he asked when he caught me staring at him. "Is my face covered in mustard?"

I laughed. "No. I was just wondering how you got to my house."

"Bus, mostly. And some very slow walking. I didn't have a lot of cash and didn't want to use cards." He held up the burger. "I ate a lot of these."

"But it was days. Where did you sleep?"

"I hid out in a cheap motel near the park until I felt strong enough to walk into town to catch the bus." He ran a hand over his shorn hair. "Did this so I'd look different."

I eyed his bruises. "I don't think you needed to worry about that."

Traffic slowed to a crawl, and high concrete walls sprang up along the sides of the freeway as we inched toward the border. Eric put on a Dodgers baseball cap and a pair of orange, mirrored Wayfarer sunglasses we'd picked up at the gas station. I sucked the dregs of my iced tea, nervous.

"We're in a Prius. We're gonna be fine," he said.

Up ahead a sign flashed ENTERING MEXICO, BE PREPARED TO STOP. I saw the weigh station and a number of booths with border agents, police SUVs with dogs searching cars, lights flashing.

We rolled up to the green-uniformed officer guarding our lane, his hand on the butt of his gun. He motioned for me to roll down the window, and I did, smiling. I handed him our passports and he stooped and looked me up and down, then glanced around me at Eric, who waved.

"Any fruits or vegetables?" the officer asked.

I did my best impression of nonchalance. "No."

He returned our passports without so much as glancing at them, and waved us on. "Welcome to Mexico."

I rolled up the window and pulled away, exhaling a sigh of relief.

Eric took a crumpled piece of notebook paper from his pocket and unfolded it. "Can I see your phone?"

I handed him the phone and he punched in an address scribbled on the paper. "Where are we going?" I asked.

"Rosarito. It's a beach town just south of Tijuana."

"Is it safe?"

"It's fine," he replied.

"That's where the doctor is?"

"Yes. I'll see him tomorrow. I'm feeling better, though. You did a good job patching me up."

I glanced at him. "That's the painkillers talking," I said. "You're still going to the doctor."

He consulted the phone. "Go left here."

I followed his directions into the setting sun as he scrolled through the channels on the radio, landing on a traditional mariachi station. My phone dinged in his hand. He raised his eyebrows. "You got a text from Summer."

"What's it say?"

"'Hey, girl.'" He put on his best Summer voice. "'John's leaving Sunday if you wanna come out for the week. LMK.'" He dropped the valley-girl accent. "Smiley winky face with heart."

"Text her back, 'Go to hell, bitch. You tried to murder Eric and pin it on me.'"

His fingers moved across the screen. "No!" I cried. "I was joking!"

"Oops. Already sent." He saw the petrified look on my face and laughed. "I'm kidding. I didn't send anything. What do you want me to say?"

I thought for a minute. "'Headed out to Lake Havasu to visit Grannie in her new condo, hit you up when I'm back.' Winky smiley face with heart."

"You two are all about that winky smiley face with heart," he said, typing the message into the phone. "Take a right up there at the gate."

I turned onto a wide cobblestone drive with a guardhouse in the center, flanked by two big white arches. A fat guard in a white uniform opened the window of the guardhouse as we approached. Eric leaned across me. "*Vamos 78 Calle Costa Azul, invitados Eduardo Garcia.*"

"*Nombre?*" the guard asked.

"Raphael Sanzio," Eric said.

The guard checked his list, then opened the gate. "*Izquierda en la fuente.*"

The road gently sloped down toward where the orange-and-pink sky met the tranquil sea, leveling out at a big fountain, lit blue. I turned left and bumped along between the pristine white hacienda bungalows that lined both sides of the road.

"That's it." Eric indicated a bungalow on the ocean side.

I parked the car in the carport and got out and stretched, then unloaded my overnight bag from the back and lugged it up the steps while he unlocked the blue door.

Inside, light from the sunset spilled through double sliding glass doors into the open living room. A colorful rug was strewn across the terra-cotta floor, and traditional Mexican blankets in deep hues of turquoise and red hung on the walls over white couches. I dropped my bag and beelined for the sliding glass doors.

Eric and I stood side by side at the terrace railing, looking out at the ocean. The air was thick with salty sea mist. A set of stairs led down to a sandy beach that stretched fifty feet to where the waves crashed.

"Raphael Sanzio?" I asked. "At the gate."

"My new name, thanks to George." He laughed. "The Renaissance—"

"Painter, yeah, I know." I laughed.

"You know your art history," he said, impressed.

"You don't have to know history to know who Raphael is. He's a Teenage Mutant Ninja Turtle, for chrissakes."

"Summer didn't."

"And here I thought you liked her for her brain." I turned and walked inside.

He followed me into the kitchen, where I opened cabinets, hunting for the liquor. "You were fooled by her, too," he pointed out.

I found a nearly full bottle of silver tequila and held it up triumphantly. "True." I set it on the blue tiled counter with a clink. "And I wasn't even getting blowies from her."

When I looked up, he'd disappeared. I took out two margarita glasses and filled them with ice from a bag in the freezer, then poured hefty shots over the ice.

Eric entered to find me rummaging through the cabinets in search of mixers. He dumped a pile of limes on the counter, laughing when he saw my expression. "There's a tree out front."

I sliced up limes and squeezed the juice over the ice. "To your new life as a Renaissance man," I said, handing him a glass.

He smiled and held my gaze. "Thank you again."

I ripped my eyes away and stared into my drink, pushing away the memory of his lips on mine. "You don't have to keep thanking me."

I studied the smashed lime floating in my tequila, struck by the thought that if Summer had tried to murder him and pin it on me, I probably didn't need to worry anymore about ruining our friendship by dating him.

The possibility lit in my chest a desire so strong, I had to walk away. I headed to the bathroom, where I stared at my face in the mirror and promised myself I wouldn't make any rash decisions. I felt sure he'd sleep with me right now if I gave him the chance, but I'd actually come to value Eric's friendship, and I certainly didn't want to ruin it over sex. Because, no matter that he'd come to me for help, no matter that I meant that much to him at least—the rest was still true: Eric had never been the type of guy who was looking for a serious relationship, and I had no interest in having my heart broken by him.

Once I'd gotten ahold of myself, I joined him on the balcony, where we sipped our cocktails, watching the light bleed from the sky. The tequila burned down my throat all the way to my belly. Emboldened by the alcohol, I ventured another of the questions that had been gnawing at me.

"What happened with John and your mom?" I knew I was prying, but he didn't seem to mind.

"My mom grew up poor in Paris. John swept her off her feet, knocked her up with me, moved her to New York. Then, when she was six months' pregnant, she found out he was married."

"To Dylan's mom?"

He nodded. "My mom couldn't work in the US without the green card he never delivered, and he wouldn't let her leave the country with me, so she was completely dependent on him. He liked it that way. She lived in one of his apartments; he gave her just enough money to scrape by. He controlled her and abused her, mentally and physically. She had to be a certain weight; she wasn't allowed to see other men. She became depressed. She drank, started popping pills. When I was eleven, I came home from school one day to find her in the bathtub with her wrists slit."

My hand went to my heart. "God, Eric, I'm so sorry."

"It was his fault. He made her miserable."

No wonder he hated his father so much. "Where did you live after that?" I asked.

"John sent me to live with his mother in France," he said. "Ironic because all my mother had ever wanted was to return to France. He was never around, but my grandmother was wonderful, and Dylan would come visit during the summer. Dyl hated John almost as much as I did."

"Does he hate him still?"

"I guess not," Eric said. "For enough money, anyone can be bought."

"Not you, apparently."

"Not by his money. Because it comes with strings. He's a puppeteer, and I don't want to be his puppet." He drained his drink and leaned his forearms on the railing, his head hanging between them. "I would like to take it away from him, though," he muttered.

"Is your grandmother still alive? Could she help you?"

He nodded. "She's in her nineties, still sharp. She owns a lot of stock in the company, but she hasn't been involved for years. She knows John's not the most honest businessman, but she doesn't know the extent of it, and I haven't told her because there was nothing she could do. I was planning to share what John was guilty of once I had the evidence in hand, but I never got the chance."

"And now?"

"I'd never risk putting her in danger." He rubbed his temples, clearly spent.

"You're exhausted," I said. "And I'm not helping, asking you so many questions. You should get some sleep. Take the bed. You're in far worse shape than I am."

He looked up, mischief in his eyes. "You can sleep in it, too. I don't bite—unless asked."

The heat in my chest flared; my resolution wavered. I looked out at the crashing waves, knowing that all I had to do was turn my face toward him...and this time we wouldn't have to stop. But it had been a long twenty-four hours, we were in an extreme situation, and neither of us was thinking clearly right now. So as much as I wanted him, I gathered my resolve and laughed it off, never meeting his eye. "Thanks, but I've got enough hand-me-downs from Summer."

"Yeah, I guess I don't need any more from my brother, either," he returned with a smile.

"Touché," I said.

In the morning, we drove thirty minutes north to the doctor George had recommended. I'd assumed, because we were paying cash for off-the-books treatment in Tijuana, that his office would be as sketchy as the transaction, but it wasn't. Far from it. The lobby boasted polished tile floors and marble counters topped with fresh flowers, the leather couches were comfortable, and racks displayed every tabloid under the sun, in both Spanish and English.

After a torturous two hours of failing to distract myself with magazines, finally the office door opened and I looked up to see a smiling Eric. His arm was in a sling and he was sporting fresh bandages. "Broken collarbone, three ribs, stress fracture in my thumb, and a sprained ankle." He beamed. "And they dressed all the cuts. The arm was a little infected, but they cleaned it out and gave me antibiotics."

"The nose?"

"Broken, but will probably heal fine, so they don't need to rebreak it. And my cheekbone is broken, but it's sitting in place, so as long as I don't cage-fight for a while, I'll be okay."

I must have looked at him funny, because he clarified. "I don't cage-fight. That was a joke. Doctor was shocked I was in such good shape, given the fall. Wanna grab a margarita and lunch?"

"How's the pain?"

"Not great, but better than it was. He gave me a prescription for painkillers, but I don't want them. I'm my mother's son—I like them too much. I'd rather hit the tequila."

We ordered lunch from a taco truck and carried it back to the house, where we sat at the table on the terrace in the shade of a big umbrella.

Eric mixed margaritas for us while whistling "Margaritaville," buoyant with the knowledge that he had no internal bleeding, no badly infected wounds, and fewer than expected broken bones.

Gazing out at the ocean, I could almost forget the circumstances of our bizarre little vacation. But I was going to have to go home and face the music tomorrow, and he wasn't going to be able to live off a hundred thousand dollars for the rest of his life. Not even in Mexico.

He raised his glass. "To heaven."

"More like purgatory," I returned. "It can't last forever."

"We can pretend," he countered.

"You need a plan."

"Who says I don't already have one?"

I raised my brows.

"I'm going to stake my claim on Lionshare Holdings."

"How? I thought you didn't want it. And he's not about to give it to you, not anymore."

"I don't want it; I just want to watch him lose it."

"But you need leverage," I said. "Right now you have none."

He nodded. "That's why it does me more good for Summer to think she got away with it, and for her to stay with my father. She's my in."

"I don't follow. You no longer have access to her," I pointed out. He looked at me purposefully. Right. "But...I do." Now I understood. My heart sank. "I'm your plan."

So this was why he'd come to me; this was why he'd been flirting with me. Of course. How could I have been so stupid?

"Summer told me she was taking you and some other girls on a trip aboard his yacht in a couple of weeks, right? It would be the perfect opportunity...."

"Fuck you." I pushed away from the table. "I can't believe I trusted you."

"Belle, I promise you can trust—"

"Why don't you go ask your brother? He knows much more about your dad and his corruption, I'm *sure*, than Summer does."

"I don't trust him."

"Just because he's at your dad's company doesn't mean he's become your dad," I challenged. "The way Dylan put it to me, he wanted to grow up, take responsibility, take advantage of the opportunities available to him. That's not evil; that's smart. Maybe it would do you some good to take a page from his book and grow up yourself."

"Belle," he said quietly.

I recognized that I was hurt and lashing out, but he was using me. "You're jealous of him because he's actually making something of himself, and you've just come to me because you thought I'd be an easier mark. But guess what? You were wrong."

He drew back, looking out at the sea, silent. I was so angry, I felt physically ill.

Finally he spoke. "I'm sorry I'm not my brother," he muttered.

"And I'm sorry I'm not Summer," I snapped. I pushed back from the table. "I need to be getting back to LA. Good luck with your scheme."

I stormed inside without a backward glance. He didn't follow me, didn't try to stop me as I gathered my things and chucked them into my car, didn't chase after the Prius as I pulled away, glancing furtively in the rearview mirror.

Day 7

Friday evening—Ligurian coast, Italy

After the twenty-four hours I've had, the lazy pace of a seaside village in the late afternoon feels like a dream. Remnants of the adrenaline that has kept me in motion all day still surge through my veins, making me jumpy, and I'm so exhausted that my whole body is buzzing, my thoughts a jumbled mess. *Your sister is on her way to your grandmother's.* What did Vinny mean by that? *Remember why you're here.* What does he know?

I can't be sure I can trust him, but there's no time to worry about it now. I have to keep moving. I need to get to the train station.

It can't be that difficult to find, right? This place isn't exactly a sprawling metropolis. I survey the old-world buildings that line the sun-drenched seaport and head toward what I'm guessing is the center of town, scanning the passing faces for hostility.

There's a group of teenage girls huddled together on a bench giggling over a cell phone, a couple making out with abandon in the midst of a crowded restaurant patio, a grown man eating gelato from a cone with gusto. None of them remotely hostile.

A young woman standing under the red awning of a restaurant offers a menu as I approach. "*Treno stazione?*" I ask.

Her face shows concern as she registers my appearance, and she begins to speak in rapid Italian. I stop her apologetically. "*No Italiano.*"

Unfazed, she calls back into the restaurant behind her, drops her menus on a table without waiting for an answer, and starts off down the bustling sidewalk, waving for me to follow. When we reach a narrow alleyway that cuts between two salmon-colored buildings, she gestures that I should go up the alley and make a left at the top.

"*Grazie*," I say, but she's already jogging back toward her restaurant.

The brick passageway is shaded and cool. I hurry up the path between the endless rows of vine-covered buildings to a set of stairs that lead up to the left. I follow the steps as my guide suggested, until they empty into a small square arranged around a fountain depicting a man wrestling with a lion.

On the far side of the square is an archway with a painted green sign above that shows a picture of a train.

I hasten across the square into the tunnel beyond the arch. The walls are rough-cut stone, the domed ceiling up-lit with blue lights. My beaten sandals slap the flagstone, echoing down the corridor as I push on for what must be a hundred yards or more, until it opens into a light-filled chamber with vaulted ceilings and brushed-concrete floors.

The station isn't crowded: a few people mill about reading their cell phones; a backpacker is asleep on a bench, his head resting on his pack in the unguarded way only a man can doze in public. To my right under a board announcing train schedules is the ticket booth, facing three sets of double doors flung open to the track beyond.

I'm nearly certain passport checks aren't mandatory between Italy and France, but I'm obviously going to have a problem if a spot check is conducted at any point. There's no way around it, though. I guess I'll just have to somehow elude the passport inspectors if that happens.

I study the board, unable to find La Quessine or Saint-Tropez. From the map, it looks like the closest station is a place called Saint-Raphaël Valescure, which I'm guessing is still a good hour from La Quessine by car, but it'll have to do.

The uniformed man in the booth looks up as I approach. "*Ciao*," I say, smiling. "*Uno ticket por treno a Saint-Raphaël Valescure.*"

Thankfully, he seems to understand my pigeon Italian. "*A che ora?*" He points to the board.

The next train is at 14:59, arriving at Saint-Raphaël after one change at 20:07. I'll just have to pray I have enough money left for a cab and that I find a driver willing to floor it to La Quessine to get me there by nine.

I have no idea how to say 14:59, so I go with *"La prossima treno."* I'm wildly guessing at the translation, but he gets what I'm trying to say.

"Quattro minuti." He points to a large clock that I somehow missed, right next to the board. It reads 14:55. I have four minutes. Not enough time to find a phone charger, but oh well. I've got the address memorized, thank God, and if I want to make it in time to meet Vinny, I've gotta get on that train. I nod wildly. *"Ventinove."*

Grateful for the low price, I hand over the twenty-nine euros and he gives me my ticket just as the train pulls into the station.

(nineteen to twelve days ago)

Mexico/Los Angeles

I was trapped somewhere in the middle of the thick line of cars inching toward the US border when the remorse set in.

I'd screwed up. I should never have said those things to Eric.

A hot wind mixed dust with the exhaust of the hundreds of vehicles behind and ahead of me, forcing me to keep the windows raised though the air-conditioning struggled to keep up. My head pounded; my tongue was thick with thirst. But what pained me most was the sinking feeling in the pit of my stomach that I'd ruined things with him. I'd been mean. I knew his brother was his point of weakness and used it against him. All because he'd asked me for help.

Had he been trying to manipulate me? He'd made no false promises, told no lies. He'd answered all my questions honestly and was nothing but gracious and open with me.

So he flirted with me; that wasn't a crime. He was just a flirt. He was French, after all; it was probably how he dealt with everyone. I was the one who had read into it, thought there'd been more between us than there was, because I'd wanted there to be. And to be fair, he probably did want to sleep with me, even if he didn't want anything further.

God, I was so glad I hadn't slept with him last night. I'd be far more mortified than I was right now.

I should go back, apologize. But there was nowhere to turn the car around in this clusterfuck.

I took out my phone and thumbed through my contacts, landing on the number for the Mexican burner he'd purchased this morning. I steeled my nerves and hit dial. The phone rang and rang, and finally a message in Spanish came on saying what I could only imagine was that the user had not yet set up voice mail. I sent a text:

I'm sorry. I want to help you. Tell me what I can do.

When I still hadn't heard from Eric a week after I returned from Rosarito, I figured it was over. I'd managed to fuck it up and I'd never see him again. I worried about him; I considered driving back down there—I lay awake nights staring at the ceiling, going over the different possible scenarios for our reunion (he loved me, he hated me, he was gone, he was dead)—but in the end I decided that if he wasn't returning my texts or calls, he probably didn't want to see me. And I desperately needed to work to pay my rent.

I did speak to Dylan a few days after I left Mexico. He didn't call me; I called him, maintaining the charade that I was simply a concerned friend. I inquired as to whether he or his father had found anything further about Eric's disappearance, hoping against hope that he'd come clean with me and admit that John was their father, who was only looking into Eric's disappearance so that he could make it permanent. For Eric's sake, I wanted Dylan to turn out to be a good brother after all, for Eric to be wrong about him. But Dylan shut me down, telling me they'd found no signs of foul play. I should let it go, he said. When I reminded him there was still no body, he gave me a rather cryptic "Let's hope it stays that way."

"Has anyone been to his loft?" I'd asked, knowing it would still be the mess he'd found after it had been ransacked, as Eric hadn't had time to clean it before Summer pushed him off the cliff. "Maybe there would be some clue there."

"Yeah," he said. "Everything was in order."

So he was lying to me. "Summer has a key," I fibbed. "Maybe I'll go by and—"

"Please don't," he said. "Belle—the kind of people Eric was involved with—even if they had nothing to do with it, trust me, you don't want to draw their attention. Promise me you won't."

He sounded genuinely worried enough that I promised, realizing that just maybe he was lying to me in order to protect me. Maybe he wasn't such a bad guy after all. Maybe he was a coward, or maybe he was biding his time to bring his father down on his own terms (though from what Eric had told me, it was doubtful). Only time would tell.

The following Tuesday night at the dimly lit swanky joint where I tended bar was slow. I was taking my time to craft the perfect Southside for one of my favorite regulars—an older actor who reminded me of my late grandfather—when I heard my name, spoken by a woman with a soft lilt to her voice. I looked up to see George. Her hair was piled atop her head in the same stylishly messy updo as the last time I'd seen her and she was wearing the same red lipstick and black-framed glasses, leaning on the bar with her gaze fixed on me. When our eyes met, she smiled.

"Fancy seeing you here!" I said, perhaps too brightly. I slid the Southside in front of my regular and made my way over to her. "What can I get you?"

"Macallan on the rocks," she said.

Of course that was her drink. I poured her glass fuller than management would be happy with and set it in front of her. She tipped it to me and took a sip. "Can we talk?"

I nodded. "Ed," I called to the other bartender, "I'm taking my break."

He gave me a thumbs-up and cast a glance around the empty bar. "Think I can handle it."

George followed me to a corner table, where we sat facing each other. I extracted a matchbook from my pocket and relit the votive in the center of the table. "What's up?"

She leaned in, her features distorted in the candlelight. "*Raphael* sent me."

My heart fluttered. "Oh?"

"He got your texts before he changed his number, but he was afraid to reach out to you himself. He didn't want to put you in danger."

A ray of hope. Perhaps he didn't hate me, after all. "What did he say?"

"He could use your help, if you're still up for it."

I resisted the urge to smile. "What does that mean?"

"He wants to stop his father doing any more damage to the world," she whispered earnestly. "He's trying to gather enough incriminating information on him to blackmail him into handing over the reins of the company."

I raised my brows.

"He realizes if he wants change he is going to have to create it himself," she went on. "His father knows so many powerful people, he has escaped accusations with hard evidence so many times. Even if Raphael were successful in exposing his crimes, he might still never go to prison, and Raphael and others would likely suffer, or die, in the crossfire. It would be a waste. Instead he has to beat his father at his own game."

"How is he planning to do that?"

She leaned in, her dark eyes gleaming in the flickering light. "He's hired someone trustworthy to build a secure server where he can store evidence against his father—evidence that if it is ever exposed, would send him to jail—which he'll keep locked away as long as his father stays in line."

"What evidence?"

"That's where you come in."

I frowned. "I don't know how much help I'm going to be in that department. I don't have unrestricted access to Jo—his father, and he certainly doesn't tell me his secrets."

"You're going on a trip aboard his yacht in a few weeks, no?"

I shook my head. I'd been using my job and a faked illness as an excuse to avoid Summer since I returned from Mexico, but hadn't yet worked up the nerve to cancel my trip with her. "No way."

"Hear me out," she said. "You may change your mind."

I took a deep breath. "I'm listening."

She removed a gold box from her bag and set it on the table between us. "Open it."

I removed the lid. Inside the box was a gold watch with a large round digital face. I took it out and slipped it around my wrist. "What's this?"

She set a user manual an inch thick on the table next to the box. "Think of it like a security camera on your wrist. It wirelessly records all audio and video to a remote server without you ever having to do a thing."

I was dubious. "So you want me to wear this on the trip? And what, try to get John to talk about illegal stuff?"

"Shhhhh..." She stiffened at the mention of his name and looked around, but none of the few patrons in the bar appeared to be paying us any mind. "This trip is really about visiting a town on the Ligurian coast that he plans to raze and turn into a resort. You girls are just decoration. He'll be taking meetings along the way, and though he's always careful, he won't suspect that one of Summer's girlfriends might be anything more than a pretty face. So you'll have a better chance than anyone of getting close to the source. You're an actress, right? All you need to do is play the part of glamorous guest—relax and take advantage of his hospitality, drink his champagne, eat his caviar, and get a tan."

I laughed. "I don't think I'll be doing much *relaxing.*" But she did make my role sound easy, for the amount of good it would do. Almost too easy. The hardest part would be pretending to be Summer's friend for a week.

"The other thing—in fact, the main thing—you need to do is log in to the computer on the boat and access the link Raphael sends you. It will allow his guys to hack into the server and cameras on the boat."

"Ah," I said, the wheels of my brain spinning. "Will they know the servers have been hacked? What if they catch me? I'm not exactly James Bond."

"They'll never know. The malware doesn't make any changes. It only allows remote access and download. And from what I understand, guests are allowed to use the desktops on board."

"How will I communicate with him while I'm on the trip? I assume we can't email or talk. How will I know it's working, or if something's going wrong?"

"He'll set up an email in another name. A friend of yours, someone you would be emailing anyway to tell about your trip. You'll send each other coded messages this way, messages that appear to be about the weather or food."

That sounded complicated. "We can't just use apps?"

"No. And you'll need to wipe your phone of anything personal. We can't be sure he won't have trackers installed on your phones once on board."

"Jesus." I bit my lip, turning over the idea. "So I just go on the trip like everything is normal. Wear this watch and click on some link. No one will ever be the wiser."

She nodded. "Simple."

But it wasn't simple. I'd have to spend a week cooped up on a boat in a foreign country with Summer. Granted, it wouldn't be just any boat—it would be a luxury megayacht, likely with plenty of room to get away from her. Wendy and Claire would be there as well, and surely Summer would be on her best behavior in front of John, her mother, and all her friends? It certainly wouldn't be the fun girls' trip I'd imagined when she'd first extended the invitation, but perhaps the week could be...doable. "Then what? When is he planning to blackmail his father with all this?"

"Once Raphael feels he's gathered enough material, he'll meet with his father and force the turnover of the company." She looked into my eyes. "Belle, don't worry. He'll do his best to make sure your friend never knows you were involved. The confrontation will be after you return, and he won't make a move until he knows he has enough to make it stick. This isn't all on you. If he doesn't get enough evidence from the boat trip, he'll find other ins, other ways to get more information."

"So I'm not totally necessary."

"You're his best bet," she said. "He can't play dead forever. Time is of the essence, and you'll be in a place to give him access to the information on all his father's servers. It's unlikely there won't be enough evidence to follow through with the plan."

It was true I had a personal stake in Eric coming back from the dead before the authorities suspected foul play and Summer pinned his disappearance on me, so agreeing to this plan could be beneficial for my interests as well. "How will I be safe, afterward? Once John sees the feed from the watch, he'll know it was me."

"That's the whole point of the blackmail," she assured me. "He won't dare touch you because if anything ever happens to you, all the videos and other information will be released."

I nodded slowly. I knew that John was a horrible person doing damage to the world on a daily basis; I believed in Eric's cause and knew that in addition to it benefiting me personally, I'd be doing my part to actually make lasting, positive change—a chance I might never have again. But this was my life, the only one I had. Did I want to stake it on this? "It's a big risk." I exhaled.

"There will be money in it for you. You just need to name your price."

Oh. "Can I talk to . . . Raphael?"

She took out her cell phone, hit dial, and put it to her ear. "I'm here with Belle. She has some questions for you." She passed me the phone.

"Hi," I said, my heart in my throat.

"Hi." I thought I detected a smile in his voice. "She told you everything?"

"Yes."

"Will you help me?"

I sighed. Would I be able to live with myself if I didn't? "It's a lot."

"I know. But I also know you can handle it. You're strong, and you're a damn good actress. If you can manage to put everything that's happened out of your mind for just one week, pretend you're still her friend—the watch and the link will do all the rest."

His voice was so close, I could almost imagine his breath in my ear. "Can I see you?" He was silent for a moment. "Hello?"

"I'm here. I . . . I'm not in Mexico anymore. I'm . . . a lot farther away. Probably better if you don't know where. George doesn't, either. But after it's over, I won't have to hide anymore."

"I talked to your brother a few days ago," I said. "He told me nothing was out of order at your apartment."

"So either he's lying or John cleaned it up," he said.

I hadn't thought about the possibility of John cleaning it up. "He said there was no reason to suspect foul play, but that I should stay out of it for my own safety. I got the feeling he knew a lot more than he was letting on."

"Of course he does," Eric said. "He's in France now, staying with our grandmother near Saint-Tropez. If you have a chance to see him while you're there, take it. See if you can find out what he knows and where his loyalties lie."

"What about your grandmother? Whose side is she on?"

"I've left her out of everything until now because I didn't want to upset her, but I'm nearly certain she'll be on our side once she learns the truth."

"What if something goes wrong? What if they find me out?"

"Remember, I'll be able to see the feed from the watch every time it connects to Wi-Fi and uploads what it's shot since the last time it was connected. If anything goes wrong, we change plans. I'll get you out of there. I promise."

"Okay," I said. "Lemme think about it. But I think, okay."

Day 7

Friday evening—Italian to French Riviera

The train careens along the lip of the cliff on rails cut into the side of the mountain, high above the glittering sea. My heart beats in sync with every rotation of the wheels as we skate along the razor's edge. It's breathtaking; one wrong move and we plunge to the rocks below.

I've failed on my mission and I'm a million miles from home. What a terrible spy I'd make. Staring out at the horizon, I catalog my mistakes: I should have taken the money Eric offered; I should have been more careful—more obsequious with Summer, firmer with Amythest; I should never have given Amythest my watch. When was the last time it had uploaded—in the port yesterday before my meeting with John? At least I'd downloaded the link. If the cameras on the boat caught Summer pushing Amythest, was Eric able to capture the recording off John's servers before the feed was inevitably wiped?

The train hurtles into a tunnel. *Your sister is headed to your grandmother's.* A threat? Or a reference to my code with Eric, a validation that Vinny's on my side? In the pitch black, I wish more than anything that I could email Lauren_Carter812 somehow, and find out who to trust.

Please, God, don't let it be a trap.

Hoping to avoid passport control, I visit the restroom as we cross the French border, taking as much time as possible to clean myself up in the small steel space. It feels immensely good to wash my face and rinse the blood, sweat, and dirt from my weary limbs, but nothing is to be done about my tangled hair or ripped dress. Thankfully, when I emerge, I find no agents have boarded the train.

When the train pulls into Gare de Saint-Raphaël Valescure just after eight, the sun has just dropped beneath the sea, leaving the sky lavender in its wake. I scramble off the train and hasten through the modern station, skidding to a stop in front of the rectangular glass information booth. "Taxi?"

"*Sortir les portes à gauche*," the unsmiling attendant informs me, pointing toward the sliding glass doors.

Outside to the left, I find a couple of taxis idling at the curb in a dedicated lane just off the busy local street. I lean into the open passenger-side window of the first one in line. "La Quessine?" I ask.

He shakes his head. "*Local seulement.*"

I move to the second taxi in line and repeat the question, only to be given another refusal. Discouraged, I move to the third and last taxi. The driver adjusts her hot-pink hijab and sighs. "*Deux cent. En especes.*"

My jaw drops. Two hundred euros? After the low cost of the train ticket, I'd been hopeful a taxi would at least be affordable. I only have eighty in cash, and I don't know whether I even have a hundred in my bank account. Regardless, I nod. "Okay," I say. "*Je vais au . . .*" I don't know the word for ATM. "ATM? Cash point?"

She nods and holds up three fingers. "*Je vous attendre trois minutes.*"

I cast a glance around for an ATM, relieved to spot one not twenty feet from where I stand, on the front of the boxlike train station. I insert my debit card and hit the balance button, hoping against hope that I have enough. Finally the spinning wheel disappears and my balance flashes up on the screen: €108.20. So I'm twenty short. Okay, clearly I'm just gonna have to make do.

Again kicking myself for being too proud to take the money Eric offered me before the trip, I withdraw the hundred the ATM will allow me and return to the car sporting my most pitiful smile. "*J'ai cent quatre-vingts*," I say. Then, remembering the three left over from my train ticket. "*Cent quatre-vingt trois. S'il vous plaît? C'est très important.*"

She looks me up and down, considering. "*S'il vous plaît*," I again plead with prayer hands.

She nods and waves me into the cab. "*Merci beaucoup*," I cry, climbing into the backseat with a sigh of relief. "*Allez au 12 Chemin de la Pommière dans La Quessine.*" She searches in her navigation. "*Combien de temps?*"

"*Une heure*," she says as she pulls away from the curb.

I'll be ten minutes late, but ten minutes is nothing considering the hoops I've jumped through to get here, and with any luck Vinny can be a little flexible.

We wind along the coast as the color drains from the sky, and I find I'm biting my nails, a habit I haven't indulged in since college. I stop myself, for the millionth time trying to focus on my breathing as I gaze out the window. I feel as though I've leaped off a cliff with no idea whether I can fly. All I need is my passport back, and to get home, where I can reconnect with Eric and be done with this whole charade.

Night has fallen by the time we drive through the gate at the address Vinny gave me. A full moon hovers over the water, casting long shadows as we roll up the gravel driveway nestled between vineyard rows. Atop the hill looking out toward the sea is a large traditional French country house, stone exterior accentuated by light-blue shutters and a steep, sloped roof. I'm not sure what I expected for my handoff with Vinny—dark alleys and abandoned warehouses come to mind—but a mansion with an unobstructed view of the Mediterranean is certainly a surprise. "*Êtes-vous sûr que c'est l'adresse?*" I ask the driver.

"*Douze Chemin de la Pommière*," she confirms.

We stop next to a bubbling fountain, and I give her all my cash, thanking her again.

She drives away in a cloud of dust as I climb the flagstone steps, for the first time reading the inscription etched in curling iron above the entryway. GRANDVIEW MANOR. I recognize the name immediately as Eric and Dylan's grandmother's estate. So this is where Vinny was leading me.

Your sister is headed to your grandmother's.

Of course. It makes perfect sense. I stare at the blue double doors, butterflies fluttering in my stomach.

Now or never.

I raise the heavy ornate knocker and rap three times.

A plump older woman in a traditional maid's black dress and white apron opens the door and looks me up and down. I'm less dirty than I'd been before I cleaned myself up on the train, but still, I can only imagine the image I must cut in my ragged dress and shoes with my wild hair and bloody knees. "*Mademoiselle,*" she says politely. "*Puis-je vous aider?*"

My mind blanks. I guess they weren't formally expecting me. I never considered the door might be opened by a housekeeper wanting to know my intentions. It's the most elementary question, and I have no idea how to answer it. Is Vinny here? Is Eric here? I seem to have traveled halfway across Europe only to turn up at his grandmother's doorstep without even knowing her name, for heaven's sake.

I smile dumbly, reaching for the one name that's still safe to use. "Um, I'm a friend of Dylan's?"

I hope he's the kind of guy who extends invitations to friends far and wide to visit him if they're passing through France. I have no idea whether he's home, but maybe that won't matter. All I need is to get inside for a few minutes, long enough for the handoff with Vinny. *Please, God, let Vinny be here . . . or Eric.*

The housekeeper moves aside, and I step into the quiet house, smoothing my hair. Iron chandeliers hang from the vaulted ceiling; a muted Oriental rug stretches across the flagstone floor. At one end of the room, a giant stone fireplace presides over a set of slate velvet couches that face each other across a wide reclaimed-wood coffee table. But what draws my eye is the art. The walls are lined with countless paintings and photographs of every different size and style, hardly an inch of wall between them.

"*Suivez moi,*" she says, beckoning to me.

My heart thuds so hard I'm surprised she can't hear it as I follow her down a hallway and into a deep-blue parlor. On the far wall, a large flat-screen television is mounted between two white bookshelves that stretch the length of the room. A glass coffee table divides two barrel-backed white chairs and a white couch.

Oh. I guess this is why she didn't hesitate when I mentioned his name: one of the chairs is indeed occupied by Dylan, staring at me with astonishment. I give him what I hope is a friendly but not too friendly nod. I still have no idea what he knows, or doesn't, or whose side he's on. Clearly this isn't the moment to find out.

In the other chair is a small, stylish woman who looks to be in her eighties. She wears a black sweater with white pants, a long strand of pearls around her neck. Her hair is pure white, and watchful eyes peer out from behind black-framed round glasses, taking me in. My most polite smile evaporates when my eyes land on the other two people in the room: John and Summer are perched uncomfortably on the edge of the low couch with their legs at odd angles, as though they might leave at any minute.

My blood turns to ice. No. No, no. It was a trap, after all.

Clearly upset by the sight of me, Summer starts to speak, but John silences her with a small movement of his hand, his countenance absent its usual charm. If he's surprised to see me, he covers it well.

I stand very still, feeling all their eyes on me. Every reflex in my body is screaming at me to run, but that would do me no good. I have to think like a predator, not prey.

"Isabelle," John says evenly.

Ignoring him, I step over the little white dog curled up asleep on the rug and extend my hand to the woman I can only assume is Dylan and Eric's grandmother. An ally, I pray. "*Je m'appelle Isabelle Carter*," I say as blithely as I can muster in my best French. "*Votre maison est magnifique.*"

Dylan stares at me like I'm speaking in tongues, but the woman smiles. "Grace." She takes my hand between hers. "*Enchantée.*"

Behind me, Dylan sneezes. "Sorry," he says automatically.

"God bless, Dylan." I turn to catch his eye, but he drops his gaze to the floor, suddenly intensely interested in the little dog that continues to snore like it's her job. To his credit, he looks as lost as I feel right now.

Grace's vigilant eyes follow me, her face inscrutable as I scan the room for a place to sit and, finding none, remain standing. My heart is beating a mile a minute, but I control my breath. "Summer, John. Fancy seeing you here," I say with false bravado. "Where are the girls?"

"On the boat, where you should be," Summer blurts. "What are you doing here?"

John gives her a sharp glance and lays a hand on her knee, then returns his unblinking gaze to me. "Why are you here?"

I strain to sound casual. "I need my passport."

The bottom half of John's face smiles, but the eyes don't get the message. "We don't have it here with us," he says. "But if you come back to the boat—"

"I'm not going back to the boat," I snap. Breathe. "I just want to go home."

John's eyes bore into me, the smile evaporated. "You can't run away, Isabelle. There's nowhere to go, nothing to do."

Why did Vinny let me run at all, if he was lying about helping me? Anger simmers inside me. None of this makes sense. I turn to the grandmother and Dylan to plead my case. "I just want to go home," I repeat, more fervently this time. "Please, tell them to let me go home. I'm not a prisoner here, am I?"

Dylan again drops his gaze and shakes his head. He doesn't look happy about any of this, but he also isn't exactly jumping to help me. Strikingly similar to his stance on Eric's disappearance. Eric was right about him, I decide. He's a pushover and a patsy.

His grandmother, on the other hand, is a different story. "John." She turns her keen gaze to her son. "Is Isabelle a prisoner?"

"This is none of your business, Mother," he growls, refocusing on me. "Summer says you have a problem with Amythest's disappearance." He waits to continue until I meet his unrelenting gaze. "It was an accident.

The report has been filed. We are offering a generous sum to each of you girls for your trouble, and that will be the end of it."

Summer smiles coldly, smug in her victory. Absent Vinny, I scramble for a backup plan, hoping I'm doing a better job of maintaining a cool exterior than I feel like I am. On the positive side, none of them seem to have any idea about the phone burning a hole in my purse, which holds evidence of both John's sexual proclivities and Summer's confession. And no one seems to know about Eric. Clearly self-preservation is priority one. I walked my ass into this trap, so I guess at this point my best choice is to take the cash and act repentant. I can worry about getting the phone into the right hands when I get home.

I place a sweating palm on my heart and smile apologetically, putting on what I hope is an Oscar-worthy performance. "I'm so sorry. I was upset, and not thinking clearly. Of course it was an accident."

"Good," John says. "You can take the helicopter back to the boat with us. Once you sign the paperwork, the hundred thousand is yours."

I don't have any time to consider how much money that is or how the hell I'm going to avoid going back to that damn boat, before my thoughts are interrupted by the sound of wheels on the gravel drive. John looks to his mother sharply. "Who is that?"

"A friend of mine," she says calmly. "I've been expecting him."

Your sister is headed to your grandmother's house.

Eric. Please God.

John narrows his eyes at her. "At this hour?"

"What, I'm not allowed to have boyfriends?"

"You should have told me someone was coming, Mother," he says darkly.

She dismisses the idea with a wave of her hand. "And take the chance you would not come *visite* your old *mère*? Never. And I wouldn't have met your *très belle, très* young girlfriend."

"We're not here to visit," he says. "We're here because you wanted to discuss the transfer of your stock."

"Oh yes, that." She smiles. "*Terminé.*"

For the first time, John looks unsettled. "What do you mean? I didn't get any paperwork about—"

"Oh." Her smile widens. "I didn't transfer it to you." Suddenly, the little dog at Grace's feet springs up and bounds to the door, yapping. "I transferred it to him."

We all turn to see Eric standing in the doorway, Vinny beside him. For a moment, the entire room is frozen.

Then, at last, John's composure fails him. "You *bitch*," he seethes.

Eric claps his hands slowly, shifting his gaze to his father. "Father of the year."

This is the first time I've seen Eric since I left him on the beach in Rosarito, and I didn't realize how much I'd missed him. He's dressed in his customary black, his hair still close-cropped, but his wounds are healing, leaving him with a scar across his cheek that somehow only makes him sexier.

John fumes, his eyes darting between Eric and Vinny. Summer's mouth opens and closes like a fish out of water, her eyes wide with horror; Dylan stares at his brother in shock, engulfed in emotion. Only Grace is composed, a smile hovering around her lips as she gazes up at Eric with affection. "*Mon chéri!*" she says as he approaches and gives her a kiss on the cheek. "*Enfin!* Took you long enough."

"I was in Montreal," he explains.

Summer gapes at him. "You're . . . " She gulps.

"Alive? Yeah," Eric says. "I hear you've gotten better at killing people." He crosses the room to me and takes my hand. "Are you okay?"

I nod and follow his eyes to my soiled dress, suddenly remembering my filthy appearance. "It's been a long day."

Summer's gaze ping-pongs between us. "I knew it," she mutters.

John watches us from under hooded eyes, his mouth in a hard line. I see his gears turning. But it won't do him any good.

Dylan clears his throat. "Could someone please tell me what the hell is going on?"

Eric takes his phone from his pocket. "I'm taking over Lionshare."

"The hell you are," John snaps.

Eric shrugs. "I think you'll change your tone when you see the mountain of evidence I've collected against you."

"I don't have to remind you what happened last time you tried to collect evidence," John warns.

Eric taps away at his phone. "But this time is different. Because this time"—he meets his father's stare—"I'm blackmailing you." He directs his attention to Grace and nods at the television. "*S'il te plaît allume ça.*"

She points a remote, and the TV comes to life with a chime.

"The input for screen casting, please."

Grace selects one of the HDMI ports, and a spinning wheel comes up, then two rows of video pop onto the screen. Eric uses his phone to scroll down, revealing rows upon rows of videos. "Vinny tells me there was some confusion over the death of one of the girls on the boat."

He selects one of the boxes and presses play. The security footage is surprisingly clear despite it being dark out, and shows Amythest and Summer on the upper deck directly under the camera, engaged in a catfight as the other girls look on.

" . . . keep your nasty little hands off him," Summer warns.

"Make me," Amythest taunts. "What do you think he would do if I told him you killed your ex?"

"What the—I don't know what she's told you, but—you wouldn't dare, you little bitch." Summer reaches out and grabs Amythest by the back of her hair, yanking her head back. Amythest brings a knee up, connecting with her groin. "Whore!" Summer slaps her across the face. Amythest tries to push her away, slipping to her knees in the process.

"Summer, leave it!" Rhonda shouts. "It's not worth it."

"Shut up, Rhonda," Summer snaps.

I can hardly watch, knowing what's coming for my violet-eyed friend.

Amythest is on her feet again, backing away as Summer stalks her toward the railing. Amythest says something unintelligible, and suddenly the two of them are a blur of hands and hair and feet, kicking and slapping and pulling. Amythest is scrappy, but Summer is angrier, with a significant height advantage. Again she grabs Amythest by the back of the hair, this time slamming her head into the railing. Nose bleeding, Amythest flails. With one hand around her throat, Summer pushes her up and back. And then, in a flash, Amythest is tumbling backward over the railing. Her bloodcurdling scream stops short with a sickening crack and a nearly imperceptible splash.

My hand flies to my mouth as I choke back a sob, recognizing the scream that's been echoing in my head for twenty-four hours. Eric strokes my arm.

Summer spins to face the other girls, huddled at the edge of the camera's eye. "She fell," she spits. "She was drunk and she fell."

I blink away tears as Eric stops the video. The room is still, all the oxygen sucked out of it. "Any questions?" he asks. No one speaks. "Good. Let's move on."

John scowls at Summer, shrunken into the couch as though hoping it might swallow her, the corners of her mouth downturned. He doesn't seem surprised—surely he'd seen the video on the boat before it was wiped—but infuriated that her stupidity is now affecting him in a way he can't control.

Eric hovers over his father, arms crossed. "My hackers have thoroughly swept your servers; Vinny can confirm—I have all the details on every shady thing you've done in the past ten years, not to mention the security footage from the boat and the additional videos from the camera watch Belle was wearing." He looks to me, his gaze softening, and I smile. "Insider trading, tax evasion, bribery, murder—just to name a few."

Vinny extends a thick manila envelope to John, who rips it from his hand, refusing to make eye contact with his former goon. "Take a look," Eric suggests. "Though that's just the tip of the iceberg."

John tears open the envelope and thumbs through the contents. "What do you want?" he growls.

"I told you. Lionshare," Eric says evenly. "You'll resign, effective immediately, or everything I have on you becomes public. So public that there'll be no one to bribe."

"You're a fool," John chides. "That'll sink the company."

Eric holds his hands up. "No fucks to give."

John rises to his feet. "You ungrateful bastard—"

Eric laughs. "Exactly."

"After everything your grandfather sacrificed to start this company—" John turns to his mother. "Mother, you're not going to agree to this, are you?"

"*Tais-toi.*" Her withering gaze sears holes into John. "You care about *rien que de l'argent.*" She rubs her fingers together for emphasis. "*Money.* For years, you are *un étranger. Je pense,* 'He is selfish. He is not good son or good father, but he has no good example in his father, *alors,* he is not a bad man.' *Mais* when I learn what you have done to your own blood, to the people who work for you, I know you are no longer *mon fils.*"

"Mother—"

But she only glares at him, tight-lipped.

"This past week," Eric says to John, "at the—shall we say—*privileged* advice of one of your Chinese partners, you adjusted your position on steel and made twenty-three million, give or take. Now, I know that's not a lot to you, but it's damn sure enough for the SEC to be interested, should they ever find out. That money's now Belle's." I inhale so quickly I cough, shocked. Eric glances at me. "Make that thirty."

Thirty million dollars. That's insane. I can't even imagine it. It would mean paying off my parents' mortgage, buying a new car...I wouldn't ever have to bartend again. It's beyond comprehension.

"And five million in a trust for Amythest's mother," Eric continues, looking to Vinny for confirmation. "For when she completes rehab. Summer"—he fixes his eyes on Summer—"you're turning yourself in for pushing Amythest over the side of the boat."

Her face crumples. Her mouth opens in protest, but no words come out. Tears spill from her eyes, leaving tracks of mascara down her face.

"That's harsh," John protests.

"What the hell do you care?" he scoffs. "She was screwing me behind your back every chance she got. Until she tried to kill me."

John clenches his jaw.

"It's not true," Summer cries to John, placing her hand on his thigh.

Eric and John both ignore her. "She turns herself in; she'll get five to ten for manslaughter, less if she behaves," Eric says.

"A small price to pay for a life," I add.

"You'll see that she complies." Eric raises his brows at his father. "Remember, if any of these directions are disregarded, or anything happens to Belle or me, or anyone we're close to, the information I have will be sent to every relevant news outlet."

"If you'd been this clever to begin with, you could have made something of yourself," John says.

"Oh, I have, Dad." Eric slaps a contract in front of his father and throws a pen down. "Your resignation."

John stares hard at his son and then picks up the contract to read it over carefully. Eric sets a one-page document in front of Summer. "Your confession."

She turns to me with tears in her eyes. "Belle, you know I'd never do anything to hurt you." For just a moment, I see my best friend again, my confidante and ally, and my heart goes out to her.

But only for a moment. Maybe someday I'll be able to forgive, but I can't forget what she's done. And I don't want to. She'd toss me aside just as easily as she tossed Amythest off that boat. "Actually, Summer, I have our confrontation last night on tape. So, as it turns out, I know you *would*."

I can feel others in the room turn to look at me in surprise as I take Amythest's bejeweled phone from my purse and hold it up for everyone to see. But I keep my gaze locked on Summer's, watching her features harden as she morphs back into the monster she's become.

"And, John," I continue, "in case you don't recognize it, this is Amythest's phone. The same one she used to record the, uh . . . *shower* she gave you." Summer casts a nasty glance in his direction as he narrows his eyes at me.

There's silence for a moment before John scribbles his name and tosses his contract at Eric, then spins on Summer. "Just sign the damn thing," he spits.

Eric gathers the two signed contracts from the table and smiles at me. "Anything else you'd like, Belle?"

I fix my eyes on Summer, Amythest's bone-chilling scream ringing in my ears. Part of me wants her to apologize—or more accurately, to grovel on her knees and beg for her life. I'm tempted to wrench that sparkling sapphire off her finger and throw it in the ocean. But no. That's not who I want to be.

I make sure she's watching as I walk over and thread my fingers through Eric's. "I have everything I need."

He looks at me, a grin spreading across his face. So I was right: the photo in his bedside drawer did mean something. We'll have a long road ahead of us, but for the moment, I feel his fingers squeeze mine and I figure we'll be all right.

"Eric." Dylan rises from his chair and approaches his brother. I'd nearly forgotten he was there.

Eric considers him for a time before nodding. "We'll talk."

Dylan throws his arms around him. "I missed you."

After a moment, Eric pats him on the back. Out of the corner of my eye, I see movement in the hall and notice that two buff guys dressed in black have taken up residence in the doorway next to Vinny.

John cuts his eyes to the men. "Unnecessary."

"You have your men, I have mine," Eric returns calmly. "This is the last time I'll see you. My men will escort you on your plane—or rather, my plane, since Lionshare is now mine—back to New York, where there's a press conference tomorrow to announce your resignation. The rest of Summer's friends will be flown back commercial, and you should know that the NDAs they signed have been voided, as I am now the head of the company. I'm sure the authorities will want to talk to them once Summer turns herself in." He glances at me. "We'll be taking the helicopter."

He leans in and kisses his grandmother on the cheek. "*Merci* for helping me make this meeting happen. *Je t'aime.*"

"*Je t'aime*," she says.

Final words I could say to Summer swirl through my mind as Eric and I exit the room, but they're all vengeful or trite, and none of them do me any good. And so I leave without a backward glance.

We sprint across the gravel driveway and through what looks to be a rose garden, to where the helicopter waits on the tennis court, headlights blazing. A smartly uniformed pilot hands us up into the cabin, and the blades begin to turn.

The inside is plush with thick green carpet and creamy leather seats, three on each side. Eric presses a button, and a partition rises between the pilots and us. He slides into the seat next to me and hands me a pair of headphones.

I feel a slight sway as we lift off, and slip the headphones over my ears. Immediately the deafening thrum of the blades subsides and Eric's voice crackles to life. We're both laughing, giddy with relief.

I'm the first to catch my breath. "Jesus Christ, Eric, couldn't you have told me Vinny was on my side all along? I was terrified."

"He wasn't," Eric says. I raise my eyebrows. "Vinny and I were always cool, but he'd stopped working for my dad last year when his mom got sick. I didn't know he'd gone back until you mentioned he was on the boat with you. And still, I couldn't be a hundred percent sure how loyal he was to John. But the minute you threw out the sea urchin SOS, I knew I had to do something fast, so I took the chance and called him. I didn't tell him about you until I knew he was on my side."

"And your grandmother?"

"I'd been in touch with her this week. Once I shared everything, she was more than happy to help by arranging that meeting with John."

He reaches under the seat and slides out a built-in icebox and bar caddy, from which he extracts a bottle of champagne and two flutes. But before he can pop the cork, I put my hand on his arm. "We need to call the Coast Guard, to make sure someone is actually looking for Amythest," I say.

"Vinny's on it," he says. "And we'll go in person in the morning." He takes my hand. "I'm sorry you lost a friend."

"Me too," I say, my heart heavy. "She was—one of a kind. I think you would have liked her."

His eyes rest on mine, the lights of Saint-Tropez glimmering out the window, and I know all my reservations about him were unnecessary. "Summer mentioned you kept a picture of me in your bedside table."

He nods. "Because yours is the face I want to see every morning when I wake up." He moves closer, a mischievous smile playing around his lips. My entire body tingles. His gaze travels to my lips. "Are you finally going to let me kiss you?"

I nod, and his lips are on mine. I melt into him, and the line between us blurs. I've imagined this moment so many times, it's almost too much. Though usually when I imagined it, the helicopter headsets weren't getting in the way.

"Where are we going?" I murmur between kisses.

"There's a beautiful little hotel near Cannes where we can stay the night," he says, nuzzling my neck.

All I want is to be alone with him, completely undisturbed. "We may need a few nights," I say, again drawing his mouth to mine. "How far is it?"

He looks out the window and points. "See that outcropping of lights? It's the next town."

He pops the cork on the champagne and pours us each a glass. I feel the now familiar fizz of bubbles in my throat, the residual sweetness on my tongue. "I have to tell you," I confess, "I don't really like champagne."

He laughs. "You know? Neither do I. So we'll change it out."

Right. Because this is all his now. Or rather, the company's—which is his. The repercussions of what just transpired are only beginning to ricochet in my mind. *Thirty million dollars.* That's going to take a long, long time to sink in.

"To be honest, there's a lot about this lifestyle I don't . . ." I pause, thinking of how to put it without sounding insolent. "That I don't ever want to be a part of."

"I know." He gently caresses my cheek. "And you won't be. We won't be. I promise."

"But now you have to run this billion-dollar company. How is it not going to devour your life?"

"I'm going to sell it." He breaks into a smile. "To someone who'll do the same amount of good with it that my father did bad."

"Who?" I ask.

"You met him, actually. Charles Bricknell."

My eyes widen with delight. "I liked him," I declare. "And his wife. Marlena. She was fabulous. And their son, too."

"Magic Mike." He grins. Then, off my quizzical look, "Long story, better told by him."

"But . . . you know them through your dad?"

"Sort of. They were never friends, but were in the same social circle. Marlena happened to see some of my art at a party at Grandview when I was in my teens, and took an interest. She's the one who encouraged me to apply to art school and everything. Charles has wanted to buy

John out for years so I knew he'd jump at the opportunity. I wasn't sure he'd want to be involved with bringing him down, though, since he'd been one of his investors in the past. But once I had enough evidence from the servers on the boat to bury John, I reached out to Charles, and he volunteered to invite him aboard his yacht and record their conversation."

I remember the discussion I'd heard parts of aboard the *Tyger*, through the office door. "So that's why we were invited to Marlena's birthday party last-minute."

Eric nods. "They're good people. I trust them."

It gives me immense solace to think of John's company in Charles's hands. "Good."

He raises his glass to me. "You did it, *sis*."

I smile, feeling so many different emotions I don't yet know how to begin to untangle them. *What a difference a week makes.*

Eric slips his arm around me, and I settle into his shoulder, our eyes fixed on the dazzling lights of the coast below. Yachts bob on the dark sea, blazing like stars in a moonless sky.

It's all very surreal, this fresh chapter in my life. But you know, I think I could get used to it.

Acknowledgments

My heart is bursting with gratitude for all the wonderful humans without whom this book would not be possible:

To my parents, Frank and Celia, for introducing me to the magic of books and always championing my artistic endeavors. To my husband, Alex, for supporting me in too many ways to count, and for not counting. You are my happy ending. To my early readers, Alice, Maria, Ashleigh, Anne, Gillian, and Dina, for giving me the confidence to send this book out into the world. To Kathryn Stockett, for your generosity.

To the brilliant team at Levine Greenberg Rostan—and most of all my fabulous agent, Sarah Bedingfield. Thank you for your insight, encouragement, and friendship, for believing in me and guiding me from concept to completion, and for always having my back. And thank you for giving me a safe space to fail, because the space to fail is so necessary in order to succeed.

To my superb editor, Millicent Bennett, for your acuity, your expertise, your attention to detail—because the little things matter!—and for always making this process fun. You are the lioness guiding this cub of a book into the world.

To my fantastic film agent, Michelle Kroes at CAA, for your discernment and always knowing the right thing to do.

And finally, to the outstanding team at Hachette Book Group and Grand Central Publishing, for making the dream a reality: Ben Sevier,

ACKNOWLEDGMENTS

Karen Kosztolnyik, Beth deGuzman, Brian McLendon, and Matthew Ballast on the executive team; Andy Dodds, Kamrun Nesa, and Ivy Cheng in publicity; Tiffany Sanchez and Alana Spendley in marketing; Alison Lazarus, Chris Murphy, Ali Cutrone, Rachel Hairston, and Karen Torres in sales; Albert Tang, Brian Lemus, and Elizabeth Stokes for the beautiful jacket art; Kristen Lemire, Jeff Holt, and Marie Mundaca in production; Nancy Wiese, Joelle Dieu, and Francesca Begos in subsidiary rights; editorial assistants Carmel Shaka and Meriam Metoui; and Lisa Cahn for producing the awesome audiobook.

I am forever grateful for all of you.

About the Author

KATHERINE ST. JOHN is a native of Mississippi and graduate of the University of Southern California. Over the years she has worked as an actress, screenwriter, director, photographer, producer, yoga instructor, singer/songwriter, legal assistant, real estate agent, bartender/waitress, and travel coordinator, but finds she likes writing novels best. Katherine currently lives in Los Angeles with her husband and children.